THE MELODY GIRLS

Anne Douglas

This first world edition published 2010
in Great Britain and in the USA by
SEVERN HOUSE PUBLISHERS LTD of
9–15 High Street, Sutton, Surrey, England, SM1 1DF.
Trade paperback edition first published
in Great Britain and the USA 2011 by
SEVERN HOUSE PUBLISHERS LTD.

British Library Cataloguing in Publication Data

Douglas, Anne, 1930-
The Melody Girls.
1. Dance orchestras–Scotland–Glasgow–Fiction.
2. Women musicians–Fiction. 3. Glasgow (Scotland)–
Social conditions–20th century–Fiction. 4. Love
stories.
I. Title
823.9'14-dc22

ISBN-13: 978-0-7278-6936-4 (cased)
ISBN-13: 978-1-84751-273-4 (trade paper)

Typeset by Palimpsest Book Production Ltd.,
Falkirk, Stirlingshire, Scotland.
Printed and bound in Great Britain by
MPG Books Ltd., Bodmin, Cornwall.

One

Edinburgh's West End post office clock was going slow. Or so thought Lorna Fernie, counter clerk, covertly glancing up at the hands in between serving customers. If the clock wasn't going slow, why was the afternoon so long? Sometimes it seemed as though leaving time would never be reached and she'd never make it to the Merchant Hall for the talent contest, which was foolish even to imagine. But then she was a wee bit nervous, wasn't she? Unusually for her.

A slim, quite small girl, not yet twenty-one, Lorna's eyes were blue and very bright beneath dark level brows that contrasted well with her auburn hair. Auburn, not to say ginger, though Lorna didn't mind if folk called it that. After all, her dad had been ginger until his later years when, of course, his hair had faded, but he'd still been called Coppers by his colleagues in the dance band where he played saxophone. The same saxophone now owned by Lorna.

On that late November afternoon, even with the Christmas rush still some way off, folk were queuing patiently in the post office. But then, in 1945, they were used to queuing. Fact of life, eh? Same as shortages and rationing. Bomb damage, too, though it had to be admitted, Edinburgh had got off pretty lightly with that. Still had some protective sticky paper on the post office windows, though – just another reminder of the war, if you needed it.

Stamps, postal orders, packages, parcels, on and on went the flow, as the clerks worked away through the afternoon, but a lull came eventually when Pattie MacDowell, next to Lorna, was able to ask in a stage whisper, 'You nervous about tonight, Lorna?'

'A bit,' Lorna answered after a pause.

'You're used to playing, though? At concerts and that?'

Yes, it was true, Lorna reflected. She was used to playing – mainly the piano – at local concerts, kirk socials, and so on, but tonight's event was different. A talent contest in aid of charity. A competition where she'd be judged. She wasn't used to that.

'I've never been in a talent contest before,' she said at last. 'And it's important, you see. There's a prize.'

'Aye, ten pounds, I heard.' Pattie, a plump little blonde, was excited. 'That's a lot, eh?'

'I'm more interested in something else. If you win, you get to play on the wireless.'

'The wireless! Where?'

'Here, in Edinburgh. At the studios in Queen Street.' Lorna's eyes suddenly shone. 'Imagine it, broadcasting!'

'And that'll be you, Lorna. I bet you win tonight. You're a lovely pianist.'

'Tonight, I'm playing the saxophone,' said Lorna.

The hands of the clock moved round at last to show the half hour after five. Going home time, thank the Lord, and as Miss Dickinson, the supervisor, closed the doors to the public, the staff yawned and stretched, buttoned up their coats and began to call out their 'goodnights'.

Lorna, of course, was wasting no time. This was what she'd been waiting for: to finish work, skid along home, have her tea – not that she'd want it – and get ready for the contest. Her mother would be coming with her, and her Auntie Cissie, over from Musselburgh, and probably Ewen MacKee, a senior postal clerk who worked in the back office after being demobbed from the navy.

'Hey, Lorna, wait for me!' He was calling to her now, as she raced out into the chill of the evening. 'You know I'm going your way.'

'Hurry up, then. I want to do some practising when I get home.'

'You don't need to do any practising,' he told her, grinning, as they set off together through the lighted, crowded streets of the West End, he suiting his long-legged stride to her quick little steps. 'You know all your piano pieces backwards, eh?'

'I'm playing the saxophone, Ewen.'

'The saxophone? Whatever for? I mean – I know you're good, but . . .'

She laughed a little at the expression on his broad, good-natured face, as he took off his cap and put his hand through his thick brown hair.

'But girls don't play the saxophone? They do, then. They can play any instrument going, don't have to stick to the piano or violin.'

'Yes, but for something like the contest, I thought sure you'd play those good tunes you know so well. I bet that's what the judges would like.'

'Who knows what they'd like? And I can play tunes on the saxophone, anyway. If you come tonight, you'll hear 'em, eh?'

'I'm coming tonight, all right. Just try to keep me away!'

They parted at the end of West Maitland Street, from where Ewen continued into the Dalry area and Lorna ran fast to a shabby old house off the Haymarket. Here she had lived all her life in the ground-floor flat of the converted building, the only child of her parents after two brothers had died in infancy. It was not a sadness Lorna herself had experienced, being too young at the time. In fact, she had known no sadness at all until the death of her father the year before, a grief that was still with her. How did you get over losing somebody who'd meant so much? 'You just take it day by day,' Tilly her mother had told her. 'And keep busy.'

Well, they were busy enough. They had their living to make, Tilly as a dressmaker, Lorna, after her war work making munitions, in the post office, For now, as she told herself, but not for ever.

There were four rooms in their flat. Two bedrooms, a kitchen and a living room, which was furnished like most of the living rooms Lorna knew, except, along with the stuffed sofa, the loaded sideboard, the table and chairs, there was a piano. Very old, with walnut casing and yellowed keys, even a pair of candleholders, but it was Lorna's pride and joy, and all thanks to Auntie Cissie, her mother's sister, who'd let them have it years before. It had belonged to her late husband's mother, given to Cissie for her children, but they'd never wanted to play and had now left Edinburgh.

'Who else would I give it to, but Lorna?' Cissie had asked reasonably. 'With her dad being a musician and all?'

'Always meant to get one,' Cam Fernie had said, thumbing through the old music that had arrived with the piano. 'Never got round to it.'

'Always needed something else first,' Tilly had put in.

'And that's where we made our mistake, eh? This should have come first.'

'You had your fiddle and your sax.'

'But we should've thought of Lorna.'

As her father sat down and ran his fingers over the keys, muttering that he'd have to tune the instrument before he did anything else, Lorna could remember standing looking on, transfixed with happiness.

'Am I going to learn to play, Dad?' she'd whispered.

Of course, she'd learned to play. As Lorna bounded into the living room now, calling to her mother that she was home, the memory of all those lessons came back. Not just for the piano, but the saxophone and violin as well, with her father patiently teaching her so thoroughly she'd never needed anyone else.

Oh, but it was hard to think he wasn't still there in his chair, smoking and smiling as she came in from school! But she wasn't coming in from school today, and it was Auntie Cissie sitting in his chair now. She was waiting to go with her and Ma to the talent contest that was looming ever nearer.

'Hi, Ma!' Lorna cried, flinging back her auburn hair. 'Hi, Auntie Cissie! All set for tonight?'

Two

It had always seemed to Lorna that her mother and her aunt were more like twins than ordinary sisters, even though there were three years between them, Cissie now being forty-eight and Tilly forty-five. Both were fair, though, and had such similar faces – long and pale, with high cheekbones and blue eyes much lighter than Lorna's – you could be forgiven for confusing them. Unless you knew them as well as Lorna did, for in character they were quite different.

Tilly was steady, never making a move until she was sure, while Cissie was bold and, as she sometimes said with a laugh, ready to jump in with both feet. 'Might get wet sometimes,' she would add, 'but never drowned, eh?'

'Here she is!' she cried now, when Lorna came to give her a hug. 'Here's the winner!'

'Och, now don't be saying that,' Tilly said reproachfully. 'Nothing's for sure in this world.'

'When the judges hear Lorna playing that lovely "Minute Waltz" thing she played at the kirk concert, there'll be no contest,' Cissie retorted. 'She'll knock 'em for six.'

'I won't be playing the "Minute Waltz",' Lorna said firmly. 'That's a piano piece.'

'So? I thought you were playing the piano?'

'I've decided to play the saxophone.'

There was a silence as the two sisters exchanged glances.

'The saxophone,' Tilly said at last. 'I don't believe it. Whatever's got into you, Lorna, to think of doing that?'

'Aye, what indeed?' Cissie asked. 'The saxophone's a terrible solo instrument, so it is. Why, you'll need somebody to play with you, eh?'

'No, I won't, I'm playing on my own. My sax sounds beautiful.' Lorna frowned deeply. 'And it was my dad's instrument, don't forget.'

'But yours is the piano,' Tilly declared. 'And he only played the sax in Jackie Craik's band.'

'I could've played it in a band!'

'But you know he always said you couldn't. I can see him now, sitting in that chair and saying Jackie and the fellows would never accept a lassie. Don't tell me you've forgotten, Lorna!'

'I haven't forgotten,' she said quietly, looking away from Aunt Cissie sitting in her father's chair.

Of course she remembered her dad saying she'd never follow him into a dance band, much as he wished she could if it was what she wanted. That had been long ago, before Lorna had heard that some women musicians had got their chances and taken the place of the men gone to war. But now the war was over and maybe things had gone back to the way they were. Lorna didn't know. All she knew was that she needed to get her foot in the door, and that this talent contest might be the door she could open.

'Ma, I'd better have my tea and get ready,' she muttered. 'Time's getting on.'

'Ah, now, you're upset.' Her mother put her arm around Lorna's shoulders. 'But it's best to face facts, pet. As your dad always used to say, even if you were given a job, a dance band is no place for a lassie.'

'Look at the hours he used to keep, eh?' Cissie added, rising from Cam's chair. 'Never home till the small hours, and then there'd be the drinking and the smoking. I always said he'd never make old bones.'

'Yes, well, let's no' go into all that now,' Tilly murmured, quickly blinking her pale blue eyes. 'Best get our tea and be on our way.'

'There are such things as all girl bands, you know,' Lorna said, passing out plates. 'Maybe they'd no' turn me down.'

'All girl dance bands?' Cissie echoed. 'Where are they, then?'

'There are plenty in America, but some in England as well. There's a lady has a band plays on the wireless sometimes.'

'But no' girl bands here in Scotland, eh?'

Lorna shook her head. 'Haven't heard of any.'

'Don't tell me you'll be running away to England, then?' her mother asked, not altogether in fun. 'Ah, look, you stick to your post office job and play your music in your spare time. That's the best for you, I'm telling you. Now, I'll get the tea.'

'What are you going to wear tonight, Lorna?' Cissie asked, as they sat down to pies and peas. 'Got to cut a dash, you know.'

'Well, I can either wear my green,' Lorna answered, smiling at last. 'Or, my dark blue. If I don't wear my dark blue, I can wear my green. That's the choice.'

'One of these days we won't need clothing coupons,' Tilly remarked. 'I'd say the blue, Lorna, the one I made for you. You suit the colour.'

'I think the blue, too. Always think it makes me seem taller.'

'Now you don't need to worry about looking taller. Leave that to the men. Which reminds me – is that nice fellow from the post office going to the concert tonight?'

'Ewen? Yes, he says he'll be there.'

Tilly glanced at her sister. 'He's a lovely laddie, Cissie. Lorna could do a lot worse.'

'Oh, Ma, stop your matchmaking!' Lorna cried, rolling her eyes and jumping to her feet. 'Ewen's a friend, that's all. Look, mind if I don't help clear away? I'm going to get ready.'

'She's a wee bit worked up,' Tilly whispered, as Lorna hurried off. 'Nerves, you ken.'

'No' like her to be nervous.'

'Seemingly, this talent thing is something special. I just hope she wins.'

'No need to worry,' Cissie said comfortingly. 'She will.'

In her little bedroom that was hardly bigger than a box room, Lorna tried on the dark blue dress. It was her belief that she had the smallest mirror in the world, perched on top of the smallest chest of drawers, yet as she twisted and turned, trying to get a view of herself, she knew she would never complain. Compared with girls in some of the tenements, she lived like a princess. Own room, own mirror, own place to put her things! Heavens, she was lucky not to be taking a turn at sharing a bed!

All the same, it wasn't easy getting ready when you had to make do with fractions of a reflection, but from what she could see, she decided she'd been right about the blue dress. It definitely made her seem taller, and once she'd put on her high heels, it would look even better. Wouldn't be warm, of course, but then the hall would probably be too hot, anyway, when the audience was all stuffed in, and for travelling in the tram she could wear a cardigan under her coat.

When she'd given her hair a good brush she was about to put on some lipstick when she paused. Better wait to do that.

With a little catch of breath, she turned to pick up her father's saxophone case from her one chair and took out the brass instrument she had so often seen him play. It was so beautiful. So lovingly crafted by someone probably long dead, for it was quite old, her dad had said, and yet shone as brightly as though newly made. Of course, that was the special lacquer put on to protect the brass, but even the well-used keys, some covered in mother of pearl, seemed to Lorna to be as good as new.

She ran her fingers down the cone-shaped body, remembering that she'd said she'd like to practise before the contest, but of course there'd been no time. Still – she put her lips to the mouthpiece – she would just play a few notes, to put her in the mood, for she did so love to hear the deep, special sound that from the first had drawn her to listen when her dad was playing his sax.

He'd been pleased that she'd liked it; the saxophone wasn't to everyone's taste. Didn't she prefer the piano? Oh, she loved her piano, but the saxophone was to her more special. Sometimes its music was so soft, so sad. Sometimes, when her dad played jazz, just the opposite: loud, bright, so full of rhythm, it set her feet dancing. One day, she used to say, she would learn to play the saxophone, and her dad would say, yes, and he would teach her. And so, of course, he had and said she was a natural. But he still didn't think she could ever play in a band.

Ah, well, best not to think of that now. Just try a few notes from the piece she'd be playing first that evening, which was a Bach suite arranged for the saxophone. Very hard, but she had to show what she could do and there was an easier piece to follow.

'Lorna, Lorna, are you ready?' came her mother's voice, before she'd scarcely begun. 'It's time to go.'

'Oh, no,' Lorna groaned, and hastily packed away the saxophone, put on her lipstick, found her cardigan and her coat, and ran out to join her mother and Auntie Cissie.

'OK, I'm ready.'

'Why, you're never wearing high heels to go out, Lorna?' Cissie asked. 'It's raining, you ken. Quick, put your boots on and I'll take your shoes in ma bag. Tilly, have you got the umbrellas?'

If we could just get going, Lorna thought, as nervous now as a racehorse under starter's orders. Just hope I feel better when I get there.

Three

Although they thought they'd given themselves plenty of time, when Lorna and her family arrived at the Merchant Hall in Newington, they found it almost full and already uncomfortably warm. Not something you normally had to complain about in Edinburgh's public rooms, as Cissie remarked, but oh, dear, what about the smell of the damp coats and wellingtons, then? It would have to be a wet night, wouldn't it?

'Just as long as we get seats,' Tilly murmured, scanning the rows of chairs. 'You'll be all right, Lorna, you'll be behind the scenes, eh?'

'I'd better go and see what's happening,' Lorna said, putting her hands to her flushed cheeks. 'Will you take my coat and cardigan, Ma? And Auntie Cissie, where's my shoes?'

'There's somebody waving to us,' Cissie said, nobly handing over Lorna's high heels in exchange for her damp boots. 'It must be that young man you mentioned, eh? I think he's got some seats for us.'

'Yes, it's Ewen!' Tilly cried. 'Oh, good lad, he's saved us some seats – that's a relief.'

As they made their way through other family members and friends of the performers searching for seats, Lorna was staring in surprise.

'Why, there's Pattie!' she exclaimed, 'And – oh, no – Miss Dickinson! Who'd have thought she'd come tonight?'

'Hi, Lorna!' Ewen cried, as they came up to the front row. 'Hello, Mrs Fernie. I made sure of some seats for you – they're in the second row – got here before they even opened the doors.'

'And I'm sure we're very grateful,' Tilly gasped. 'Well done, Ewen.'

'Never thought to see you here, Pattie,' Lorna was murmuring. 'And Miss Dickinson – it was nice of you to come.'

'Why, Lorna, we had to come and give you our support!' cried Miss Dickinson, who was looking younger and smarter than when at work. 'And it's in aid of the children's hospital, too, isn't it? I'm always one for a good cause.'

'Wanted to come and wish you luck,' Pattie said earnestly. 'We'll all be cheering for you, Lorna.'

But Lorna's eyes were on three men and one woman taking their seats in the front row. One of the men she recognized as being the conductor of a local orchestra and another the head of a school music department – their photographs were often in the local papers. So was the woman's – she was a well-known soprano. But the fourth person Lorna didn't know and could only guess who he might be. From the BBC, perhaps? For these, of course, were the judges.

'I've got to go,' she muttered, and holding tight to her saxophone case, made her way towards the platform, just as a middle-aged man came out to speak. She didn't need to wait to hear what he said, she knew he was from the hospital for sick children and would be thanking everybody for the shilling entrance fee they'd paid to hear the contest and wishing all the entrants good luck. All she wanted now, as she moved to join her rivals in a small room at the back of the platform, was for it to be her turn. But of course, they were all wishing the same.

Although there were only ten talent hopefuls – five young women, five young men – the room seemed full, for some had brought their accompanists, and there were also several women organizers, ticking off names, setting out chairs and trying to put everyone at ease.

'Not long to go now,' one of these said brightly. 'There's Mr Dean making his introduction. Before you know it, it'll all be over!'

'We're supposed to be enjoying it,' one of the girls murmured, at which a small ripple of laughter ran around the room.

Another girl – tall and pale with anxious eyes and brown hair unevenly cut short – laid her hand on Lorna's arm. 'Have you seen the judges?' she whispered. 'Are they out there?'

'In the front row. Want to take a peep?'

'No, no, I think we'll be starting any minute. Where are you on the programme they sent? I'm fifth.'

'I'm fourth. Just before you, then. Before the interval, as well. That's good, eh?' Lorna introduced herself, adding that she would be playing her saxophone.

'Oh, my, a saxophone! Is it as difficult as it looks?'

'Worse.'

'My name's Hannah Maxwell. I'm just playing the piano.'

'Well, that can be difficult, too. What are you starting with?'

'Chopin's "Minute Waltz".'

'Oh, nice,' Lorna murmured, looking down at the girl's hands on her roll of music. Strong, pianist's hands, with spatulate broad fingers. She had the feeling that this girl was good. Probably she could play the "Minute Waltz" in under the time. So, what a bit of luck, eh, that she, Lorna, had decided to play her sax?

'Why in God's name aren't we starting?' a young man with a tenor's voice asked. 'It's ridiculous, keeping us hanging about like this.'

'Are you first on?' Lorna asked kindly.

'Yes, and I can't decide whether that's good or bad.' He gave a tremulous grin. 'I'm dead keen to win, you ken. No' for the money, but the spot on the wireless.'

'We all want that,' said a tall statuesque young woman, who looked to Lorna like a singer. 'But I want the money as well.'

'Ladies and gentlemen, may I have your attention?' boomed the voice of a stout woman, one of the organizers. 'The contest is about to begin. Could Anthony Baird step forward please?'

'Oh, God,' said the young tenor, swallowing hard. 'That's me. Where's my accompanist? Janet, Janet!'

'I'm here, Tony,' a girl said comfortingly. 'No need to panic. I've got the music.'

'This way, please, Mr Baird,' the organizer told him, holding his arm as though he might suddenly run away. 'You, too, dear, if you're accompanying him. And when you've finished your pieces, could you both just move into the audience? No need to return here.'

'Oh, listen, they're clapping,' someone said. 'That's nice, eh? If they clap when we come on.'

'Hope they clap when we've finished, as well,' the statuesque young woman sighed, at which Lorna smiled.

'Are you joking? They're all friends and relations out there. They'll clap, all right.'

'But maybe no' for everyone.'

'Never mind the audience,' Hannah said sharply. 'Think of the judges.'

'Everyone keep quiet,' hissed the organizer, returning. 'Mr Baird is beginning.'

And as the strains of Sullivan's 'Take a Pair of Sparkling Eyes' came back to them, the contestants fell silent.

Four

Exquisite agony, was how some later described it, having to sit and wait to go on, while listening to others performing and wondering how good they were, and whether it was worth even stepping out on to the platform, as confidence gradually drained away.

Whatever happened, Lorna knew that she would go on, do her best, even if all seemed hopeless, for you could never be certain what the judges were looking for – it might be something you'd never expect and you might have it.

All the same, when her name was called and she had to walk out on to the platform, it took all her courage to smile around the hall, pretend to be at ease, pretend, in fact as that girl had said, to be enjoying herself. And then there were the moments when she had to stand, still smiling, as Mr Dean introduced her and read out what she was going to play on her unaccompanied saxophone, a most unusual, but welcome choice, as he was sure everyone would agree.

'A little Bach first, then a rhapsody by Eric Coates, and then something I expect Lorna thought we'd all know.' Mr Dean laughed a little. '"Red Sails in the Sunset", a very pleasant tune.'

'Ah,' murmured the audience, and Lorna, sensing their approval, felt a sudden surge of confidence and knew at once that it was going to be all right for her. And so it proved. She played better that evening than she'd ever dared to hope for, and though the applause for the Bach and the Eric Coates was muted, when she finished with "Red Sails in the Sunset", after being accompanied by half the audience singing along, the clapping was so deafening, she almost felt like shedding a tear or two. She didn't of course, but waved and smiled to her mother and the rest of her supporters, while thinking with relief that no matter how well Hannah Maxwell played the 'Minute Waltz', she couldn't possibly do any better.

And when Hannah appeared, looking paler than ever, and Mr Dean announced that she'd be playing Chopin, Schubert and Beethoven, Lorna was still very sure she'd got nothing to fear. Even when Hannah began to play and it was clear she was as good as Lorna had guessed, with a beautiful touch and solid technique, Lorna didn't allow herself to waver. Good pianists were, after all, not hard to find. There was nothing special about them, nothing different, which was why Lorna had decided against playing the piano herself. Her sax would carry the day, she was sure of it, and in the interval, so many people – apart from her family – were congratulating her, she felt she was walking on air.

Until, at the end of the contest, after the judges had deliberated in the now empty back room and had appeared to give their verdict, for the first time she felt doubt. Glancing at Hannah, who was trembling beside her, and then at the rest of the entrants, it came to her that she had been far too confident. Worse, big-headed. Why, any of these could win! The tenor, the singers, the fiddle players, or, of course, Hannah. What had possessed her to think her sax would single her out?

But when the local conductor stepped forward to speak on behalf of the judges, Lorna couldn't help herself. She still thought, maybe . . . maybe she had won.

First, of course, there had to come the nice words about all the entrants, to make them feel better over losing. Such a high standard . . . everyone deserving of a prize . . . particularly liked . . . there was the tenor's name . . . and, oh no, her own! Too soon, if she was going to win. Oh, too soon!

And, yes, that was right, for here came the final announcement. By unanimous decision, for her professionalism, her sensitivity, and her most talented piano playing, the winner was . . .

'Hannah Maxwell!'

Everything after that was a blur, as the bitterness sank in. Even when Lorna's name was called as runner-up and she had to go up to the judges with Anthony Baird who'd taken third place, she felt quite unreal. Perhaps he did, too, for his grin was forced as he accepted his prize of three pounds and later congratulated Lorna on her five.

'No' bad, eh? Better than nothing.'

'I'll say,' she heard herself heartily agreeing. 'It's more than twice my wages.'

'But no' a chance to broadcast.'

'That's only for Hannah.'

And then, of course, they joined in the congratulations being given to Hannah, now scarlet in the face and being embraced by her parents and a girl who might have been her sister, before turning away to be consoled by their own families.

'Ah, pet, what a shame, eh!' Cissie was crying, and Tilly was just putting her arm around Lorna and Pattie was saying, well, never mind, five pounds was a fortune, eh? And Miss Dickinson was saying she'd been so thrilled by 'Red Sails in the Sunset', and Ewen was declaring that Lorna should have won, and she was shaking her head and telling him to keep his voice down, when another voice cut through to her and she turned in surprise.

'Miss Fernie – forgive me for interrupting – but could I have a word?'

A tall well-dressed man of about forty, carrying a hat and a raincoat over his arm, was standing at her elbow. He had dark hair that was mixed with grey and a sharp, dark gaze, and as her eyes went over him, the world for Lorna suddenly became real again. She had no idea who he was, but she knew somehow that he was important. Or, might be – to her.

'Yes?' she asked, standing aside from people leaving, as her mother, Auntie Cissie, Ewen, Pattie and Miss Dickinson, all stood staring at the newcomer.

'I'm Luke Riddell. From Glasgow. You may have heard of me? I have a dance band there. Luke Riddell's Orchestra?'

Five

He had a dance band?

Lorna's eyes on Mr Riddell were not just bright, but starry. He had a dance band in Glasgow, and he'd asked to speak to her? Could it mean anything? Such as what? Take a hold, she told herself, stop staring, stop thinking, say something!

But Mr Riddell's gaze had moved to Tilly, standing close to Cissie, both looking wary, though Cissie, Lorna could tell, was excited. She always loved the unexpected and to have this well-dressed stranger coming up to speak to Lorna was unexpected, all right. Tilly, though, just wanted to know what was going on and perhaps sensing this, Mr Riddell guessed correctly that she was Lorna's mother. Again apologizing for interrupting, he asked if Tilly was Mrs Fernie.

'That's right,' Tilly admitted cautiously. 'I'm Mrs Fernie.'

'Well, then, I knew your husband. We met from time to time, as folk in the same line of business do, and I always admired his music making. I was very sorry to hear that he'd—'

'Yes, he died last year,' Tilly said quickly. 'But why did you want to speak to my daughter?'

'I wanted to compliment her on her playing. In my opinion, she should have won.' Mr Riddell turned to Lorna. 'When I heard your name announced, I guessed you were Cam Fernie's daughter, and when you took up that tenor sax of his – it was his, wasn't it? – I knew at once that you were going to be good. And might be what I'm looking for.'

'Looking for?' Lorna repeated, swallowing hard.

'What do you mean?' asked Tilly, as Cissie's eyes widened and a frown creased Ewen's brow.

'Well, when I thought I'd look in on the contest – I happened to be in Edinburgh on business and somebody told me about it – I never expected to find a sax player. But the way things are, with some of my guys not coming back to the band after the war, I've got vacancies and one's for tenor sax.' Mr Riddell gave a brief smile. 'And yes, I do take women in my band. I've got two already.'

'Are you . . .?' Lorna began, then stopped. She couldn't put it into words, she couldn't say, as though it was something quite to be expected: 'Are you offering me a job?' He was, though, offering her a job. She knew it. Just couldn't believe it.

'We can't talk here,' Mr Riddell was saying quietly. 'Perhaps you'll take my card, Miss Fernie? Discuss it with your mother, and then, if you're interested in playing with the band, give me a ring.'

'Interested? I am interested, Mr Riddell.'

'It's out of the question,' Tilly said, her voice shaking. 'Lorna could never go to work for a band in Glasgow.'

'That's right, she's got a job here,' Ewen declared. 'In the post office.'

'The post office?' Mr Riddell repeated.

'I really think we should be going,' Miss Dickinson said abruptly. 'Pattie, Ewen—'

'I'm no' going anywhere.' Ewen's face was dark red. 'Except with Lorna and her folks.'

'We're all leaving now,' Cissie told him cheerily. 'It's like Mr Riddell says, we can't talk here, anyway.'

'Miss Fernie, I look forward to hearing from you,' the bandleader said smoothly. 'And Mrs Fernie, please don't worry. Your daughter can talk it over with you and it can all be sorted out for the best. It's been very nice meeting you, and everyone.'

And having politely inclined his head and put on his hat and raincoat, Luke Riddell walked swiftly from the emptying hall.

'Well!' Cissie exclaimed, laughing a little. 'Talk about a surprise, eh? Imagine a guy like him coming up to speak to Lorna, then! And he knew Cam, and all!'

'Let's just get home,' Tilly said shortly. 'We're going to be the last out at this rate.'

'Aye, we'll be sweeping the floor, next,' Ewen said glumly, his eyes fixed on Lorna, who in fact was incapable of seeing him, or anything, except what was in her own mind.

'I'm away for my tram,' Miss Dickinson murmured, her eyes, too, fixed on Lorna. 'Pattie, I think you're going my way?'

'Yes, Miss Dickinson.'

'Ewen?'

'I'm going back with Lorna.'

'Right. Well, I'll see you tomorrow, then. And Lorna, be sure to do as Mr Riddell said, my dear. Discuss everything with your mother, that's always best. We wouldn't want you to . . . get carried away.'

'Don't worry, we'll discuss it, all right,' Tilly said coldly.

Only Cissie kept up a stream of chatter on the tram going home, with Tilly and Ewen keeping a stern silence and Lorna still lost in her own thoughts. Back at the flat, however, Tilly managed to be polite and asked Ewen in for a cup of tea, and a slice of cake. Yes, she'd managed to get a Dundee cake from the Stores, wonders would never cease.

'Probably be dry as dust, but seeing as I've no eggs left, there's no baking for me, eh? Come on in, anyway.'

'Thanks, Mrs Fernie, it's nice of you to ask me, but I think I'd better get off home. You and Lorna, you've things to talk over.'

'If you're sure, now? Come some other time, then. You're always welcome.'

As he murmured his thanks again, Ewen's gaze rested on Lorna. 'You'll no' rush into anything?' he asked in a low voice. 'You'll think about what's best?'

Focusing her eyes on him at last, Lorna gave a radiant smile. 'Of course I'll do what's best, Ewen. No need to worry about that.'

'No need at all,' her mother said with meaning, and as Ewen touched his cap and slowly left them, the three women went into the flat and busied themselves making tea.

'Doesn't it seem a long time ago since we were last sitting at this table?' Lorna asked, avoiding her mother's eye. 'So much has happened, eh?'

'You won a lovely big five pound note for a start,' Cissie remarked, studying her cake as though to decide on its dryness. 'A very nice consolation prize, I'd say. You going to put it into your post office savings tomorrow?'

'Haven't thought. Probably.'

'Let's stop beating about the bush, Lorna, and get the talking out of the way,' Tilly said sharply. 'Won't take long, seeing as you know what I've got to say.'

'Oh, Ma, you're never going to try to stop me going to Glasgow, are you?' Lorna asked, setting down her cup. 'You know it's all I've ever wanted, and seeing Mr Riddell this evening, it was like the answer to a prayer.'

'We were supposed to be having a discussion, Lorna. That's what Mr Riddell said himself. Talk it over with your mother, he said. Nothing about making up your mind without a minute's thought!'

'How can you say I'm going to do that?' Lorna cried, her cheeks pink, her blue eyes flashing. 'I've done nothing else but think about being in a band for ages!'

'Aye, this is Mr Riddell's band we're talking about. I can tell you're planning to go over to Glasgow and take whatever's going.'

'Let's leave the lassie to think about it, Till,' Cissie put in quickly. 'If you go on about it now, you'll only make things worse.'

'I've a right to say what I think, Cissie. I've a right to stop my daughter making an awful mistake.'

'All Ma wants is for me to keep on at the post office and then get married to Ewen,' Lorna said bitterly. 'That'd be the mistake, that would.'

'See the way her mind works?' Tilly cried to Cissie, suddenly bursting into tears. Shaking her head, she fixed her eyes on Lorna. 'Of course I want you to marry Ewen, Lorna! What mother wouldn't want to see her daughter settled, instead of going off to Glasgow to play in a band!'

'Oh, Ma!' Lorna left her chair and ran to put her arms round her mother's shoulders. 'Don't cry! I'll be settled one day, but for now, I just want to have a go at what I really want to do. I'm like Dad, that's all. I want what he wanted, eh? If I'd been a laddie, you'd never have said a word, would you?'

'Thing is, you're no' a laddie,' Tilly sighed, wiping her eyes. 'And what's this Mr Riddell really like, I'm wondering. Your dad was never a special friend of his, as I remember.'

'If they only met now and again, he wouldn't have had the chance to be his friend,' Cissie remarked. 'I must say, I thought Mr Riddell seemed very nice. Very gentlemanly.'

'I thought so, too,' Lorna said eagerly. 'And did you hear him say he already had two girls in the band? When other bandleaders don't want any!'

'So, you'll be hoping to be number three.' Her mother sighed. 'I wish you'd think what it'll mean, Lorna, if you do take a job with him. Remember, you'll have to live in Glasgow, you'll be working too late at night to come home.'

'Ma, it's too soon to go into all that. I haven't even arranged anything yet. And then I might have to have an audition. Nothing's for sure.'

'You won't need an audition, Lorna!' Cissie cried. 'Mr Riddell's already heard you play at the talent contest.'

And of course Ma wishes he never had, Lorna thought glumly as she began to clear the table.

'I'll do these cups and then make up the sofa,' she murmured. 'My bed's all ready for you, Auntie Cissie.'

Ignoring Cissie's protests that she'd be quite happy to take the sofa herself, Lorna removed and washed up the cups, just managing to overhear before she returned, her aunt saying quietly to her mother, 'You'll have to let her go, Till. It's the way of the world. Young folk have to lead their own lives. No point trying to stop 'em.'

'Oh, Cissie, I know, but she's all I've got. You canna blame me for worrying.'

'Lorna's a sensible lassie. You'll see, she'll be fine.'

I hope that's true, Lorna thought, lying awake on the old sofa, trying to avoid, and failing, its malevolent springs. I just hope it all works out. But why shouldn't it? Never in the world had she dreamed she'd have this wonderful chance, but here it was, offered to her just when she'd been so low, and though the last thing she wanted was to upset her mother, she knew she must take it. It was – if it didn't sound too pretentious – her destiny.

Six

All the same, when it came to making the call to Mr Riddell, Lorna found herself hesitating. Not because she'd changed her mind – that wasn't going to happen - but because every time she thought of using the public telephone kiosk outside the post office, her mother's sad face came into her mind. And then her steps faltered and her hand fell to her side.

A piece of nonsense, that was what it was! Lorna was twenty years old. She'd a right to her own life. Hadn't Auntie Cissie said as much? And Glasgow was no distance from Edinburgh, she'd be able to pop home often enough. Ma would just have to accept the situation and would soon get used to it, anyway. Why not?

Well, of course, Lorna knew the answer to that. Her dad was gone and so recently the wound was still raw. Before that, Ma had been happy, with her husband and daughter as part of her life; she'd never have imagined that within a year, she might be left on her own. Husband gone, daughter gone. Which was why Lorna's steps had not taken her to the call box; why her hand had not stretched out to put in her coins and make the call to Mr Riddell. If she didn't do that, her mother would at least still have her.

Aware that both Ewen and Miss Dickinson were beginning to wonder what she was going to do, and with Pattie seeming ready to ask her, Lorna still kept quiet. She knew that she was right about her destiny and that to take the first step on the road towards it, she must make that call, but still she havered.

'Haven't you phoned that fellow yet?' Ewen asked at break time a couple of days later, as they drank pallid coffee together. 'From the look of him, I'd say he wouldn't be one to wait around for folk.'

'I know, and I'm going to ring him. Definitely.'

'When?'

'Soon.'

Ewen finished his coffee. 'You thinking of your ma?' he asked shrewdly.

'Yes, I am!' she answered, glad now for the chance to talk. 'I know it's only going to get worse, the longer I leave it, but I'm all she's got, you see, that's the trouble.'

'But it isn't just that she'll miss you, Lorna. She feels like me. Worried about what you'd be going to.'

'Oh, you're as bad as she is, Ewen – going on about the band! I can take care of myself!'

He shook his head. 'Maybe. The truth is, I think you're just as worried as your ma and me. Why don't you just forget the whole thing?'

'I will not!' she cried, jumping to her feet. 'I'll have another talk with Ma and ring Mr Riddell tomorrow.'

The unbelieving smile on Ewen's broad face only strengthening her resolve, she felt immensely relieved. Tomorrow it would be. All she had to do was put her mother's fears to rest.

The amazing and wonderful thing was that she didn't have to do that. For, as she later sat at home, staring at the evening paper, waiting for the right time to speak, it was Tilly who spoke instead.

'Oh, for goodness sake, Lorna!' she suddenly cried from her seat at her old treadle sewing machine. 'Ring that Mr Riddell and be done with it!'

Lorna's jaw dropped. Her eyes widened. The evening paper slipped from her grasp. 'What's that, Ma?' she asked faintly.

'You heard. I said to ring Mr Riddell. You've been sitting around moping ever since he offered you that job, and I just wish you'd get on with it.'

'Ma, do you mean it?'

'I do. It came to me in the night. I thought, Lorna's got to go. She's got to find her own way. That's what Cissie says, and it's true. So, I've made my decision. If you take the job in Glasgow, if you want to be like your dad, I'll say no more.' Tilly gave a sigh. 'But just get on with it, eh? So that I know where I am.'

'Oh, Ma!' Lorna ran to her mother, swung her round from the sewing machine and hugged her fiercely. 'You don't know what this means to me. I've been so worried, I can't tell you.'

'Aye, I know, and that's no' right. You're a grown up lassie, you shouldn't have to be worrying about me.' Tilly planted a quick kiss on Lorna's cheek and then turned back to her work. 'Now, make us a cup of tea, eh? While I finish this sleeve for old Mrs MacIntyre's new blouse.'

The tea tasted like nectar. After she'd drunk it, Lorna danced into her room, took out her saxophone, and played for so long her mother had to come in at last and remind her that not everybody in the neighbourhood was as keen on the saxophone as she was. At which, Lorna gave a rueful smile, thinking that some folk, at least, would not be minding if she moved on to Glasgow.

Would she be moving to Glasgow, though? All depended on Mr Riddell, and when she finally got through to him from the call box the following morning, it seemed to her that he sounded rather different. Had he already forgotten who she was?

'What name did you say?' he was asking, as she hung on to the phone with a trembling hand. 'Sorry, there's a lot going on here, could you speak up?'

'It's Lorna Fernie, Mr Riddell,' she cried, as loud as she could. 'Speaking from Edinburgh. You asked me to ring some time.'

'Did I?' His voice was more hoarse than she remembered, and in the background, she could hear chatter and laughter and somebody on a trumpet playing a scale. 'Lorna Fernie? Oh, wait a minute. Cam Fernie's daughter, eh? The little sax player from the talent concert?'

'Yes, that's me,' she answered, breathing a sigh of relief. 'You said to give you a ring.'

'So I did, I was thinking of you for my missing sax, wasn't I?' Suddenly Mr Riddell shouted, 'Hey, you folks, cut the noise, eh? I've got somebody on the phone – you still there, Miss Fernie?'

'Yes, Mr Riddell.'

'Nice of you to call. I remember now, I was hoping you would. When would you like to come over, then?'

'To Glasgow?'

'Of course, of course, to Glasgow. I take it you're interested in the band?'

'Oh, yes, Mr Riddell, I am.'

'Well, can you make it this Saturday, then? Say, two o'clock? I'll call a rehearsal for half past, so you and I can have our talk and afterwards you can meet the band.'

'That would be good,' she told him, trembling with a mixture of excitement and apprehension. 'Saturday's my half day.'

'Excellent. You know Glasgow at all?'

'No' really.'

'Not to worry. I'm easy to find. I rent a rehearsal studio in Light Street – back of Cowcaddens. Next to a disused church. You can't miss it. See you then, Miss Fernie. Now, I've got to go.'

And without waiting for her to say goodbye, he was gone and

the line was dead. For several moments, she stood without moving, breathing in the smoky, sweaty atmosphere of the call box, going over the practicalities of getting to Glasgow on Saturday in time for two o'clock. Of finding her way to Light Street, wherever that was. Of what music she should take with her, because Mr Riddell would be sure to want her to play. And carefully putting to the back of her mind the thought of meeting the band.

Though, of course, it was what she wanted, as she had to admit, as she left the call box at last to return to work. Of course, she wanted to meet the band, and become part of it as soon as possible. It was just that to begin with, it would be difficult. Like reliving the first day at school or in a new job. Everyone knowing everyone else, everyone knowing what to do. Except you.

On the other hand, it was a challenge, this coming meeting, and Lorna, young as she was, had already learned that you never got anywhere in this world unless you could face challenges. So, head up, shoulders straight, she told herself, and prepare for whatever was to come on Saturday.

Only nothing could have prepared her for the shock, when Saturday eventually arrived, of walking into Luke Riddell's rehearsal studio and meeting what seemed to be a sea of eyes fixed on her. Head up, shoulders straight. How could she remember her own instructions, when the entire band, it appeared, had arrived at two instead of half past and was looking at her?

Seven

If the eyes of the band Lorna met at the door of the large echoing studio were not exactly a 'sea', it was certainly true that they were looking at her, and with a good deal of interest, too. Twelve men. Two women. All taking stock of her, as they busied themselves setting out chairs and stands for the rehearsal. So, why were they early? What had gone wrong?

'All my fault, Miss Fernie!' Mr Riddell cried, as though reading her mind, and hurrying forward to greet her in shirt sleeves and without a tie, yet still seeming as spruce as though in his formal suit.

'Now, how did I get it wrong, then? I should have asked the band to come at half past two, but I forgot and they usually come at two, so of course they came at two. Mea culpa, eh? You find us all right?'

'Oh, yes, thanks,' Lorna murmured, keeping her eyes down in the hope that other eyes would be turned away. No need to say that she'd lost her way twice and by the time she'd found the studio, was rather wishing she'd let her mother and Ewen come with her, as they'd wanted to do.

No, no, it would've been foolish to let them come. Would have given quite the wrong impression, if anyone here had seen them. As though she, a girl of twenty, couldn't find her way around.

'No trouble at all,' she added, clearing her throat, and heard someone laugh a little. No doubt thinking she looked so hot and worked up it was obvious she'd had trouble.

'Good, good,' Luke Riddell said cheerfully. 'Well, guys – and ladies – as you're all here, I'll introduce you to Lorna Fernie from Edinburgh who might be joining us as tenor sax. Maybe some of you knew her dad – Cam Fernie? Coppers as some called him. Played with Jackie Craik's Edinburgh band?'

Coppers Fernie? Yes, some of the men were nodding their heads. They remembered Coppers.

'Great player,' put in a comfortably plump man of forty or so with an alto sax, who introduced himself as George Wardie. 'Good arranger, too. I heard he was better than Jackie at working out who played what from a melody.'

'Each to his own,' Luke Riddell said with a frown. 'You may be a damn good arranger yourself, George, but I know exactly who should play what in my band, believe you me.'

'Oh, sure, Luke, sure,' George said hastily. 'Everybody knows that.'

'Yes, well, come on, Miss Fernie.' Smiling again Luke Riddell took Lorna's arm. 'You take off your hat and coat and we'll go into my little office and let these characters wait a bit, eh? Be looking over the parts for "I'll Get By", everybody. I want to open with that tonight.'

The office at the rear of the rehearsal room was little, all right. Cramped, might have been a better word, Lorna thought, squashing into a flimsy chair opposite Mr Riddell's desk that was piled high with sheet music and papers, plus a telephone, a typewriter and several used cups and saucers. Round the walls were photographs of well known jazz and swing musicians, and a few group photographs of the band, some posed with young women in evening dress who were probably vocalists, as they were not shown with instruments.

Yet those two girls Lorna had spotted out there in the rehearsal room must have instruments? When were they going to make it to the group photographs? It would be interesting to find out just how far they'd been able to integrate with the men, Lorna thought, and hoped she'd soon be able to find out.

'Fancy some tea?' Mr Riddell asked. 'I would, anyway.' He leaped to the door and called through it. 'Anybody making tea out there?'

'Yes, Luke,' a woman's voice answered. 'I've just been volunteered to put the kettle on.'

'Flo Drover,' he told Lorna, returning to his seat. 'She plays guitar in the rhythm section. Know what a rhythm section is, Miss Fernie? Or, may I call you Lorna? But why not let's have a look at that sax of yours while we wait for the tea? Then we can get down to business.'

Business? What did that mean, exactly? A proper audition? Or, just a little run through of some of the music she'd brought? Lorna hadn't forgotten that word the bandleader had used when he'd introduced her to the band: 'might'. 'Might be joining the band', he'd said. Which could equally well mean that she might not.

'What a beauty,' Mr Riddell was murmuring as he ran his fingers down her father's sax. 'Ah, these older horns are good, you know. Give you a head start with the tone, and the thing that's most important about sax playing is getting the tone. That's what I noticed about your playing, Lorna. That's why I asked you if you were interested in my band.'

'Tea's up!' cried a thin, dark-haired young woman entering the office with a tray on which were two mugs of tea and a plate of biscuits. Attractive, with high cheekbones and hazel eyes, she gave Lorna a friendly smile, as she told them they'd got the last of the shortbread. 'Who'd think the war was over, eh?'

'Lorna, meet Flo Drover,' Mr Riddell said, taking a cup of tea. 'Flo, Lorna's going to play for me when she's had her tea, so better shut the door, then we can't hear the racket from out there.'

'Right you are,' Flo replied, with another smile, before going out and carefully closing the door behind her.

'What would you like me to play?' Lorna asked, drinking her tea as fast as possible. 'I've brought some music with me.'

'Oh, we won't use yours, my dear. I've got something here I'd like you to try.' The bandleader smiled as he handed her a piece of sheet music. "September in the Rain" – a lovely melody, and a fine foxtrot. How's your sight reading?'

'Not too bad,' she answered bravely, for though her father had given her practice, reading a piece of music at sight had never been one of her favourite things. She'd always felt annoyed when she made a mistake and would stop and try again, while Cam would be shouting, 'Keep going, keep going!' Which of course, she'd be expected to do, if sight reading in a band. Now, why hadn't she thought Mr Riddell might give her this test, and done some preparation? Too late to think of that now.

As she picked up her instrument and prepared to play the music Mr Riddell had set on a stand for her, she remembered her own instructions. Head up, shoulders straight – here was a challenge, all right. But maybe not one she could meet.

Eight

Luck, however, was with her. As soon as she ran her eye over the music of 'September in the Rain', Lorna could see that it wasn't too difficult, which gave her the confidence to think that her technique might see her through.

And so it proved. She breathed well, she made the right notes, she kept going, and the beautiful tone Mr Riddell so much admired did not desert her. In fact, by the end, she was almost enjoying herself, for the melody was the kind she liked – sweet, melancholy, ideally suited, in her view, to her instrument. And the fact that the bandleader was sitting broodingly listening, no longer mattered. Until she'd finished, of course, when she had to wait for his verdict.

'Pretty good' he said at once, blandly meeting her anxious gaze. 'Not perfect, but pretty good for somebody without band practice. You liked the melody, didn't you?'

'Yes, I did.'

'Always shows. Well, let's move on. You heard a fellow say just now that your dad was a good arranger. Somebody who could take a piece of music and score it for the band in the right way? You ever do anything of that kind, Lorna?'

'No. My dad wouldn't have taught me.' She smiled faintly. 'Never thought I'd have anything to do with a band.'

Mr Riddell's answering smile was broad. 'That's why you think I'm an oddball because I have women in my band? I'm not the only one, you know. Oh yes, I can give you the names of one or two guys who took on the lassies. But it's not popular, I'll admit. Not popular at all.'

'I think it's wonderful that you do,' she said earnestly, and he laughed.

'Maybe. Just one more question, if you don't mind. I realize you've no band experience, but you probably know that most players at some time or other have to play solos. In fact, they like it. Like to have the spotlight. Maybe improvise, though I don't go for that too much. We're a dance band, not a jazz band. But, how d'you feel about solos, then? You'd like to take a turn?'

'Oh, yes! I'd love to play solos!'

'And you'd be good. I can say that because I've heard you already.'

He gave her a long considering look. 'So, I guess decision time has come. Would you like to join Luke Riddell and his Orchestra, Lorna?'

Her lips parted; for a moment she did not speak. 'I would, Mr Riddell,' she said at last. 'I'd like to, very much indeed.'

'That's grand. I'm very glad to have you and I think you've made the right decision.'

He put out his hand and she shook it, hoping hers was not trembling, for she did feel rather strange. Excitement and relief seemed to be hitting her like strong drink – not that she'd had experience of that – and she knew she should try to appear calm and matter of fact, especially as there would be things to discuss.

Her wages, for one thing, and when she should start work. If she need only give a week's notice, perhaps in two weeks' time? No point in hanging about, eh? No, definitely not! Lorna couldn't wait to begin. So, what about the money, then? Not that her wages mattered, the job was all that was in her mind. Still euphoric, still feeling she should be trying to calm down, she waited for Mr Riddell to tell her how much he would be offering.

But when he did, she knew she needn't try any more to settle her floating head. The sum was like a splash of cold water in her face, instantly sobering, instantly bringing her back to earth.

'Three pounds, ten?' she repeated. 'Three pounds, ten shillings?'

'More than you're getting now, I expect?' he asked easily.

'But I live at home now, Mr Riddell. If I join the band, I won't be able to do that.'

'True. I don't run a part-time band – we've too many engagements. You'd have to go into lodgings, but they're cheap enough.'

She looked at him worriedly. 'But would I have enough left to live on?'

'Lorna, how much did you expect? Your dad, of course, would be getting a good salary – he was very experienced. You've no experience at all. I'll have to teach you everything about being in a band, and while you're at that sort of stage, I really don't feel I can offer any more.'

'I see,' she said blankly.

'Maybe you don't realize how much the average wage is these days? I tell you, three pounds ten is good money for someone your age.'

The bandleader's tone was testy, his dark gaze cold, yet Lorna, in desperation, somehow found the courage to reinforce her point. 'I don't care about making a lot of money, Mr Riddell. It's just that I have to be sure I can manage.'

He was silent for a moment, as though gathering patience, finally managing to produce an encouraging smile. 'Tell you what, then, have a word with Flo Drover – the girl who brought us the tea.'

'Flo Drover?' Lorna, gathering her belongings together, rose, as Mr Riddell jumped up and opened the door.

'Yes, you can ask her about her lodgings. Well, I think it's a bedsit she has, but pretty cheap. There may be another one you could try for. And while you're with her, I'm going to tell her to explain what you should wear and what the rhythm section is for. You looked a bit blank when I asked you about it, didn't you?' As he held the door for her, Mr Riddell's smile had faded. 'As I told you, Lorna, you have a lot to learn.'

Nine

Following Luke from his office, Lorna found herself hard put to know what she was feeling. Elated, that she'd been offered a job in a band? Yes, she should have been feeling that, for it was all she wanted, and in a way she did feel it. But then that little crossing of swords with the bandleader over her wages had rather spoiled things. Taken some of the gilt off the gingerbread, as the saying went. For she couldn't help wishing that he'd been more sympathetic to the point she was trying to make. Living at home on three pounds ten was one thing. Living away, was quite another.

Striding into the studio where the band had obviously made themselves at home, dumping cups and glasses all around, sending cigarette smoke rising like a forest fire to the ceiling, Luke was, to Lorna's surprise, in a jovial mood. Is he a weathercock? she wondered. Swinging every way, one minute, mad at her; the next, telling everybody to be delighted she'd be coming to work with them?

For that was his message, as he put his arm around her shoulder and called, 'Hi, fellas – and young ladies! Come meet our new second tenor sax! Because I've given Lorna here a job and she starts two weeks on Saturday. Give her a big hand, then!'

There were a few claps, a few calls of 'nice to have you', and certainly the two young women were all smiles, but for the most part the men only shrugged and raised their eyebrows, and one good-looking, dark-haired man seemed almost taken aback.

'Josh Nevin,' Flo whispered, nearing Lorna in answer to Luke's beckoning finger. 'You'll see a lot of him, you know, seeing as he's lead tenor sax. Thinks he's the tops.'

'Now, now, Flo,' Luke remonstrated, shaking his head. 'Remember, Josh is one of our stars. I'm going to introduce Lorna to him, soon as you've told her about your digs. Also what she should wear – you know the sort of thing – and what the rhythm section does.'

'Oh, my, when do we get to the rehearsal?'

'Aye, when?' asked the handsome Josh himself, strolling over and staring hard at Flo as though he'd guessed she'd been talking about him, before shaking hands with Lorna.

'Congratulations, Miss Fernie, on getting into the band. I look forward to playing with you.'

'Thank you,' she answered. 'I'll be doing my best.'

'Hey, what's got into you, coming over all formal?' asked a fair-haired young man with a trumpet, slapping Josh on the back. 'Just give the new tenor sax a smile, eh?'

'I am smiling!' Josh snapped, and as he moved away, followed by Luke who appeared to be trying to placate him, Flo touched Lorna's arm.

'Take no notice, Josh'll settle down. He's seen your lovely hair and thinks folk will notice you instead of him. But he is good, he'll be a help to you.'

'Just don't play his solos,' the fair young man warned, gazing himself at Lorna's striking hair, as Flo laughed and introduced him.

'This here's our Roderick – as you can see, he's a trumpeter.'

'Rod!' he corrected quickly. 'Rod Warren. Only my mother calls me Roderick.'

'Well, nobody at all calls me Florence!' Flo retorted. 'But what's all this about the rhythm section, Lorna?'

'Seems I should know about it,' Lorna replied. 'I'm afraid I don't.'

'Can't be expected to know everything before you start,' Rod Warren said kindly.

In fact, thought Lorna, he had a kind face. Not so obviously handsome perhaps as Josh, but undoubtedly attractive, with a wide smile that made his blue-grey eyes crinkle, and an ease of manner that made her feel welcome. At least, here was a man not sulking over her appointment. She gave him a warm smile.

'The rhythm section in a band usually has a drum set, a guitar, string bass and piano,' Flo was explaining. 'That tall guy over there is on drums, the one next to him is on bass, Ina at the piano is, guess what, the pianist, and yours truly is on guitar. The front players in a band carry the melody, but the rhythm section behind provides the beat. Very important, eh?'

'Key,' put in Rod. 'And also accompanies soloists. Oh, wait till you hear me, Lorna! The great Harry James has got nothing on me!'

'That's enough blow from you,' Flo said with a laugh, 'if you'll pardon the pun. Push off now, I have to tell Lorna about dresses and digs.'

'Nice guy,' she murmured to Lorna, as Rod moved on. 'Half American, you know. Me, I'm from Glasgow. Ina, come over a minute – what's your place like? Lorna has to find somewhere to live.'

'My place? It's terrible!' Ina, small, fair-haired and freckled, smiled at Lorna. 'A wee bed sitter, the cheapest I could find, and everything's shared and nothing works. Wouldn't recommend it, Lorna, but welcome to the band, anyway!'

'Where I am sounds better than that,' Flo told Lorna. 'Shall I ask about a vacancy? They charge fifteen bob a week, room only, no food. Any good?'

'Sounds perfect!' Lorna cried, shaking hands with Flo. 'Could you let me know, if I give you my address?'

'Edinburgh, eh?' Flo grinned. 'Oh, posh!'

'Hey, I didn't say it was the New Town. But Flo, what did Mr Riddell mean about the clothes I'd have to wear? I've a couple of nice dresses – I thought they'd do.'

'Are they short or long?'

'Oh, short.' Lorna caught Flo's look. 'No good?'

'Well, Luke's very particular about what the band wears. He likes the girls to match the lads, so, we wear white in summer when they wear white dinner jackets, and in the winter when they switch to dark blue, then we wear dark blue, too. Dresses can be any style, but Luke prefers long. Likes the formal look, you see.'

'And what'll all this cost? Supposing I can find a dress, anyway?'

'No need to worry,' Flo said, looking embarrassed. 'If you can't afford it at the time, Luke pays and takes the cash out of your wages.'

'Now, why am I no' surprised to hear that? How many dresses will I need, then?'

'Two, at least. In case one gets damaged, you know. Got any clothing coupons left?'

'No, but if my mother can find the material, I might sweetheart her into running something up for me. She's a dressmaker.'

'Wow, that's a bit of luck, eh?' Flo's brow cleared. 'I was going to offer to lend you one, if all else failed, but looks like you'll be OK.'

'As though I'd be able to get into one of yours!' Lorna laughed. 'Thanks for the thought, anyway.'

'I think we're going to start,' the bass player said in a low voice. 'His Nibs is getting restless, better get in place. Lorna, hope you'll be happy with us. I'm Dickie Tarrant. You going to watch?'

'Sure,' Lorna said, with a return to euphoria. Oh, forget the money, eh? Things were going to work out, weren't they? If she could get a room for fifteen bob, and not have to shell out too much for food, she'd be OK. And she was in the band! As her new colleagues under Luke's direction moved in to 'I'll Get By', it was no wonder her heart was singing along with them.

Ten

It was late when Lorna got home, travelling on wings, or so it seemed, and of course her mother was waiting and worrying. And so was Ewen.

'Why, Ewen!' Lorna exclaimed, 'whatever are you doing here?'

'He looked in to see if you were back yet,' Tilly said coldly. 'I must say, we never thought you'd be so long.'

'I had to stay to see the rehearsal, and that took a while, and then I'd to get to the station. I was as quick as I could be, Ma.'

'Point is, did you get the job?' Ewen asked, then shrugged. 'Silly question. You must have done, if you were asked to watch the rehearsal.'

'Yes, I got the job.' Lorna, suddenly returning to earth, sank into a chair. 'I start in two weeks' time. Listen, is there any tea going? Nothing to eat, thanks, I had a sandwich at the station.'

'A sandwich at the station – I can guess what that was like!' Tilly commented. 'But I'll just put the kettle on.'

'OK, then,' Ewen said quietly. 'Tell us about it.'

Tell them about it? She didn't know where to start. But Ewen saw the smile that curved her lips as she remembered, and he sighed a little.

'That good, eh? Beats the post office, I suppose?'

'Well, it's different. I think the best part was watching the band play. Oh, it was so thrilling! All the time I was just dying to join in, and even now, the tunes are still going through my head. And you know what happened when they were playing "September in the Rain"? That was the one I had to sight read for Mr Riddell . . .'

'No, what?' Ewen groaned, as Tilly came in with the tea tray.

'Well, Mr Riddell suddenly stopped conducting and came up to me and asked me to dance, and there we were, doing the foxtrot, and everybody was laughing, but he was telling me to notice that his tempo wasn't the strict tempo some bandleaders liked but what he thought was best, and I thought so too. And when we came to the end of the music, everybody clapped!'

'This guy married?' Ewen asked, after a silence. 'This Mr Riddell?'

'Yes, he is. Flo and Rod – two of the people in the band – told me on the way to the station. He's married to the vocalist, Suzie Barrie. She wasn't there this afternoon, but apparently she's very glamorous.'

'Never mind his wife,' Tilly said swiftly, as she passed cups of tea. 'What's he going to be paying you?'

Lorna drank some tea and set down her cup. 'Three pounds ten a week.'

Tilly and Ewen exchanged glances.

'And you've to pay for lodgings out of that?' asked Tilly. 'You're no' going to have much left.'

'Flo – she's a guitarist – is going to see if there's a bed sitter going at her place. That would be cheaper than lodgings.'

'And you'd do your own cooking and starve to death, I suppose?' Tilly shook her head. 'Oh, Lorna!'

'Ma, I'll be all right. I can cook, you know.'

'Know how much your dad was getting from Jackie Craik?'

'He was experienced. I've got it all to learn.'

'Fifteen pounds a week,' Tilly said quietly.

Lorna's jaw dropped; so did Ewen's.

'Ma, I never knew that!' Lorna cried.

'Mrs Fernie, are you sure that's right?' Ewen asked. 'Why, it's a fortune! I mean – most folk are no' earning anything like that.'

'It's what he got, all the same. Jackie Craik never minded paying good money to get the best.'

After a brief silence, Ewen said he'd better be going, and when Lorna went to the door with him, managed to say he was pleased for her. If she'd really got what she wanted.

'Oh, I have, I have!'

He gave her a long serious look. 'And who did you say took you to the station?'

'Flo, the one who plays guitar, and Rod – he plays the trumpet.'

'Why'd you need anybody to go with you to the station?'

'I didn't need anybody! We were all going the same way, that was all.'

'Rod's Flo's boyfriend?'

'No!' Lorna was growing impatient. 'They just live near each other. Had to go back to change before work at the ballroom. What's the matter with you, Ewen? Asking all these questions?'

'Nothing.' He put his collar up, pulled his cap down. 'See you Monday, then. Goodnight, Lorna.'

'Goodnight!'

Closing the door on the wintry night, Lorna hurried back to the living room, where her mother was sitting by the fire.

'You'll be ready for your bed?' she asked, looking up wearily 'I am, anyway. Better fill the kettle for the hot water bottles.'

'Ma, I'm still amazed by what you told me about Dad's wages. If he earned so much, how come we didn't . . . well, spend more?'

Tilly smiled. 'Because your dad spent plenty anyway. And you know what on.'

Lorna lowered her eyes. 'I never saw him drunk.'

'Och, no, it was all just drinking and relaxing with the boys after they'd finished playing. But he got through quite a bit of cash, until he started thinking about us and took out some insurance. That's all put away for the future – your wedding, maybe.'

'My wedding? Oh, Ma, if there's any money, it's for you.'

'Now, what would I do with it?' Tilly rose, rubbing her back. 'Still think that Luke Riddell could be paying you more. Ask around, see what the others are getting.'

'The main thing is I've got the job I want, Ma. My foot's in the door.'

'Don't I know it,' Tilly sighed.

Lorna, feeling guilty, said hastily, 'I'll be popping over from Glasgow all the time, Ma, you'll see!'

'Aye, if you can afford the train fare.'

'There's always the bus.' Lorna took a deep breath, watching her mother carefully. 'But, listen, Ma, could you do me a favour? I don't like to ask, when I'm going away, but I'm pretty desperate.'

Tilly gave her a long enquiring look. 'Oh? Sounds bad. Better tell me what it is, then.'

'Well, looks like I'm going to need a couple of new dresses. Seemingly, the men in the band all wear dark blue jackets, and Mr Riddell likes the girls to wear long dark blue dresses to match.'

'Does he indeed?' Tilly frowned. 'Sounds particular. And why do the dresses have to be long? You've got the nice blue one you wore for the talent contest – surely that would do?'

'It's just that Mr Riddell likes something more formal.'

'Well, the problem will be to find the material. I've some blue stuff left but I might need more. And how much is it all going to cost?'

'It's OK, Ma, I'll pay out of my wages.'

'Oh, what a piece o' nonsense! Couldn't Mr Riddell pay for what you have to wear in the band?'

As Lorna said nothing, Tilly shook her head. 'We'll just have to hope that my material will be enough, then. So, when do you want these dresses? I've a lot on at the moment.'

'Just for when I go away, Ma.'

'For when you go away . . . All right, I'll do what I can.'

'Oh, Ma, you're an angel!' Lorna hugged her mother again. 'I don't know what I'd do without you!'

'You'll soon find out,' Tilly said dryly.

Eleven

When the time came for Lorna actually to leave instead of thinking about it and talking about it, the parting was just as bad as she'd guessed it would be.

'The end of an era,' Cissie said cheerfully. 'Comes to us all, Tilly. Still, Lorna's only going to Glasgow, eh?'

But Tilly, carefully folding the new blue dresses for Lorna to add to her case, knew that Cissie had got it right. When a child grows up and departs, yes, it was the end of an era. And yes, it came to all parents sooner or later, but that didn't make it any easier.

'Won't be easy for you, either,' Cissie told Lorna the night before her departure. 'You'll be all excited inside, but sort of sad as well, eh? I mean, you've had to say goodbye to all your friends at the post office. They'll be a big miss.'

'I'll still come back to see them,' Lorna muttered, just wishing Auntie Cissie would go for her bus to Musselburgh. 'As you say, I'm only going to Glasgow.'

'And Ewen's coming with us tomorrow,' Tilly said firmly. 'We're going to see Lorna into her new bed sitter.'

'Ah, the faithful Ewen!' Cissie cried. 'He's no' ready to forget you yet, Lorna.'

'No one's forgetting anybody, Auntie Cissie,' said Lorna.

Although Lorna considered herself lucky to have been able to rent a room at Flo's place, an old tenement house off Buchanan Street, Tilly, naturally, didn't think much of it. True, it was very small, with only the basics of furniture, a washbasin and a miniature cooker, but what could you expect for fifteen bob a week? Lorna said it would suit her fine.

'And you think you're going to be able to cook on this?' Tilly asked, running her finger round the hotplate. 'First, it'll need a good clean. Have you got some scouring powder? I'm sure I canna think how you're going to manage.'

'Don't worry about Lorna, Mrs Fernie,' Flo told her earnestly. 'I know that's easy to say – my folks are dead now, but my mum used to worry about me, too. I'll see Lorna's all right.'

'That's very kind of you, Miss Drover,' Tilly said, studying Flo's thin, intelligent face, and seeming reassured by what she saw. 'I must admit, I feel better, now I see she's got a friend. I know the band scene, you see, I know what she's up against.'

'Oh, Ma,' Lorna sighed, glancing at Ewen, who was too despondent to join in the conversation.

After they'd had something to eat at a small cafe with Flo, there was the melancholy walk to the station where Lorna, having embraced her mother, even kissed Ewen, which would once have cheered him up, but now had no effect. He did manage a wave with Tilly however, as they were carried away on the train to Edinburgh, while Lorna waited until it was out of sight,

'Sad for your mother,' Flo commented. 'Even though you're no' far away. And your young man looked pretty glum.'

'Oh, Ewen's isn't my young man, Flo!'

'He'd like to be, then. My guess is there'll be a few feeling like that in the band, too. Once they've got over the shock of having a girl sax player. I mean, you'll be sitting on the front line, eh? We other lassies are at the back, out of the way – they hope.'

'You talk about young men for me – how about you?' Lorna asked with some hesitation. 'I bet there's someone.'

'Wrong.' Flo studied her nails. 'I've had my fill of affairs that have gone wrong. At the moment, I'm no' interested.'

'That makes two of us. All I want at the minute is to be a success in the band. Mr Riddell says I've a lot to learn. That's why he's no' paying me much.'

'If you don't mind me asking, how much is he paying?'

'Three pounds, ten.' Lorna hesitated. 'How about you?'

'I'm on six.'

'Six!'

'You think it's good? Know how much Dickie Tarrant gets, who stands right next to me playing bass? Twelve.'

'Dickie gets twelve pounds a week?'

'Aye, and he's no' been with the band five minutes and I've been with it two years. All the guys get twelve, and think they should get more – that's why Luke's always losing fellas. He'll no' pay the right money, so some just move on, if they can find another band. Some stay because they think he's good, or they don't want to go to England where there's more work. Of course, he banks on that.'

'But girls accept less, anyway?'

Flo shrugged. 'And play as well as the men. To be fair, Luke wouldn't take them on if they couldn't, he thinks the world of his band. But he's certainly thinking about taking on more women, so's he doesn't have to pay too much.'

'And yet he can seem so nice.'

'Oh, a charmer. But there's a dark side to him. Sometimes have to watch your step.'

Yes, perhaps she'd already seen that dark side, thought Lorna, but said nothing, as Flo, looking at her watch, told her they'd better be going. Lorna wouldn't want to be late for her first rehearsal with the band.

'Oh, Lord, no!' Lorna had cried, as she was seized with an attack of nerves that set her wondering how she would ever find the courage to play again to Luke's satisfaction, or under the sombre gaze of Josh Nevin, whose chair would be next to hers.

But it was all right. It was fine. That first time with the band, she played as though born to it, which was what she'd always dreamed of doing, and when it was over, though not a great deal was said by the men around her, she felt she'd proved herself. It might be, that however well she played, some men would never accept her, but she knew and they knew that she was worthy of acceptance and that was what mattered.

Certainly, Luke himself was pleased with her, and when he came up and praised her performance, she found herself again forgetting about her wages and remembering only that he'd given her the chance to do what she wanted. Her smile was radiant.

'Did well, didn't she?' Luke asked Josh, who gave a quick nod.

'Sure she did. But, Luke, I take it I'm still on for my solo tonight? You didn't ask me to rehearse it.'

'I'm not sure, Josh. Suzie wants to put in an extra number tonight.'

'Suzie does?' Josh's brow was like a thundercloud. 'She doesn't need an extra number, does she?'

'You're telling me what my wife needs?' Luke asked icily. 'Who's leading this band, Josh, you or me?'

'OK, forget my solo tonight. Sorry I spoke.'

'I'm sorry you did, too. You're not the only tenor sax around, Josh.'

'And you're not the only bandleader!'

A frozen silence descended on the band, as Josh and Luke seemed to be attempting to outstare each other, and then, as quickly as the row had blown up, it died down, and Luke clapped Josh on the back.

'What the hell are we arguing about?' he asked. 'You know your solos are a star turn, Josh. Would I want to lose them?'

'So, I play one tonight?' Josh asked quickly.

'Make it next week,' Luke told him easily. 'I sort of promised Suzie her extra spot tonight. You understand?'

'As long as I do get to play it next week.'

'No question.'

A long whistling sigh ran round the band as the tension faded, and as Luke and Josh walked away together, Rod appeared at Lorna's side, brows raised, eyes dancing.

'Oh, oh,' he whispered. 'Now you've soon seen us kids at play, eh? But don't worry about it. You did well just now – that's what matters.'

Lorna, still looking apprehensive, managed a smile. 'Nice of you to say so. I feel it's good I've broken the ice.'

'And there's always plenty of that,' said Flo, joining them. 'Come on, Lorna. We've just got time to get home, get changed and grab a bite to eat before we head out. No rest for the wicked they say.'

'I don't need any rest,' Lorna said at once, though it suddenly came to her that her real test with the band still lay ahead, playing that evening at the Atholl Rooms. Not so much a grand ballroom, but a lovely, friendly venue, Ina told her. And peaceful, too.

'What she means is, nobody fights,' Flo remarked, smiling wryly. 'Unlike some dance halls. Where we don't play, let me add.'

'No, really, you'll be all right there, Lorna,' Ina said encouragingly. 'Just the place to start.'

With real dancers, Lorna thought. Would they notice if she made any mistakes? Maybe not, but Luke would. And so would Josh. If he'd got over his little spat with the bandleader.

'Come on, don't look so worried,' Rod whispered. 'No need to be nervous at the Atholl.'

'I'm no' nervous!' Lorna cried. 'Well, just a bit.'

Twelve

The Atholl Rooms were in a part of Glasgow unknown to Lorna, and not one that seemed the likely home of a dance hall. On a wet night in December, in a street of converted office blocks and dark tenements, the tall building that was the band's destination seemed quite uninviting.

Yet when the doors folded back and Lorna, clutching her raincoat around her shoulders, followed Flo inside, she was surprised to see a fine, spacious dance floor, well lit and warm, with chairs and a stand, known as a platform by the band, and Luke's name in large letters on a banner twisted high.

'Luke Riddell and His Orchestra' it read, and below it, arms outstretched amongst the players arriving, stood Luke himself and Suzie, his wife, the vocalist.

'Come in, come in,' Luke cried, in his most cheerful tones. 'Nasty night, eh? But won't put anybody off, I can guarantee it. Lorna, meet my wife, Suzie. Suzie, meet our new tenor sax.'

'Delighted!' cried Suzie, moving forward to take Lorna's hand. 'Oh, what a pleasure to have another girl around! I keep telling Luke, that's what folk want, to look at pretty girls, not guys in jackets!'

'As though anybody looks at the band anyway,' someone said, but though Luke turned his head sharply, he couldn't see who it was, and Suzie only laughed her singer's melodious laugh. Because, thought Lorna, she would know very well that if people didn't look at the band, they would certainly look at her.

Blonde, with scarlet lips and round brown eyes, she was just the sort of woman who would always be looked at, especially when poured into a slinky black dress, with chunky beads at her throat, bangles glittering on her narrow wrists, and dark red polish on her fingernails. She was everyone's image of a vocalist, and whether she could sing or not, wouldn't really matter. Except that Luke would probably want a vocalist who could sing, as well as look like Suzie, he being a perfectionist.

And at that thought, Lorna began to feel worried again and instinctively looked round for Rod, who obligingly came up to her.

'Why, Lorna!' he cried, taking in her mother's carefully stitched dark blue dress that showed off her delicate colouring and the flame of her auburn hair, 'you look terrific!'

'Do I?' She looked towards the clock that showed only a few minutes to the opening of the hall. 'I'm beginning to feel a bit wobbly.'

'Wobbly? In that dress and with your gorgeous hair, you're going to knock 'em dead!'

'Gorgeous hair?' Her smile vanished. 'I'm hoping folk will like my playing, rather than my hair.'

'Ah, come on, it's just a compliment. Don't take it the wrong way.'

'Why do men always concentrate on what women look like?'

'You mean you mind?'

'When I play the same as they do, I mind.'

'Well, here's something else to think about. If Josh doesn't turn up, you might end up lead tenor on your first outing playing for a dance.'

'Oh, no!' Her eyes widening, she looked at once for any sign of Josh, half hoping he would come, half hoping he wouldn't. Lead tenor sax! Why not? Then she laughed inwardly at herself, as Josh came sauntering up to take his seat next to her. As though she could be lead tenor sax!

'All right, Josh?' George, the lead alto, called, at which Josh looked down his fine nose and shrugged.

'Sure, why shouldn't I be?'

'Just wondered,' George said with a grin.

'See you at the intermission,' Rod whispered to Lorna. 'We'll have a drink, eh?'

She nodded, keeping her eyes on the hall doors which were now opening to admit the evening's dancers, young men in suits, with slicked back hair, and girls in short skirts and high-heeled shoes, noting that immediately the atmosphere was changing. They might be here to dance, but these young people were an audience, and playing with an audience was always different to playing without. As excitement began to exert its grip again and the band members took their seats, Josh bent his head towards Lorna.

'All set? You remember we're starting with "I'll Get By"?

'Yes, thanks,' she murmured, thinking that his words were the first sign of his being helpful. Never mind, she was grateful, anyway. 'I remember.'

'Luke's going to beat us in. Ready?'

'Oh, yes!'

And there was Luke, elegant in his formal evening clothes, standing up in front of his band, the only one that Lorna could now see, or needed to see, as the dancers took their partners, the lights went low, and the music began.

Her first true test of playing with the band was upon her, and though her concentration had to be focused on her own part, suddenly into her mind came the face of her father. He'd always said she'd never play in a band, yet somehow he must always have known that she could, and perhaps in the future, would, or why would he have taken so much trouble training her?

Oh, Dad, she murmured silently, be pleased for me, be proud.

But as the first number ended, with clapping from the dancers and Josh actually smiling, there was, of course, no way of knowing how her dad would have felt. If only he hadn't had that heart attack. If only she could have asked him to come and hear her play. He would have been proud, she told herself, and believed it.

Thirteen

Foxtrots, quicksteps, modern waltzes, old time waltzes, tangos, even a rumba for the brave-hearted; the music rolled on effortlessly until Suzie came on to sing 'All of Me' and, as usual, according to an aside from Josh, stopped the show. The combination of her looks and her voice, which was in fact, very attractive, was too much for the young folk, who kept calling her back until she'd agreed to sing more numbers, and only let her go when she waved her arms, smiling widely, and said she'd be along later. Which was the signal for Luke to produce his own smile and announce the intermission.

'Thank God for that,' the band muttered, claiming they were dying of thirst, but when Rod came up to Lorna, she said she'd like a coffee, if there was any to be had.

'Sure there is. You can get coffee or tea at the bar.' Rod laughed. 'Must admit, this'll be the first time I've had coffee here.'

'You'd rather have alcohol, I suppose?'

'In moderation. I'm not a great drinker. See too much of it.'

'Occupational hazard, my dad used to call it.'

'He was right about that.'

After they'd found somewhere to sit with their coffee in the bar, they exchanged glances, each taking pleasure in the little interlude.

'Mind if I speak of it, but are you really partly American?' Lorna asked, stirring her coffee which was so weak, it looked as if it needed help. 'Sometimes, I think I can hear the accent in your voice – other times, you sound quite Scottish.'

'Border Scots,' he answered readily. 'But yes, I'm half and half. My dad's American.'

'Exciting.'

'I don't know about that. My mother was a Scottish nurse working in the south of England when my father came over in the First World War. They married and after the war, he took her back to Los Angeles, where my brother and I were born. But things didn't work out.'

'Oh, I'm sorry. I shouldn't be prying . . .'

'No, no.' Rod put his hand over hers. 'I don't mind talking about it. All settled years ago, quite amicably. Mother came back home to the Borders when I was ten and Leland was eight and she's been there ever since.'

'Where did the music come from?' Lorna asked softly, looking down at Rod's hand which he at last withdrew from hers. 'I mean, for you?'

'No idea. No one else in the family was interested, but as soon as I heard my first trumpet, that was it, I was sold. Took lessons and when the war came and I joined up, I played for army dos whenever I could.' Rod shook his head. 'Not that there was much music around at El Alamein, for instance.'

'And now you're with Luke Riddell. You happy, Rod?'

'Sure. He's a great bandleader. Not keen to pay well, but I get by. Got a flat I share with a couple of office workers, see my mother when I can, and Leland in Perth – he's a trainee accountant.'

'What about your father?'

'Been too difficult to see him, though now the war's over he's asked us to go to the States. And one of these days, I plan to do that. Want to check out the music, get to hear some of the American big bands.' Rod finished his coffee. 'But all this is about me, Lorna. What about you? I know you're from Edinburgh and your dad was with Jackie Craik. That must have given you a head start, eh? To have a father who played sax.'

'Yes, it was wonderful.' Lorna smiled reminiscently. 'We were very happy, Ma and Dad and me, though there should have been two boys, as well. They died very young.'

'I'm sorry.'

'Yes, well, Ma got over it, of course, but then Dad had his heart attack last year, so there was only me.' Lorna fixed Rod with an earnest gaze. 'That's why I feel bad about leaving her, even though I'm only in Glasgow. I know she wishes I'd just get married and give up my sax, but I'll never give up my sax.'

'Might get married, though. If there's anyone special?'

'There's no one special. Ma thinks so, but I don't.'

'You mean, there is someone?'

'No. I just said.'

Rod glanced at his watch. 'Better make sure we're not late back. Luke flies off the handle if anybody's late.'

'Oh, quick, let's go.'

'It's all right, not time yet. And you haven't finished telling me about yourself. I was wondering – didn't your father try to get you into Jackie's band, then?'

'Jackie's band? No. Dad thought girls would never play in dance bands with men. Just said they weren't for the lassies.'

'Guess he was thinking of the life. Can be tough.'

'But we all make music, we should make it together. You agree, don't you?'

'Let's say, I'm glad you're making music with me.'

Rod was laughing gently at himself, when he looked around the bar and suddenly his laughter died.

'Oh, God, Lorna, everybody's gone! We'd better get moving. Back to the dance hall, quick!'

'You said it wasn't time!' she cried, her heart thumping.

'I know, I got it wrong. Come on, run!'

But though they did run to the dance hall, they were still too late. The dancers were all there, waiting. The band was on the stand, waiting. Worst of all, Luke was walking up and down, moving his stick from hand to hand, and he was waiting, too.

'I'm sorry, Luke,' Rod said in a low voice as he leaped on to the stand. 'It's my fault, I mistook the time. Lorna's not to blame.'

'We're very sorry,' Lorna murmured, her scarlet face contrasting with Luke's furious pallor. Picking up her sax with a trembling hand, she took her place next to the impassive Josh, while Luke with a supreme effort at control, turned to the hall and smiled.

'Ladies and gentlemen, will you please take your partners for a ladies' excuse-me, in our quickstep medley.'

And turning back to the band, he raised his stick, murmured to the players, and gave them the beat for the first melody, which Lorna was always to remember. 'Jeepers, Creepers'. Oh, Lord, would she ever forget trying to play her best to that tune, when under sentence of telling off? For it would come, she knew it would.

And it did. At the end of the evening, when Suzie had sung her last song, the last waltz had been played, and the dancers had left, the band left too. Except for Rod and Lorna, standing, waiting, for Luke to speak.

He wasted no more time.

'Can you just tell me what got into you, Rod?' he demanded coldly. 'You know what I think about people in the band who come in late. I don't care whether it's for a rehearsal, or a broadcast, or a dance programme, or what the hell it's for, but everybody who plays for me turns up on time. So, how come you made Lorna – who's playing with us for the first time – as late as you? How come you kept everybody waiting? Everybody in the band, everybody on the floor, and me, for God's sake?'

'I don't know, Luke,' Rod answered tightly. 'It was a natural mistake. We were having a coffee and talking, looked up, saw the time and ran.'

'A natural mistake? You're not in this band to make natural mistakes, Rod!'

'OK, I've said I'm sorry. It's not exactly a hanging offence. If you want to sack me for being five minutes late, go ahead. But Lorna's not to blame, so leave her out of it.'

'I'm as much to blame as Rod,' Lorna declared, clearing her throat. 'But it's just like he said, it was a mistake. We were talking, we missed the time. It won't happen again.'

Seeming stunned by the way they were answering him back, Luke stood perfectly still, his pallor turning to scarlet on his cheekbones, his dark eyes moving sharply between the two young people. Then, as Lorna had seen him do before, he suddenly relaxed.

'I take it you don't want me to sack you, Rod?' he asked smoothly.

'Of course I don't, Luke. I like working for you.'

'And Lorna?' Luke gave her a wry smile. 'You've not had much experience yet, but you're doing so well, just try to remember my rules in the future, eh?'

'I will, Luke.'

'OK, let's forget this and say goodnight. Enjoy your day off tomorrow.'

At these words of farewell, on to the stand swept Suzie, in fur wrap and silk headscarf, followed by Flo, wearing her coat and carrying Lorna's.

'Now now, tough guy!' Suzie cried. 'That's enough of blowing people up. Let's get home.'

Luke frowned. 'Everything I do is for the audience, Suzie. I don't make the rules for myself.'

'Oh, come on, you know you like throwing your weight about!' She laughed and took his arm. 'That's it for tonight, though.'

'I was thinking we'd go for a drink with the lads.'

'No, we're going home. Goodnight all!'

As Luke was led away, Rod turned uneasily to Lorna and Flo. 'You two coming for a drink?'

'I think I'll just get off home, Rod, thanks all the same,' Lorna murmured.

'Me, too,' Flo said, passing Lorna her coat.

'I suppose I'm in the doghouse, am I?' Rod asked, gazing at Lorna. 'Got you into a row with Luke. Thanks for supporting me, anyway.'

'I missed the time as well. Why should just you be blamed?'

He put his hand through his short fair hair. 'If you really don't blame me, thanks again.'

'OK, OK, let's break this up,' Flo said crisply. 'I'm dying to get home. Come on, Lorna.'

'Maybe I can see you to the tram? Or are you getting a taxi?'

'Too dear and the tram's just up the road. You go and join the lads, Rod – you look as though you could do with a drink. We'll see you Monday.'

'Lorna, how about Sunday?' he asked eagerly. 'Can we meet?'

'I'm sorry, Rod, I said I'd go over to my mother's tomorrow. She'll be wanting to know how things went.'

'Say they went well,' he said glumly.

'As though I'd say anything else! See you Monday, Rod.'

'At the rehearsal studio,' Flo called over her shoulder. 'Luke wants to tell us his plans.'

'Monday,' Rod agreed, as a caretaker appeared with a broom and meaningful scowl, at which they all three hurried away.

'Somebody's smitten,' Flo whispered to Lorna, when they'd hitched up their long skirts and climbed on to a late tram. 'Rod can't take his eyes off you, eh?'

'What a piece of nonsense, Flo! You've got a wonderful imagination.'

'No wonder he forgot the time, talking to you. But he's a nice guy, you know.'

'If you say I could do worse, like my mother, I'll throw you off the tram.' Lorna laughed. 'I told you, I'm no' interested in young men at the minute.'

'Only your career, eh?'

'That's it, exactly.'

'Well, maybe you're right. As I told you, falling in love never did me any good.' Flo gave a long sigh. 'Och, when you see Luke in full flow, don't you wish we could just run away and start our own band?'

'Start our own band?' Lorna stared. 'As though we could!'

'Has been known. What about Ivy Benson, in London? And a few others I could mention.' Flo took out her cigarettes. 'Oh, forget it! Just a pipe dream, as they say.'

'A lovely pipe dream, I say.'

⋆ ⋆ ⋆

But in her bed that night, picturing herself with her own band – as though it could happen – Rod's rueful face suddenly came into Lorna's mind. 'A nice guy', Flo had said, more than once, and of course he was. Not that Lorna was interested. Still, before she finally fell asleep, she was smiling.

Fourteen

Plans. Seemed Luke had plenty, and when the band gathered in the studio on Monday afternoon, looks were exchanged and shoulders shrugged, because no one ever knew with Luke what might be coming.

As there was no rehearsal scheduled, people sat where they liked, and it didn't take long for Rod to find Lorna and join her, at which point Flo, some distance away with George, gave a knowing smile.

'Enjoy Sunday?' Rod asked.

'Yes, it was good to be back home.'

'See the young man who isn't your young man?'

'As a matter of fact, I didn't.' Lorna, who was feeling bad that she hadn't contacted Ewen, changed the subject. 'Why no rehearsal today? I thought we were playing for a private dinner dance?'

'True, at the Commodore Hotel, but they don't give a damn what we play. It's some rich young fellow's birthday and we know what those dos are like. Everybody playing the fool and racketing about the place.' Rod laughed. 'So, Luke picks out the numbers we all know backwards and that's it. No rehearsal needed.'

'Attention everybody!' Luke, immaculate in fine wool sweater and perfectly pressed trousers, was on his feet, controlling his band as though he was about to conduct. 'Just want to put you all in the picture with what I've got lined up for you.'

'Hope it's something good!' came a cheeky call from Dickie Tarrant, whose size matched the bass instrument he played in the rhythm section.

'Damned good!' Luke retorted. 'First off, what would you say to a broadcasting contract?'

Broadcasting? A murmur of interest ran round the band, and Lorna, her eyes shining, caught her breath. Broadcasting? Could it be that what she'd failed to achieve at the talent contest was coming to her at last? Seemed so, for as Luke explained, he'd managed to negotiate a six-week contract with the BBC in Glasgow to begin mid January. A half-hour slot, five evenings a week.

'We'll be able to fit them in before our other engagements,' he said happily. 'And who knows where it'll lead? It's about time we got on the airwaves again – haven't had a spot since pre-war days.'

'That really is good news,' George commented. 'Broadcasting will give us just the publicity we need.'

'Exactly.' Luke nodded. 'All you read about in the papers are the big names down south – Ambrose, Jack Hylton, Geraldo – all great bands, but where's Scotland? We've got good bands too.'

'We'll need the latest numbers, Luke. Want me to get started on arrangements?'

'Too right, but we mustn't forget the old favourites. We'll have to work out the right balance, and see what Suzie thinks. The BBC's keen to have a vocalist.' Luke smiled indulgently. 'She could end up being famous – me too!'

'This is so thrilling,' Lorna whispered to Rod. 'It's what I've always wanted, to be on the wireless, playing to all those unknown people out there – I can't wait to start!'

'Not going to be nervous of the red light?'

'The red light?'

'Means you're "On Air".'

'Oh, no, I see what you mean!'

'Don't worry, you'll be OK. Soon as you begin to play, you'll forget where you are. I know – I did some broadcasts for the Forces radio.'

'Everybody – hush!' Luke suddenly shouted, raising his hand. 'I haven't finished yet. Thing is, I've been thinking for some time that we ought to be playing more theatres. Yes, I know, we're a dance band and always will be, but a theatre engagement's also good publicity, and should be worth considering. I'm looking into it and I'll let you know what happens.'

'Sounds good,' Josh remarked. 'I'm all for a bit of variety.'

'I'm glad you said that.' Luke grinned. 'Because the next thing on my programme is touring.'

Touring? At the word there was a general sagging of jaws and quiet groans, which Luke of course did not miss.

'Come on, come on,' he said irritably. 'What are you complaining about? Most of you never played the army camps during the war with George and me, and the few guys we could manage to scrape together – my God, you'd have had something to moan about then!'

'Oh, the freezing barracks, the freezing food,' George agreed, nodding. 'But they were grand lads, you know. Grand audiences. And never knew when they were going out to meet Jerry. Bravest of the brave.'

'Yes, well it should be more comfortable for us now,' Luke went on. 'I'm arranging bookings for next March, which is when we'll be free of contracts here and the radio contract as well.'

'Booking where?' asked Dickie Tarrant. 'Don't say the Highlands. They'll probably still be under snow in March.'

'The Borders, as a matter of fact, but taking in Ayr, Carlisle and Berwick as well. And we needn't start worrying about snow at this stage. Come on, we've just said we want to get the band better known. Touring's a way to do it.'

'Should be going to London, then.'

'That'll come, just give us time!'

'Bags I sit next to you on the coach,' Rod said in Lorna's ear, as people began to drift away. 'And don't think I'm joking.'

He touched her arm. 'Listen, tonight we'll be finishing late, I won't have the chance to ask you to go on anywhere, but tomorrow we'll be free until the evening. Couldn't we meet for lunch somewhere?'

Still starry-eyed from the news of the broadcasting engagements, she said at once, 'Why not? If you know any good places to eat?'

'You mean you're interested in the food?' He gave a mock groan. 'And I'm only thinking about seeing you.'

'Ah, you are joking, aren't you?'

'Honestly, I'm not.'

Now, she really looked at him. 'We have only just met, Rod.'

'What's that got to do with it?'

'Well – nothing, really, I suppose. Where shall we meet, then?'

'I'll call for you at twelve. No trouble, it's on my way. We can go into town together. All right?'

'Oh, yes. Fine. But I'll see you tonight, anyway.'

'Not going home now? We could get the tram.'

'We're going shopping,' Flo interrupted, coming up with Ina. 'Have to fit shopping in sometime, you know.'

As Rod left them, saying he'd see them at the hotel dinner dance, Flo shook her head at Lorna.

'Well, that frightened him off, eh, talking about shopping? But honestly, he's turning into a limpet. If you don't want him, you might have a job to get rid of him.'

'I'd hang on to him, if I were you,' Ina said with a smile.

Do I want him? Lorna asked herself. Apart from her unwillingness to be sidetracked from her career, it was true what she'd said – they'd only just met. But that didn't seem to matter to him.

'Great news about the broadcasts, eh?' Ina asked, as they set off for the shops, and Lorna, glad not to have to think any more about Rod, eagerly agreed.

'Oh, it's grand, really grand. Couldn't be more thrilled.'

Fifteen

For lunch next day, Rod took Lorna to a pretty little tea room in Sauchiehall Street.

'No, not the famous Willow Tea Room,' he told her apologetically. 'You know, the one designed by Charles Rennie Mackintosh way back. I thought we'd never get in there, and this place seems right for you.'

'Right for me? How?'

'Well – pretty and sort of feminine.'

'Feminine?' Lorna, looking round at the elegant little cafe, smiled a little. 'You mean, for the little woman?'

'Ah, now, come on, Lorna! What's wrong with being feminine?' Rod passed her a menu. 'The light lunches are right for everybody, anyway, in spite of rationing. I think you'll find them OK.'

'Of course I will! Everything's perfect. No, I mean it, Rod. I think you've got hidden depths to choose a place like this. And knowing about Rennie Mackintosh, as well. I must say, I don't know much about him myself.'

'That's because he was a Glasgow artist, and you're from Edinburgh.'

'Ah, now, that's unfair!' Lorna flushed. 'As a matter of fact, I don't know much about art at all. Music's all I've been interested in up till now.'

'Snap, then!' Rod's eyes were dancing. 'I don't know much about art, either. It was Flo who told me about Rennie Mackintosh, after we all went out to the Willow Tea Room one time. And did you know that "Sauchiehall", as in the street, is really "Sauchiehaugh" which means willow meadow? She told me that as well.'

'Flo's very clever,' Lorna murmured. 'Very intelligent. And deserves better from Luke than she gets.'

'How do you mean?' Rod asked with interest, but when a waitress came to take their order for soup and herb omelettes, Lorna made no reply.

'Are you talking about money?' he pressed. 'I've often heard her and the girls complaining.'

'Well, you might hear me complaining, too.'

'I won't ask you what you get, but I know Luke pays girls less than the men. Can't blame him, I suppose. It's usual practice.'

'Can't blame him? What are you talking about, Rod? How can it be fair to pay women less than men if they do the same work?'

'Lorna, the men are the breadwinners. They have families to support.'

'Oh? So where's your family, Rod?'

He looked a little abashed and seemed at a loss for a reply, until the waitress brought their soup and he gave a sigh of relief.

'Hey, this is good, eh? Want a roll with it?'

'You must admit, it would be fairer if single men and single women at least were paid the same.' With unusual force, Lorna tore her roll apart. 'Come on, Rod, agree with me!'

'Yes, maybe that would be more fair,' he said hastily. 'Can we talk about something else now?'

For a moment or two, she studied him, thinking, yes, his was a fine face, with wide, benevolent brow and generous mouth, those eyes that crinkled when he smiled. So, why were his views so different from hers? And, oh God, why did she mind?

For the rest of the meal, they trod very carefully, saying no more about money or women's rights in the workplace, and by the time they came out into driving rain and decided to go to the pictures, they felt remarkably in tune with each other.

'Good idea to come here,' Rod remarked, as they stepped into the vestibule of the cinema where a small queue was forming at the box office. 'Best place to get out of this downpour, eh? And who cares what's on?'

'Why, I do!' Lorna cried, brushing her damp hair from her brow. 'And it just so happens, it's something I want to see. Look – it's a Hitchcock picture – *Spellbound*.'

'With Ingrid Bergman – my favourite!'

'Gregory Peck – mine! Oh, Rod, I do hope we're no' too late for the beginning.'

'Exactly in time for the matinee, from what it says on that board. Our lucky day, eh? I'll just find some money.'

Standing to one side, Lorna averted her eyes as Rod sorted through a handful of coins from his pocket. Sometimes, in the past, going out with boys who weren't earning much, she'd offered to pay her share but they'd always refused, just as Rod would refuse if she offered now, she felt sure.

It would not be his style, to let a woman pay for anything, and the truth was, he did earn more than she did. All the same, she wondered if she should make a stand – let him see that they were equals, even if Luke didn't think so? But he'd already reached the front of the queue and was buying their tickets while she was still debating what to do, and in the end she let it go. Why make a fuss and cause more arguments?

'Thanks, Rod,' she said quietly, as the usherette showed them to seats in the back stalls, and at his smile, decided she'd done the right thing.

She was even more relieved they hadn't had another argument when, as the lights went down, he took her hand and she sensed his pleasure in just being with her. He really wanted that, didn't he? Was really happy in her company, even though he scarcely knew her? And already, as his warm hand rested round hers, she was wondering if she might be feeling the same about him.

There was certainly something about his presence that stirred feelings that were new to her. And exciting. Trouble was, she'd meant it when she'd told Flo she wasn't interested in young men 'at the minute' – only in her career. Anyway, it was all too soon and she had other things to think about. The broadcasting contract, for instance. Whenever the thought of that came into her mind, she hugged it to her as something warm and comforting. But then – she couldn't deny it – holding hands with Rod was having something of the same effect.

Better concentrate on the film, she thought, for the Lord knew, it was exciting enough, with its Salvador Dali dream sequences, and dear handsome Gregory Peck being suspected of murder, and lovely Ingrid Bergman trying to protect him. But why did the pattern of lines upset him? And who was the mysterious proprietor, haunting the mountain slopes? By the end of the thrilling denouement, Lorna found herself quite forgetting to analyse her feelings about Rod and she was just clinging on to his hand like a lifeline.

'Oh, Lorna,' he whispered, laughing, as the credits rolled up and the cinema lights came on, 'you weren't scared, were you?'

'No, of course I wasn't!' she declared, finally loosening her hand from his. 'But I thought it was a terrific picture, didn't you?'

'I did. Just wish we didn't have to come back to reality.' Rod tapped his watch. 'Must go home, though. Get ready for this evening. Because, this evening, we're not going to be late, right?'

'Right. I'm never going to be late for Luke again, that's for sure.'

As they stood at the tram stop in the still falling rain, she glanced at Rod who was looking a stranger with his fair hair so wet it seemed dark. Yet his friendly smile was his all right, and so was the blue-grey gaze he turned on her in the fading December light.

'Thanks for a lovely day, Rod. I really enjoyed it.'

'Not over yet. We'll meet tonight. Maybe go for a drink afterwards?'

'Maybe.'

But already she'd decided that she wouldn't. Better go carefully, eh?

'Very sensible decision,' Flo told her later. 'It isn't just that you might have problems with Rod if you encourage him, but you could be in trouble with Luke as well.'

'Luke? What's he got to do with it?'

'Well, he's like a lot of bandleaders – they don't want their musicians getting involved in relationships. Within the band, I mean. Usually falling for the vocalist, of course, and thinking more about her than their playing.'

'I don't see that it's any business of Luke's to interfere in people's private lives.'

'He reckons it is his business when their private lives affect the performance of the band. Look, don't worry, you're being sensible about Rod, and we'll hope he'll get the message, eh? There won't be anything for Luke to complain about.'

'I'll have to admit, I'm sort of attracted to Rod,' Lorna said slowly.

Flo gave her a long steady look. 'You'll have to make up your mind, then, what you want.'

'Well, it's early days, isn't it? I'm just starting out. I have to think of that.'

'Quite right. Stick to concentrating on your career. Find time for Rod later. If he cares for you, he'll wait.'

'I suppose he will.'

'And in the meantime, have you thought about what solos you might play? I'm sure Luke will be asking you soon.'

'Solos? Help, I did say I wanted solos! But what will Josh say?'

'Who on earth cares? It's Luke you have to worry about not Josh.'

But Lorna was still really worrying about Rod.

Sixteen

In the weeks that followed, all went well. Better than Lorna could have hoped.

First, there was Christmas and though she'd been thinking she might not be able to spend it with her mother, Luke having booked the band for a Christmas Eve dance, she did manage to get a train early on Christmas morning which meant she could be home in good time.

'And you've got Christmas Day and Boxing Day?' Tilly asked, looking pleased when they opened their presents together. 'I never thought you'd get the time off at all. You remember your dad was always playing somewhere and I'd to fit the dinner in when I could.'

'I never thought I'd get it myself,' Lorna told her. 'But now we can have a lovely day to ourselves, eh?'

Tilly looked a little apologetic. 'As a matter of fact, Cissie's coming over with your cousins and I've invited Ewen and his mother as well.'

'You haven't!'

'Aye, I have. Thought we could have tea and then a sing-song, with you playing the piano like you used to do. Mrs MacKee's really looking forward to it.'

Bet she is, Ewen, too, Lorna thought, but her expression softened. Actually, she was quite looking forward to it herself, and in the event found it really did her good to be home again.

It was a relief to be free of worries about her solos – though her first had gone well on Christmas Eve, with praise from Luke and no adverse comments from Josh. Free, too, of having to watch out for Rod, to see if he was upset that they weren't going out together, though in fact, he seemed to be taking it rather well. Accepting her excuses, smiling his pleasant smile, 'getting the message', as Flo had put it. What a relief!

Even when, on Christmas afternoon, Ewen looked so happy to see her, which should have made her feel bad, and his mother complained about her rheumatics, which was always her way, seasonal spirit got Lorna through and she saw to it that they had a wonderful time. Auntie Cissie and her cousins, Pippie and Alex, were kissed and embraced, too, and after Tilly's Christmas cake and mince pies, there came the sing-song with Lorna playing the piano and people shedding a tear or two, for this was the first peacetime Christmas and they had to remember those who would not be celebrating as they were.

'The poor folk no' coming back from the war,' Cissie murmured, when the singing was over and Ewen was opening the bottle of port he'd brought. 'Let's drink to them, eh? And absent friends.'

'And Dad,' Lorna whispered, her eyes misting again.

'Aye, to Cam,' Tilly said. 'And your Jamie, Cissie.'

'To our dad,' said tall, blond Pippie and Alex in unison. They were both working as teachers, one in Jedburgh, the other in Hawick, but fascinated by Lorna's new job, and after the toasts, keen to get her to talk about it. When might they hear her play then? Would the band be touring, for instance? When she told them they'd be touring the Borders and the south in March, there was great excitement, and though Tilly put on her dubious look, even she couldn't find anything to worry about when Lorna casually threw in that the band would be broadcasting in January.

'Oh, my, you're going to be famous!' Pippie cried. 'Wait till I tell them at school!'

'Playing on the wireless,' Cissie sighed. 'Hear that, Ewen?'

'I hear,' he answered cheerfully. 'Congratulations, Lorna. I'll be sure to tell 'em all at the post office.'

It was only when he and Lorna went for a walk on Boxing Day, that he seemed unable to keep up his pretence of being happy for her and admitted that he was feeling very low.

'Aye, low's the word for me,' he muttered. 'Seeing you flying, eh?'

'Flying, Ewen?' Lorna repeated. 'I'm just a very ordinary part of the band. I'm no' flying anywhere.'

'Yes, yes, you are. I feel it. And I bet there's some guy for you over there already, isn't there? I don't know why, but I feel that, too.'

'No, no,' she said quickly. 'No one special.'

'It's all right, Lorna, I never expected to be the one for you.' He smiled grimly. 'The boy next door, eh? I'm the one that's no' special.'

'Oh, Ewen, you're very special to me. My special friend.' Lorna's eyes were searching his face which was pinched and reddened with the chill of the air. 'Doesn't that mean anything?'

'In a word, no.' He took her arm, as they turned from the banks of the Water of Leith and retraced their steps. 'It's cold, eh? Let's get back to your ma's. She promised me more of her Christmas cake.'

Just before they went inside the house, however, Ewen took out a notebook and pencil. 'When do you say you'll be on the wireless?' he asked quietly, and when Lorna told him, wrote the dates in his book. Then he kissed her cheek and very swiftly her lips.

'I'll be listening,' he whispered, and followed her into the house.

Seventeen

After Christmas and Hogmanay came what Lorna and the band had really been waiting for: the January broadcasts. Yet it appeared to some that the idea of being back on the air had gone to Luke's head, for not only had he called in two extra arrangers to score new numbers, he'd taken to drilling the band so hard in rehearsal, some felt like going on strike. Always a perfectionist, he'd now become obsessed with finding fault, and shouted so loud at unfortunates who played a wrong note, or displeased him in any way, by the time the first broadcast was due, many were succumbing to nerves.

'It's just because he's setting such store on making his name with the publicity,' George explained. 'It's important to him to do well, so you just have to go along with it.'

'It's important to all of us,' Flo snapped. 'But we aren't driving everybody mad because of it.'

'Ah, but he's the bandleader,' George reminded her. 'He gets the kudos if we're a success, he carries the can if we're not.'

'Well, thank God, the whole thing will soon be over,' Josh put in. 'Then we can relax.'

'When we go on tour?' Flo asked with raised eyebrows. 'Are you serious?'

Lorna was saying nothing, thinking only of the broadcast ahead. Like everyone else, she was on edge, yet so consumed by excitement, she seemed able to put her nerves aside. This was an experience she had looked forward to for so long, she wasn't going to let anything spoil it.

Arriving early for the brief warm-up before they went on air, she looked around, as she so often did, for Rod – not to talk to, just to see how he was looking. She found his eyes, as they so often were, fixed upon her. She smiled a little. He smiled back. But they did not speak.

In fact, after the producer had finished telling everybody what to expect, it was Luke who was doing most of the talking, walking round, reminding everybody of things they already knew, even tweaking people's jackets, as though they were going to be seen, which was absurd.

'I feel like telling him, this is the wireless we're on, Luke, not the films!' Ina whispered, nudging Lorna's arm. 'Will you just look at him with Suzie? He's more like a fashion plate than she is!'

'Talk about a peacock,' Dickie Tarrant commented. 'Just hope he doesn't forget where he is and shout at us if we get something wrong'

But all fell silent as the producer showed them into the studio to take their places. The clock showed it was time. They were on air.

Somebody was introducing them: 'Tonight we have one of Scotland's best known dance bands – Luke Riddell's Orchestra – playing to you from the BBC. And here is Luke himself, to tell you something of the programme. Ladies and gentlemen – Luke Riddell!'

'Good evening, everyone,' came Luke's especially smooth tones. 'Can't tell you how much pleasure it gives my band and me to be playing to you this evening, and we hope you'll enjoy the music we've chosen for you. A medley of old and new, beginning with that catchy number, "On the Sunny Side of the Street", followed by "Anything Goes", "I'll Be Seeing You", and that old favourite, "Harbour Lights".

And then Luke was turning to the band, raising his stick, beating them in, and at last, long last, they were off. Nerves forgotten, they played their best, Suzie sang her best, Luke introduced more numbers, and the time flew by so fast, before they knew it, he was at the microphone again, wrapping things up, telling everyone to tune in tomorrow for more music from Luke Riddell and his Orchestra! They were off air.

'Well done!' cried the producer.

'Well done,' Luke agreed, walking amongst his band as they were leaving the studio. 'Just one or two wobbles – nothing to speak of – very good on the whole.'

'What wobbles?' asked Josh. 'If you ask me, we've never played so well.'

'I agree,' the lead trumpeter, Bob Kenny said truculently. 'If you've found anything wrong, just spit it out, Luke.'

'He hasn't found anything wrong,' Suzie declared. 'We were all perfect. Now, let's get going. We've another show to do tonight, remember.'

'Oh, no!' people began wailing, as they prepared to face the January night. 'We've still to play at the Atholl!'

'Don't tell me you've forgotten,' Luke said grimly.

* * *

Having observed everything and soaked up her new experiences like a sponge, Lorna hurried home with Flo, her thoughts now with the mainly unknown audience who might have heard her play that evening. Only as a part of the band, of course, not in a solo spot – that honour had gone to Josh, as was only to be expected, he being lead tenor sax. But still part of the Luke Riddell sound, which must have gone out to so many homes, so many folk she would never know and yet could feel affinity with, simply through her instrument and the music it played.

'Enjoy it?' asked Flo. 'Did it come up to expectations?'

'Oh, yes. Yes it did!'

'Well, don't take too long getting ready now. We haven't got a lot of time.'

'Don't I know it!' Lorna answered, rushing to wash and change and put on the kettle. But when she was almost ready, just brushing her hair, she couldn't believe how quick Flo had been, knocking at her door.

'Come in, Flo!' she called. 'Door's not locked!'

But it wasn't Flo at the door, it was Rod.

Eighteen

Snow was covering his overcoat and melting from his hair as he stood in her doorway, gazing at Lorna.

'OK to come in?' he asked huskily.

She had risen from her chair, putting down her brush, and for a moment did not speak. Was she just surprised to see him? Or, not surprised at all? Had she always known that some time, in spite of all her efforts to stand aloof, he would come to her? Anyway, she finally nodded and he took a step towards her.

'A fellow coming out let me in your main door. I told him I was from the band, come to collect you.'

'I see.'

'He saw my trumpet case.' Rod showed it, with a smile, then set it down. 'Must have believed me.'

'Are you collecting us?'

'Well, it's snowing – I thought for once we'd share a taxi.' He was very close to her now, close enough to touch her, but staying still, keeping his eyes upon her. 'I see you've already changed. So have I. Into my awful blue jacket.'

'You look nice in that blue jacket.'

'Not half as nice you look in your blue dress.'

'Got my old cardigan over it for now.' She laughed uneasily. 'No' so warm in here.'

'Believe me, you look beautiful. But here am I, covering everything in snow.'

Unbuttoning his overcoat, he let it fall and after a long moment of silence, put out his arms to her and, still in silence, she went to him. It seemed right, it seemed natural; something they could not deny themselves, and for some time they stayed together, letting the feeling wash over them that some great step had been taken, that nothing would be the same for them again. Then they kissed, and kissed again, ecstatically, until Rod drew away, holding Lorna from him so that he could look into her eyes.

'Oh, God, Lorna,' he said in a low voice, 'why have you been running from me? What makes you so afraid?'

'I wasn't afraid, Rod. Well, not of you. I just – I felt it was too soon.'

'What was?'

'Oh, you know – to be having a relationship. I'm just starting out on what I want to do. I didn't want . . . to be serious.'

'You thought you could choose?' Rod smiled and held her close again. 'Lorna, darling, you can't choose to be serious or not serious. You can't choose to love or not love. It happens, that's all. And it's happened to us.'

'We can't be sure, Rod. Folk often think they love someone, and then they find it wasn't real.'

'Mine is real. Yours is real. Lorna, promise – you won't run from me again?'

Her lips parted, she was ready to speak, when another knock came at her door.

'Lorna, are you ready?' came Flo's voice. 'It's snowing, so I've booked a taxi.'

'I'm ready!' Lorna called back, hurriedly giving Rod his coat and running to open the door. 'Flo, look who's here! Rod had the same idea as you – he wanted us to take a taxi.'

'Well, well, Rod, eh?' Flo, in heavy coat and gloves, with a scarf wound round her head, looked at Rod and smiled a little smile. 'Nice, we're all going in together then. The taxi's due in five minutes, so we may as well go down to wait for it.'

'May as well,' they agreed.

There it was, the taxi, waiting; headlights blurring in the whirling snow, the driver reluctantly climbing out to open his doors.

'I'll be pig in the middle!' Flo cried, making Lorna go before her, so that she could sit between her and Rod, and looking from one to the other in the gloom of the interior, her eyes sparkling.

Oh, Flo, you tease, Lorna thought. She knows, doesn't she?

But trying to separate herself and Rod, the way they felt at that moment, was pointless. Each was so conscious of the other, so dwelling on every look, every movement, Flo might just as well not have been there.

It was only when, as usual, she was absorbed into the music at the Atholl Rooms, that Lorna's thoughts moved away from Rod, but they returned in full force at the intermission, only to be kept hidden when Ina came up to join them for coffee.

'Just making sure you don't forget the time,' she cheerfully announced, but at the look on Rod's face, hastily added, 'only joking, of course!' and asked if they were going for a drink later. 'I thought I might, if the boys don't get too noisy.'

Rod's eyes met Lorna's. A drink with the boys? They'd rather be on their own. Separately, they came to the same conclusion, though. Better not push it, eh? Better not cause talk at this early stage. What had happened between them that evening was their secret, something to be held close and marvelled at, not revealed too early.

'I think I might go along,' Lorna said carefully.

'I might, too.' Rod cheerfully finished his coffee. 'Hey, isn't it time we were on our way?'

All three were the first back on the stand, except for Luke, who graciously inclined his head at them and said, 'Well done!'

Nineteen

In the time following that first broadcast, Lorna thought she'd never been so happy. Everything in her life seemed to be combining to give her what she wanted – well, perhaps not quite all, for she and Rod were having to be very careful. Not only to keep their new-found love a secret from the band and sharp-eyed Luke, but also to keep within the limits they'd set themselves. No sex, then, but love-making as near as they could get to it without taking risks. Risks Lorna never put into words but which Rod perfectly understood.

'Need the ring on the finger?' he asked once, lying with her in the battered armchair of her bed sitter, having taken her hand and kissed it. 'How about I get one?'

She had hesitated. Engagement, marriage: they represented huge changes for which she wasn't quite sure she was ready. Though she knew she and Rod were truly in love, the path ahead wasn't as straightforward as it might be. Commitment was involved, and she'd already made a commitment to her career. How would it work out to have two commitments? That was the question she had to answer.

'You're thinking you're too young?' Rod had asked quietly, but she'd shaken her head.

'I'm twenty-one now – loads of women marry at that age.'

'But you're not ready?'

She shrugged. 'We could maybe wait a while?'

'Fine. Just as long as you don't desert me.'

'As though I would!' she'd cried and the discussion ended in passionate embraces until it was time to get ready for their evening booking.

With the ending of Luke's dance hall contracts and the blustery arrival of March, came the time to begin preparing for the tour. There were low-voiced grumbles from certain members of the band.

'If we have to go on tour, why not somewhere abroad?' asked Bob Kenny. 'Somewhere warm?'

'Good idea,' voices agreed, until Josh reminded them that foreign travel was still much restricted, unless you were entertaining the troops somewhere.

'Could do that,' Dickie Tarrant said with enthusiasm. 'Could go to Germany, maybe. Let's suggest it to Luke.'

But no one volunteered to do that, Luke being well known for not accepting suggestions from anybody.

'While we're talking about suggestions,' Flo murmured to Lorna, 'mind if I make one to you? Don't let Rod sit next to you on the tour coach too often. I think Luke is watching you more than you realize.'

'You really mean he'd tell us we shouldn't be together?'

'You know he would. Haven't I said he doesn't approve of love affairs between people in the band? And he's no' the only one.'

'Can he honestly say we don't play as well because of our feelings for each other?' Lorna cried angrily. 'As soon as I pick up my sax, that's all I'm thinking about, and Rod's the same with his trumpet. I'll tell Luke that, if he says anything to me!'

'Be careful, then. Remember, he's the boss.'

Lorna hesitated, looking at Flo's strong thin face 'If Luke knows about us, I suppose other people do?'

'Only Ina and me. I don't think the men have noticed anything yet, but might when we're all together on that coach. Better watch your step, eh?'

'I do get tired of doing that,' Lorna admitted. 'But I'm still looking forward to going on tour. I mean, it has to be interesting, seeing different places and new audiences, hasn't it?'

'Are you joking? First, the coach will be freezing. Likewise, the digs. Likewise, the halls. Probably the food, too.'

'Have you actually been touring?' Lorna asked, laughing, and Flo shrugged and laughed herself.

'No, I'm just going on what folk tell me.'

'Well, this one might be different.'

'Ah, you're thinking of spending more time with your Rod, eh? Just remember what I said, though. Watch your step.'

Twenty

Kilmarnock, Ayr, Peebles, Moffat, Dumfries, Carlisle, Alnwick, Berwick-upon-Tweed . . . Just names on the map to Lorna, until on a bleak March day, the band set off on its travels.

'Oh, what did I tell you?' Flo cried, as they entered their coach for the first time. 'It's freezing!'

Well, it was true, it wasn't warm, but Lorna, ready to get the most out of this new experience, scarcely noticed, and anyway, in spite of all Flo's warnings, she had Rod next to her, his comforting hand in hers covered by his folded overcoat – why should she mind the chill?

It soon became apparent, however, that everything Flo had said about touring was turning out to be true. The coach was cold; their lodgings spartan; the local dance halls where they played, always icy until halfway through the evening when the audiences added some warmth. As for the food, with rationing still in force, there was no point in expecting too much. The local people did their best, and if it felt as though the war was not yet over when the spam came out again and there were no eggs for breakfast, well, what could anyone do?

Go to the pub after they'd finished playing, maybe, or huddle round the fire in their digs – and wait for better times.

For Lorna, still determined to enjoy herself, the thing she couldn't help noticing about being on tour was that it seemed to have an odd effect on some of the men in the band. Their playing was fine, just the same as always, but in the coach they seemed to revert to being schoolboys again, playing practical jokes, singing bawdy songs, drinking, shouting and pointedly excluding the women in a way that hadn't been obvious for some time.

'Och, guys are often like this on tour,' George told the girls, when they'd arrived in Peebles after a particularly rowdy session on the coach. 'Just high spirits, nothing to worry about.' He laughed. 'You've just got to dodge the paper pellets they fire around, eh?'

'They wouldn't be behaving like this if Luke travelled with us,' Ina commented. 'Why does he have to use his own car?'

'He's the bandleader!' George answered, scandalized. 'Got to allow him some perks. And he has Suzie with him, too, remember. She likes her comfort.'

'I think it's a pretty bad way to go on,' Rod remarked, joining the girls. 'I know we all like to relax but some of the fellows go too far.'

'They're just having a bit of fun,' George told him. 'And if you're thinking about the lassies here, they're tough, eh? Not going to be upset by a few blue songs!'

'Sez you,' Flo retorted. 'I agree with Rod – some of the guys go too far. Not all, of course.'

'Well, don't say anything to Luke, will you? There's no need to get him involved.'

'Wouldn't dream of it, George. We don't want any trouble.'

Rod's eyes, though, were on Lorna.

'Sure, we don't want any trouble,' he murmured later, when they were managing to walk home alone to their lodgings. Which were not, as Rod had already secretly complained, in the same guest house, for Luke had made the bookings and carefully arranged for the three girls to be together and the men apart.

'But I don't want you upset by those fellows, and I've a damn good mind to say something.'

'Rod, don't worry about it. It's the way a few guys like to go on when they're with other guys.'

'Yes, but it's quite unnecessary. They're grown men, for God's sake. They needn't behave like kids.'

'I think it's because Luke's not around. A chance to let off steam.'

'Just as I say – they're like school children when teacher's away.'

Rod suddenly took Lorna into his arms and kissed her hard.

'Listen,' he whispered against her face. 'Why not give all this up? Why put up with it?'

'Put up with what?' she asked, pulling away.

'Well, this band thing. I mean, I know you enjoy playing and you're good – really good – but it's no life for someone like you. Mixing with the guys and having to pretend you don't mind how they go on.'

'Look, I don't care about being one of the boys, I just like being in the band. Playing my sax, trying to improve. If the men want to play the fool on the coach – so what? It's our playing that's important.'

'Well, there is an alternative to the band, you know. One you might like just as much. One you will like, in fact.'

'What are you talking about?'

'You know,' he said softly. 'I'm talking about that ring on your finger. I'm talking about being married to me.'

For a long time she was silent, her eyes searching his face in the poor light of the street lamps.

'That's an alternative?' she asked at last. 'We're talking "either or" here? I never knew when we discussed rings on fingers that it meant giving up everything else.'

'Well, it would have to, wouldn't it? Luke would never want us as a married couple, but that's not important. We wouldn't want it ourselves, would we? Most guys in the band are married. Their wives aren't in the band too.' Rod laughed a little. 'Hell, if they were, there'd be no more bawdy songs or practical jokes on the coach, eh?'

'Let me get this straight,' Lorna said evenly. 'You're saying that if we get married, I'll be staying at home while you'll be playing in the band as usual?'

'Well, it is usual, isn't it?' Rod's eyes were puzzled. 'For the wife to be at home and the husband to be at work? That's how it's always been.'

'There has just been a war, Rod, when women did all kinds of jobs. They were even called up to make munitions, as I was. They even went to war, didn't they?'

'Yes, but that was hardly normal, was it? Now that the war's over, things will get back to how they used to be. There'll be no need for women to do those things.'

'So, what do they do? Give up work, stay at home and do the dusting?' Lorna's eyes were flashing. 'I'm sorry, Rod, that isn't for me. I've found the job I've always wanted and I shall never give it up. If I marry, I keep on in the band, that's all there is to it.'

'For God's sake, Lorna, you must see that that's not possible!' Rod's arms were raised, his hands waving, as he stared into Lorna's set and determined face. 'There's no way we could be married and play in the same band! It would never work out, we'd have no home life at all. And, as I say, Luke would never permit it.'

'I don't see what it would have to do with Luke. He wants good players. We're good players. Why would he want to let us go because we were married?'

'Because it's just the way things are, Lorna. You tell me how many married couples you know playing in the same band!'

'Well, there aren't many women in bands anyway, are there? But, there's Luke and Suzie.'

'Suzie's a vocalist. It's not the same thing at all.' Rod ran his hand over his brow and groaned a little. 'Look, please think about this rationally—'

'Just because I don't agree with you, I'm no' being rational?' Lorna shook her head. 'Rod, let's leave this for now, OK? I'll say good-night and see you in the morning.'

As she moved quickly away from him, Rod ran after her and tried to take her arm but she shook it away.

'In the morning, Rod. I said we'd leave it for now.'

'Please, Lorna, let's not part like this. You know we won't sleep a wink.'

'Goodnight, Rod.'

'Lorna, I'm not saying goodnight—'

But it was too late for him to say anything else. The door of Lorna's lodgings had opened and closed, and she was gone.

In the morning, when they met at rehearsal, their faces were alike: white, strained and desperately unhappy. Even though they knew others were watching, they clasped hands and gazed into each other's eyes, not speaking until Luke came in, when, very hurriedly, Lorna leaned forward and whispered in Rod's ear, 'Oh, Rod, no more arguing, eh? Let's just keep on as we were.'

'For God's sake, let's!' he whispered back.

'When you're ready, you two!' Luke cried, frowning, and tapping his stick on a music stand. 'Perhaps we might start?'

'Sorry,' Lorna murmured, hurrying to her place next to Josh.

'Sorry, Luke,' Rod added cheerfully, joining the trumpet players.

And as the first number got under way, it was amazing to everyone how well the two of them played when they should have been in disgrace. And might still be, if Luke took exception to all that holding of hands and looking into eyes, thought the rest of the band, awaiting events with interest.

Twenty-One

What happened was nothing to do with Lorna or Rod.

Dickie Tarrant, returning to his digs in Moffat, the small town that was their next venue, took a tumble down a flight of stone steps after a pub session, not only dislocating his shoulder but also breaking a bone in his hand. No bass playing for him for some time was the doctor's verdict when Luke drove him to the local cottage hospital, which so enraged Luke, he almost threw a tantrum in Casualty. For where was he going to find a replacement bass player?

'Talk about blue songs,' Ina said at breakfast the morning after the accident. 'George said we should have heard Luke in the car after they'd left Dickie at the hospital. Oh, my, the air was blue then, all right!'

'But poor old Dickie,' Lorna commented sympathetically. 'He's got to stay in hospital?'

'Just overnight. They thought he might have a bit of concussion as well.' Ina's normally pale face was flushed, her expression anxious. 'I might try to get to see him today. Maybe cheer him up. I mean, it's worse for him, not being able to play, than for Luke, eh?'

'And you will cheer him up,' Flo said kindly. 'Might as well admit you've been going out with him quite a lot lately.'

Ina's flush deepened and she glanced at Lorna. 'All right, I have, but you know what Luke's like – tries to control our whole lives. Dickie and me've been keeping things quiet.'

'I'm a bit tired of Luke's control,' Lorna muttered, and Flo, eating a last slice of toast, nodded.

'Aren't we all? But Lord knows where he's going to find a new bass player at such short notice. He'll be on the phone now, I expect, ringing round his contacts. Might even try poaching. You know what these bandleaders are like, always pinching other people's players.'

'Oh, I hope Luke doesn't try that!' Ina cried. 'He'd have to make the job permanent to get anybody, and then what would Dickie do?'

'Don't worry,' Flo told her. 'No one from a good band will want to join us in the middle of touring, eh?'

It seemed she was right about that for the bass player, found for

Luke by one of his Glasgow contacts, was not from any other band but a young fellow named Sorley Simpson, just out of the navy who was looking for a job. Tall and well built, with a head of curly dark hair and a cheerful grin, he seemed nervous when he arrived two days later and had to run the gauntlet of the band's stares and Luke's keen ear.

'Of course, I'm out of practice,' he murmured, after his first run through, and was not made to feel better when Luke coolly agreed that he could tell. Still, beggars couldn't be choosers, a bass player was needed and Sorley was taken on as temporary replacement for Dickie.

'Only temporary – that's a relief,' Ina sighed. 'I was afraid Luke might give him Dickie's job.'

'Don't think he'd do that,' Flo said grudgingly. 'But what I'm wondering is how much he'll be paid. Having heard him, maybe we needn't worry, eh? Luke won't push the boat out for him.'

'By which you mean he won't get more than you?' Lorna asked with interest.

'He'd better not!' Flo cried.

Rod said, if they liked, he'd tactfully find out what the new guy had been offered.

'But don't blame me if it's more than you,' he told Flo with a grin. 'I'll only be the messenger, and you have to remember Luke just does what's usual.'

'Pays a man more than a woman however badly he plays?' Flo shook her head in exasperation. 'Go ahead, then, Rod, tell us the worst.'

And the worst was just what the girls had half feared. Sorley Simpson was to be paid twelve pounds a week, the same as Dickie.

'I don't believe it!' Flo breathed, turning pale. 'Luke wouldn't be such a fool. He knows he needn't pay Sorley as much as that. He wants the job, eh?'

'Seems he's had another offer,' Rod said quietly. 'From some band in England. And he knows it's Luke who wants him, so he's held out for the going rate.'

'Going rate for men!' Flo cried. 'But what about women? I'm going to have it out with Luke, I'm going to tell him straight, if I don't get the same as this new fellow, I'll be the next one to go!'

'Better not, better calm down,' Rod advised. 'Luke's not the type to respond to having a pistol at his head. And remember, Sorley's only temporary. He'll be gone as soon as Dickie recovers.'

'It's the principle of the thing!' Flo answered, now turning scarlet with anger. 'You agree with me, don't you, Lorna?'

'Yes, I do,' Lorna declared. 'It's disgraceful that we're paid the rate we are. I'll go with you, Flo, if you want to talk to Luke.'

'That wouldn't be a good idea,' Rod said at once. 'You won't be doing yourselves any good, threatening Luke, and with all due respect, Flo, guitarists are easier to find than bass players.'

'Thanks so much, Rod! It's nice to know that I'm expendable!'

'Look, I didn't mean—'

'Why don't we wait a bit,' Ina asked reasonably. 'Say, till we get back to Glasgow? By then, Luke will have seen that Sorley's not worth the extra wages and might cut him down anyway.'

'I just want him to put us *up*!' Flo retorted, but after a few moments of consideration, seemed calmer and agreed to wait until they returned home before tackling Luke.

'I'm wondering if she's right to wait,' Lorna said worriedly to Rod. 'I think we should have this pay business out in the open. We girls need to make a stand.'

'I don't agree,' Rod said firmly. 'It's always best not to do anything in the heat of the moment.'

'You just don't want me to get the push and depart,' she said teasingly, but his face remained serious.

'Wrong. If you get the push, Lorna, I might have more chance of getting you to marry me.'

Her smile faded. 'I thought we'd agreed to put talk of marriage on hold, Rod?'

'For now,' he answered softly.

Twenty-Two

Lorna's first tour, which had not in the end been as enjoyable as she'd hoped, finally closed in the ancient border town of Berwick-upon-Tweed. Long a battleground between England and Scotland, continually swapping nationality depending on which side had most recently won, it was now officially English, but very appreciative of a Scottish band. Which at least gave the players a warm feeling of a job well done, as they piled into the coach for the last time.

'Not much to look forward to now,' Flo sighed, taking a farewell look at the wide mouth of the Tweed and the sea that lay beyond.

But Ina smiled and said, 'Oh, I don't know.'

'Well, of course Dickie's recuperating back in Glasgow, eh? Nice to know someone's happy.'

Lorna, loosening her hand from Rod's, leaned over the back of her seat to tap Flo on the shoulder. 'Don't worry,' she whispered. 'It'll be all right. Luke will have to see our point of view.'

'Think so?' Flo turned round, her eyes wary, for George had come to sit beside her. 'We'll soon know, anyway.'

'What's all the mystery?' George asked genially. 'You two cooking up something good?'

'Why, George, you know we can't cook!' Flo answered with a laugh, and Lorna, sitting back, glanced at Rod whose face was expressionless, yet conveying his feelings, all the same.

'Wish you'd stop being so disapproving,' she whispered, but he only covered her hand with his.

'How could I disapprove of you, Lorna?'

'Maybe just of what I do.'

'Never!

She wasn't sure she could believe him.

They had just one day to sort themselves out back home, Luke had decreed, and then he'd be calling a rehearsal for their new engagements. Not only two spring balls, but a week's playing at the Royal – second only to top of the bill, so they'd better sharpen up after the tour.

'Aye, he's like a cat in the cream over all this,' George said, grinning.

'And guess who'll be arranging into the small hours – yes, you're right, yours truly!'

'Oh, why is George always so cheerful?' Flo groaned, as she and Lorna arrived back at their digs. 'Thank God he doesn't know what we're up to.'

'What's the plan, then?' Lorna asked, putting her key in her door. 'See Luke after the rehearsal?'

'No, before. We'll get there early, catch him in his office.' Flo tightened her lips. 'When I say we, I mean just me, Lorna. I really don't want you to be involved.'

'Want some beans on toast? I'm starving.'

'You're just not listening, are you?'

'No, I'm not. Look, come in when you're ready, and I'll open the tin.'

'Rod not coming round?'

'I told him I wanted an early night, which is true. But I do want to work out exactly what I want to say to Luke tomorrow.'

'That's if I let you say anything,' Flo said firmly.

Luke seemed surprised when they arrived early at his office the following afternoon, and unwilling to be interrupted.

'You both want to see me?' he asked, staring from Flo to Lorna, his brows drawn together. 'I've got George here, we're going over his arrangements.'

'Luke means he is,' George said, rising from his chair. 'Putting a note here, a note there, the way he always does.'

'I know what I want,' Luke said shortly. 'OK, you two had better come in, then, but whatever you want to say, make it snappy, eh? You won't mind if George stays?'

'As a matter of fact, Luke, we'd like to speak to you on your own,' Flo told him. 'This is personal.'

'No trouble.' George, carrying an armful of scores, moved into the rehearsal hall, his look curious, but he made no further remark. Only gave them a grin as they shut the office door.

I expect he's guessed what we're going to say, Lorna thought, taking a chair next to Flo, her mouth dry, her hands damp. And probably Luke had, too. But what his answer would be was anybody's guess.

'So, what's this all about?' Luke asked, sitting at his desk and pointedly looking at his watch. 'Not come to complain about young Simpson, I hope? He's only holding the fort, you know.'

'Only holding the fort?' Flo's colour had already risen. 'But very well paid, all the same.'

'Ah, so that's it, is it?' Luke's smile was pinched. 'Money. I should have known. Perhaps I did. It's not the first time, you've raised the subject, Flo, but I'm sorry to see that this time you've involved Lorna here.'

'Flo didn't involve me!' Lorna cried. 'I wanted to speak to you myself because I feel the same as she does.'

'Well that's a shame, then, because I'm just going to have to tell you what I tell her, it's not possible to pay you girls any more.' As they opened their mouths to reply, he held up his hand. 'I'd be going against all accepted practice. Women get less than men. Can't be helped, it's the way things are.'

'And you don't think it's unfair?' Flo asked, breathing fast. 'To pay an inexperienced player like Sorley more than you pay me?'

'You're not doing too badly, Flo, in the circumstances. As for Lorna, I shall be increasing her wages after she's been with us a little longer. I might remind you, that both of you are earning more than many working men at this time.'

'That's beside the point,' Flo declared. 'We're only comparing our wages with people who do the same as we do, and sometimes no' as well as we do. And if you're going to say that men need more money because they're the breadwinners, Sorley isn't keeping a wife and family, any more than I am!'

Very deliberately, Luke rose to his feet. 'I'm sorry, girls, you can argue as much as you like, but the truth is I can't change the situation. Now, if you please, you'll have to excuse me, I've things to do before the rehearsal.'

'That's it?' asked Flo, rising to her feet. 'You're no' going to listen to anything else we have to say?'

'There's no more to be said.'

'There is from me, then.' Flo, shaking with emotion, glanced at Lorna. 'Only me, though, Luke, Lorna's out of this.'

'What do you mean?' Lorna cried. 'I'm with you all the way, Flo!'

'No, because there's no need for you to say what I'm saying.'

'Which is what, for God's sake?' Luke groaned. 'Flo, will you get on with it, so that we can get back to work?'

'But maybe I won't be going back to work.' Flo took a deep breath and steadied herself. 'Because I have to tell you, Luke, that if you can't see your way clear to paying me what you should, I'll have to think about leaving the band.'

There was a long moment of silence, during which Luke's eyes locked with Flo's and Lorna gave a low groan. Then Luke strode to the door and opened it.

'No need to think about leaving the band, Flo, you are leaving it. You've made it plain you aren't happy with me, you do nothing but moan and complain, and quite frankly, I've had enough. Yes, you're a competent guitar player but not indispensable, so, I'm putting you on a week's notice, which I can do according to your contract, and after that, I'd like you to go.'

As Flo stood very still, her face pale, her eyes flashing darkly, Lorna cried, 'Luke, you can't do that! You can't sack Flo!'

'Think yourself lucky I'm not sacking you as well,' he answered coldly. 'I'm prepared to keep you on, Lorna, because I think you've been led astray by Flo, but I don't want to hear one more word from you about money, is that clear?'

'You won't hear any more from me on anything,' Lorna retorted, trembling. 'If Flo goes, I go. I'll take a week's notice as well.'

'No, Lorna, no!' Flo shouted, but Luke only shrugged.

'So be it. If that's what you want, Lorna, that's fine by me. Better get going now, we have a rehearsal due in ten minutes.'

'Never mind the rehearsal.' Flo suddenly stretched out her hands towards Luke. 'Please, Luke, don't sack Lorna. She's worked so hard for her job and she's first rate, you know she is. You can't let her go, just for trying to support me!'

'I don't want to let her go, but it's her decision. Isn't that right, Lorna?'

'It's my decision and I'm going,' Lorna said quietly. 'Now, if you want us to join the rehearsal, we will. I don't want it said I didn't honour my contract, so if I'm supposed to be working a week's notice, I'll work it.'

'Well done, Lorna!' Luke cried. 'That's the right attitude. Now, as I say, I've things to do, so can we bring this meeting to an end?'

'So, that's it, then?' Flo muttered to Lorna, as they stood in the rehearsal hall, watching members of the band beginning to drift to their places. 'Luke's won and we've lost. I've never been so humiliated in my life.'

'He didn't humiliate you, Flo. You stood up to him, you told him we wanted what was right!'

'And look where it got us.' Flo shook her head. 'I'm out of a job and so are you, and that's upset me, Lorna. I told you I didn't want you to be involved.'

'I'd never have forgiven myself if I'd stayed on when you had to go. Anyway, it's for the best, isn't it?'

'For the best? How can you say that?'

Lorna's eyes were sparkling. 'Because it'll make us do what we should do.' As Flo only stared, clearly lost, Lorna clapped her on the shoulder. 'Don't you remember what you said you wanted?'

'What? What did I say I wanted?'

'Your own band, of course!' Lorna's face was triumphant. 'Now's our chance, Flo, to strike out on our own. We can do it together, create an all-girl band here in Scotland. Wouldn't that be worth getting the sack for?'

'Oh, Lorna!' Flo was looking as though she didn't know whether to laugh or cry. 'It sounds wonderful, but it isn't possible. We could never have our own band. For a start, you'd need capital and we've none.'

'We could get it. We could get all we need, if we try hard enough. How does anybody start in this business? We can succeed, if we want to – it's as simple as that.'

'You're so young, you don't appreciate the difficulties—' Flo was beginning when Lorna put her fingers over her lips.

'Ssh, don't say any more just now. I see Rod coming over. Let's talk about it later. But it's something to think about, eh?'

'You can say that again!'

'Hi you two,' Rod said, smiling. 'What's going on? You look like you're planning to blow up the Houses of Parliament, or something.'

'I wouldn't mind blowing up somebody,' Flo said tightly. 'No name, no pack drill, as they say.'

'Tell me after the rehearsal.' Rod jerked his head towards the office door. 'Here comes His Nibs. We'd better get moving.'

Twenty-Three

After the rehearsal, Rod asked Lorna if he could come back with her to her bed sitter.

'You know I've been suffering withdrawal symptoms all the time we've been on tour,' he said in a low voice.

'Missing me?' she asked. 'But I was always there.'

'Missing your room, where we could really be alone. Didn't you feel the same?'

'Yes, I did, but we won't have much time together now, when we have to play at this ball Luke's booked us for.' She hesitated. 'Besides, I've something to tell you.'

'Just as long as I get to kiss you first.'

That would be just as well, Lorna thought. After she'd given him her news, they might not feel so much like kissing.

In fact, in her little bed sitter, where the tea she'd made grew cold in the cups, Rod soon sensed anyway that something other than his kisses was on her mind, even though she appeared to be as passionate as he and might have fooled someone less understanding.

'What is it?' he asked at last, drawing away and studying her face. 'Lorna, what's wrong?'

'Nothing's wrong.' She made a nervous attempt to tidy her hair. 'Between us, anyway. But Flo and me – we've got the sack.'

Rod's eyes widened; he caught his breath. 'You asked for more money? Both of you?'

'Yes, today, before the rehearsal.'

'I told you that was a damn fool thing to do. You know what Luke's like – why in hell did you still risk your job by tackling him?'

'It's the principle of the thing, Rod. He's wrong and you know it, to pay somebody like Sorley Simpson more than Flo – and me so little, come to that. We had to speak to him, we had to make our case.'

'And the result was, he sacked you both? Just like that?'

'Well, Flo said she was thinking of leaving the band if he wouldn't consider paying her what he should, so he told her she would be leaving the band anyway. As for me, if I agreed not to talk about my wages, he said I could stay.'

'You could stay? Then why did you get the sack?'

'I suppose I sacked myself, because of course I wasn't going to stay if Flo had to go.' Lorna took Rod's hands in hers. 'Surely, you can understand – I couldn't let her down?'

'You didn't think you'd be leaving me as well as the band?'

'Leaving you? No!' Lorna laughed a little. 'I never thought of that for a minute. Why should I leave you?'

'You'll be staying on in Glasgow, then? Not going back to Edinburgh?'

'No – well – I'm no' sure . . .'

'You see, you haven't thought it through,' he said gently. 'But I'm ahead of you. As I said before, you needn't leave me if you leave the band, because now we can get married.' He was beginning to smile, his eyes to dance. 'This is it, Lorna. Marriage is no longer an unspoken word. We can get married as soon as we like and you won't have to worry about anything ever again. From now on, I'll take care of you.'

Lorna stood very still, letting his words wash over her, but when he tried to take her in his arms, she pulled away.

'I did say, didn't I, Rod, that if I got married, I wouldn't be giving up playing?'

'Yes, but that doesn't matter now. You're out of the band, you won't be playing anyway.'

'I'm hoping that's isn't true, because the fact of the matter is . . .'

'Is what?' he asked, as she paused.

'Well, it's only just come to us, Flo and me, as something we could do – though we have kind of discussed it before . . .'

'Discussed what? For heaven's sake, Lorna, what are you talking about?'

'Our band,' she said simply. 'We're going to start our own all-girl band.'

It was something he had so clearly not even thought about, she could tell that he couldn't at first take it in. But he had turned very pale, and the dancing light faded from his eyes.

'An all-girl band,' he repeated. 'Lorna, are you crazy? How are you going to start such a thing? What are you going to use for money? Where are you going to get the women to be in it? It's the maddest idea I've ever heard in my life.'

'Is it?' Her tone was icy. 'Let me tell you that there are girl bands all over America, and in England, too, and they're all very successful. So, there's no reason why we shouldn't run a band here in Scotland that would do just as well, and if you're asking about money, we'll get it, and the girls to join us – why not? Why shouldn't there be all-girl bands, when there are all-men bands and no one thinks they're crazy?'

'They're just not the same. OK, maybe it's not logical to say they're different, but you have to go by what people are used to.' Rod gave a groan. 'All I care about now, Lorna, is that if you go ahead with this mad plan, it'll mean the end for us. I'm serious. It will drive us apart, just as surely as though we didn't care for each other any more.'

'Why? Why should it?' Lorna's eyes on him were stormy. 'I don't understand you, Rod. Why should my running a band drive us apart?'

'Because it'd be even worse than if you were just in Luke's band. You'd be completely wrapped up in what you had to do, just like he is. Worrying about bookings and agents, finding money, checking on the players. There'd be no home life, no life for us at all.'

'No, Rod, no! I wouldn't let it happen!'

'You couldn't help it.' He slowly shook his head. 'And all the things I want from marriage, they wouldn't count, would they? I mean, having you by my side, making a home, having our children, going through life together. If you had your band, could you give me those, Lorna?'

'No,' she said after a silence. 'Maybe I couldn't. No' all of them, anyway.' She rose and picked up her teacup, looked at its contents, set it down. 'I could give you love, though, but maybe that wouldn't be enough.'

Rod stood up and reached for his coat. 'In the sort of marriage we'd have, it wouldn't last, would it? That's what I'm saying, Lorna. It's what I *have* to say, in fact, not what I *want* to.'

'Are you going now?' she asked dully.

'Yes, got to get ready for tonight.' He looked at her for a long time. 'Lorna, is there any chance you could . . . change your mind?'

'No, Rod, I can't. I can't do what you want.'

Slowly, he buttoned on his coat. 'I'll see you at the hotel, then. For this ball.'

'Yes, all right.'

When he had left her, she sat for some time, staring into space. Then she washed up the teacups and slowly, like a person moving under water, began to get ready for the evening engagement she'd promised to keep. Working her notice, she thought, and not just from the band.

Twenty-Four

That last week with Luke's band passed with agonizing slowness for Lorna and Flo. If they hadn't agreed to work out their notice, they could have been away, out of reach of sympathetic looks and questions, but for Lorna, all that mattered was avoiding Rod. Not seeing the suffering on his face that mirrored her own. Not having to hold back the words that might have brought them together again: 'I love you, Rod, I'll do what you want, I'll give up my plans for a band.'

So far, every time those words had come to her lips, she had stopped herself from saying them. For why should he not have said to her: 'I love you, Lorna, I'll be glad for you to do what you want, so, just start your band and we'll be married and live happily ever after'?

He never spoke such words to her, she never spoke her words to him. And she was sure they never would.

At least, the idea of the all-girl band had not gone away, even though Lorna's pleasure in it had temporarily faded. Flo, in fact became more and more enthusiastic, and Ina was quite bowled over by it. She had, of course, been stunned by the news of the sacking of Flo and Lorna, and was all for going to see Luke herself, until Flo talked her out of it.

'What good would it do if you were to lose your job as well?' she asked sensibly. 'Might as well stick it out, until we get going. Then you can come and join us.'

'You mean your own band? Well, I'm thinking of it. If you're sure you need a pianist.'

'You bet we do, we need everybody. But, as I say, you'd do better to stay with Luke until there's an actual band to go to. Sure you'll be all right to leave Dickie, Ina?'

As she hesitated a little, Flo said brightly, 'Come on, you know you can still see each other. We won't be going far.'

'Well, how about you and George?' Ina asked, with a sudden, cheeky grin.

'George?' Even Lorna, deep in her own thoughts, looked up at the name. 'What's George got to do with anything?'

'Didn't know he had a thing going for Flo?' Ina asked. 'See, she's blushing!'

'I never knew about you and George,' Lorna said, frowning a little. 'Why'd you never tell me, Flo?'

'For pity's sake, there was nothing to tell!' Flo cried irritably. 'OK, he's been asking me out for some time and I haven't gone, so maybe we've both missed that particular boat. I've got more important things to think about now, anyway.'

More important things . . . Lorna's heart was like an unbearable weight in her chest, as she considered what was important and what was not. At one time, she'd thought her life would be so simple. Get a job in a band. Be happy. End of story. Now she felt tossed on violent seas, caught in emotions she didn't know how to handle, yet clinging on to what had driven her so far, the feeling that she must be true to herself, true to what she could do and wanted to do. And if someone didn't want that for her, then she needed to admit that he was not for her.

But, oh, that was so hard!

When the week of notice finally ended, there was an emotional drink with the band on the last night, with even Luke shaking the leavers' hands and wishing them all the best, and being described by Flo under her breath as 'the great hypocrite'. Still, it meant there was no unpleasantness at the end.

And then George, for once not seeming cheerful, took Flo home, and Lorna, not looking out for Rod, who had kept his distance all week and particularly that last evening, went home alone.

Still wearing the dress she'd worn for her last time with the band, she sat in her room, thinking she should make a start on her packing, but instead doing nothing at all. Tomorrow, she would be returning home to Edinburgh, where she would look for a temporary job to keep her going while she worked out her plans, while Flo, in Glasgow, did the same. Lorna was too weary and too dispirited to look forward to her new life.

Where had all her energy gone? Vanished with her love for Rod? No, because that love was still with her. Gone with her hopes of love, then? Maybe. Perhaps all along she'd been foolish to think she could have everything she wanted? Folk always said that women couldn't expect to have it all.

With tremendous effort, she finally rose from her chair, deciding to change into something casual and begin work on the packing, when a light knock came at her door and her heart lurched. Flo, perhaps? No, not Flo, who was giving George a farewell drink. Who, then? The knock came again. 'Oh, God,' she whispered, for she thought she knew.

'Lorna?' came Rod's voice. 'Are you there? Please open the door.'

She opened it and he came through, gasping a little, as though he'd been running.

'No snow today.' He smiled faintly. 'Remember that time in winter when I came to you?'

'I remember.'

He had changed from his band uniform into shirt and slacks and was not carrying his trumpet, so he must have gone home first and then come running to her. She began to tremble, wondering what it might mean, as his eyes went over her as though they would never look away, and he drew her into his arms.

'Still in your blue dress,' he whispered. 'So beautiful . . . Lorna, I had to see you.'

'I didn't expect you.'

'You thought I wouldn't come to say goodbye?'

'Why should you come? You haven't spoken to me all week.'

'I know, I didn't dare. If I'd spoken to you, I might have disgraced myself. Burst into tears, or something.'

'As though you would!'

'Well, how have you been feeling this week, then?'

'Like bursting into tears.'

'There you are, then.'

'Oh, Rod, this is hopeless.' She pulled herself from him and sank into her chair, real tears stinging her eyes. 'I don't know why you've come, it can't do any good.'

He knelt at her side. 'I had to say goodbye, Lorna.'

'I'm only going to Edinburgh.'

'Thing is . . .' He took her hands. 'I'm going away myself.'

She gave a start, staring at him with huge, apprehensive eyes.

'Where?'

'America.'

'America?'

It was worse than she'd ever expected. Terrible, awful news, because it really was the end of hope. She knew now, as she looked desolately away from him, that all along, secretly, she'd been hoping that there might still be a chance of reconciliation. Even that short while ago, when she'd blamed her loss of energy on her loss of hope, there had been a spark flickering, so tiny she'd not even allowed herself to recognize it. But it had been there, and now it was gone. Extinguished by that word he had just said. America.

'You're going to your father?' she asked, trying to appear calm.

'Yes, he's written to Leland and me. Thinks it's time we saw each other again. Asked my mother to go out, too, but she says better not. There's nothing for her now in America.'

'But plenty for you?'

'More than here,' he said quietly. 'I can't bear the thought of staying on without you.'

'I feel the same.'

'But you're starting a new life, aren't you? A life where there's no place for me?'

'You say that, but it isn't true.'

'I wish to God you were right.'

He stood up, then drew her from her chair back into his arms, and for some time they stood together, trembling and caressing, until quietly he slipped her dress from her shoulders and she began to unbutton his shirt. In the corner, as they both knew, was her narrow bed; something they'd always averted their eyes from in the past, but now it seemed to burn its way into their consciousness. No words were spoken except their names that they repeated over and over, as they moved across the floor, scattering clothes as they went, until they reached the waiting bed and sank into joy.

I never meant this to happen, Lorna thought for a brief moment, but then there was no space in her mind for thoughts any more, no space except for feelings that were the most intense she had ever known. Would she remember them for ever, these feelings of her first time?

Oh, but not the last? Surely not the last time with Rod, lying beside her, looking still so happy, with all the wretchedness of the past week wiped clean from his dear face?

'Oh, look,' he whispered, 'there's your dress on the floor. Your lovely blue dress. But you look even more beautiful without it.'

'I should pick it up,' she said lazily. 'I should pack. I'm going to Edinburgh tomorrow.'

'Ah, don't go to Edinburgh, darling Lorna. Come to America with me.'

America. It was as though a cold wind was sweeping over their nakedness, and Lorna sat up, gazing down at Rod, who had put out a hand to hold her. Quietly, she unpicked his fingers and stepped from the bed. Her dressing gown hung from a peg on the door and she put it on, tying it round her waist, while he, as sensitive as ever to things unsaid, left the bed and came to her.

'Lorna, I'm sorry. I never meant us to make love. But, oh, I can't really regret it! You don't, do you? You don't regret it?'

'No, I don't regret it,' she said shakily.

'I thought you were upset.'

'No' about making love. It was the most wonderful thing I've ever known.'

'Thank God for that!'

'But I am upset. About America.'

'You needn't be.' Rod had begun to dress. 'You can come with me. I haven't booked a sailing yet, we could do it together.'

'You know I can't come with you to America.' Lorna picked up her dress and put it on a hanger. 'It's out of the question.'

'After what's happened between us?' Rod was standing very still. 'You don't want to marry me?'

'I'd marry you tomorrow, if you'd let me have my band.'

Every remnant of joy that had been showing in his face left and a strange flatness of expression took its place, making him appear, as had happened before, a stranger.

'You're still wanting that,' he said slowly. 'I don't believe it. You're choosing something that may never even happen over happiness with me? How can you do that, Lorna?'

'I could be choosing happiness with you,' she said eagerly. 'If you'll say you'll just accept what I want to do. Then we can marry and be happy. Please, Rod, say it. Say I can at least try to get my band together, because if you really love me, you'll want me to do that.' She went to him and took his hands, looking pleadingly into his face, but he only shook his head.

'It's impasse time, Lorna. We love each other, we've just made love, too, but we'll neither of us give in to what the other wants.' He gave a short laugh and released her hands from his. 'What sort of love is that?'

'You're saying it isn't real?

His face twisted with pain. 'Can it be? Oh, God, I can't give you up, yet I know what you're offering would never work out. Would never work out for me. I told you why, and nothing's changed. We want different things, so we have to face facts. If we married, it would be a disaster.'

'I'm desolate,' she whispered. 'Desolate.'

'Then come with me! Give up the band and come with me to America!'

'So, I'd be the one to give in?'

'You'd be happy, I promise you.'

'No, because there'd always be something missing.'

'I wouldn't be enough?'

She slowly shook her head. 'I suppose I want it all. Marriage and my career. As you do.'

Those words seemed really to bring everything to an end, and when they kissed and embraced at the door for the last time, finality and a terrible sadness covered them like a soft grey cloak.

'I do love you,' Lorna said. 'Whatever you say, our love is real to me.'

Rod kissed her cheek gently. 'And I still love you – always will.'

'Can we keep in touch?'

'Think there's any point?'

'Maybe not.'

'Goodbye, then, dear Lorna. I wish you luck, I want you to be happy.'

'And you. Goodbye, Rod.'

When he had gone and she had heard the outer door bang, she sat in her chair again, her head bent, and let the tears flow. What had she done? What had she done? She wanted to leap up and run after him, crying to him to come back, come back, she'd give everything up for him. But some iron in her soul made her stay where she was. Maybe Rod was right, they'd be facing disaster if they married. The fact that he had said it – was that not disaster, anyway?

Twenty-Five

'Well, so this is what going to Glasgow has meant!' Tilly cried on Lorna's first day home. 'Trouble, and nothing else, as far as I can see.'

'Oh, don't go on, Ma,' Lorna sighed, studying the job vacancies in the evening paper. 'It wasn't all trouble. I got good experience in Luke Riddell's band.'

'Aye, and the sack, too.' Tilly's pale eyes sharpened. 'And what about this young man of yours, then? The one you never brought home? How come all that ended in tears?'

'I was going to bring him home.'

Oh, that hurt, didn't it? Her mother's talk of tears? Lorna, steadfastly keeping her eyes on the newspaper, was wishing herself anywhere except under interrogation by Tilly. 'Anyway, he wasn't my young man at all, as it turned out.'

'Just a heartbreaker, eh?'

'I wouldn't say that.'

'Going off to America, though.' Tilly pursed her lips. 'Some of the lassies who married Yanks in the war were awful disappointed, you ken, when they got to the States.'

'I'm sure some were very happy, too.'

'It's always better to stick to someone of your own kind. Somebody who knows what you know.'

Ewen, of course, Lorna said to herself, circling a job in a flower shop and another in a bakery, and smiled as Tilly told her Ewen had asked after her and might come round tomorrow.

'You could maybe ask him if there's anything going at the post office, Lorna?'

'Thanks, but I am not going back to the post office, Ma.'

'Well, what are you going to do? There are precious few band jobs for girls round here, as you know.' Tilly rose and set out cups for their last cup of tea before bed. 'I suppose you might ask Jackie Craik if he's got anything, but like your dad used to say, he never wanted women in his band.'

'I'd never ask Jackie Craik for a job,' Lorna said firmly. 'I know his views too well. No, what I'm planning to do is to get some temporary job and then do what I really want to do.'

'Which is what?' Tilly asked, swinging round with the teapot in her hand.

Lorna, folding the newspaper, finally looked up and met her mother's eyes. 'Run my own band.'

'Oh, my Lord!' Tilly set down the teapot with a thump. 'Oh, Lorna, whatever next? Your own band? That's crazy talk. I – I'm speechless.'

'It isn't crazy talk, Ma. Flo and me, we've discussed it and we think we could do it. There are women's bands in America and England and they're popular. We reckon we could make a band popular here. We're going to give it a go, anyway. Just got to work out the details and get the finance.'

Turning back to her tea making, Tilly appeared quite taken aback, as though Lorna had surpassed herself this time in surprising her.

'Your Auntie Cissie always said you'd be a law unto yourself,' she said over her shoulder. 'And she's absolutely right, eh? I just don't know what to say to you, Lorna.'

'Needn't say anything, Ma. Leave everything to me.'

'Including this finance you talk about?' Tilly sniffed. 'We used to call it money. So, how are you going to get it?'

'Well, we wouldn't need all that much,' Lorna said eagerly. 'Just enough to hire a room and pay for advertising and wages, until we begin to get engagements. I thought I'd ask a bank about a loan.'

'A bank! Lorna, banks don't lend you money unless you can pay it back. You'd have to have some capital.'

'I could see what they said. After all, other people must have had the same problem starting off.'

'I suppose your friend Flo can't help?'

'No, we're both in the same boat.'

'And she's going to be the bandleader, is she?' Tilly looked dubious. 'A very nice lassie, but are you sure she's got what it takes to lead a band?'

'Of course! She's older than me and she's knows more.'

'But you've got the personality and the looks, Lorna, though I say it myself.'

'Looks don't come into it, Ma.'

'No?' Tilly smiled. 'Looks come into everything, I'd say. Now, have your tea and get to bed, you look exhausted. Tomorrow, you could discuss things with Ewen. He'll be dying to help. No' that he's got any money, of course.'

* * *

The following evening, Lorna and Ewen went to the cinema, where they saw a re-run of the film *Great Expectations* with John Mills.

'That's what you've got, eh?' Ewen asked fondly, when they came out blinking into the light of the May evening. 'Great expectations of being a lady bandleader. I'll bet you succeed, too.'

'Don't see why I shouldn't. Once I get started.'

'Need cash, though. Wish I had some, I could be your backer.' He grinned, as they began to walk home along Princes Street. 'To be honest, I have got fifty quid in the post office. Would that help?'

'Oh, Ewen!' Lorna hugged his arm. 'As though I could take your money! But it's nice of you to offer.'

'Och, you'd need a lot more, anyway.' He looked down at her worriedly. 'Do you really think the bank will lend you something?'

'Ma doesn't think so, but I'll have to ask. Nothing ventured, nothing gained.'

They paused to sit down on a bench near St John's, a fine West End church, watching the cars go by and the pedestrians enjoying the still warm evening.

'About that fellow you knew,' Ewen began, but Lorna immediately became rigid, her face a mask and he faltered. 'I suppose you don't want to talk about him, eh?'

'No, I don't.'

'You said once there was no one special, but I always knew there was. Then your mother dropped a hint or two. Said you might be bringing someone over.'

'And now you realize that won't be happening?'

'I don't want to make things worse for you, Lorna, but if he's hurt you, just tell me where he is and I'll go over and give him what for.'

'He's about to sail for America,' she replied, surprised she could smile at Ewen's vehemence. 'You'd be too late. Anyway, the truth is, we've hurt each other. He wanted one sort of life, I wanted another, so we had to agree to part.'

'What sort of life do you want, then?' he asked quietly. 'One that doesn't include marriage?'

'One that might include marriage, as long as it had my band as well.'

Ewen's brow cleared. 'That's good, Lorna. That's OK. Because anybody who cared for you would want you to have both, eh?'

For some time she watched the passing show of evening Edinburgh without speaking.

'Yes, that's true,' she said at last. 'Anybody who cared for me would want that. Shall we make a move, then?'

'Just let me say first, if you ever need any help, if there's ever anything I can do . . . I want to tell you I'll be there.' Ewen looked steadily into her eyes. 'I mean it, Lorna.'

'I know you do, Ewen.'

Linking arms again, they continued their walk back to Tilly's flat, where Ewen came in for a little while before saying goodnight at the door and they exchanged brief kisses.

'You'll let me know how you get on at the bank?' he pressed, and she promised she would, as soon as she'd had the interview for which she'd have to brace herself.

'Such a nice laddie,' Tilly remarked, when Lorna returned.

'It's no use, Ma. No point in hoping.'

'You mean, about you and Ewen? No, I stopped long ago. But he is a nice fellow.'

'He is. And you're right, he would he helpful, if he could.'

Tilly was mending a stocking, screwing up her eyes over the ladder as her needle went in and out. 'Maybe I can help, Lorna.'

'Ma, don't worry. Any money you've got you need. I don't want to be a drain on you.'

'Have you forgotten?' Tilly clipped off her thread.

'Forgotten what?'

'The insurance money.'

Lorna sat up in her chair, the colour heightening in her cheeks, her eyes very bright. 'The insurance money,' she whispered. 'Yes, I had forgotten. But that was supposed to be for my wedding.'

'Aye, well, what wedding? Seems to me it'd be more useful to you now. If you're really serious about this band business.'

'Oh, I am! I am!'

'Came to me in the night,' Tilly went on. 'I woke up in the small hours, couldn't get back to sleep, and I thought about your dad and what he would've wanted for you. I reckon it'd have been the band, if it was to be just for girls, no' a wedding. I mean, my folks had no money when your dad and me got wed, so we did it all ourselves on a shoestring.' Tilly smiled at the memories. 'And look how happy we were, eh?'

'Oh, Ma, you're my saviour, you always are!' Lorna ran to Tilly and flung her arms around her neck. 'But are you sure, though? Are you really sure you want me to have it – the insurance money?'

'Aye, I'm sure. It's in the building society at the minute – that's where your dad said we should put it. I'm no' certain how much there is – should be some interest – but there'll be enough to start you off, eh?'

'Look, I'll pay you back. Soon as I get some money coming in, I'll put it all back in the building society.'

'What a piece of nonsense! When it was for you, anyway.' Tilly smiled affectionately. 'But if you ever do get wed, you can maybe pay the bills then.'

'You bet I will!' Lorna was dabbing at her eyes. 'Though I can't see it happening for a long, long time.'

'Best get your band started first, eh? We'll go to the building society tomorrow and find out just how much there is, and then you can tell Flo.'

'I'd tell her now if she had a phone. Maybe I'll write a letter. Have you got any ink? Any writing paper?'

Lorna was almost dancing round the living room. 'Oh, Ma, I can never thank you enough. And Flo will feel the same. She'll be over the moon.'

'Here's the ink, here's the paper.' Tilly was rooting in her purse. 'Got a stamp?'

Only a few minutes later, the letter was written and Lorna was flying out to the post box. She pictured Flo's delighted surprise at the news she was sending, and of all they could now do to turn their plans into reality. She was so grateful to her mother, so glad of the money, and for the first time since saying goodbye to Rod, felt the pain of loss might one day ease.

Twenty-Six

At first, it seemed as though everything was going to be so easy. The insurance money – four hundred pounds – turned out to be more than expected and would certainly be enough to pay rent for premises until money could be made; wages, too, though they would have to be low at first.

'There was far too much for just a wedding,' Lorna pointed out. 'I mean, what were you planning? Something in St Giles's Cathedral?'

Tilly shook her head. 'I suppose we always thought there'd be some over for you to start married life with. So, now you can have it to start something else.' She sighed a little. 'Just hope it's successful.'

'It will be, Ma, it will be. Flo and me – we know we can do it. Isn't that right?' Lorna appealed to Flo, who had come rushing over from Glasgow specially to thank Tilly.

'Oh, that's right, Mrs Fernie,' Flo said earnestly. 'All we needed was some help and you've given it to us. We couldn't be more grateful.'

'The money was never meant for me, so no need to thank me. I know you'll both make the best use of it you can.'

She could be sure of that they told her.

Euphoric days, then, to begin with, when the two young women felt they were walking on air and that everything was going their way. Until they met the problems.

First, it took some time to release the money, and even when it was in Lorna's new bank account, it looked as if it wouldn't be used, for she couldn't find anywhere to rent for their studio. All they needed was somewhere to rehearse and do the paper work, but finding properties to rent in post-war Edinburgh was, it seemed, almost impossible. Everyone was looking for houses, flats, rooms – anything – but those few that were available were too expensive for most people.

'I give up!' Lorna cried, after some weeks of searching had gone by without success. 'I don't think we're ever going to find anything.'

'Looks that way,' Flo agreed gloomily, who came over from Glasgow when she could to help in the search. 'It's lucky I have my typing job.'

'Oh, don't say that!' Lorna cried. 'To think of you typing, and me in the bakery, instead of running our band! It's heartbreaking. I mean, we can't even advertise for any players until we get premises, and we haven't even got Ina now.'

Flo sighed. 'She said she felt pretty sad about letting us down, but I always had the feeling she wouldn't want to leave Dickie.'

'Can't blame her for that,' Lorna said quietly. 'If she's found the right one, good luck to her.'

Flo put a sympathetic hand on Lorna's arm.

The breakthrough came in the end from Ewen, who arrived at Tilly's flat one June evening with great news.

'Got the very place, Lorna! Come on, I'll take you to see it. I've got the keys.'

'Where is it?' she cried, leaping up. 'Ewen, tell me!'

'Aye, tell her,' Tilly ordered. 'She's been like a wet weekend lately, with no' finding anywhere.'

'Well, don't expect too much, but a pal of mine told me there are some disused premises off the Leith Walk, back of one of the cinemas. Used to be a boys' club, but it's no' been used for years and hasn't got planning permission for housing, so nobody's bought it and it's still for rent.'

'Would it do for rehearsals?'

'Be ideal. Nobody around to hear you.' Ewen hesitated. 'Need a ton of paint, though, to smarten it up, and I don't know what else.'

'I can do painting. But what's the rent?'

'No' bad. But there might be others in for it, so better come round now and have a look at it.'

'I'm on my way.' Lorna was already scrambling into her jacket. 'Ma, do you want to come too? It's a lovely light evening.'

'No, pet, you decide if it's what you want.'

It was exactly what she wanted. The electricity was not connected, of course, and the grime-encrusted windows made it difficult to see the place clearly, but potential screamed out to Lorna as soon as Ewen opened the door. There was a large main room that would do for rehearsals, plus a smaller room that would serve as an office. There was a tiny kitchenette with a sink and a gas ring, a terrible lavatory, a stack of old chairs, a table tennis table on its side, and waste paper rolling in the corners.

'Plenty to do,' Ewen observed.

'It's perfect. Oh, Ewen, you're another saviour, eh? Give me the agent's details. I'll go round first thing in the morning.' Lorna stood very still, her hands clasped together. 'Oh, but what'll I do if I don't get it?'

'I have a feeling you will. Everybody's luck turns some time. It's your turn.'

Impulsively, she kissed him and he flushed, but made no attempt to embrace her.

'Here, take the keys. You can return 'em tomorrow.'

'I'm so grateful, Ewen.'

'Aye, well, wait until it's all sealed, signed and delivered.'

'Then we can have a celebration.'

'Then we can start buying paint.'

In the event, they did both, for Lorna, sending up prayers of thanksgiving, got the lease of the premises, and a celebratory meal was fixed up at a restaurant they couldn't normally afford. Flo came over from Glasgow and Cissie from Musselburgh to join Tilly, Ewen and Lorna, and if the food was only the usual post-war fare, everyone was so cheerful it tasted far better.

'Didn't I always tell you, Lorna would do something like this?' Cissie cried, her face flushed with excitement for her niece. 'A law unto herself, eh? Well, I think it's wonderful. When do you want me to come over with my paintbrush, then?'

'Be careful, Aunt Cissie,' Lorna cried happily. 'We might just take you up on that!'

Later, when the party was over and she was preparing for bed, she reflected on how rapidly things could change for people. One day down, the next up, then down again, up again. If only she and Flo could now stay up, not floating above the clouds, but doing well, achieving what they wanted. At least, now they had their studio, there was hope of that. Next job would be to advertise for players. Oh, and find a name for themselves. So far, they'd thought of nothing suitable.

It was only as sleep began to claim her that another little worry crept into her mind, but it wasn't enough to keep her awake and in the morning, she had work to do.

Twenty-Seven

'Talk about transformation scene!' Flo cried, when at last their restoration work was done and the new studio had risen from the ruin of the old club. 'Who'd have thought such a wreck of a place could look like this?'

The little team of Lorna, Ewen and Flo stood looking round at their handiwork with deep satisfaction, though, of course, it hadn't all been theirs. They'd had to employ a builder and a roof firm to make the club really habitable, and professional cleaners to make inroads on the years of accumulated dirt, before they could begin on the decoration themselves. Then, however, the place had really begun to shine, and with its gleaming walls and windows, its polished floor and brightened chairs, it represented all that Lorna and Flo could have wanted.

'If you ask me, the owners should be jolly grateful to us for doing all this,' Flo remarked, dropping into one of the chairs. 'If they want to try to sell it again, they'll have better luck, eh?'

'Who's going to let them try to sell it?' Lorna asked sharply. 'We've got our lease and we're going to stay.'

'Sure, I was just talking.' Flo glanced at her watch. 'Say, are you folks hungry? How about getting some fish and chips?'

'Terrific,' Ewen answered. 'I'm starving. Have to do one last wash of the brushes, though.' He grinned. 'Then tomorrow you two can start thinking about finding some girls for your band, eh?'

'I'll just have to have my piano brought over,' Lorna said, sitting next to Flo. 'And find a second-hand desk for the office.' She yawned and coughed a little. 'I don't think I'll have any fish and chips, though – the smell of the paint is getting to me.'

'I know, it hangs, doesn't it?' Flo leaped up and joined Ewen in the washroom to clean her brushes. 'It's really nice of your ma to put me up tonight, Lorna. I'm so glad I haven't to go back to Glasgow till tomorrow.'

'We'll have to think about getting you a place to live here, now that we're ready to advertise for players.' Lorna was yawning again, her face rather pale. 'Shall we all go to Ma's, then? You could have your fish and chips there.'

'Fine, I'll lock up for you,' Ewen said cheerfully. He stood, smiling, taking a last look round the studio. 'Looks grand, eh? All ready for the lassies. You girls decided what to call yourselves, then? Flo and Lorna's Band, or what?'

'We're still thinking.' Flo was putting on her cardigan. 'Got any ideas? Apart from Flo and Lorna's Band, which doesn't exactly appeal!'

'Ivy Benson calls her band the Ladies' Dance Orchestra,' Lorna said thoughtfully. 'I can't think what we should be.'

'I think we should go for girls in the title,' Flo suggested. 'But Rhythm Girls, that's been used, and All Girls Band as well.'

'I know!' Lorna cried. 'How about the Melody Girls?'

'Inspired!' Flo cried.

'The Melody Girls it is,' Ewen said. 'But, like I said, you'd better get on with finding other people to play. You're going to need more than two Melody Girls to get your show on the road. Wish I could've joined you somehow.'

'Wrong sex, Ewen!'

'And then there's the little problem that I can't play anything, either.'

'Shall we go?' Lorna asked, leaning against the door. But as the others came up and she took a step away, she seemed for a moment to waver.

'Hey, are you all right?' Ewen was grasping her arm.

'Oh yes, thanks. I just need to get some fresh air.'

'You're right, it's the paint,' Flo said, opening the door. 'Might be a few days before the smell clears.'

Both she and Ewen watched anxiously as Lorna stood taking deep breaths of the fine summer air, until her colour returned and she smiled at them. 'Told you, I feel much better now. Come on, let's go for the tram.'

'Wouldn't like to take a taxi?' Ewen asked, rattling coins in his pocket. 'My treat.'

'A taxi? What a piece of nonsense! No point in wasting money. You know what, I might even have some fish and chips when we get back. There's quite a good shop near us.'

They had a very pleasant evening at Tilly's, all four eating excellent fish and chips with bread and Tilly's butter ration, and afterwards sat talking of plans for the Melody Girls until Ewen reluctantly took himself home and the others prepared for bed.

'Sure you'll be all right there?' Lorna asked Flo on the sofa, to which Flo of course answered that she was fine.

'It's been a grand day, eh?'

'Lovely. I feel we've really done well. Goodnight, Lorna.'

'Goodnight, Flo. We'll write the advertisement for the girls tomorrow, shall we?'

'Can't wait to see what replies we get!'

But in the morning, when Lorna came to breakfast she was not looking well. Seemed she had been quite sick.

'Must have been the fish and chips,' she muttered. 'I shouldn't have had them.'

'Never did suit you,' her mother said, fixing her with a thoughtful gaze.

'We needn't do the advert today, if you don't feel up to it,' Flo suggested. 'I've got to go back to Glasgow, but you could maybe put something in the paper later?'

'Yes, I'll do that.' Lorna drank some tea and cautiously ate some toast. 'I'll go with you to the station.'

'No work today?' Tilly asked, still watching her.

'No, we took a couple of days off to finish the painting.'

'Grand that it's all done, eh?'

'Yes.' Lorna rose. 'What time do you want to leave, Flo?'

'Any time now. I'm catching an early train. Mrs Fernie, I'd like to thank you again, for putting me up. And for everything.'

'Get on with you!' Tilly answered, smiling. 'Always glad to see you. And I'll be seeing you again, when the band gets going.'

'I'm looking forward to that.'

As soon as they were outside, Lorna grasped Flo's arm with strong fingers. 'Oh, Flo, something's happened. Something awful.'

Flo's dark eyes widened. 'What? What are you talking about?'

'I don't know how to tell you . . .'

'For God's sake, spit it out! What is it? What's wrong?'

'I think I'm going to have a baby.'

Flo stopped in her tracks. 'Lorna, that's nonsense. Heavens above, you're sick once and you think you're in the club? Come on, be sensible!'

'I was already worried before I was sick. Thing is, I've missed two.'

'Oh.' Flo looked away.

'Yes, oh.' Lorna smiled drearily. 'I felt pretty odd yesterday, but I kept telling myself no' to worry, I'd be OK, but then this morning, when I was sick – Flo, I just knew.'

'You can't know until you've seen a doctor. I mean, for sure.'

'I tell you, I feel it in my bones. I'm no' mistaken.'

They began to walk slowly towards the tram stop, Flo looking as though she'd taken a few steps that weren't there, Lorna as though her world was collapsing around her. Which, in fact, was how she'd felt, ever since she'd sat on the side of her bed that morning after the sickness and looked into her future. It couldn't be, it couldn't be, but it was. She was going to have Rod's baby.

'I didn't even know you were sleeping with Rod,' Flo said after a time. 'Suppose I should have guessed.'

'It was only the once. That last night before I left.'

'Only needs to be once.'

'We were always so careful, not to – you know – go all the way and then, that last night, it just happened and it was so wonderful . . .'

Tears were gathering in Lorna's eyes, her voice sounding strained and choked with the effort of not letting them fall. 'When Rod asked me if I regretted it, I said no . . .'

'And now you do?'

'What do you think? My whole life has changed. All my plans – our plans.'

'You haven't thought of . . .' Flo hesitated. 'No, of course not.'

'No, of course not,' Lorna echoed. 'If you mean am I going to find some little old woman to poke me about in a back street basement? No thanks. I'll keep the baby. How, I don't know at the moment.'

'Well, are you going to tell Rod? It's his baby as well, you know.'

'No, I'm no' going to tell him. We don't want to marry now. What's the point?'

They had reached the tram stop to stand some way away from the other people waiting, their eyes on each other's faces.

'I think we could still go ahead with the band idea,' Flo said uncertainly. 'I mean, we've rented the premises now and done all the work.'

'You could go ahead, but without me.' Lorna shook her head. 'Can you see me conducting the band, getting bigger and bigger? Having to tell the girls I'm expecting and no' married? And what would the public think, if they got to know? It's out of the question, Flo. I have to accept, it's just the end for me.'

'There's no way I'll be trying to run the band without you, Lorna.

Let's just put everything on hold and see how things go. There's no need to make decisions now. First, you have to see the doctor.'

'I'll see him,' Lorna agreed, 'but I know what he'll say.'

What would her mother say, though? That, Lorna couldn't even guess.

Twenty-Eight

Though she'd been praying she might be wrong, Lorna was right about what their old family doctor would say. She'd been his patient since she was a little girl, and guessed he'd be cheerful when he broke his news, which indeed he was.

'Middle of January is your date,' he brightly told her. 'Looks like you'll get Christmas over, anyway, though can't be sure about Hogmanay. Might be early. Come on, now, lassie, don't be looking so glum! These things happen.'

'Never thought to me,' she sighed.

'Well, how about the father? He going to do the right thing?'

'He doesn't know, he's just gone to America.'

'Well, you tell him to get himself home again and take you down the aisle. In the meantime, put a ring on your finger and call yourself Mrs. Makes life easier.'

Could anything make her life easier? Laura wondered, returning home. She didn't think so. Certainly not buying herself a ring and calling herself Mrs Warren. No, she couldn't do that. But what was she going to do? Letting herself into her mother's flat, she could only think of the next step to be taken. Telling Ma.

Tilly was busy unpicking a customer's dress which she was to refashion into a more modern style, and looked up quickly when Lorna came in. 'Another afternoon off!' she exclaimed. 'That shop hardly sees you, Lorna. What was it for this time?'

'Shall I make some tea?' Lorna asked, not meeting her mother's eyes.

'Aye, I'm parched. It's warm today.' Tilly sat back, removing her thimble, as Lorna made the tea and looked in the tin for biscuits. 'What an appetite you've got these days, lassie! You'll soon be putting on weight.'

Lorna's cheeks were scarlet. 'Eating for two,' she said quietly. 'I bet you knew that, eh?'

'Guessed,' Tilly said, with equal quietness. 'I've heard you in the mornings, you ken. Why didn't you tell me about it before?'

'Wanted it confirmed.' Lorna crunched on a digestive biscuit. 'Saw Dr Atkins today.'

'Whatever did he say?'

'He was very nice about it. Said these things happen.'

'I never thought to you.'

'No.' At last, Lorna's eyes rested on her mother's face. 'Well, it did happen, Ma. Just the once.'

'All it takes.'

'And my life is ruined.'

'Oh, now, that's no way to talk. It's no' the end of the world.'

'Well, you tell me how I'm going to start my band when I'm expecting? And when the baby's born, I'll have to look after it.' Lorna looked desolately into her teacup. 'It'll be years before I'll be free, Ma.'

Tilly sat with her finger to her lip, a considering look in her eyes. 'I could look after the bairn,' she said slowly. 'I'd no' mind.'

Lorna looked up, her lips parting, unable to speak.

'Aye, it'd be no trouble,' Tilly went on. 'A babby in the house again! When I lost your wee brothers, I always wanted more children, but none came after you.' She leaned over and looked into Lorna's face. 'Well, what do you say?'

'Ma, I don't know what to say. You're always saving me from something!' Lorna tried to laugh. 'Do you mean it, though? Would you really do that for me?'

'You're so set on this band thing, and I'm thinking now you'd be good at it, it'd be a sad day if you had to give it up. So, if I can help, Lorna, I will.'

'Ma, you're a saint! Yes, you are.' Lorna's voice was trembling. 'It'd make all the difference if I could just look forward to getting the band going. All the difference in the world!'

'Well, you can look forward to it. Though you'll have to wait a while longer than you thought.'

'I know, I know. But if I can be sure it's going to happen, I can put up with that.' Lorna hesitated. 'But might it be too much for you, Ma? Folk always say babies are terrible hard work.'

'Och, I'll be fine! And the best thing would be I could still do my dressmaking, seeing as I work at home. Look, let's say I'll take charge, then, but in the meantime, as I say, you'll have to put off starting the band. No point in booking lassies to play for you if you don't want 'em to know about the bairn.'

'That's right,' Lorna agreed. 'What I'll have to do is keep on with my job as long as I can to pay the rent for the studio, and it'll be the same for Flo. She'll have to stay with her typing job and I'm sorry about that, but she says she doesn't want to start without me.' Lorna's mouth twisted. 'Och, I was a fool, eh, to get caught in this trap?'

'No doubt of that.' Tilly began stitching again. 'But what about your young man, then, the one I never saw? You've never even mentioned him. I suppose he is the father?'

'Of course he is!' Lorna drew her brows together. 'I only had one young man, Ma.'

'Sorry, it's just that you've never said anything about him. Have you told him yet?'

'He's in America.'

'You could still tell him. He should know. Should help to support the bairn when it comes.'

'I haven't told him. There'd be no point. We'd already decided no' to marry.'

'Oh, Lorna! So he just skips off to America leaving you in the family way. That's what men do, of course.'

'I told you, we never meant it to happen. And I don't want anything from him, I'll bring the baby up myself.' Lorna suddenly smiled, leaped to her feet and hugged her mother. 'I mean, with your help. Oh, Ma, you'll never know how grateful I am! Somehow, I'll make it up to you. I will, I promise.'

'You just think about keeping well and having that grandchild.'

'And then starting my band.'

They were both quiet, contemplating the differences in their lives that would soon be upon them, when a knock sounded at the front door. Lorna said she would answer it.

'Canna think who it'd be,' Tilly said, beginning to fold up her work.

It was Ewen.

'Hi, Lorna!' His broad face was lit by smiles. 'I'm just on my way home. Wondered if you'd like to go for a walk later on? It's sunny again.'

She hesitated, swinging the door. 'Yes, I think I would. That'd be nice.'

'I'll call for you, then.'

'OK. As a matter of fact, I've got something to tell you.'

'Oh?' He grinned. 'Sounds interesting. Why no' tell me now?'

'Later. See you, Ewen.'

'See you, Lorna.'

As she closed the door, she asked herself why she'd decided to tell Ewen her news then; she could have waited, until she had no choice. But somehow she felt she wanted to tell him as soon as possible. She wanted to be honest with him, who'd always been her most loyal friend.

Twenty-Nine

At first, Ewen seemed to be taking her news well. They had walked quite a way through the streets before she had found the courage to speak, finally reaching the Water of Leith in the Coates district of the city, where his kind eyes rested on her.

'What's up?' he asked gently. 'I know something's bothering you.'

'I hope you won't be upset, Ewen. Or, angry with me.'

'Angry? I'm never angry with you, Lorna.'

'Well, disappointed. The fact is I'm . . . going to have a baby.'

He had been smiling, but instantly the smile was wiped away as the kind eyes were lowered and, for what seemed an age, he bent his head away from her. At last, he looked up, though not into her face.

'A baby? Oh, Lorna!'

'I know. I've been a fool. I feel terrible.'

'And that fellow is in America?'

'It was just the one time, Ewen. I keep saying that, as though it makes things better, but of course it makes no difference at all. We were just crazy, that's all.'

As he said nothing, she touched his hand. 'You can imagine how it was.'

'Imagine?' His tone was suddenly rough. 'Oh, yes, I can imagine.'

He walked a little way away to stand looking down at the sluggish water winding its way towards the Dean Village, his shoulders hunched, his head again bent. It was clear her news was now sinking in and he was not at all taking it well. She had hurt him, grievously hurt him, and there was nothing – nothing – she could do.

'Shall we go back?' she called at last.

He nodded, turning, his face very pale, and came towards her, but still he didn't look at her.

'I knew you'd be upset,' she said in a low voice. 'But I wanted to tell you, Ewen, because I couldn't face keeping it a secret until the time you'd have known anyway.'

'Something of a shock – to know now.'

'Yes. I'm sorry.'

'Hell, I don't know why I'm so cut up. It's none of my business what you do.' He ran his hand over his face. 'Except, we're friends. I care for you.'

'That means a lot to me.'

'Me too. I just never . . . I never thought . . .'

'I know.' She shrugged. 'I never thought, either, that this would happen to me.'

'What are you going to do? I mean, about the band?'

'Put it on hold. Until after I've had the baby. Then Ma's offered to look after him – or her – for me. That's wonderful, eh? Letting me have my chance. I'm so grateful.'

'Yes, your ma's wonderful, but what about the father? What's he doing for you?'

'He doesn't know.'

'You haven't told him? Lorna, you have to tell him. It's his responsibility, this bairn, no' just yours.'

She had begun to walk back. 'I don't want to tell him. I don't want him to marry me, because it would never work out. We had a terrible row that last night, when we realized we wanted different things, but I'd rather bring up the baby without a father than give up my band.'

'Aye.' He gave a long sigh. 'But it'll be hard for you. Even with your ma's help.'

'Life's always hard for women. Especially if they want more than men think they should have.'

Ewen suddenly laid his hand on her shoulder, finally meeting her eyes as he made her turn to him. 'I always said I'd be there for you, Lorna, and that's still true. If it's going to be tough for you, I want to help. If you need anything, just ask.'

'You really mean that, Ewen?'

'I said I did. It's still true.'

'I don't know what to say, then. Think I don't deserve you.'

'For God's sake, don't let's talk about deserving. You loved somebody, you couldn't help that. It's no' something you can order.'

Slowly, they hugged and stood together for a few moments, before walking on, each feeling rather better, Lorna because she'd told Ewen her news, he because he had gradually begun to accept it.

'How about the folk you know here?' Ewen asked. 'Are you going to tell them? I'm thinking of people like Pattie and Miss Dickinson.'

'I'll be telling Pattie, and I suppose Miss Dickinson, too. They'll keep it to themselves.'

'But you don't want to tell these girls who might be in your band?'

'No. If I can, I'm going to keep the two sides of my life separate.'

'Won't be easy.'

'It's the way it has to be, Ewen. I can't set out as a new band-leader with everyone knowing I've a baby but no husband. I wish things could be different, but even today folk are still ready to sit in judgement.'

'Seems ridiculous to me. What's it matter, anyway, when it's your music that counts.'

'Ah, that's a lovely thing to say, Ewen. It is the music that counts, but some will no' see it that way.'

'So, the poor bairn has to be a secret? It isn't a good start, Lorna.'

'It's the best I can do,' she answered, her voice thick with tears, and he said no more.

At the door to Tilly's flat, he told her he wouldn't come in, but he'd keep in touch, see her again very soon.

'I'm glad you haven't cast me off, Ewen.'

'As if I could.'

'I was thinking, would you be godfather? It'd mean a lot to me if the baby had someone like you in its life.'

'Godfather?' He gave a rather pleased smile. 'Wouldn't mind, Lorna. Wouldn't mind at all.'

'That's settled, then, and thank you very much.' Her face grew bleak. 'Of course, it'll be some time before there's a christening.'

'It'll pass.' At last, Ewen was sounding more his old self. 'That's the thing about time – it passes.'

Thirty

On the last Sunday of January, 1947, in the middle of one of the coldest winters of the century, Samuel Cameron Fernie was baptized at his family's local kirk, Ewen MacKee standing as godfather and Flo Drover and Pattie MacDowell as godmothers. He was already by then almost a month old, for, as Dr Atkins had said he might, he'd arrived early at his grandmother's flat – on New Year's Day, in fact – a fine, lusty child, who looked like his father, though only Lorna and Flo knew that and they did not dwell on it. When ginger hair replaced the dark fuzz of his early days, everyone in the family was pleased, with Tilly saying and Cissie nodding agreement, that he was Cam Fernie to the life. But, of course, anyone who really remembered Cam knew that wee Sam looked like someone else.

Never mind, the christening went off well, with the handful of guests who'd braved the severe weather returning to Tilly's flat for tea and the christening cake she'd somehow managed to find ingredients for, while Sam behaved beautifully, seeming not to mind being passed from hand to hand for cuddles.

'Looks like he's going to be a good baby,' Cissie remarked to Lorna, now her old slim self again. 'How do you feel about leaving him, then?'

'Why, I'm no' leaving him yet, Auntie Cissie. We don't start rehearsals for the band until next week.'

'Aye, but then you're hoping to get taken on for the dances, eh? You'll no' have much time after that.'

'Ma will be taking good care of Sam for me,' Lorna replied a little coldly. 'And she's just as keen as I am, to see me get started.'

'And I'm keen, too.' Cissie's pale blue eyes were earnest. 'I'd like to see you do well. But don't be paying too high a price, eh?'

'Just leave the price to me, Aunt Cissie,' Lorna told her, turning away, her eyes filling with tears.

'Why am I such a target?' she asked Flo and Pattie when they came to sit by her. 'I'm sure everybody thinks I'm a criminal because I'm trying to do my job.'

'No, no, it's just unusual, that's all.' Flo's gaze was very direct. 'As long as you're happy about it yourself, don't worry about it.'

'I wouldn't say I was happy. When I look at Sam, I know I want to be with him as well as doing my job.'

'Whereas men aren't usually geared up to feel like that, are they? Still, as I say, try no' to worry, eh? Sam'll be safe with your ma and you'll see him as often as you can. And remember, it won't be long before we'll be trying for engagements, and when the money starts rolling in, think what you can do for Sam and your mother!'

'As long as it does. As long as we're a success.'

'I'm sure you will be,' Pattie said quickly. 'I think you're both terrific!'

Even disregarding her loyalty, it did seem true that their plans, after the long wait, were working out wonderfully well, and the goal that had once seemed so far away was now actually in sight. Imagine, rehearsals starting next week!

'I still can't believe that we had so many replies to our advertisement,' Lorna said, thinking back to the auditions they'd held, with all the girls playing with their coats on and their hands blue with cold, as there was no way the studio could be kept warm in January during a national fuel shortage.

'Oh, the poor things, Flo, remember them trying to play for us, and all the instruments kept going flat!'

'Poor us, too, we were as cold as they were.'

In the end, though, they'd found almost all the players they wanted. Apart from Flo on guitar, they'd selected four trumpeters, three trombonists, five saxophone players, one string bass player and a drummer. That had left a pianist to find, and things were getting a little desperate when, as Lorna recalled, one came unexpectedly strolling into the studio, closing the door behind her on flurries of snow, and asking if she was too late to apply for the band, she'd only just seen the advert.

'And you are?' Flo had asked.

'Claire Maxwell.'

'And what's your instrument?'

'Piano.'

The girl was tall and slender, rather pale, with a straight nose and brown eyes. Her hair, when she pulled off her woollen hat, was brown and unevenly cut, and something about that hair and her looks in general made her seem familiar to Lorna, though she couldn't place her.

'That's lucky,' Flo was saying, 'we're short of a pianist. Any experience of dance band music, or are you mainly classical?'

'I've played for dancing in a three-piece trio at one of the hotels. The classical stuff I leave to my sister.'

And then it dawned on Lorna who the girl must be and she gave a beaming smile. 'Why, I think I know your sister!' she exclaimed. 'Is she Hannah Maxwell, who won a talent contest some time back? I was playing my sax, but she pipped me to the post and I wasn't surprised. She's brilliant!'

'Yes, that was Hannah. She's in London now, at the Royal Academy of Music, doing really well.' Claire was coolly studying Lorna's face. 'So, you were the sax player she beat – I vaguely remember seeing you at that contest. Are you really forming your own band?'

'Sure, I am, with Flo Drover here. A swing band, playing dance music, so your experience might be useful. But what happened to the trio?'

'Collapsed when the fiddle and cello decided to go to London. I've been working in a stationery shop ever since.' Claire made a face. 'Can't wait to get back to the piano.'

'Well, here it is,' Lorna told her, gesturing to the piano in the corner. 'My old Joanna. Like to play us something?'

'You bet,' said Claire.

As soon as she began to play, Lorna knew why she'd left the 'classical stuff' to her sister, for she had none of the delicacy of touch or feeling that Hannah, or even Ina, could display. But, oh heavens, she had something else, all right, something that Lorna and Flo were looking for, and that was rhythm!

As she hit the keys with a medley of well-known tunes, both Flo and Lorna's feet were tapping, their shoulders moving, their hands wielding imaginary batons, and Flo was even singing.

'"I got rhythm, I got music, I got *my* man, who could ask for anything more?"'

Who indeed?

As Claire finished and swung round for their verdict, Flo and Lorna exchanged glances.

'Well,' Claire asked abruptly, 'how did I do?'

'Very well,' Flo told her. 'Of course, we'll have to discuss the matter—'

'No need,' Lorna declared. 'I think we should offer Miss Maxwell a job.'

'Claire, please.' The pianist's brown eyes were alight. 'Thank you very much, I'd like to take it.'

'We can't pay much at the moment,' Flo said hastily. 'Three pounds a week, until we get going when we hope it will be more.'

'That's OK. It's more than I'm getting at the stationer's. When do I start, then?'

'We're holding first rehearsals next Wednesday, and as soon as we think we're ready for auditions, with any luck we'll be finding engagements. But we have to show that we can play together and know what we're doing. There will be training involved.'

'Oh, sure,' Claire agreed. 'I'm expecting it.'

'But you'll be a natural,' Lorna told her, and shook her hand. 'Very nice to have met you, Claire, and I'll be in touch about formal details. Please remember me to your sister.'

'Lorna, I think we've done well to find her,' Flo remarked, when Claire had left them. 'So, now we're all complete. Next thing will be the first rehearsal.'

'No,' Lorna said with a smile. 'Next thing is Sam's christening. You hadn't forgotten, had you? When you and my friend, Pattie, have starring roles, no less?'

'Forgotten I'm one of the fairy godmothers? No fear! I've got the christening mug in my bag at this very moment. Oh, but Lorna, isn't it grand that everything seems to be working out?'

In fact, after the christening party was over, when George Wardie suddenly arrived from Glasgow, it appeared that things might work out even better than they'd hoped. As their very good friend, the one person from Luke's band who knew their secrets and had their interests at heart, George should have attended the christening, only Luke had decided to call a snap rehearsal which he could not avoid. As it was, he'd rushed over to Edinburgh as soon as he could, clearly bursting to announce something exciting.

'George, how nice to see you, after all!' Lorna cried, opening the door to him. 'Come on in and meet my mother.'

'Thanks, I'd love to.' In spite of the cold, George was mopping his brow. 'But, girls, I can't wait to tell you – I've got great news.'

'Lorna, is that one of your friends out there?' Tilly called. 'Bring him in beside the fire!'

Thirty-One

Though on tenterhooks to hear his news, Lorna and Flo waited as patiently as possible while George shook Tilly's hand and gave a little bow.

'Mrs Fernie, I'm George Wardie, from Luke Riddell's band. It's lovely to meet you. So sorry I couldn't make the christening.'

'Why, we understand, Mr Wardie,' Tilly told him, presenting Cissie and Ewen, 'and it's nice to meet you, too. We've heard a lot about you. But come away in and get warm.'

'Not that there's much of a fire,' Lorna said apologetically, as George sat down and smiled at Sam, sleeping in Cissie's arms. 'The coal's just about to run out.'

'But what's this great news?' Flo asked, unable to contain herself any longer. 'Have you found anything for us, George, is that it?'

'Well, you know I've been looking for bookings. But just let me give Lorna this wee present for the baby. Not very original, I'm afraid.'

'Why, George, they're lovely!' Lorna exclaimed taking out silver cufflinks from the little box he gave her. 'You're so kind! And they are original, because he hasn't got any.'

'What a lucky boy,' Tilly said, smiling, as Lorna kissed George, who blushed, and Flo, having praised the cufflinks, shook his arm.

'So, have you found anything?' she asked again. 'Come on, George, out with it!'

'I certainly have.' He gave a broad grin. 'How about an audition at the Carillon Ballroom?'

The Carillon? It was one of the city's premier dance halls. Flo and Lorna were almost squeaking with excitement.

'I don't believe it!' cried Flo.

'I said I'd scout round for you, eh?' George tapped his nose. 'And I've got my contacts. Anyway, I've booked you for an audition in February. You'll have about three weeks to get your girls into shape.'

'February? We'll never do it!' Lorna wailed.

'We will, we will.' Flo was laughing with delight. 'They're all good lassies and by the time we've drilled 'em, they'll be fine. George, give us the details now!'

'But maybe Mr Wardie would like some tea first?' Tilly asked. 'We did have some wine, but I'm afraid it's all gone.'

'Tea would be nice, Mrs Fernie, thanks, but please call me George,' he told her, his eyes lighting up as she sliced him a piece of christening cake before leaving to put on the kettle. 'My, I never expected this. And what a grand baby you've got there, Lorna. Looks like it'll not be long before he's borrowing your saxophone!'

'The details, George,' Flo reminded him. 'What'll we get, if we're taken on?'

'Well, if you pass the audition, you'll be given a spot to see how you go for a couple of weeks, alternating with Chris Darley's band – think they do a lot of old time and Scottish, as well as ballroom. Pretty good, I've heard.'

'No' my dad's old band, anyway,' Lorna said with relief. 'I don't particularly want to meet up with Jackie Craik.'

'And what time's the audition?' Flo asked, as Tilly came in with the tea.

'Ten o'clock, on a Wednesday.' George scrabbled in his pocket. 'I've got the date here, Flo. But don't worry about it, you'll sail through it, I'm telling you.'

'When we have to start from scratch?' Lorna asked. 'Flo, we're going to have to get down to intensive rehearsals as soon as possible.'

'I told you, you wouldn't have time to come home much,' Cissie said, rocking Sam who had begun to whimper, but Lorna took him in her arms and soothed him.

'Sure, I will,' she said softly. She raised her bright eyes to George. 'But I'm very grateful to you, George, for getting us this chance. We shan't let you down.'

'How about a toast?' Ewen asked, passing round tea. 'Have to be teetotal, I'm afraid. But how about we all raise our cups, anyway?'

'Hang on, I'll just put Sam down in his basket,' Lorna said. 'Wait for me, I want to make the toast, too.'

'What is it, then?' asked Tilly.

'Why, the Melody Girls!' Ewen replied, and when Lorna came back, to take up her cup, everyone rose, smiling over the non-alcoholic toast.

'To the Melody Girls!' they cried, and then there were hugs all round, and a few tears and kisses.

'May you have all the success in the world!' Cissie cried, embracing Lorna to make up for her earlier criticism.

Ewen, his eyes on Lorna, sighed. 'Don't worry,' he told her, 'they will!'

Thirty-Two

Rehearsal time, and the day, in August, 1948, was sunny. Too nice, to be inside. Ah, but if you didn't rehearse, you didn't play well, and if you didn't play well, you might end up having nowhere to play at all. So Flo reminded her Melody Girls – those who sighed for fresh air and a bench in Princes Street Gardens. Or, even, if they could afford it, tennis.

'Tennis, would you credit it?' Flo whispered to Lorna, fixing her eyes on Bridie, a trumpet player, who'd been moaning that if it hadn't been for the rehearsal she might have been at the club she'd joined, flashing her legs in her wee tennis skirt and making up to the pro.

Drawing her brows together, Flo said she'd have to have a 'word', and beckoning Bridie over, told her in a loud enough voice for any other would-be tennis players to hear, that if she wanted to play tennis instead of her trumpet, she knew what she could do.

'Why, Flo, I never said I'd no' want to play ma trumpet!' Bridie exclaimed. 'I'm a Melody Girl, and that's what counts.'

'And that applies to everyone?' Flo asked, and at the chorus of agreement, nodded. 'OK, then, let's get started. "Buttons and Bows", Lorna?'

' "Buttons and Bows",' Lorna replied, her eyes taking in the girls who'd ranged themselves in their usual places, remembering how she'd once thought she'd never get to know them all, but now counted herself an expert on everyone's character, looks, talent and problems. And, oh heavens, didn't they have problems, then? More than the men? Well, more worries over love affairs, that was for sure. Or, maybe the lassies just talked about them more.

Sweet girls, though, all of them: Bridie, Alison, Katie, Jeannie, Sylvia, Nancy, Rhona, Vinnie, Trish, Win, Lynne, Madge, Heather, Gloria, and Claire – so happy to be in a band that in quite a short time was already achieving some success, in spite of those men who said they'd never make it. Bookings at the Carillon, at good hotels and occasionally the theatre, with possible radio contracts to come and maybe tours – och, the world was their oyster! They all knew that, and if they complained about rehearsals in good weather, what of it? Both Lorna and Flo knew quite well that none of their girls was going to give up her chair in the band. Especially not when wages were up too!

As she picked up her baton, however, Lorna, still smiling, suddenly met Claire Maxwell's dark eyes upon her and felt for a moment the oddest feeling of unease. Someone walking over her grave, perhaps? Wasn't that the way folk described the feeling? How ridiculous! As though Claire's gaze could make her feel like that! With a little shake of the head, her smile fading, Lorna looked away and called to her girls,

'Now, remember, this is a new song and full of rhythm, so, give it your best, eh? It's our opener at the hotel tonight.'

And off went the rehearsal. Situation normal.

Later, over a cup of tea in their tiny office, Flo and Lorna relaxed, enjoying that time of day when they could just, as they described it, flop. The rehearsal over, the girls had departed – probably for belated sun bathing or tennis – and the time to play for dancing was a lovely long way off.

'So, a cup of tea and a cigarette, what could be nicer?' Flo asked, as though she were truly at ease. But it had come to Lorna, watching her, that she was not as relaxed as she was pretending to be.

'Why the smoking, Flo?' she asked at last. 'It's no' like you to smoke so much. You got something on your mind?'

'Och, nothing gets past you, does it?' Flo shook her dark head and with a quick movement, stubbed out her cigarette. 'Makes me sure I'm right in what I'm thinking.'

'Why, what are you thinking, then?'

'That you should take over this band completely.'

Lorna's blue eyes widened, and she caught her breath. 'Whatever are you talking about, Flo? You know we're a team, we're partners, we have been from the word go. What's got into you, saying I should take over the band?'

'I think it would be better with just you, Lorna. You're a natural at the conducting, and you've got the personality as well.' Flo smiled a little. 'No' to mention the hair.'

'Oh, come on!' Lorna's cheeks were suddenly as bright as that auburn hair Flo seemed to think had something to do with the argument, which Lorna considered to be a piece of nonsense. 'Look, you're much more knowledgeable than me, much more experienced. If anyone should be leading the band all the time, it's you. Folk look at me and they're probably thinking, what does she know, then? Why, she's no' been around five minutes!'

'That isn't what they're thinking at all.' Flo was lighting another cigarette and shaking her head. 'They're admiring you, seeing somebody who's absolutely right for what she's doing. Now, for me, it's a struggle. I hate having to stand up in front of everybody, always have, so when it's my turn to lead the band, all I'm wanting is to play in the rhythm section the way I usually do.'

Lorna was silent for a moment, trying to take in this aspect of Flo she hadn't known existed. 'You've always seemed so positive to me,' she murmured. 'So good at getting what you want from the players. I never dreamed you weren't happy.'

'I wouldn't say I wasn't happy. I'm really glad we've got the band going and that we've done so well. It's just that we learn by what we do and what I've learned is that the band would be better as just yours, and not shared with me.'

'We have done well,' Lorna said softly. 'Think back to when we first started. At the Carillon that time – remember?'

'Sure, I remember. George got us the chance and we took it. I'm proud of that.'

'They thought we'd be a novelty, didn't they? They thought we'd be a flash in the pan. But then we got the hotel bookings and the King's Theatre that time, and the publicity was so good—'

'"Flame-haired band leader sets feet tapping" was one headline I seem to recall,' Flo said with a grin. 'See what I mean, Lorna?'

'"Flame-haired",' Lorna repeated with a grin. 'When they probably meant ginger? But, look, tell me you aren't serious about this. Why can't we keep on the way we are?'

As Flo drew on her cigarette, hesitating, Lorna, with the quickness Flo had already observed, said, quietly, 'There's something else, isn't there? Something you haven't told me yet?'

'OK, clever clogs.' Flo shrugged. 'The truth is, George has asked me to marry him.'

'George?' Lorna sat, stunned. 'George has proposed? What – what did you say?'

'I said yes. Well, I'm very fond of him, you know. In fact, we do love each other. He's a bit older than me, but that doesn't matter.'

'No, of course not.'

'And we think we can make a go of it, anyway.'

'But, Flo, you're no' leaving me, are you?' Lorna was winding her fingers together. 'Has all this about me running the band been just a way of telling me you're going?'

'No!' Flo ground out her cigarette, her gaze on Lorna very steady.

'There's no question of me leaving. What George wants to do is join us.'

'Join us? As a sax player? Flo, we're an all-girl band. And he's never wanting to leave Luke, is he?'

'He is, then. Luke's even more difficult than he used to be and George has had enough. No' the only one, either. Josh Nevin's already left to join Jackie Craik's band, here in Edinburgh.'

'Josh has?' Lorna was bewildered. 'I can't take all this in. I know Luke's difficult – I mean, look at the way he treated us, and once he heard about our band, he never once came over to hear us play, or even wish us luck. But he runs a good band and George would surely be better off with him. I mean, he can't play with us, anyway.'

'He doesn't want to play with us. He wants to be taken on as agent. You know how helpful he's been so far, with his contacts and so on. And then he found us an accountant and he's helped us with publicity. He's just wondering if we could find enough money in the kitty to pay him to work full time.'

'He's certainly been helpful – I don't know what we'd have done without him.' Lorna's face was thoughtful. 'And we probably are making enough to pay him as agent, though I don't know the going rate. The thing is, Flo, he's a saxophone player. I can't see him giving that up.'

'He's been a saxophone player for a long time, Lorna. Feels like a change.'

'Especially if it means he can marry you?' Lorna asked with a smile.

'Well, there's that.' Flo smiled, too. 'But the other thing he wants to do for us is more arranging. He's first rate – much better than me.'

'Flo, you're very good!'

'Not compared with George. But, listen, what do you say? Can we at least consider this? Discuss it with the accountant?'

'Sure, we can!' Lorna leaped up. 'Just as long as you don't depart to Glasgow, Flo!'

'No need to worry about that. So, I can tell him you approve, then? He's . . . well, he's coming over this evening, told Luke he'd urgent business, would you believe? We're going to have dinner before I've to be at the hotel.'

'You devil, Flo! You were pretty sure what I'd say, eh? Oh, but I'm so happy for you, and for George. I'm planning what to wear for the wedding already!'

Thirty-Three

It soon became clear that taking on George as agent was one of the best things Lorna and Flo had done. He was so knowledgeable about every aspect of big band life; he had such a vast experience of other bandleaders and musicians, of where to get bookings, of wages and practical matters, Lorna felt she was learning more and more just by having him around.

'To be honest, he's as much manager as agent,' she told Flo, as the summer progressed into autumn. 'And I never wanted a manager, I wanted to do everything myself, but now I feel I'm learning so much from him, I couldn't do without him.'

'Don't forget the arranging,' Flo replied, her face showing her pride. 'You must admit he's creating a special character for our band, the way he blends the instruments in a particular way.'

'I'm learning to do that, too, in case I ever lose George!' Lorna said with a laugh. 'Hope things don't change when you two get married, eh?'

'Och, that's a long way off. Next spring, I should think.'

'And then I'll be losing my flatmate,' Lorna sighed.

Some time before, she and Flo had finally been lucky enough to find a place they could afford in the New Town, which had given Lorna more flexibility than living at her mother's could provide. Of course, it had been a wrench to leave Sam, but she visited whenever she could and shared her mother's joy in watching him change from baby to toddler. He was, though, still a secret from her girls in the band and her public, and she couldn't see that changing any time in the near future.

One dark Sunday afternoon in early November, when she was visiting at Tilly's, Ewen looked in, hoping for a walk, but the weather was too bad and he had to settle for tea instead. While Tilly bustled about in her little kitchen, preparing sandwiches, Lorna and Ewen sat playing with Sam, who was piling up bricks and enjoying knocking them down.

'Oh, dear, hope he isn't going to grow up into a vandal!' Lorna said, laughing as she helped Sam pile up his bricks again. 'Or, do you think he might become a demolition expert?'

'I think he's going to be something pretty good,' Ewen said earnestly, touching Sam's auburn head with a gentle hand. 'He's a grand little boy. Who does he look like, then?'

'Nobody, really. He's just himself.'

Not true, of course, for in looks Sam was undeniably Rod Warren's son, but if she didn't admit it, Lorna didn't mind. As time had progressed and her heartache had eased, she sometimes liked to remember the good times with Rod. It was right, she thought, that her son should have been the result of love, even if the love had faded.

'Still haven't told folk about him?' Ewen whispered. 'I mean the lassies in the band and such?'

'No, I don't see the need.'

'Yet the neighbours all know, eh?'

She shrugged. 'They have to. But what's your point, Ewen?'

'I just feel a fine little laddie like Sam shouldn't be kept under wraps. You've put him in one compartment and your work in another. It doesn't seem right.'

'I've told you, it's the way it has to be. People aren't ready to be understanding yet. They aren't all like you, Ewen.'

He was opening his mouth to continue his argument, when Tilly came in with a loaded tray which she set on the table and called out cheerfully, 'Tea's ready! Ewen, you're looking awful serious, come away and pull up a chair.'

'Tea!' Sam cried. 'Tea for Sam!'

'What would you like?' Lorna asked fondly, taking him on her knee.

'Cake,' he answered promptly. 'Bickie.'

'Bread and butter first,' Tilly ordered. 'Then a sandwich. And then, if you're a good boy, cake.'

'Good boy,' he repeated, contentedly eating the bread and butter he'd been given, but then his face changed, his eyes filled with tears, and he looked accusingly at Tilly. 'Jam, Gramma, jam!'

'But you're going to have a nice sandwich, Sam – see, I'm cutting it up for you now.'

'Jam,' he continued to wail. 'Jam, Gramma!'

'Here,' Ewen said, hastily spreading jam on Sam's bread. 'Here you are, Sam. Don't cry any more.'

And as Sam's tears amazingly dried and he smiled sunnily over his bread and jam, Lorna and Tilly shook their heads and told Ewen he would spoil him.

'I would if he was mine,' Ewen agreed.

'I know the feeling,' Lorna said. 'And he is mine.'

'You're lucky, eh?'

'Yes,' she said slowly. 'I am. Very lucky.'

Some days later at the studio, before the girls had arrived for rehearsal, George came in with a bottle of wine and a corkscrew. He was grinning cheerfully and said they were to have a celebration.

'Whatever for?' Flo asked.

'Why, the new prince, of course. Princess Elizabeth's baby.'

'Heavens, was that in the papers?' Lorna asked. 'I've been so busy, I missed it.'

'On the wireless.' George drew the cork and looked round. 'What, no glasses?'

'You know cups are all we've got,' Flo said, passing them out. 'The wine'll taste the same, anyway.'

'No, it won't,' George said seriously. 'I can see I'm going to have to educate you, Flo, when we're married.'

'If you find the wine, I'll take instruction!'

'Well, there's more of it around. Things are gradually coming back, eh? One day we'll be rid of rationing.' George poured the wine into the cups. 'Here you are, anyway. To Prince . . . what's his name again?'

'Charles,' said Flo.

'To Prince Charles, then. Drink up, girls.'

'Prince Charles,' they echoed.

'My, isn't it nice, drinking wine when we should be working?' Lorna put down her glass. 'But now I'd better put out the sheets for "It's Magic". We haven't played it before.'

'Maybe we could have another celebration some time?' Flo suggested. 'I mean, before our wedding.'

'Think we might,' George said, pouring himself more wine. 'I wanted to sound you out on dates for a tour. Then if you agree, I could book it and that'd call for another celebration, I reckon.'

'A tour?' Lorna asked. 'I've been thinking for some time we should get something arranged. I'd prefer the spring, though.'

'I don't think we need wait for the spring for this one. It's to entertain our troops in Germany – British Army of the Rhine.' George grinned. 'Fancy it? I think it'll be interesting, anyway.'

'BAOR?' Lorna's face lit up. 'Why, George, that'd be wonderful. Flo, what do you think?'

'Terrific. George top up my glass, eh? The only thing is, we might leave half the girls behind once the army gets to see them!'

'Occupational hazard,' George agreed. 'Keep a close watch on 'em, eh? Or you'll find yourself with no sax players, or a trombonist missing, or something.

'Then you and I'll have to play,' Lorna told him, but his eyes were on the door.

'Well, speaking of sax players, look who's just walked in, then!'

And, turning her head, Lorna was astonished to see Jackie Craik at the door, with, behind him, Josh Nevin.

Thirty-Four

'Nice,' Jackie Craik commented, advancing into the studio and looking round. 'Very nice, isn't it, Josh?'

'Very smart,' the handsome Josh returned. 'I'm impressed.'

'So, to what do we owe this honour?' George asked warily. 'Haven't seen you at any of the girls' venues, Jackie.'

'No, but I've been meaning to look in. We were passing the studio – thought we might catch the lassies at rehearsal.'

Jackie, in his fifties, a lean, almost scrawny figure yet with powerful arms and strong features, gave a polite nod towards Lorna and Flo. 'You don't mind us calling without notice, ladies?'

'Not at all,' Lorna answered coolly. 'But the girls aren't here yet and I'm sure you won't have time to wait.'

'Ah, come on, now, Lorna, don't get on your high horse! I remember you when you were a wee girl, you know, when your dad used to bring you in sometimes to say hello.'

'Yes, and I always loved seeing the band, but when I was grown up, you never wanted me in it, did you?'

'And you've never forgiven me, have you? Still, you got into Luke's band, eh? And so did Miss Drover here.' Jackie nodded again to Flo. 'And now you've both deserted him, like George and Josh. Only I poached Josh, of course.' Jackie laughed heartily. 'Didn't take much poaching, did you, Josh?'

'Couldn't wait to get away,' Josh agreed. 'Hello, Lorna, hello, Flo. I must congratulate you on what you've achieved.'

'Always so formal,' George sighed. 'Why don't you both just say you've come to do a recce on the opposition?'

'Thought never crossed my mind,' Jackie said blandly. 'But now we're here, how about a drink, then? Or, is that bottle empty?'

'It's empty, we've been toasting the new prince.'

'Oh, very loyal. Well, perhaps we'd better be on our way. Honestly, we just looked in on the off chance of seeing your band in action, Lorna. We're probably playing ourselves at the same time as you – I mean if you're playing a lot.'

'We are. Sorry, not to offer you a cup of tea, but we are pretty busy.'

'Right, then we'll leave you to it. Nice meeting up again, eh?

George, Luke told me you'd flown. He's pretty cut up, you know. Didn't you two go back a long way?'

'He'll get over it,' George said shortly, as Jackie and Josh moved slowly to the door. 'Goodbye, Jackie, Josh.'

'Perhaps we'll meet again in the not too distant future?' Josh asked, his dark gaze on Lorna.

'Doubt it. We're planning a tour of BAOR, Germany.'

'Germany, eh?' Jackie grinned, but his eyes flickered. 'Guess not everybody would want to go there, eh?'

'How do you mean?' George asked.

'Well, if you remember, it's not so long ago we were fighting the Germans.'

'So? We'll be entertaining our soldiers, not the locals.'

'They say the country's in a mess, though. Rebuilding and such.' Jackie shrugged. 'Still, you'll probably be OK where the troops are. I've heard they're practically making new towns for 'em.'

'As long as there's somewhere for the girls to play, they'll be fine. And what's so unusual about people entertaining the troops? They even did that during the war. It's called keeping up morale.'

'Sure it was and the lassies will be doing a good job.' Jackie, at the door, smiled briefly. 'You've done very well, Lorna, you and Flo, and I'd be the first to say so. Josh, you ready?'

'So, what was all that about?' Flo asked, looking from Lorna to George when the visitors had departed. 'Why the sudden interest in our band, do you think?'

'Because you're a success,' George answered. 'Jackie never cared a tinker's cuss when you first started out, but now you're getting the bookings, you've become a threat, so he's interested.'

'Flattering, I suppose. But next thing, he'll be trying to spot our best players and start poaching. What's the betting?'

'That would mean having to have women in his band,' Lorna said, turning away. She gave a little sniff. 'He'd never agree to that.'

'Hey, what's wrong?' Flo turned Lorna round and studied her face. 'You're no' crying? Has the awful Jackie upset you?'

'It was just, talking to him, made me think of my dad again. When he took me to see the band, like Jackie said, he was so pleased I liked it all.' Lorna blew her nose. 'But, you see, when it came to it, he was just like Jackie, said I'd never play in a band.'

'No, he wasn't like Jackie.' George put his arm round Lorna's shoulders. 'Jackie didn't want you, but your dad just thought it wouldn't be possible. There's the difference.'

'You believe that?'

'Sure. Don't tell me he wouldn't have been proud of you now, because I knew your dad and I tell you he would have been thrilled. Another copper-haired saxophone player just like him, but running her own band? He'd have been over the moon.'

'I'd like to think so.' Lorna smiled faintly. 'Anyway, we managed to see Jackie off, didn't we? Even though I had to romance a bit about the tour to Germany.'

'That wasn't romancing, that was fact. We'll be going to Germany, all right. I'm planning to start setting the wheels in motion right away.'

'Can't wait,' Flo said, hugging Lorna. 'But, here come the girls – wait till they hear!'

As the players began to stream in for rehearsal, Lorna straightened her shoulders, put up her head, and dabbed again at her eyes. 'Tell 'em, George,' she whispered.

And when he'd told them and the excited buzz over the news had finally died down, she and Flo managed to get them into place for their new number, 'It's Magic', which went down well. Catchy, agreed the girls, and good lyrics.

'Think we'll be magic, over in Germany?' Bridie asked cheekily, and Lorna, laughing with Flo, said she wouldn't be surprised.

Thirty-Five

It was January before the Melody Girls went to Germany. Christmas had been suggested for their tour, but Lorna would not give up being with Sam at that time, and George finally made arrangements for travel after Hogmanay. Not a time to see the country at its best, he admitted, but they were not, after all, going for the scenery, and to play for the troops in dreary January might be just what they wanted.

All the same, the girls, on first arriving, confessed to some disappointment. Not with the winter weather, but because they'd thought they'd be in the famous Rhineland and instead found themselves in the industrial north.

'Well, the whole country is zoned for occupational purposes, you see,' a woman officer explained. 'The French are in Baden, the Russians in Saxony, the Americans in the Rhineland and the British in places like Dortmund and Düsseldorf.' She smiled. 'But you'll be given a good time wherever you are, I can promise you!'

Which proved to be the case. Bands for dancing were popular anyway with the troops, both women and men, but bands with girls – well, the male soldiers couldn't believe their luck. So many good looking girls, all in matching evening dresses, all playing away with such talent and energy, their leader a stunning redhead – what more could anybody want?

'We're really going to have to keep a watchful eye,' Flo remarked to Lorna and George, after the Melody Girls had responded to their welcome with even more enthusiasm than they showed at home. 'It's just like I said, the girls are bound to meet guys who'll be chatting them up and before you know it, we'll be losing players.'

'I said the same thing,' George replied. 'On the other hand, chatting up falls short of making proposals, eh? And even if things get serious, maybe we can put it to the lassies that we don't want to be leaving 'em behind when the tour's over.'

'I'll have to have a word,' Lorna sighed. 'But they're having such a good time and playing so well, I don't want to spoil things.'

'Let's see how things go,' Flo advised. 'After all, we don't stay in any place too long. They maybe won't have time to make relationships.'

'Don't bank on it,' George said with a grin. 'Some of these guys are fast workers, eh?'

In the event, only two of the girls – Nancy, one of the trumpet players, and Trish, an alto sax player – confessed to Lorna that they'd both met the men of their dreams. Och, she'd no idea! It was love at first sight, so it was, and the young soldiers were just as serious as they were.

'Now, look, you've only just met,' Lorna told them. 'You don't know these chaps and they don't know you. Things seem different in different surroundings, you know, so go home and see how you feel then.'

The two girls looked at each other, sighed, but said nothing.

'You probably wouldn't be allowed to stay here, anyway,' Lorna went on. 'You must just be sensible and no' rush into anything.'

'It's all right for you, Lorna,' Trish, a round-faced blonde murmured. 'I bet you've always been sensible, eh?'

'Me?' Lorna, her heart lurching, pretended to laugh. 'I don't know about that. But I do understand how people can feel.'

'Is that right?' Nancy, vibrant and black-haired, with vivid green eyes, shook her head. 'Don't think anybody knows how I feel!'

'Nor me,' Trish said mournfully.

But all ended well. When the time came to go home, there were sad partings but no players lost, and if there were promises to write and meet later, Flo said she wouldn't mind taking bets that those particular romances would soon be forgotten.

'Which is not to say, you won't lose some lassies back home to wedding bells and prams,' George said cheerfully. 'Another thing that's different about girl bands, you see. It's no easy job for a woman to combine being in a band with running a home.'

'No need to tell me,' Lorna said quietly. 'I'm only managing courtesy of my mother.'

'George, try a bit of tact,' Flo whispered, at which he looked contrite and Lorna told him not to worry.

She looked away for a moment or two. 'What got me about Nancy and Trish, though, was that they thought I couldn't understand how they felt because I was too sensible . . .' She laughed a little harshly. 'Me? Sensible?'

'So you are,' Flo said quickly.

'Wasn't always, was I?'

'One lapse – no need to worry about it. You've a grand little son, anyway.'

'Who's kept a secret.'

'Maybe that's for the best,' George said after a pause. 'Have to be careful when you have a public to consider.'

'What do you think?' Lorna asked Flo, who had said nothing, but Flo was diplomatic.

'I think it depends on what each individual wants. There's no rule about these things.'

Lorna, nodding, suddenly gave a little cry. 'Help, I've just realized! You two might be getting married this year. You sure that doesn't mean you'll be giving up the band, Flo? If George thinks it's hard to combine being married with playing your guitar in a band?'

'Hell, I never said that!' George cried, putting his arm round Flo's shoulders. 'I was speaking generally, not particularly.'

'Because he knows I'd rather die than stay at home all day,' Flo said, laughing and pushing him away. 'Don't worry, Lorna, you won't get rid of me so easily. The truth is, though, you could perfectly well manage on your own now, and you know it.'

'I could not! I want you both around. They say two heads are better than one, well maybe three are better than two!'

'Really mean that?' George asked. 'Because there's a suggestion I'd like to make, if it's OK with you?'

'Sure, fire away.'

'Well, it's something I know you two will have considered, but haven't taken on board so far. I'm talking about taking on a vocalist.'

'A vocalist?' Lorna glanced at Flo. 'You're right, George, we have thought about it, but there are problems. Finding the right person, I mean.'

'Can't all be as lucky as Luke, finding Suzie,' Flo put in.

'No, well, I hadn't given it much thought myself,' George said, 'but Claire Maxwell asked me recently if you were interested in taking on a singer.'

'Claire did?' Lorna frowned deeply. 'Why? Why ask you, George?'

'I've no idea. I suppose she's a bit shy, eh? Thought I might be easier to approach.'

'What are you talking about?' Flo cried. 'For a start, Claire isn't shy, and as for finding you easy, since when has she found us hard, then?'

'And who's she got in mind for vocalist, anyway?' Lorna asked. 'Wouldn't be her sister – she's destined for a career as a concert pianist.'

'And wouldn't be Claire herself,' Flo laughed. 'She's a pianist, too.'

'As matter of fact, she did tell me that she'd done quite a bit of singing,' George said awkwardly. 'Says she'd like to be considered, if you ever did want a vocalist.'

'Claire, a vocalist?' Flo shook her head. 'I don't see it. She's got a good sense of rhythm, yes, but what about her personality? You need to be very outgoing to sing with a band, and she's the opposite.'

'Maybe we should give her an audition, though,' Lorna said slowly. 'Let's just see if she can sing, or not. I think maybe the time has come to have a vocalist, anyway. You never know – she could be the one.'

Thirty-Six

For a reason that wasn't hard to understand, Lorna constantly found herself putting off arranging Claire's audition. Ever since that time she had found the young pianist's eyes fixed on her in a strangely speculative way, she'd felt uneasy in her presence. It was foolish, she knew, but there was something about the girl that made her believe there was antipathy there, and try as she would to behave the same towards her as she did to everyone else, she couldn't always manage it.

Still, she couldn't put off the audition for ever. No point in causing further hostility, and she couldn't ask Flo to do the job on her own when she'd asked to step down from being joint leader. Nowadays, they'd hit on a compromise, with Lorna acting as official bandleader but Flo being available for joint discussions, of which this matter of Claire as vocalist would be one. Maybe George should come into it, too. But after a moment's thought, Lorna decided against including him. He'd already appeared to be rather indulgent towards Claire, and she really needed objective views.

'You're actually going to give me a try-out?' Claire asked when Lorna approached her concerning the audition.

'Yes, why not?'

Claire shrugged, her flat brown eyes searching Lorna's face. 'Thought you'd decided against it.'

'We hadn't actually decided on having a vocalist at all until recently, but now that we're going for it, there's no reason why we shouldn't audition you.' Lorna, trying to look friendly and at ease, took out her diary. 'I believe you did tell George you'd had a lot of experience?'

'Not professional experience, but yes, I've sung in amateur musicals. Hannah never wanted to get involved in that sort of thing.' Claire's lip twisted. 'Far too intellectual, of course, but I wasn't.'

'How's Hannah getting on, then?'

'Oh, need you ask? Very well. Certain to hit the big time.'

Lorna hesitated for a moment. 'You're doing well, too, you know. Just because you play swing doesn't mean you're no' as good as a classical pianist.'

'Are you joking? There's all the difference in the world in the way people see you.'

'That's absolutely untrue, Claire, but we won't argue about it. Can you come to the studio next Tuesday afternoon at about three? We'll just see how you get on with Flo at the piano to begin with, maybe try with the band later. All right with you?'

'Hedging your bets?' Claire asked coolly. 'Needn't involve the band unless you like me?'

'Thought that's what you'd prefer.'

'Yes, well, it is. Thanks, then, I'll come at three.'

So, now I know what's really wrong with her, Lorna thought, making a note in her diary. She's just eaten up with envy of Hannah, who's the sort of pianist she could never be, but no one's explained to her that she's just as good in her own way. What a shame! She'd clearly been quite damaged.

This explanation of Claire's attitude made Lorna feel much better, for it seemed obvious now that Claire had nothing against her personally, she was just at odds with the world, which was much easier to understand. And perhaps might make it easier to feel more sympathetic towards her singing, though there was no way they could take her on if she wasn't good enough.

They must just hope that that wasn't the case, Lorna told herself, hurrying along with Flo to the studio some days later for the audition. The February afternoon was cold and wet, with no hint yet of spring, enough to depress anybody, as Flo remarked.

'And we'll be even more depressed if we have to turn Claire down, eh? It might make things awkward afterwards.'

'At least, we won't have to find another pianist for the rhythm section.'

'I was thinking she might be able to keep that job on, anyway. Just get up from time to time to sing.'

'We'll have to wait and see if we want her first.' Lorna was narrowing her eyes as they reached the studio. 'Who's that waiting at the door, Flo? Don't tell me it's Josh Niven!'

'It is, then. Whatever does he want? Maybe he's got the sack from Jackie's band.'

Flo laughed, but Lorna was shaking her head, as she put down her umbrella.

'No point coming to us, is it? We don't want any fellows in the band, however good looking.'

Certainly, Josh was good looking, even standing in the rain with the drops falling from his sodden trilby and running down his fine nose. There was something slightly foreign looking about him, Lorna always thought, and remembered someone saying that he had an Italian mother. Perhaps it was from her that he got his formal way of speaking? Perhaps his temperament, too, but that might just as easily have come from his Scottish father. Who knew how the genes worked?

'Hello, there!' he cried as they came up to him. 'I was wondering whether to give up and depart, but here you are, thank the Lord.'

Lorna unlocked the door and ushered him in, glancing uneasily at her watch, for Claire was already due.

'Better take your hat off,' she advised. 'It's soaking – so are you. Did you want us for something? We're just going to hold an audition.'

His face fell, as he took off his hat and put a hand through his damp black hair. 'Ah, that's a shame. I was just passing – thought I'd drop in and see how it went for you in Germany. We never heard.'

'Can't think why you'd be interested.' Flo was shaking her coat. 'But I can tell you that it went really well. We all had a great time, didn't we, Lorna?'

'Certainly did,' Lorna answered. 'But here comes Claire. She's trying out for vocalist, Josh, and I don't suppose she'd want some guy she doesn't know listening in.'

'Vocalist, eh?' As Claire came in, putting down her umbrella and staring at Josh, he looked not at her, but at Lorna. 'Jackie's found a terrific girl for us. She can certainly put over a number.'

'OK, Josh, it's been nice talking to you, but I think we want to get on,' Flo said briskly, steering him towards the door. 'Come and see us some other time.'

'May I not be introduced?' Claire asked, putting out her hand. 'I'm Claire Maxwell. Pianist for the rhythm section, actually.'

'Josh Niven. I play sax in Jackie Craik's band.'

The two shook hands, with Claire's eyes still running over Josh's face and Josh looking polite.

'Best of luck, with the audition,' he murmured.

'Thank you. Perhaps we'll meet again?'

'Perhaps.' He nodded, smiling, then glanced again at Lorna. 'I'm sorry to have held you up, Lorna. I'll be in touch, shall I?'

'If you like,' she answered impatiently. 'Goodbye, Josh. As Flo says, we have to get on. Claire, hang up your coat, then, and say when you want to start.'

'Oh, right.' Claire watched as the door closed on Josh, then turned, smiling brightly.

'What was that Romeo doing here, then?'

'Romeo? That was just a fellow we knew in Luke Riddell's band,' Flo said smoothly. 'Now, I'm going to be accompanist for you and I've got a note of what you want to sing. Which one first, then?'

Claire, realizing that her testing time was finally upon her, turned a little pale. 'I thought – maybe – "Begin the Beguine"?'

'Oh, help, that's the most difficult.' Flo gave a grin designed to put Claire at her ease. 'You sure you want that one? How about "Harbour Lights" – nice and easy, to get you started?'

'I don't mind. Whichever you think.'

'OK, "Harbour Lights" it is, then.' Flo hummed a little of the tune herself as she settled herself at the piano. 'I'm no great pianist, remember – I reckon Lorna should be doing this. How's it go – "I saw those harbour lights, they only told me we were parting . . ." Right you are, then, Claire. Let battle commence.'

Thirty-Seven

Oh, dear, she is so nervous, Lorna thought, much more nervous than when she played the piano for us. Just hope all this strain is going to be worth it.

But it wasn't long before she realized that it was not. As soon as Claire, standing very straight in a pale green dress, began to sing, Lorna's spirits fell so fast, she almost thought she could physically feel her heart leaving her. It wasn't that Claire sang badly. No, her voice was pleasant, a light crooning mezzo-soprano which she had no trouble keeping in tune, but that was all it was. A pleasant voice that would have been an asset to a chorus or a choir, but could never in the world put over a melody with a band. Where was the rhythm Claire had shown in her piano playing? Where was the personality, the charisma, of someone like Luke's Suzie?

Was she being unfair? Lorna asked herself. Was she judging too soon? It was the first song, after all, and the girl was nervous. Give her a bit of time to warm up. Decide nothing until she'd finished all that she wanted to do.

Song after song, however, showed the same lack of feeling, the same absence of power that could draw and hold an audience, and when it came to the great Cole Porter number, 'Begin the Beguine', Lorna knew that there was no getting out of it. She was going to have to tell Claire that not only was she not going to take her on as a vocalist, it was very unlikely that anyone else ever would. Her talents lay with the piano, and she must recognize that and build her career on what she could do. But, oh Lord, how was Lorna going to tell her?

'"Let the love that was once a fire remain an ember!"' Claire was crying as her final song came to an end, and she was lifting her hands, doing all she could to fill the room with her emotion, to sway the two women listening. And the trouble was, it wasn't bad. Not bad at all.

But it wasn't good, either. Not good enough. As Flo still sat at the piano with her hands folded, Lorna knew, because they were on the same wavelength, that she was sharing exactly her thoughts. So, maybe Flo would tell Claire? No, it must be Lorna herself. She felt that, knew that.

Rising to her feet, she cleared her throat. She looked at Claire and Claire looked at her.

'Thank you, very much—' Lorna began, but Claire cut her short.

'Don't bother saying anything,' she said coldly. 'I don't need any words, I can tell by the look on your face. You don't want me, do you?'

'I thought you were very good, Claire—'

'Oh, so did I!' Flo said quickly, moving to stand beside Lorna. 'You have a very good voice, Claire, no doubt of that.'

'But not good enough for you?'

'To be a vocalist,' Flo said gently.

'And why not, then? Could you please tell me why not?' Claire's eyes were hard as stones, her tone truculent. 'I've been told by some very good teachers that I've got real talent as a singer. I believe that there's nothing the band could play that I couldn't sing. Yet you tell me I can't be a vocalist?'

'It's a question of – it's hard to explain – presentation, I suppose you could say. A vocalist has to have a good voice, but also a way of putting a song across. So that it reaches the audience, sort of thing.' Flo glanced at Lorna. 'Wouldn't you say that, Lorna?'

'I would. She has to be able to present a song – and herself.'

'And I couldn't learn that?' Claire snapped.

'Well, I think maybe it's . . . inborn.'

A bright red colour had touched Claire's cheeks and her still hard eyes moved rapidly between Flo and Lorna.

'This is just prejudice, isn't it? You've no real reason for turning me down, you just don't want me. Well, maybe I don't want you, either. I don't want your rotten little job in the rhythm section, with you two bossing me around the way you'd never have dared to do if I'd been somebody like Hannah. If I'd been to college, if I'd been promised recitals, you'd never have turned me down, would you? You bet you wouldn't!'

Snatching her coat from the rack, Claire began to pull it on, her face still red, her voice thick with tears. 'I'm away,' she muttered, fumbling for the door handle. 'You won't see me again. Find yourself another pianist – and a vocalist, if you can.'

'Claire!' Flo cried, running to her and grasping her arm. 'Now this is just a piece of nonsense! Nobody wants to boss you around, nobody gives a damn here about college or recitals! We want you to stay because you're good at your job. That's the truth, isn't it, Lorna?'

'It is,' Lorna agreed, coming to Claire's side. 'Why, didn't I tell you, Claire, that you were as good as your sister though in a different way? Please don't throw up your own career for no reason. We do want you in the band, honestly we do.'

As the two women gazed earnestly into Claire's face, they sensed her mood relaxing and knew that the battle was probably won. For the way she would see it, she was going to stay, not as a loser, but as a victor. They'd had to come, pleading with her not to leave them, though they must have known, as she knew, that they could probably find another pianist. But she was good, she had rhythm, they wanted her and it was her decision, whether she said yes or no.

In the end, as Flo and Lorna had guessed she would, she said yes. Grudgingly and with the same hard unrelenting gaze, she agreed to stay on with the band as rhythm section pianist, and it was tacitly agreed that no more would be heard of her bid to be a vocalist.

'See you tonight, then,' Flo said cheerfully.

Lorna chimed in, 'At the Carillon, Claire.'

With one last dark look, Claire muttered that she would be there, then snatched up her umbrella and went out, banging the door behind her.

'Phew!' Flo whispered, sinking into a chair. 'What a struggle, eh? Was it worth it? Do we really want her?'

'I feel sorry for her,' Lorna murmured. 'Otherwise, I'd have told her what she could do, when she started raving on about us.'

'She's obviously got a chip on her shoulder big enough to sink her, but for heaven's sake, let's forget her for the moment. I've got news.'

'Good, I hope?' Lorna sighed.

'Very. George and I have decided to get married in April. Small affair at the register office, lunch afterwards. You coming?'

'Oh, Flo!' Lorna rushed to give her a hug, crying she couldn't be happier. 'Of course, I'm coming!'

'Lovely. You can be my bridesmaid, if you like, if they have bridesmaids at the register office. And then after a wee honeymoon in London, we'll come back to George's flat. So, you'll be free of me, Lorna.' Flo smiled. 'Have the whole place to yourself!'

'Oh, Flo, I'm going to miss you.'

'Well, I'll still be with the band, you know. As I said, there'll be no giving up work for me.'

'And I'm grateful for that.'

When they were putting up their umbrellas outside the studio, Lorna glanced at Flo, a little frown between her brows.

'Why do you think Josh Niven really came today, Flo? Just to find out how we got on in Germany? Seems odd, don't you think?'

'No' really.' Flo locked the studio door and put the keys in her bag. 'He had to find some excuse, I suppose.'

'Excuse for what?'

'To see you, of course.'

Lorna, astonished, burst into laughter. 'Flo, that's ridiculous. Josh isn't interested in me. When we sat next to each other in Luke's band, he scarcely took any notice of me at all!'

'That was because he was worried at first that you'd take all his solo spots, and then you were so striking to look at, he thought you'd steal his thunder. And when he stopped worrying about all of that, you'd made it pretty plain which fellow was interesting you.'

Lorna lowered her eyes as they began to walk home, dodging puddles, listening to the rain splashing on their umbrellas.

'I still don't think you're right,' she said slowly. 'Girls can usually tell if a man is keen.'

'You just haven't been noticing, that's all. Mark my words, he's going to get in touch, now that there's no rival, so be prepared. And to be honest, it's about time there was someone in your life again. Why shouldn't it be the handsome Josh?'

'You know why, Flo.' Lorna lowered her eyes. 'Do I have to spell it out? I can't get involved with anyone.'

'You're never thinking of Sam?' Flo's look was outraged. 'Lorna, that's ridiculous! You can't live like a nun all your life because of that one mistake with Rod!'

'Flo, I love Sam more than anything in the world, but I have to face facts. What man is going to want to take me on when I have someone else's son in my life? I couldn't ask it, could I?'

'Of course you could!' Flo cried robustly. 'If a fellow loves you, he'll be happy to take on Sam. These things happen, it isn't the end of the world. He'll understand.'

'Think so?' Lorna looked unconvinced. 'Well, I needn't worry about it at the moment, anyway. There's no fellow around that I can see, and don't mention Josh. You're all wrong about him.'

'We'll see.' Flo put her hand on Lorna's shoulder. 'Don't rule him out, is my advice.'

Thirty-Eight

At first, Lorna thought she had been proved right, for no move was made by Josh to contact her.

'There you are,' she told Flo, 'it's just as I said, Josh has no interest in me. Which lets me off the hook.'

'Don't talk like that,' Flo said sharply. 'I've told you, you can't cut yourself off from possible happiness because of what happened years ago.'

'Oh, Flo,' Lorna sighed. 'Don't go on.'

'Well, Josh is coming to the wedding, anyway. George invited him, just like he invited Luke and his whole band, don't ask me why. And I bet Josh will make his number then.'

'I can't think what I'll do, if he does.'

'You'll know what to do, all right,' Flo told her firmly.

Still unconvinced that Josh was interested in her, Lorna couldn't help looking out for him at the wedding reception, and the curious thing was, as soon as he arrived, he appeared to be looking out for her. Or, at least, as soon as his dark eyes found her, he was swiftly by her side.

'Lorna, there you are! There's such a crowd here, I couldn't at first see you.'

'It was supposed to be a quiet wedding,' she said with a smile.

'With two bands?'

'Only one's going to play, and that's the Melody Girls.'

'Minus you and Flo, of course.'

'Of course.'

They stood together, each with a glass of something sparkling, eyeing each other as though they were strangers. What is he thinking? Lorna wondered, and knew that what she was thinking of him was that he had never looked so elegant as he did now, in his formal suit with a flower in his buttonhole and a crisp white shirt contrasting with his dark good looks.

'You're looking very smart,' she murmured, and took a sip of wine. 'As though you don't always.'

'And you're looking very lovely – as though you don't always.'

'I'm by way of being a bridesmaid.' She looked down at her dark blue dress with a smile.

'Flo was fortunate to have you.'

'She's looking lovely, that's for sure.'

Josh's gaze went to Flo, in the middle of a crowd of guests, looking spectacularly slender in a cream two-piece, with a wisp of a hat on her dark hair, and her face flushed and pretty.

'She is,' Josh agreed. 'I've never seen her look better. Don't they say all brides look radiant? Bridesmaids, too, I think.'

'Never knew you were so practised at flattery, Josh.'

'It's my Italian heritage,' he answered gravely, then relaxed and gave an easy open smile that quite transformed him. 'Ah, Lorna, it's so wonderful to see you. I've been wanting to get in touch, but . . . I don't know – couldn't summon up the nerve.'

'Since when have you needed nerve to speak to me?'

'Since I've spent my time regretting I missed out in the early days, when you first joined the band.' Josh looked down at his glass. 'Didn't exactly welcome you, did I?'

'Let's forget all that now – there's someone I'd like you to meet.' Lorna was waving to her mother who was searching the crowded room for her. 'Ma – over here!'

'Lorna – I didn't see you!' Tilly came up, looking flustered in a patterned pink dress of her own making and a matching hat that was perched precariously on her newly waved hair. 'Such a crowd, eh? I thought this was going to be a quiet wedding?'

'Seems it snowballed. Ma, this is Josh Niven, who used to play sax for Luke – now he's with Jackie Craik. Josh, meet my mother.'

With a courtly gesture, Josh bowed over her hand, causing Tilly to look surprised and pleased. 'Nice to meet you,' she murmured. 'My husband used to play sax for Jackie – did you hear that?'

'Oh, yes, and they still talk about him, you know. A great loss, they say.'

'Aye, well, Lorna here is following in his footsteps. I see her band's gearing up to play now, and there's Luke Riddell watching.' Tilly laughed. 'Realizing all he's missed, eh? Lorna, shall we go over?'

'Yes, will you excuse me, Josh?'

As Lorna took her mother's arm, Josh said with a look of appeal, 'I'll see you later, Lorna?'

'Yes, of course. I just want to check that the band's OK. George is going to conduct for me.'

But out of earshot of Josh, Lorna quickly asked her mother about Sam. 'He's all right with Auntie Cissie, Ma?'

'Oh, happy as a sand boy! Cissie's always been good with bairns, and I didn't want to miss Flo's wedding.'

Of course not, Lorna thought, and an arrow pierced her heart as she realized it went without saying that young Sam couldn't come too. But she hadn't time to dwell on her feelings, for Tilly was looking back at Josh and murmuring what a nice, handsome fellow he was, then.

'How come you never mentioned him before, Lorna, if you both played sax in Luke's band?'

'Oh, I don't know. We weren't particular friends, I suppose.'

As her mother gave her a long considering look, Lorna knew exactly what was in her mind. Now with Sam in the background, might it not be hard for Lorna to be particular friends with any man?

'Think these babies can manage without us?' Flo in front of the band asked cheerily, carefully not letting her gaze go to Luke who was standing to one side with Suzie.

'As long as they've got George,' Lorna told her.

'We should have been playing ourselves, eh?'

'No, we should not. Flo, you're the bride, I'm the bridesmaid. Let them play for us for once.'

'Well, George is the bridegroom,' Flo said reasonably. 'But he was dying to conduct, anyway. George, George, what are you going to open with?'

Bursting with pride, George, in his dark suit and white carnation button hole, gave a grin. ' "Ain't she sweet?" ' he answered. 'That's you, Flo! I chose it specially.'

'Oh, get on with you!' she cried, embarrassed, but laughing. 'Make a start, then.'

And at George's beat, the Melody Girls, all in their matching dresses, their hair specially done, their smiles wide, began to play, as the guests, Tilly among them, stood around, listening, and Flo and Lorna each felt identical rushes of sentimental pride.

Only one girl was not smiling as she played, Lorna noticed, and that was no surprise for it was Claire. There hadn't been many smiles from her since her failed audition, but at least she was still with them, playing her piano, contributing to the rhythm section. Flo, in fact, had said she thought there'd be no more trouble from her; they had, after all, fallen over backwards to make her happy. But then maybe she was not the type ever to be happy, whatever anyone did.

Lorna, not wanting to catch her eye now, looked quickly away, returning with relief to the pleasure of listening to her band.

And as they moved through their programme of old songs and new, there was plenty to take pleasure in, as even Luke admitted when the girls had finished playing and were mingling with the crowd.

'I'll have to hand it to you, ladies,' he told Flo and Lorna, while Suzie, startlingly dressed in red with a large feathered hat, beamed, 'you've done a good job with these girls you've found. I never thought you'd manage it.'

'Will you listen to him?' Suzie cried. 'He's just so green with envy, he can hardly speak! All these lovely lassies playing for you and no' for him!'

'His bad luck, eh?' asked George, who'd joined them.

'I think he's been very fair,' Flo said coolly. 'Thanks, Luke, we appreciate all you've said. But you've got something we haven't, and that's a wonderful vocalist.'

'Ah, you're too kind.' Suzie gave her a hug. 'Just wish I could sing for you girls, too.'

'No question of that,' Luke said firmly. 'Come on, Suzie, mustn't monopolize the bride. We'll circulate, eh?'

As he swept Suzie away into the crowd, Lorna caught Flo's arm. 'Do you think she heard?' she whispered.

'Who?'

'Claire. She was just turning away when you mentioned Luke having a lovely vocalist. I saw her colour rise. I think she heard.'

'So what?' Flo asked. 'I don't see that it matters.'

'She's very touchy on that subject,' George murmured.

'Well, we haven't got time to worry about her now.' Flo took his arm. 'I think they're wanting to make a toast to us, George, and then we've to get to the station.'

'London, here we come!' George cried. 'And all the big bands we're planning to see. Just to find out if they're any better than ours.'

'I'm sure they're not!' Tilly told him. 'Now, where's this toast you're having, then?'

When the toasts had been made and George had responded to a chorus of cheers and jokes, a wedding car appeared at the hotel door and the bride and groom were driven away, amid more cheers and throwing of confetti.

'Ah, it's all over,' Tilly said sadly. 'Always an anticlimax, eh, when the bride and groom have left?'

'Yes, I feel a bit low,' Lorna admitted.

'Come back with me, then. See Sam.'

'I was planning to. I've got plenty of time before our booking.'

'I'll just get my coat, then.'

As Tilly hurried away, Josh quietly took her place. 'Lorna,' he said softly, 'any chance of our meeting some time?'

'Meeting?'

'Maybe for dinner one evening?'

'You know what the evenings are like, Josh. We're both booked to play, aren't we?' She gave a teasing smile. 'Unless we're doing better than you and you've got spaces?'

He laughed. 'No, we're fully booked, all right. But daytime, we're free. Couldn't we meet for lunch sometime?'

Couldn't we meet for lunch somewhere?

Rod Warren had asked her that once, but she swiftly put the memory from her.

'I suppose we could,' she said slowly, half turning to see if her mother was on her way back. 'Why don't you give me a ring?'

'No, let's fix it now. How about next week – say, Wednesday? I could pick you up from your studio, if you like, if you're doing a morning rehearsal?'

'Wednesday would be fine. Shall we say twelve o'clock?'

'I'll be there,' he said quickly, as Tilly, in her coat, arrived back, smiling to see Josh.

'So, he turned up again?' she murmured to Lorna on the way to the tram. 'Seems keen, eh?'

'I don't know about that.'

Again, her mother studied her, but said nothing of her thoughts.

Sometimes, she was perhaps deciding, it was better not to put thoughts into words.

Thirty-Nine

Clang! It was only when Josh appeared at the door of the studio the following Wednesday, ready to meet her, that Lorna realized what she'd done. Allowed him to collect her in front of her whole band, that was all! How could she have been so stupid? She, who needed to be so private, as good as announcing to all her girls that she was going out with Josh Niven from Jackie Craik's band, a fellow they all knew and no doubt had their eye on, he being such a heart-throb.

If she'd planned it, she couldn't have given them more cause for giggles and gossip, and as she saw their eyes avidly sliding over him as he came directly to her, her heart sank to her best court shoes she'd put on for the occasion.

'Hi, Josh!' Bridie cried. 'Looking for somebody?'

'Found her,' he answered easily, putting his hand on Lorna's arm. 'We're just going for a little lunch.'

Did he have to say that? Lorna groaned to herself. Did he have to spell it out? They might just have thought for a moment that he'd come on business, mightn't they? No, they wouldn't have thought that. From the minute he'd stepped in the door, searched for her and found her, it had been clear enough to anyone that he'd come for one reason only and that was to see her. There was nothing for her to do, except to look happy, which in fact she might have been, if only she'd had the sense to meet him somewhere else. Or, if things had been different, anyway.

'Come on, come on,' she called, swinging her keys. 'I want to lock up, so let's get going.'

'Going anywhere nice for lunch?' young Trish, who'd once lost her heart to a soldier, asked eagerly, but Claire, who'd been standing by with her usual sour expression, only laughed.

'As though there's ever anywhere nice to go these days! It'll be spam and salad again, I bet.'

'No, I think spaghetti,' Josh replied, turning to look at her. 'I'm taking Lorna to a little Italian place I know.'

Claire shrugged and made for the door. 'Best of luck, then,' she called and left, leaving Trish and others around to smile.

'In one of her moods,' Bridie whispered.

'Ah, she has moods?' Josh asked lightly.

'All the time,' Trish told him. 'Nobody crosses Claire.'

'Never mind her now,' Lorna murmured, shooing her girls before her out of the door. 'Josh, are you coming? I have to lock up. Girls, see you tonight – eight o'clock sharp, eh?'

'Don't make a mistake and join our band at the Adelphi,' Josh called with a grin.

'Don't tempt us!' Bridie fired back.Then laughed at Lorna's expression. 'Only joking, boss!'

'Honestly, they're like a class of school kids,' Lorna muttered, as she and Josh walked away together. 'They're the same as the men – a lot of Luke's fellows always reminded me of boys at school. Except you, of course.'

'Hope so!' He took her arm and pressed it to his side. 'Listen, are you feeling cross about something, Lorna? Has something happened?'

'No, no.' She sighed 'I suppose it's just that I know I'll be in for a lot of teasing, now that the girls have seen you coming to collect me.'

'Teasing? Why?'

'Oh, you know what girls are like. Always looking for romance, and if they can't find it, they make it up.'

'You think they're making up romance between you and me?' His dark eyes glittered a little. 'I'd like to think they needn't do that.'

'I'm sure you're right.'

'No, you misunderstand.' He drew her to a halt beside a small dark blue car. 'I mean, they needn't make up something that already exists.'

'Come on, Josh.' Lorna laughed uneasily. 'There's no romance between us. We're going out together for the first time, remember.'

'As though people need to go out at all, to have certain feelings.' He studied her for a moment, then took out a car key and opened the doors of the little blue car. 'Like to jump in? This is my new baby, a Morris Eight. Well, it's more an old baby, really, but goes pretty well.'

'I didn't know you had a car!' Lorna exclaimed, climbing readily into the passenger seat. 'I've been thinking of having driving lessons myself. I could do with some transport.'

'New cars are hard to get, but I could help you to look for something second hand, if you like. Give you driving lessons, too.'

'If we ever find the time together.'

As he drove smoothly away, he gave her a quick sidelong glance. 'I intend to find the time for that, Lorna.'

The little Italian place he knew was in a West End side street, owned by his cousin, Silvio, who greeted him with a beaming smile and a volley of Italian, before changing to English and shaking Lorna's hand.

'Welcome, signorina, welcome to my restaurant. It's good you bring Joshua here, for he is always so busy, playing and playing, he never has the time to come and eat!'

'So does the Signorina Fernie spend her time playing,' Josh told him. 'She plays the saxophone, like me, and has her own band.'

'No! Her own band! This I must hear. But now you must come and eat and I will help you choose.'

Small, plump Silvio bustled them along to a window table for two, setting menus in front of them but telling them firmly what was best and then snapping his fingers to a waiter for a bottle of wine.

'On the house,' he whispered. 'In celebration of seeing you again, Joshua, with this lovely lady. Now, I will see to your antipasto.'

'You'd never think he was born and brought up here, would you?' Josh whispered with a grin. 'He likes to put on the Italian accent for the benefit of his customers, but when he feels like it, he sounds like a Scotsman, just like me.'

'Josh, I'd never take you for a Scotsman,' Lorna said, smiling. 'Somehow, I wasn't surprised to find you had an Italian mother.'

'Sister of Silvio's mother, yes, but my father was a Scot. He was an organist – played for a time at the cathedral where my mother was in the choir. It was love at first sight for them, even though their families didn't approve. They married, though, and had me, but my father died when I was only a boy.'

'Ah, I'm sorry, Josh. I know what it's like, to lose a father, but at least I knew him until I was grown up.' She drank a little of the wine the waiter had brought. 'Are you and your mother very close, then?'

'Pretty close. One day I'd like you to meet her, but at present she's in Italy, looking after my grandmother. The whole family was here at one time – no surprise if I tell you they were in the ice cream trade – but my gran went home eventually.' Josh twirled his glass. 'I suppose, that side of my family will always think of Italy as home.'

To Lorna, listening intently, all this sounded very romantic, but after what she'd been saying about a different kind of romance, she didn't dare to make the comment. Still, there was no doubt, as their lunch progressed, Josh seemed to be taking on a romantic haze of his own, even when he was only teaching her how to eat spaghetti and they were both laughing at her efforts. The question of how things were going to develop between them was very much in her mind.

Forty

'A little lunch you call this?' she asked, when the waiter had whisked away the plates for the main course that had followed the spaghetti. 'I don't feel I can ever eat again. How does Silvio do it? I mean, with the rationing and shortages and everything?'

'Ah, you never ask,' Josh answered, putting his finger to his lips. 'Ways and means, he might say if you did, but he'd never explain. Like coffee? It's very strong.'

'Perhaps I need it, though.'

'Right, we'll have coffee, then I'll settle up.' He gave her another of his long intense looks. 'It's very nice here, watching Silvio at work, being waited on, but all I want, really, is to be with you.'

'You're with me now.'

'You know I mean just the two of us, on our own.'

'That can be difficult.'

'You're forgetting my car.'

It was true, she had forgotten it, but now understood what he meant. A car could be a little world quite separate from the real one; a refuge, a safe house. A place to be so close with someone, you need think of no one else.

'I don't think we have time to go driving today,' she told Josh, as the waiter placed their espresso coffee before them. 'With George and Flo away, I'm working on arrangements. Not my forte, really, but I'm improving.'

'Arrangements? You have to do arrangements? The first time I persuade you to be with me?' Josh drained his coffee at a gulp and set the cup down. 'Why do you do this, Lorna? Why do you push me away? Hold me at arm's length?'

She sat back, fingering her own cup, not willing to meet his eyes. 'I'm sorry, Josh. I know it seems like that.'

For some moments, he sat staring into her face, as though he would read it like a book. Then he leaped up and signed to their waiter.

'This is hopeless,' he whispered. 'We can't talk here. Let's go.'

'Was good?' cried Silvio, running over. 'Signorina, you enjoy it?'

'Oh, yes, thank you, it was wonderful. A wonderful experience, my first Italian meal.' She managed a radiant smile. 'Now I know what spaghetti should really be like.'

'So, Joshua must bring you again! And soon, eh?' Silvio, delighted, was all for waiving the bill, but Josh paid anyway and, after managing to make their farewells, he and Lorna left the restaurant.

'So friendly, your cousin,' Lorna murmured. 'So – what's the word – outgoing.'

'You're thinking, not like me?' Josh asked wryly as they drove through the West End.

'I didn't say that.'

He shrugged over the wheel. 'Look, can you really not spare more time for me this afternoon? Maybe we could just go to the Botanics? Walk a little?'

'All right,' she conceded, 'but I really don't want to be out too long.'

'Fine. I promise I'll get you back to those damned arrangements any time you say.'

Neither spoke on the short drive to the Botanic Gardens, favourite walking place for Edinburgh folk and visitors, the Scottish answer to Kew, complete with Palm House, glasshouses, exotic trees and a lake with ducks.

Lorna was thinking of what she could possibly say to Josh. Tell him the truth? She had a son, who was Rod Warren's boy, back home with her mother? Even to imagine his reaction was too much for her mind to accept. All that would happen, she knew, was that this budding relationship would snap as easily as one clipped off a flower. At this early stage, it would be easy for him just to give her up. A woman with another man's child, and that man being Rod Warren? Tell him, tell him, she told herself. Watch his face.

But as he parked the car and turned to look down at her, his gaze melting into hers, she felt the sharp pain of rejection almost as though it had already happened and decided she need say nothing yet. Obviously, he would have to be told of Sam if their relationship really developed. But why not wait till then? With huge inward relief, she made the decision.

They left the car and began to walk through the tree-lined gardens, pausing at the lake to watch children feeding the ducks, smiling at the activity.

'Here's a bench,' Josh said, when they turned towards one of the great glasshouses. 'Like to sit for a while, if it isn't too cold?'

The April wind was certainly not warm, but they sat close on the bench and after a moment held hands and looked at each other.

'May I ask you again why you're holding away from me?' Josh said quietly. 'Don't say we are together now. You know what I mean, don't you?'

'Yes,' she said with a sigh. 'I know what you mean.'

'Is it because of Rod? Is he still in your mind?'

'No, he's water under the bridge.'

'He hurt you, though, didn't he? Maybe he's made you afraid? Of being hurt again?'

'We hurt each other. Because we wanted different things.'

'If it isn't Rod,' Josh said slowly, 'it must be me. Maybe you haven't forgiven me yet, for the way I used to be?' He pulled his hands from hers. 'Certainly haven't forgiven myself.'

'Most men in bands feel the way you did. I don't know why, but they're just suspicious of women players. See them as rivals, I suppose, because they have to admit, the girls know how to play.'

'So childish,' Josh was muttering, as two red spots burned darkly in his cheeks. 'Can you believe it – I thought you'd be taking all my solos? You were so lovely, I guessed Luke was going to push you forward, make you the star. It didn't seem fair.'

'And it wouldn't have been, only he never wanted to do that. I was just somebody he could pay less money to, that was all.'

Scarcely listening, Josh was dwelling on the past. 'So, I threw away my chances, didn't I? For the sake of pride, I let Rod Warren move in and by the time I realized what I was feeling for you, it was too late.' He raised his eyes to hers. 'Too late to make you think of me.'

When she looked away, he caught her hand again. 'It's not too late, though, is it? Because Rod's gone. He's water under the bridge. That's what you said, isn't it?'

'Yes, and it's true. I don't think of him now.'

'So why won't you let yourself think of me? Is it because you remember the way I was?'

'I do think of you, Josh. I like to be with you.'

'But you're afraid of getting in too deep? Just want to get on with your career?'

'Maybe.' She pushed her bright hair from her face. 'Maybe it's that, Josh.'

'Lorna, don't be afraid!' he cried, putting his arms around her, holding her tightly against him. 'Please, just relax. Meet me, go out with me, see how things go. And I promise, if you do, there'll be no strings.'

Were there people around? She found she didn't care. As she drew away to let her eyes go over his face so finely lit with feeling, she knew she was going to see him again, whatever the cost. Maybe she was taking a risk, but life was full of risks. 'Meet me, go out with me, see how things go,' he'd said . . . That's what she would do.

'The problem's going to be,' she whispered, her voice shaking a little, 'that we have so few chances to meet.'

'Don't you worry, we'll make chances,' he told her, his own voice shaking. And then they kissed, very gently, as though honouring a pact, and stood up together, to walk slowly, arm in arm, back to the car.

Outside her flat, they stood on the step, their eyes examining the new person each had become, for already their commitment had brought change. They were not the same people who had set out to the Italian restaurant earlier that day.

'Good luck with your arrangements,' Josh said hoarsely.

'To tell you the truth, I'm just longing for George to come back.'

'You'll do well. I know your talents.' He laughed a little. 'Used to think I could give you some tips for the sax – you know, different fingering, glissando, all that stuff. Found you knew it all.'

'Oh, my sax playing is OK, but with arrangements, you need to know everyone else's instruments, too, and what goes where.' She was still studying his face, not really caring what she was saying. 'As I say, though, I'm improving. I hope.'

'Of course, you are improving.' Josh looked round at passers by, then kissed her briefly on the cheek. 'When can we meet, then?'

'I don't know. We'll have to see.'

'I'll ring you?'

'Yes, ring me.' As he reluctantly turned to go, she called to him. 'And, Josh, thank you for the lunch. I loved it.'

'The first of many, I hope. But thank you for coming.' He smiled, slightly bowing his dark head. 'Better find my car, I suppose. *Arrividerci*, Lorna.'

She made no reply, only waved, until he had turned the corner of the street, making for where he'd parked the car, and was lost to her. Now, she thought, pretending to be her old efficient self, for those arrangements. But it took her some time to do anything, except sit in her chair and face what she had taken on. Taken on and would not let go. For, already, she was looking forward to another meeting with Josh.

Forty-One

He did ring, and soon. The next morning, in fact, as Lorna was cleaning her teeth.

'Why, Josh, it's you!' she cried, through a mouthful of toothpaste. 'I thought it was an emergency, someone in the band.'

'Only me, I'm afraid,' he said smoothly. 'This seemed the best time to be sure of catching you.'

'It's certainly early enough. What did you want to ask me?'

'You know what I want to ask you. When can we meet?'

'Honestly, Josh, I've only just got up – can't think straight. When do you suggest?'

'This afternoon? Jackie's called a rehearsal this morning, but we'll be finished by lunch time.'

'I'm afraid I've an appointment at the King's. We're playing there next week. I want to see the set up.'

'Tomorrow, then? Anything wrong with tomorrow?'

'Tomorrow will be fine. But make it after lunch and meet me here.'

'Too late to worry about the girls at the studio, isn't it?' he asked, and she could tell he was smiling.

'Maybe, but I'd be happier if you came here.'

'Anything to make you happy, Lorna. I'll be with you at one.'

When he had put the phone down, she stared at it for a moment, then moved to the bathroom where she looked at her face in the mirror. Oh, Lord! Good job Josh couldn't see what a fright she looked, with her hair uncombed and a white ring of drying toothpaste round her mouth! Time to make herself look normal. Her hand on the washbasin tap was trembling.

When he arrived at the flat the following day, punctually at one o'clock, she had regained her calm. A little time away from him had made her wonder if she might be over emphasizing his feelings – and her own. There would be no point in seeing more than there was in this new relationship. For the more there was, the more there would be to worry about.

As soon as he came in, though, and stood looking round at where she lived, all her doubts of his feelings and hers were swept away in a rush of pleasure at seeing him again. Worry was there, of course, but lost in the cascade as she worked hard to regain her earlier composure, while looking around for her jacket and fussing with her hair.

'Nice place,' he murmured, helping her to put the jacket on. 'You shared this with Flo?'

'Yes, she still has stuff here, but she'll be moving into George's flat when she comes back.'

'You'll miss her.'

'I will. She's great company.'

'But then it might be good to have the flat to yourself.'

'Oh, yes.' She glanced at him from the hall mirror. 'You don't share with anyone?'

He grinned. 'No one would put up with me. Anyway, my place is nothing like this. Just a one-bedroomed flat in a modern block near the infirmary. People all around, making as much noise as possible.'

'Well, I've an old biddy on the ground floor who acts like she's my keeper, and upstairs there's a family who wear clogs day and night – or seems like it.' She waved a hand. 'But, I like it here and reckon I'm lucky to have it. Like to look round?'

'Please.'

Her high-ceilinged sitting room, still showing New Town elegance, he had already admired, but then she let him peep into the kitchen, created from somebody's long ago study, and the well-appointed bathroom. When they reached the bedrooms, Lorna pointed out first Flo's, then her own, but Josh, making no comment, only nodded from the doorway and returned to the hall.

Had he been embarrassed to see her bed? Lorna wondered, for he seemed to be avoiding her eye. Normally as straight as a soldier, his shoulders were a little hunched as he looked down at his car keys in his hand.

'Seems funny,' he said, at last raising his eyes.

'What does?'

'Well, your having a place like this on your own. An Italian girl, you know, would never be allowed it.'

'Why not?'

He shrugged. 'Parents like to keep tabs on daughters.'

'Heavens above, Josh, I've had the key of the door for some time. I'm fully grown up, I have my own band, I'm making my way – why on earth shouldn't I have my own place to live?'

'Oh, no reason at all,' He took her hand. 'I don't necessarily agree with Italian ideas.'

'That's a relief.'

'So, where shall we go?' He was brightening as they left the flat and walked to his car. 'How about Peebles? Have tea at a hotel – and be anonymous?'

'You think I want to be anonymous?'

'You give me the feeling you'd like to be.'

'When I'm a bandleader?'

'That's the role you've taken on. When you step out of it, you're . . . someone else.' His voice was low but strong, filled with sudden emotion. 'That's the person I want to know.'

Lorna, opening the passenger door of the car, took her seat without at first answering. But as Josh drove smoothly away, she turned to look at his fine profile.

'I do want you to know me, Josh. The real me, just as I am.'

'I'm glad. I want us to know each other.' He flashed her a quick glance. 'Without secrets, without reserve.'

'Next stop, Peebles,' she said lightly.

In the splendour of the tea lounge of a grand hotel in Peebles, an ancient royal burgh some miles from Edinburgh, they sat facing each other across scones and fancy cakes the likes of which Lorna hadn't seen for years.

'Never mind anything else,' she said, delightedly pouring tea, 'I'd come here for the cakes alone.'

'Ah, Lorna, it's so good to see you relaxing.' Josh leaned across the table towards her. 'Now you're becoming your real self, aren't you?' He covered her hand with his. 'And not shutting me out.'

'Everything all right, sir?' a waiter asked before Lorna could speak, but Josh nodded.

'More than all right, thank you.'

'Very good, sir.'

When the waiter had withdrawn, Lorna looked about her and breathed a sigh of contentment. This vast dining room, where a trio played light music to guests who were only interested in one another, wonderfully suited her mood.

'It's true, you could be anonymous here,' she said softly. 'Big hotels – they're the places to lose yourself. I've often thought that, playing at some of the Glasgow ones, and in Edinburgh.'

'You're not lost now, though,' Josh murmured, playing with her hand. 'Because I've found you.'

She smiled indulgently. 'Think I could get my band an engagement here, Josh?'

'Too noisy. It'd be like playing in a cathedral.'

'Bet they have a ballroom. We wouldn't be too noisy for that.'

'I'd better tell Jackie to get in first,' he said impishly. 'We are rivals, you know.'

She only gave a light-hearted laugh, and Josh raised a hand for the bill.

On the way home, which led through pleasant countryside just coming into the beauty of late spring, their good spirits lasted, buoying them up on billows of well being. It might work out, Lorna, was even thinking, it just might, but when Josh stopped the car in a quiet lay-by, he surprised her by speaking again of Rod.

'You know we were talking about Rod the other day?' he began. 'Mind if I ask you something?'

'About Rod?' she asked uncertainly.

'Yes. I've been wondering what you meant when you said you both wanted different things. What sort of things?'

Lorna's lips tightened. She stared straight ahead without speaking.

'I'm sorry if it upsets you to talk about it, don't worry,' Josh said quickly. 'I needn't know. It's none of my business.'

'No, it's all right. I don't mind telling you. We were thinking of getting married—'

'Married?'

'Well, yes. We were sort of engaged.'

'Go on, then.'

'Well, we discussed things and it turned out that Rod didn't want me to continue with my music.'

'What – give up your sax?'

'Professionally, anyway. He thought – it's what a lot of guys think – that once we were married, he'd be breadwinner and I'd keep house.' Lorna slid her gaze to Josh, whose fine eyes had widened. 'Are those your ideas, Josh? I bet it's what Italian men think.'

'I'm only half Italian, Lorna. It's not what I think.'

'You mean that?' Her eyes had begun to shine. 'You'd let your wife work? Have a proper job?'

'Yes, I would. Why not? If it was what she wanted.' Josh was shaking his head. 'Think of the waste, if you had to give up your band!'

'Oh, Josh!'

Before she could stop herself, she'd flung her arms around him, pressing her face to his, at which his mouth found hers and together they kissed, long and slowly, finally drawing away and gazing at each other.

'You know what's happened, don't you?' Josh said, touching her cheek. 'Lorna, I'm in love with you.'

Though her thoughts were whirling and words were almost tumbling from her lips, she said nothing, and he put his hands on her shoulders and gently shook her.

'Is it such a surprise? Surely, you knew?'

'Sort of,' she said huskily. 'But maybe it's too soon, Josh, to be talking about love.'

'No, it's not too soon. When I say it's happened, it hasn't just happened. I've cared about you for a long time. I told you, didn't I, how it was? That I left it too late to tell you? That Rod stepped in where I wanted to be?'

'Yes, you told me.'

'And during all those early days, you never thought of looking my way, because of him, but now that he's gone, you're free, aren't you?'

His gaze on her was so intense, she felt for a moment that he would see into her mind, read her secrets. But free, he thought her, so that couldn't be true. For she wasn't free – and didn't want to be – of what might come between them. Only, as she looked at him, so handsome, so yearning, she felt she would have given a great deal to be able to say she loved him. To be free, in that way.

'We'd better go,' she told him, sighing. 'We've work ahead.'

'You haven't said yet, that you love me.'

'Let's no' put things into words just yet, Josh. Let's just see each other, the way you said, and—'

'And see how things go?' He groaned a little. 'I already know how they've gone for me.'

'Come on.' She kissed him again, gently and sweetly. 'Let's get back. No need to look sad, this isn't goodbye.'

'Feels like goodbye to me.'

'More, *arrividerci*,' she whispered, and at that he smiled, reluctantly straightening himself in the driving seat and starting the car's engine.

'Home, then, sweetheart, but not before you promise to see me again as soon as possible.'

'You know I will.'

At her flat, disregarding old Mrs MacAllan's twitching of lace curtains, they kissed swiftly, Josh's eyes alight, Lorna's closed, until she opened them and ran to her front door.

'Ring me,' she cried.

'I will!'

And then they were apart and she was in her bedroom, trying to think of the time and the evening's engagement, what she would wear, what her band would be playing . . .

And, oh, God, little Sam. When would she see him? Tomorrow. Tomorrow, after morning rehearsal, she'd go round to Ma's, see Sam, take him something special.

As she began hastily to prepare to go out, to put on her professional facade, tears began to fall, gathering and spilling, and she had to stop, to wipe them away.

Forty-Two

When Flo and George arrived back from honeymoon, they were, of course, full of all they'd seen in London. The sights, the plays, the concerts, but mainly the big bands.

'Oh, God, those guys, those bandleaders!' George exclaimed. 'You wouldn't believe how good they are. The panache, the professionalism – I'm not running down Luke or Jackie, you understand . . .'

'Or Lorna!' Flo said crisply. 'And they weren't all men, remember. How about the wonderful Ivy Benson?'

'Oh, Ivy – she's a stunner,' George agreed. 'And her girls are top notch, no doubt about it. But that's what I'm saying, there are so many top notch bands down there, so many classy leaders – Ambrose, Jack Hylton, Ted Heath – they really inspired us, eh, Flo? To put the Melody Girls on the map.'

'Make it sound as though we'd have to be in London for that,' Lorna remarked.

'You're right!' cried George. 'That's where the venues are. So many of 'em, you see. Fancy clubs, theatres, dance halls, not to mention the BBC. You should hear these London bands broadcasting! Now, if we could only land ourselves their sort of contracts!'

'The thing is, we're a Scottish band,' Lorna told him. 'We might do a few bookings in London, but we'd never make it our base. Edinburgh's our base and that's where we'll stay.'

'OK, OK.' George gave a regretful sigh. 'But let's at least see if we can get an English tour, eh? Want me to get on to it?'

'Sure. I'm all for a tour. Just as long as we come back here.'

'So, now we've sorted out our future, can I get on with packing up my gear?' Flo asked, for they had been sitting for some time in Lorna's flat, showing their honeymoon snaps and drinking coffee. 'George, how about you bringing up the cases from the car?'

'It's good that George has a car, too,' Lorna said, moving with Flo to her old bedroom. 'Josh has a Morris Minor.'

'Oh, yes?' Flo gave her a curious look. 'Been seeing Josh, have you?'

'We've been out a couple of times.'

'I told you he was interested, didn't I? And you see I was proved right.' But Flo, still studying Lorna, was shaking her head. 'How come you're looking far from over the moon?'

'You think I should be over the moon, to be going out with Josh?' Lorna opened a wardrobe and took down some of Flo's clothes. 'Shall I put these on the bed for you?'

'Oh, never mind about my things. Tell me what's wrong. Come on, tell me, Lorna. No point in bottling it up.'

'I should've thought you'd know what was wrong, anyway.' Lorna looked down at the dresses in her arms. 'I haven't told him about Sam.'

'Oh.' Flo's expression changed. 'I think I understand, then.'

'Got the cases,' George called, putting his head round the door. 'Want 'em here?'

'Yes, please,' Flo answered. 'Then why don't you read the paper next door and I'll give you a call when we're ready?'

'Suits me,' George said with a grin. 'I'd be no good at packing your stuff.'

When he'd retired to the living room, Flo, having closed the bedroom door, made Lorna sit on the bed and took her place next to her.

'What are you going to do? I have the feeling that Josh is keen and so are you. You must work something out.'

'By work something out, you mean, tell him.'

'Exactly. There's nothing else for it, Lorna. Bite on the bullet. Explain how it was.'

'How it was!' Lorna leaped up. 'The truth is I made love with Rod Warren, the last person Josh would want to think of with me. He'd never be able to accept it, he'd drop me without thinking twice.' Lorna's voice trembled. 'And to have him despise me – I'd feel so terrible, Flo. Because I have begun to care for him. It took me a long time to get over Rod, and I never thought Josh could replace him, but now I don't want to give him up.'

'He won't despise you!' Flo cried. 'He'll understand. These things happen. It was just the one time – you got carried away. Tell him, and you'll see.'

'He won't understand. Because Sam's father is Rod. It would just be too much.'

'The thing is, Lorna, you have no choice in this,' Flo said steadily. 'If you want a future with Josh, he has to know about Sam. You can't hide your son away for ever.'

The colour rushed to Lorna's face and tears began to thicken her voice. 'I will tell him,' she said in a low voice. 'But I'll wait a while. Until the time is right. That would be best.'

'Lorna, the time is now.' Flo rose and began to pack her dresses into one of the suitcases George had brought. 'What does your ma think, then?'

'I haven't said anything to Ma about Josh yet.'

'Haven't said anything to your ma? Honestly, Lorna, for such a strong person, you're behaving like some poor old ostrich! Come on, get a grip. Sort out your life. It can only be for the best.'

'All right, all right.' Lorna began to hand clothes across to Flo. 'I suppose I should tell Ma,' she said thoughtfully. 'I'll do that next time I see her.'

'That'd be something done, at least,' Flo commented. 'But Josh is the one who counts.'

'You've made your point,' Lorna said shortly. 'Let's leave this for now.'

She had thought her mother's advice would be the same as Flo's. 'Tell him. Bite on the bullet.'

But when, the following afternoon, she told Tilly that she was seeing Josh, the look on her mother's face only seemed to confirm her own fears.

'Going out with that handsome young man?' Tilly murmured, as she and Lorna watched Sam rolling one of his cars up and down the sofa. 'I had an idea he was keen when I saw him at the wedding.'

'It's early days,' Lorna said hesitantly, 'but I think . . . I think we are beginning to care for each other.'

'And you've got a problem.' Tilly's eyes moved from Sam to Lorna. 'Because he doesn't know yet?'

'He doesn't know.'

'But you're wondering how he'll take it?'

'I've a pretty good idea.'

'Aye.' Tilly sighed. 'I've known one or two lassies in the same situation. Worrying what to do, when they met a new fellow.'

'What did they do?'

'Had to tell the men, of course.'

'And what happened?'

'One fellow didn't mind. He married the girl, anyway.'

'And the others?'

Tilly shrugged. 'Cried off. Didn't want another man's child to bring up.'

'I see.'

'You can understand their feelings, eh? I mean, a babby to think about before they'd even got wed, and no' theirs?'

'Oh, I understand, all right. All too well.'

'Better to tell Josh and get it over with, before you're in too deep, eh?'

'Maybe. But I think I'll leave it for a bit, Ma. See how things go.'

Tilly's gaze returned to Sam, who was now singing to himself as he tried to fit a toy soldier into his car.

'He's a lovely little lad,' she whispered. 'Anybody could be proud of him.'

'I am proud, Ma, I am.' Lorna stood up. 'And I will tell Josh. As soon as I can pick the best time.'

'Just don't get your hopes up, then,' her mother said quietly. 'It's a lot to ask a man. Don't blame him, if he can't do what you want.'

'The only person I'm blaming is myself,' Lorna answered. 'If I hadn't been such a fool . . .'

'You wouldn't have had Sam.'

'Oh, Ma!' Lorna wailed, bursting into tears, at which Sam, looking worried, ran to her and gave her his car, and Tilly, shedding a few tears herself, said she'd put the kettle on.

Forty-Three

As summer followed spring, bringing long, long days, trees in full leaf, folk feeling relaxed now that winter was a memory, Lorna and Josh began to live for each other. Every time they could, they met. To drive somewhere, if Josh could get the petrol, to walk, to kiss, to hold, to sigh over their sweet passion, never actually making love, or even talking of it, but feeling it there, all the time, in the background of their lives.

Usually, of course, because of their evening commitments, they had to meet by day, but a night did come when both their bands were free of engagements, and they were able to meet for dinner and the theatre. It was then that Lorna suggested Josh should come in to her flat with her, for previously he had shown a strange reluctance to do so when he brought her home in the daytime.

'Come in for coffee,' she had urged. 'Josh, why don't you?'

'Ah, it's that old lady twitching her curtains,' he'd told her, his expression uneasy. 'It would just put me off being with you, wondering what she was thinking.'

'Heavens, you don't have to worry about her!' Lorna had cried. 'What she thinks is of no importance.'

'To me, it is,' Josh answered seriously. 'For your sake. I don't want people to get the wrong impression about you.'

'She's one old lady, Josh, no' people. It isn't going to hurt me, what she thinks of me.'

'Reputation is very important. Particularly for young women.'

'Now you're talking like an Italian,' Lorna had said uneasily. 'And I don't see why young women's reputations should matter more than young men's.'

'But you know they do,' Josh replied. 'Even today.' He looked about him. 'And you see, it's broad daylight. Anyone could see me going into your flat.'

'You didn't mind coming in that time you came to collect me, did you?'

'I knew I wouldn't be staying long.' Josh's look softened. 'It would be different now.'

After they'd been to the theatre, however, the daylight had faded when they arrived back at Lorna's flat, and the old lady's curtains were firmly drawn across her window.

'Are you coming in, then?' Lorna asked, standing with her key in her hand.

'Thank you,' Josh said quietly. 'This time I'd like to.'

In her flat, Lorna drew the curtains, slipped off her coat and went to the kitchen to make coffee.

'You sit down, Josh,' she called. 'I won't be long.'

But he had followed her and before she could even put out cups, had taken her in his arms. For an eternity of bliss, they clung together, kissing more and more passionately, until they moved into the living room where they lay together on the sofa, half out of their clothes, lost to a rapture that if it wasn't true rapture was as near to it as their barriers would permit.

But suddenly Josh leaped up, buttoning his shirt, putting on his jacket, his face a mask of desire as he looked down at her, but his decision very clear. 'Oh, God, I'm sorry, Lorna,' he muttered. 'This isn't how I meant things to be tonight. Not at all what I'd planned.'

'Why, what had you planned?' Lorna asked, rising and straightening her dress. 'I didn't know you'd planned anything.'

'How about making the coffee?' he asked with a smile. 'That should sober us up.'

'We haven't exactly been drinking, Josh.'

'Haven't we? I feel intoxicated, anyway.'

And so do I, Lorna thought, making the coffee with trembling hands. For how else had she come close to letting herself go with Josh, in just the same way as she'd done with Rod? How else had she almost given way to feelings that might end in disaster? Only, of course, tonight they hadn't. Josh had kept his head, drawn back, and now here was she, making coffee, and acting as though nothing had happened.

'Black for you,' she murmured, taking in her tray to the living room. 'And no sugar? I've made it nice and strong.'

'Thank you.'

They sat down on the sofa, both looking quite correct, clothes neat, hair tidy, only their eyes so full of feeling giving them away.

'Tell me what you'd planned, then,' Lorna murmured.

'You make it sound so formal.'

'You're the formal one, Josh.'

'Maybe. I like to do things by the book.' He gave an uncertain smile. 'But that's not always possible. Depends what other people want.'

'I wish you'd tell me what you're talking about.' Lorna, sensing that Josh was nervous, was nervous, too, drinking her coffee quickly, dabbing at her lips with a still shaking hand.

'Never thought this would be so difficult.' He bent his head, staring into his cup, then set the cup aside and looked up, straight into Lorna's eyes.

'Lorna, will you marry me?'

Long afterwards, she was to remember that moment. The way she had caught her breath, felt her heart drumming, her head swimming. And how Josh's eyes, so dark, almost black, so intense, had held her as though in thrall, so that her thoughts were flying everywhere, but her body remained still.

'Well?' he asked, with stiff lips. 'What do you say?'

'Josh – I – I'm stunned.'

'Stunned?' His mouth relaxed, curved into a smile. 'Is that good or bad? For me?'

'Good,' she gasped. 'Oh, Josh, of course it's good!'

'You still haven't answered. Haven't said yes, or no.'

'Yes!' she cried. 'I'm saying yes! I will marry you, Josh. If you want me.'

'Want you?' He drew her to him. 'Lorna, you know I want you. I want us to be man and wife, to be together always. Isn't that what you want, too?'

'Yes, yes, it is. But it's all happened so quickly, Josh . . .'

'No, you keep saying that, but it hasn't been quick for me. I told you, you've been in my mind a long, long time. I even told my mother about you, before she went to Italy, to prepare the ground, I suppose.' Josh laughed. 'Even though I'd no real hope of love from you at the time.'

'You told your mother?' Lorna freed herself from his arms. 'Did you think she wouldn't approve? I know I'm the wrong religion.'

'No, we're not a religious family. My mother wouldn't be too worried that you're not a Catholic. Just as long as you are right for me, someone she could love as a daughter, and I said you would be just that.' Josh leaned forward and kissed Lorna on the lips. 'So, you see, my darling, we're halfway there, already. Now, we only need permission from your mother, and I think she liked me, didn't she? That time we met at the wedding?'

'My mother?' Lorna stammered. 'Josh, I'm sure she did like you, but there's no need to ask her permission. I can say what I want to do.'

'I know it's not legally necessary, but it would be correct.' Josh was smiling indulgently. 'When can we meet? May I visit her at home?'

A cold hand grasped Lorna's heart, as she thought of her darling Sam, at home with her mother, and as the colour faded from her cheeks, she knew the time had come to be honest with Josh. Tell him, her inner voice ordered, tell him now. You have no choice, it has to be now.

But the words did not come. Instead, she said quickly, 'Oh, yes, I'll fix it up, but she does dressmaking, you know, and works at home, so it might be easier if she came here and we all had a meal, or something. Yes, that's what we'll do, because of course she'll want to meet you, when you're going to be her son-in-law.'

'Fine,' Josh murmured, his expression a little puzzled. 'I'll look forward to that, then. But now, let's get down to business. When can we go out to choose the ring?'

'The ring? Oh, Josh, we don't need a ring. No' yet.'

Though a ring from him would mean so much to her, Lorna instinctively shied away from wearing one until she had leaped the barrier that still stood between her and happiness. When she had told Josh the truth about Sam, when she had got her tongue round the words and he'd accepted the situation, then she could wear his ring. If he accepted it, she corrected herself. If. And it was a big if, one she could scarcely face.

In the meantime, it would be better if they were not to announce the engagement. Maybe just tell Ma and Flo, and keep it as their special secret.

'Let's wait a while, Josh,' she said persuasively. 'Let's enjoy our love all to ourselves for the time being.'

'Why? Why not tell people, Lorna? I'm proud to be engaged to you, I want to shout my love from the housetops. Don't you?'

'Yes, but later. The thing is, George is planning an English tour. We'll be separated for a while, and I'd have to put up with all the teasing, you know from the girls . . .'

It sounded weak, and she knew it, but Josh, gazing at her stead-fastly, seemed eventually prepared to let her have her way. 'If it's what you really want,' he said slowly. 'We'll wait a while. But what's all this about a tour? How can I bear it, if you leave me, Lorna? I can hardly manage to say goodnight.'

And it was only after a long sweet kiss that he did say goodnight, moving ever more slowly towards her door, still holding her close.

'Why did you apologize for kissing me before?' she whispered, smoothing her fingers down his cheek. 'When you were planning to propose?'

'Ah, that was just the Italian coming out in me,' he answered easily, pressing his lips to her hand. 'We're taught, you know, to respect women, especially a woman we intend to marry. I was overstepping the mark, then, wasn't I?'

'Those kisses were different from now?'

'You know they were.' He gave her one last hug. 'Oh, God, Lorna, let's get married soon, eh?'

'Let's,' she answered fervently.

But when he had left her and she sat alone, she felt her earlier euphoria fast draining from her and only apprehension taking hold.

Forty-Four

Sometimes, in the days that followed, it seemed to Lorna that those she cared about were making things difficult for her. Not Josh, of course, for he had no idea of her dilemma, but her mother, Auntie Cissie, Flo and George, were all, as she saw it, being unsympathetic.

Her mother, for instance, had flatly refused to come to Lorna's flat for a meal with Josh, and had declared that Lorna should not even consider herself to be engaged until she'd told him what he needed to know. And Cissie had fervently agreed.

'Why, pet, you're walking on a knife edge!' she exclaimed. 'You should have found out right at the start what this laddie would think of the situation, before you got yourself in too deep. Too late now!'

'Aye, did I no' tell you the selfsame thing?' Tilly asked, turning to Lorna. 'Och, I thought you'd have had more sense, eh?'

As for Flo and George, they tried to appear pleased about the engagement, but made it plain, all the same, that they believed Lorna to have been foolish, leaving it so late to explain Sam to Josh.

'He's a formal sort of guy,' George muttered. 'Lives in the past, expects everybody to live by the rule book. Comes from his mother's influence, eh?'

'Flo, you said once he'd understand!' Lorna cried. 'Now you say he won't?'

'Because, maybe, you've left it too late.' Flo's look softened as she took in Lorna's pale, strained face. 'But, then, I could be wrong. I hope I am.'

Only one person gave her comfort at this time, and he was someone she felt guilty about, anyway.

'Oh, Ewen,' she murmured, when she met him by chance one lunch time at the tram stop near her mother's. 'I feel so bad, I haven't seen you for so long. I don't know what you'll think of me.'

'It's all right,' Ewen told her, looking down at her with a compassionate gaze. 'I know you've got your problems.'

'You do? Has Ma been talking to you?'

'Aye, I've seen her once or twice. Said you'd a new admirer who was very keen, but she didn't know how things would go. Somebody in your dad's band, I believe she said.'

'He's a saxophone player, like me. Used to have the chair next to mine in Luke Riddell's band, then he moved to Jackie's.'

'And very good looking, I heard.'

'Yes, he's handsome.' Lorna looked down at her hands clutching her bag and heard her voice cracking with emotion. 'Oh, Ewen, I'm so worried, I don't know where to turn.'

'Come and have a drink,' he said kindly. 'There's a wee hotel in Shandwick Place where it's nice and quiet and you can tell me what's wrong.'

'As though you couldn't guess,' she said miserably, taking his arm with some relief when they walked from the tram stop.

'I suppose it's Sam who's the worry, is it?' Ewen asked, when they had settled into the lounge bar of the small hotel, he with a beer, she with a gin and tonic. (Not too much gin, she had insisted, she had a rehearsal that afternoon.)

'Yes, it's Sam.' She raised her eyes to Ewen's. 'I'm no' ashamed of him, Ewen. I love him dearly. But – well, you can imagine the situation.'

'Aye. Another fellow's son.'

'And Josh knows who he is – the father, I mean. Everyone says I should have been open about things from the beginning, but I was just too afraid. Couldn't bring myself to say anything. And now, he's asked me to marry him, and I'm going to have to tell him about Sam. But I don't know how.'

'Poor lassie,' Ewen murmured. 'It'll be hard, but maybe he'll understand.'

'People say it's too much to ask of him.'

'He might surprise you.'

'Think so?' For a moment, her eyes shone, but the light soon faded. 'I know you always said I shouldn't have kept Sam a secret, anyhow.'

'That's true. My advice is still to tell folk, no' just your young man. At least, the girls in the band. Be proud of the little lad, Lorna. It isn't his fault that he has no dad.' Ewen drained his glass. 'Maybe he will have, though.' He leaned forward to take Lorna's hand. 'Tell the chap soon, eh? Whatever happens, you'll feel better. It's tearing you to pieces at the minute, not knowing what he'll say.'

'You're right,' she said quietly. 'I'm seeing him tomorrow. That will be the time.'

Back at the tram stop, she reached up to kiss Ewen's cheek. 'I'll let you know how I get on.'

'And I'll be thinking of you. Good luck.'

'Thanks, Ewen, thanks for everything.'

It helped – it was always a help – for Lorna to be lost in her music, and conducting the rehearsal that afternoon, going through her arrangements, keeping up with the chatter and jokes from the girls, relieved her anxiety for at least a little while. And, of course, apart from Flo and George, no one had any idea of what she was concealing. Or, so she thought.

At the end of the rehearsal, however, she was surprised to find Claire Maxwell at her elbow, asking if she could have a word.

'Why, of course, Claire – come into the office.'

Claire took a seat facing Lorna's desk and fixed her with her usual expressionless gaze. She was, however, Lorna thought, looking more attractive than usual, with a better haircut and some carefully applied make-up, almost as though she'd made a special effort for this meeting.

'What can I do for you, then?' Lorna asked pleasantly.

'I was thinking that you might pay me more,' Claire replied without hesitation. 'It's really time I had a rise.'

'We'll be reviewing salaries in the new year. That's our usual practice.'

'Quite a long way off, the new year.' Claire examined her nails. 'I think it might be worth your while to consider me a special case.'

Lorna's heart was beginning to beat fast, but she made no sign of losing her calm. 'Why would that be, Claire?'

'Well, I get the impression that you and Josh Niven are very close these days. Perhaps planning to make a go of it? I don't think he'd be too pleased to hear about that lovely little boy of yours, would he?'

The colour leaving her face, Lorna snatched up a pencil and rolled it rapidly between her fingers. 'How do you know about my little boy?' she asked, breathing hard.

'I followed you one day.'

'Followed me? Why? Why should you do such a thing?'

'Because I always had my suspicions that you had some sort of secret. You never brought your mother here, you never said where she lived.' Claire smiled. 'I asked myself, what could Lorna be hiding? And one day I found out.'

'That's despicable!' Lorna cried. 'To follow me, spy on me!'

'I've never pretended to be a nice person, have I? Anyway, all I wanted was to see what you were covering up, and when I saw you walking with your little laddie, I knew. Lorna, he's so sweet. Anybody'd fall for him. Except maybe Josh.'

'How much do you want?' Lorna asked, after a pause.

'Oh, just a few pounds extra. Say five a week. I don't want to be greedy.'

'I suppose it hasn't occurred to you that Josh might know already?'

Claire smiled again. 'He doesn't know. If he did, he wouldn't still be around you. He's not the type to forgive, is he?'

'I don't know what you're talking about!'

'Oh, come on. If you've got a child, you've been with some other guy, right? That's what'll upset Josh. He won't want to think of it.'

Lorna stood up and walked to the door. 'Will you leave my office, please? I have nothing more to say to you.'

Claire shrugged. 'You're going to leave it to me to tell him, then?'

'No, I am going to tell him myself. That was always my intention.'

'Best of luck, then.' Claire stood at the door, her dead, brown gaze going over Lorna's face. 'You're going to need it.'

'Wait.' Lorna reached out and touched Claire's arm. 'Just tell me, will you, why you hate me so much? What did I ever do to you?'

'Oh, you're just one of those people who win all the prizes, eh? Like my sister.'

'I didn't win the prize your sister won, did I?'

'No, but you got a place in a man's band.' Claire's lip curled. 'And praised my sister to the skies. But when you could help me to do something I wanted, you turned me down.'

'Claire, I said at the time—'

'Oh, never mind what you said at the time! I knew you'd never let me be vocalist, whatever I was like. But if you've got any sense now, you'll agree to pay me to keep your secret and keep your little boy under wraps. Or you'll lose your precious Josh, I'm telling you!'

With a last look of contempt, Claire let herself out of Lorna's office and banged the door.

Feeling ill, feeling hollow, Lorna moved to her desk and sat down. This was nightmare land, wasn't it? Claire Maxwell, knowing her secret. Claire Maxwell, threatening to tell Josh. What should she do? What could she do?

With a sudden decision burning through her mind, Lorna leaped to her feet and ran from her office.

'George!' she cried, her eyes frantically checking to find him, and also to see that Claire had left, as she had. 'George! Flo! Oh, thank heavens you're still here.'

'Why, what's up?' George asked, as he and Flo were stacking up copies of the music they needed.

'I want one of you to do me a favour. If I'm not back in time, could you conduct for me tonight?'

'George'll do it,' Flo said promptly. 'Won't you, George?'

'Sure, I will. Be glad to.'

Two pairs of eyes studied Lorna's distraught face, and Flo sympathetically touched her arm. 'Are you OK, Lorna?'

'I'm fine. Just have to go out for a bit.'

'Saw you had a visit from madame,' George murmured. 'What did she want, then?'

'You mean Claire? Oh, a rise. I told her what she could do.'

'A rise? The cheek of it!'

'Yes, well, look, I'd better go. You're sure you don't mind standing in for me?'

'I told you, I'd be happy to. I like a bit of conducting. But, listen, Lorna, I've got some petrol in the car. Would you like me to drive you – to wherever you're going?'

She wanted to say, 'No, I can manage', but at the understanding look in his eyes, and Flo's, too, her lip trembled and she heard herself answering, 'All right, then, if you don't mind, I'd be glad of a lift.'

As they waited to find out where she wanted to go, she raised her head and straightened her shoulders in the old way she used to do when courage was needed.

'I have to see Josh,' she said quietly. 'Before he leaves for the next engagement. You know where he lives, George?'

'Oh, yes,' he answered heavily. 'I know where he lives. And don't worry, he won't have left yet. Plenty of time before Jackie's band will get round to tuning up. Let's get going, eh?'

No one spoke on the drive to Josh's flat, and when George drew up at the thirties block Lorna had never actually visited, no one moved.

'There it is, then, that's his place,' George murmured at last. 'Know which floor?'

'Yes, the third.' Lorna was opening the car door. 'Many thanks, George. I'm really grateful for this.'

'Want us to wait?' Flo asked.

'No, better not, thanks all the same.' Lorna swallowed hard. 'I don't know how long I'll be.'

'Oh, Lorna . . .'

'Don't worry about me. Should have done this long ago.'

'But why now? Has something happened?'

Lorna's eyes slid away from Flo's intelligent gaze. 'Claire's found out about Sam. She's threatening to tell Josh, unless I give her money every week.'

For a moment there was a stunned silence, before Flo cried, 'How could she? How could she do that to you, Lorna?'

'Never mind what she can do,' George said grimly. 'She's going to be out on her ear, eh? We'll give her the sack tonight, soon as we see her.'

'No, don't do that,' Lorna said quickly. 'She might cause more trouble then. Just leave it for now and I'll see her myself.'

'Good luck, then.' Flo was trying to smile. 'See you soon.'

'Need to discuss the tour,' George called, starting the car. 'Haven't forgotten it's next week?'

'George, Lorna isn't interested in that now!' Flo told him sharply, but Lorna only shrugged.

'I might be very much interested,' she said quietly. 'It might be just the thing I need.'

And she turned, to make her way to Josh's flat.

Forty-Five

When he opened the door, wearing a white shirt and dress trousers, she thought he was looking particularly handsome. He had not yet put on his bow tie or the blue jacket Jackie had chosen for his boys to wear that year, but she could see the jacket beyond Josh, draped on a chair in the entrance to a bedroom she had never been shown.

Strange, wasn't it, that she was now, of all times, in the flat where he lived, which he'd always been reluctant for her to visit, saying that it was no place to entertain. As though she needed entertaining! Her own theory now was that he hadn't wanted to be alone with her in his own home, for fear of losing control, but whether that was true or not, she'd no way of knowing. Certainly didn't matter now, anyway.

'Lorna, what a lovely surprise!'

He was ushering her into his neat little sitting room. 'I'd no idea I'd see you this evening.'

'I know you've to go out soon, Josh. I won't keep you, but I have to talk to you. It's important.'

'Well, let me get you something first. Coffee? Or, tea? Think I've got some tea somewhere . . .'

'No, thanks, Josh, I don't want anything.' She sank down on a small settee. 'Just want you to come and sit next to me. I have something to show you.'

'I'm intrigued.' As he sat close to her, he put his arm around her, but she moved away to open her bag and after a moment, he let his arm drop, remarking that she seemed very serious.

She made no reply to that, but took out the photograph of Sam she always carried and after a tiny hesitation, showed it to him.

'I'd like you to look at this picture, Josh.'

He took it from her and studied the small smiling figure of Sam, sitting on a trike.

'A charming little boy,' Josh observed. 'Who is he?'

At long last, she brought out the words she'd thought about for so long, and they were no easier to say than she'd feared they would be.

'He's my son. His name is Sam.'

Then she sat back and with huge brave effort looked at Josh.

He'd gone so pale, his dark eyes seemed black. They burned on her own face with an intensity that was like a flame, and in their depths was the look she'd always hoped not to see. It was one of horror.

'What . . . what are you saying?' he whispered. 'You have a child? A son? You are married already?'

'No, I'm no' married.'

'Not married?'

He leaped up and began to pace the room, his hands clasped tightly together in front of him, as though to prevent himself from wringing them. Wringing hands . . . Was he really doing that? Lorna wondered, feeling strangely detached. Did anyone wring their hands these days? Had she made Josh want to do it now?

Maybe she should just go. There was no point in staying when she was already looking at the ruins of a relationship, caused by her and her alone.

But Josh was back at her side, desperately searching her face for some hope that all this wasn't true, couldn't be true, couldn't be happening. Yet, when he gazed into her eyes and read their sadness, he could do nothing but turn his head away.

'Who is the father?' he asked at last. 'Do I know him?'

He has seen the likeness in Sam to Rod, she thought, and it has put Rod into his mind, that's why he's asked that question.

'There's only been one man in my life apart from you,' she told him. 'And you know who it is.'

'Rod Warren? Oh, God, Lorna, you slept with Rod Warren?'

He could no longer look at her, but she seized his arm and made him turn to face her. 'Once, Josh, only once. You remember I told you we had decided to marry, and then discovered we were poles apart, wanted different things from marriage. The night we agreed to part, somehow we lost our heads – the way you and I did the other night, only you were in control and we weren't. We made love and we said goodbye.'

'Goodbye,' Josh repeated. 'You never saw him again?'

'I never saw him again. He went to America and I never told him about the baby. He still doesn't know about Sam.'

'And who has been looking after the child? Your mother?'

'Yes, my mother. She's been wonderful.'

'That was why you didn't want me to go to her home, because your son would be there?'

'That was why. But I'm no' ashamed of Sam, Josh. He means

everything to me.' She hesitated. 'And I think now I shouldn't have tried to keep him a secret. I was selfish, thinking about my career.'

'But when you met me, saw how I felt, why didn't you tell me? You knew you'd have to tell me sooner or later!' Josh's face was moving with emotion, his lip trembling. 'For God's sake, why did you let me go on loving you, even wanting to marry you, when you had this secret in your life? A son you adored and I never knew! How could you do that to me, Lorna? How could you?'

She burst into long strangled sobs. 'Because I knew you would give me up. I knew you wouldn't be able to accept Rod Warren's son, and I didn't want to lose you. So, I just pretended I could leave it – tell you later, make you understand. But I knew all along you wouldn't. Couldn't, I suppose I mean.' She took out a handkerchief and wiped her eyes. 'But I didn't let you give me a ring. I knew I shouldn't do that, when you didn't know the truth about me. And it's made it easier, hasn't it? Not being formally engaged?'

'Easier?' He sat with his head bent, holding his brow. 'You think anything could make this easier?'

She shook her head. 'No. No, I don't.'

After a little while, he looked up. 'I blame Rod Warren. He's the one who should have thought of you, respected you. But he only thought of himself, and now you have a son to bring up on your own.'

'We neither of us thought at all, Josh. And he doesn't know about Sam.'

'You could have told him.'

'No, he'd have wanted to marry me and it wouldn't have been right, to marry because of a baby.'

'Wouldn't have been right? To give your son a name? Lorna, I don't feel I know you at all. You're a stranger to me.'

'A stranger?' she cried. 'Josh, don't say that, don't say that! I love you!'

'And put a dagger in my heart.'

'I'm sorry, I'm sorry.' She was sobbing again. 'Can't you see how much I feel for you? I never wanted to hurt you, never!'

Josh moved away, flinging himself into a chair, where he sat looking broodingly across at her. 'Shouldn't you be leading your band tonight?' he asked coldly.

'I asked George to take over for me.'

'Such forethought. Well, I'm not going to be able to play tonight.

I'll have to ring Jackie and tell him I'm sick.' He gave a harsh laugh. 'Which is quite true. I am sick. I've never felt so sick in my life.'

'Josh, I'm so sorry,' she said, weeping again, and trying to take his hand. 'I'm so sorry for what I've done to you. Can you forgive me?'

He moved his hand from hers. 'I told you, I blame Rod.'

'Can we . . . can we meet again?'

'I don't know. I have to have some time to myself.'

'I understand.' Lorna picked up the photograph of Sam from the table where Josh had dropped it, and put it in her bag. 'Next week, we're going on the English tour. I don't know if you remembered that?'

He shook his head. 'No, it had gone from my mind.'

'We'll be away a month.'

'I'll see you on your return.'

'You will?' A tiny hope flickered in her heart. 'I'll ring you, then.'

He inclined his head, not looking at her, and after a long moment, she moved to the door.

'Goodnight, Josh.'

'Goodnight, Lorna.'

As she turned from him, he touched her arm. 'I wonder if you know,' he said, breathing hard, 'how much you have damaged me?'

'I know, Josh.'

Their eyes met; hers were the first to look away.

'I still can't believe what you've told me,' he burst out. 'It's . . . a nightmare.'

'It needn't be,' she said eagerly. 'If we love each other, we can come through this. We can, Josh, we can!'

'Maybe. But I need time.'

'I know, I know. Remember, I'm going away. But then I'll ring you when I come back, like I said.'

'Yes, ring me.'

After a little hesitation, she began to go down his stairs, turning as they curved, to look back to see if he was still there. He was, and watching, his eyes dark as night fixed on her, but as she gave the faintest of smiles, he went into his flat and closed the door.

Going home on the tram, she kept her mind blank, as though she could save herself pain if she didn't allow herself to think. Of course, it was impossible, and by the time she'd reached home, she was back to thinking and nursing the little flame of hope he'd given her when he'd said she might ring him, risking future anguish if the hope turned out to be false. She had wounded him so severely, she knew there was every chance that the time he'd said he needed would work against her. Still, she would cling to her hope.

Back at the flat, her phone rang when she was drearily making tea, and she dived at once to answer it, thinking it might be . . .

It was Flo, wanting to know how things had gone.

'Intermission here at the moment,' she told Lorna, 'and we're all missing you, but you're no' the only one who hasn't come. Claire hasn't turned up, either. Probably didn't dare to show her face.'

'I daresay.'

'But, Lorna, I've been on pins all evening, thinking of you with Josh. How did he take it?'

After a lengthy pause, Lorna answered, 'He asked me if I knew how much I'd damaged him.'

'Oh. Well.' Flo was clearly having trouble thinking of what to say. 'We knew he'd feel like that, didn't we? But he wasn't . . . violent, or anything?'

'No.' Lorna's voice trembled. 'I suppose I was lucky. He was . . . just very shocked.'

'What about Sam? Can he accept Sam?'

'I don't know. But I don't think he can accept Rod as his father. He blames Rod for what happened.'

'And doesn't blame you? Lorna, that's hopeful!'

'No, because he blames me for not telling him earlier. I should have done, I see that now.'

'You didn't want to lose him. Surely he understands? Can't he see it's been hard for you, too?'

'Might be too soon to expect that. All he can see is that I've let him down.'

'Look, why no' try to look on the bright side? He's upset, but he didn't throw you out or anything. And he hasn't said he doesn't want to see you again, has he?'

'No. In fact, he said he'd see me when I got back.'

'There you are, then! Lorna, I'm sure he doesn't want to lose you. By the time you get back from the tour, he'll probably have reconciled himself to the whole thing. And at least he knows the truth now. You'll feel better about that.'

'Yes, I suppose I do.'

But when she lay in bed, sleepless, Lorna felt a deep and impossible regret for the time that already seemed so long ago, when Josh had not known the truth. When she had not had to hurt him. And had not hurt herself.

Forty-Six

The English tour, so carefully planned by George with Lorna's help, turned out to be strikingly successful. The way it had been planned, they travelled directly to the south coast, moving on from there to the major towns of Surrey and Hampshire, and then to London, which so excited the girls they could scarcely be persuaded to pack for the strung out journey back home. The Midlands beckoned, however, and then Yorkshire, Northumberland and the Scottish Borders. Finally, garlanded with praise, they arrived home.

Everywhere they went, they'd received rave reviews, with Lorna being described as their Titian-haired leader, and the Melody Girls themselves as 'gorgeous Scottish lassies, who certainly know how to beat out a tune . . .'

'Watch out, lads, the girls are here!' ran one headline in a music paper, and another sent similar warnings to the big band leaders of the day.

'Och, I'm sure Ted Heath and company are all crying over their bank accounts,' George commented with a grin, but he was as delighted as everyone else with the girls' success.

'Particularly here in London,' he told Lorna and Flo, when they were talking in their hotel. 'Now didn't I tell you it was the place to be? I could find you a dozen venues tomorrow that'd be desperate to have you.'

'Maybe only because at the moment we're a novelty,' Flo suggested. 'A Scottish all-girl band, but the emphasis is on Scottish. If we gave up that, we'd lose a lot of our appeal, is my view. Don't you agree, Lorna?'

'Oh, yes, I've said all along that we're a Scottish band and have to stay that way.'

Lorna's words were definite enough, but her tone, as both listeners noticed, was listless. There was nothing unusual in that; when she was conducting the band, giving interviews, or posing for photographs, she seemed to find reserves of strength and vitality. Away from the professional scene, however, she drooped and withered like a flower out of water.

'Aye, she's been an unlucky lassie, in some respects,' George remarked. 'Not because of having Sam, because he's a grand little lad, but splitting up with Rod the way she did, and now this business with Josh. I never did think he'd be the one for her.'

'Neither was Rod. Had all the wrong ideas. She seemed to have settled for Josh, but now she's told him about Sam, I can't think what's going to happen.'

'Surprised he hasn't already said goodbye.'

Flo looked thoughtful. 'The fact he hasn't, could that be hopeful, do you think?'

'Who knows? What we have to think about now is finding another pianist. Doesn't look like Claire is going to return.'

'We've managed without her so far. Let's leave it till we get back home, eh?'

'Suits me, just as long as we don't have to see her miserable face again.'

When it came to it, most of the girls were happy enough to be back in Auld Reekie, even if it didn't have as many clubs, restaurants, and theatres as London. After all, it was home and there were families to see, and young men, and you couldn't stay away for ever, could you? Even Lorna was looking happier, and there were those who'd noticed she'd been looking anything but when down south.

As their coach came over Carter Bar and the volcanic rock that was Arthur's Seat came into view, it was in fact noticeable how much brighter the leader of the band was looking.

'Been missing Josh,' Trish whispered to Bridie, and those girls nearest nodded their agreement. 'Tough, being away so long, eh?'

'Tough for us all,' said Nancy, who'd found a new boyfriend since the German tour. 'But I wouldn't have missed the trip away, would you?'

'Sure wouldn't!' came a chorus, until somebody murmured, 'Wonder what happened to Claire?'

'As though we cared,' Flo murmured to Lorna.

'I can't say I'm worrying about her,' Lorna answered. Keeping her voice down, she added, 'All I want now is to see Sam.'

'You're going round to your mother's when we get in?'

'Oh, I am. I've missed Sam so much, and Ma said on the phone that he's been missing me.' Lorna smiled a little. 'She rang from a call box, you know. Said she wished I could've seen Sam's face when he heard my voice coming out of the telephone!'

'I thought you might be going to your flat first,' Flo said delicately, giving George a sideways glance.

'You mean to check my post?' Lorna shrugged. 'Josh never said he'd write.'

'You're going to ring him, anyway?'

'Tomorrow. I'm going to stay the night at Ma's. Help Sam play with the toys I've brought him.'

'Must be fun, playing with toys again.' George laughed self-consciously. 'Sometimes we think about being parents, don't we, Flo?'

'Thinking is as far as we get.'

'I can recommend it.' Lorna glanced round at her girls who were all talking to one another. 'In spite of everything.'

'Princes Street coming up,' George said cheerfully. 'Want a hand with your luggage, Lorna?'

'Don't worry, the driver will take it out for all of us. Listen, we're going to take a couple of days off to get sorted out, aren't we? I'll be in touch later, then.'

'Don't forget!' Flo cried, when the coach drew up in Princes Street under the sombre stare of the castle, and the girls began to disembark, still talking and laughing.

'Poor old Lorna,' George murmured, as he and Flo watched her flag down a taxi and disappear towards the West End. 'Hope she gets some good news.'

'Wouldn't bank on it,' Flo answered.

Forty-Seven

Oh, it was so good to be home, Lorna was thinking as she hugged first Tilly and then dear Sam, holding him close, putting her cheek against his soft little face, as he smiled radiantly and said 'Mammy, mammy' over and over again.

'You see, he's missed you,' Tilly said fondly. 'Couldn't understand why you weren't coming to see him.'

'But then you spoke to Mammy on the telephone, didn't you?' Lorna asked. 'Didn't you hear my voice on the funny black thing in the glass box?'

'Mammy's voice!' he cried joyously. 'In the glass box!'

'And now you'll want to look in my bag, eh? I've got some exciting things, and all for you.'

They spent a wonderful time, unpacking the small cars, the fire engine complete with ladders and little firemen, the tractor with levers and imitation bundles of hay, while Tilly made tea and produced the scones she'd managed to find, and the cake she'd made with eggs brought by Cissie.

'And isn't it a shocking thing that we're still rationed?' she asked as they finally sat down at the table, Sam clutching one of his new cars. 'Sometimes I wonder if we won the war or not. Oh, and by the way, I saw Ewen in the street this morning – told him to come for a cup of tea, but he said he'd look in later. Knew you'd want time with Sam, you ken. Such a thoughtful laddie, eh?'

'I'd like to see Ewen,' Lorna said with truth. 'In fact I was hoping he'd come round.'

As Sam asked if he could get down and tore off to play with his fire engine, Tilly looked at Lorna strangely and poured her some more tea.

'Someone else came round the other day,' she whispered. 'Asked if you were here.'

'Who?'

'Josh Niven.'

Lorna set down her cup, spilling tea into the saucer. 'Josh came here? Here, Ma?'

'Yes, a few days ago.'

'I don't understand. Why would he do that? He knew I wouldn't be back.'

'I'm no' sure, of course, but I think he wanted to see Sam. You said you'd told him about your boy, eh?'

'Yes, I told him.'

'Well, maybe he wanted to see what the boy looked like. Seemed very impressed. Said he was a fine child, and gave him a pound note for his money box.'

'A pound note?' Lorna bit her lip, frowning. 'And then what happened?'

'He gave me a letter for you. I put it in the sideboard. Wait, I'll get it for you.'

While her mother found the letter, Lorna sat very still, bracing herself for – what? She would know very soon.

'Here it is!' Tilly cried, placing a small white envelope in Lorna's hand. It bore her formal name, Miss Lorna Fernie, in Josh's firm black handwriting.

'Now if you want to read it in private, go in the bedroom, pet.'

'No, I'll just read it here.'

Taking a knife from the table drawer, Lorna slit open the envelope and took out the single sheet it contained. How cool she was keeping! Sometimes, she could really put on a good act.

> I am so very sorry, my dear Lorna, but I can't do it, I can't see you again. I still love you, I think I always will, but too much has changed for us to have a future. We are not the people we thought we were, and must face that.
>
> Thank you for giving me so much happiness in the past. I wish it hadn't had to end, but I wish you all the best for the future with your band and your fine little boy. By the time you read this, I will be in London where I've been given a job with Ted Heath's band, so it's unlikely that we will meet again.
>
> I send you my love and my good wishes,
>
> Josh.

When she had finished reading it, Lorna laid the letter down. What a lucky thing it was, she thought, that her mother was with her, which meant she must keep up her acting and not burst into tears and frighten Sam. Later on, it would be different, of course, but now, she could be brave. Except that her eyes were swimming.

'Are you going to tell me what he says?' Tilly asked.

Lorna picked up the letter and smoothed it out.

'"I'm so very sorry, my dear Lorna",' she was beginning, when Tilly stopped her.

'You don't need to read it to me. Just tell me what he says.'

Lorna raised her eyes to her mother's. 'He says goodbye,' she said quietly, and gave a sob. So much for acting, she thought.

'Oh, poor lassie!'

'Only what I expected, Ma.'

'But still – oh, listen, there's a knock at the door. That'll be Ewen. Now, if he wants to go for a little walk, you go, Lorna. Sam'll be all right with his new toys. Go on, Lorna. You couldn't have a more sympathetic fellow to talk to than Ewen, eh?'

They walked again by the Water of Leith where, because the evening was fine, others were walking too, looking down at the floating weed that covered the stream and the reeds lining the bank.

'It's all over, Ewen,' Lorna told him. 'I sort of hoped it might not be, but I knew all the time there wasn't much hope.'

'Soon as you told him about Sam, that was it?'

'About Sam and Sam's father. Josh could never have been step-father to Sam, thinking of Rod.'

'And you had to get through your tour, knowing everything was over?' Ewen pressed her hand. 'Must have been terrible.'

'No, I was still hoping then. He said I could ring him when I got back. He even said he'd see me. But he came to Ma's house when I was away and left me a letter.'

'Your ma's house?' Ewen shook his head in disbelief. 'Fancy him doing that. Sounds like he couldn't face you. But what happens when you meet again?'

'He's thought of that. Got himself a job in London.'

'Lucky you didn't see him when you were down there.'

'He can only have just left Edinburgh.' Lorna stood aside to let some children run past. 'But thinking about it, Ewen, he could have behaved much worse, could have thrown me out of his flat, or hit me, or something.'

'No, no, Lorna!' Ewen suddenly held her close. 'Don't say things like that, or I'd go find him and punch him one.'

'What I'm saying is, he didn't do that. And I really hurt him, you know. He said I damaged him, and I know I did.'

'You've been hurt yourself, Lorna.'

'Yes.' She blinked a little, not wanting to cry again. 'And now we've both got to get better.'

'Takes time.'

'Well, I've been through it before.'

'You know what I think you should do now? Well, I've said it already, so you'll know what I'm on about.'

'What? What should I do?'

'Tell your girls about Sam. Tell the whole damn world, come to that. Let folk see you're no' ashamed, you're proud of your son.' Ewen nodded. 'Yes, that's what I'd do in your place, Lorna. Then you'll never be hurt in the same way again.'

'I don't know about the whole world,' she said slowly. 'My Sam isn't anything to do with people who don't know me. But, my girls . . . yes, Ewen, I think you're right.'

'You mean that?'

'Yes, I mean it. When I see my band again, there'll be an end to secrets. Thanks, thanks for everything. What would I do without you?'

'Won't have to,' he said brightly, and they turned for Lorna's old home and Sam, who was waiting to be played with before he went to bed.

The night was bad, as she'd known it would be, and for a long time she lay without sleeping in Sam's room that had been hers, just staring into the darkness, seeing Josh's handsome face. If only she hadn't made love with Rod! And yet, it was true, she had loved Rod and sometimes still thought of him. In many ways, he was an easier man to love than Josh, but there was the great divide between his views and hers and always would be.

Josh would have accepted that she wanted her career, and if things had been different, maybe they could have been happy together. But then, maybe not. She didn't blame him for giving her up. She had tried to understand what it had been like for him, to find out about Sam. But with a different sort of nature, might he not have tried to understand how things had been for her?

There was little point in going into it all now, for another thing she had to remember was that in the background there had always been his mother. An unknown quantity, but somebody who probably would never have welcomed Lorna as a daughter-in-law, even if she hadn't had Sam. With Sam, she would certainly never have stood a chance.

The way things were, maybe she had better just put all thoughts of relationships from her and concentrate on her music. That was what she'd always wanted to do, after all. And she still had Sam.

Rising carefully, she tiptoed across the bedroom floor to the cot where he was sleeping. By the light of a tiny lamp, she saw that he was curled up peacefully, scarcely stirring, and she bent down to kiss his cheek and move from his warm little hand one of the cars she had given him. Yes, she still had Sam. What more could she ask?

Forty-Eight

Two days later, Lorna having called a rehearsal for the following morning, asked her mother if she could have Sam ready to be collected at about ten o'clock.

'Collected?' Tilly repeated. 'Why, who's collecting him?'

'I am. George is going to drive us. I'm taking him to see my band.'

Tilly's pale blue eyes widened. 'Your band? How come you're doing that? You've never wanted them to know a thing about him!'

'Yes, well, it's all going to be different from now on.' Lorna's gaze met her mother's bravely, then wavered and fell. 'I've decided to have no more secrets, Ma. It's done me no good and it's never been fair on Sam.'

'Aye, that's sounds grand, but are you sure about it, Lorna? Folk are funny, you ken. For somebody like you to have a bairn and no husband, it might no' go down well.'

'That's what I used to think, and there probably would be some who'd blame me, but only folk who don't know me. For the moment, I'm just telling my girls and friends.'

Lorna hesitated, and as her mother said nothing, went on to make her case. 'It was Ewen, as a matter of fact, who first said I shouldn't make a secret of Sam, but I would never listen. Then, when I had to tell Josh, and I saw the way he was so shocked, I realized I should have told him before. So, I decided Ewen was right. I shouldn't hide Sam, I should let people see I'm proud of him. Then they might understand the situation.' With a quick toss of her head, Lorna looked again at her mother. 'And that's what I'm going to do.'

'You've certainly thought it through,' Tilly commented. 'I just hope it works out.'

'So, you'll have him ready?'

'Aye, but what do I tell him?'

'That he's going for a drive in Uncle George's car to see Mammy's band. He knows about the ladies playing trumpets and so on.'

'You want me to come?'

'Of course! The girls will want to meet you too.'

Tilly looked thoughtful. 'I'll put Sam in his blue shirt and wee new trousers. But, Lorna, what do you think I should wear?'

'Ma, you'll look fine whatever you wear, and nobody dresses up for rehearsal.'

'But you'll want Sam to look his best?' Tilly asked with a smile.

'Oh, yes,' Lorna agreed, feeling nervous already of her boy's reception.

She was still nervous when she arrived with George at Tilly's flat next morning, but as soon as she saw Sam, looking so smart in his blue shirt and new trousers, with his auburn hair damped down and a great smile on his little face, she felt such a rush of pride she hugged him close and asked George if he didn't look grand.

'Grand's the word,' George agreed. 'But how about the fire engine – is that coming, too?'

'It's his favourite,' Tilly told him. 'He might want to play with it when the music begins.'

'Wonderful!' George laughed, as they went out to the car. 'Got an arrangement for four saxophones, three trombones, three trumpets and fire engine, Lorna?'

'Would be quite a novelty, eh? Come on, let's get going. I don't want to be late this morning.'

'Nor me,' Tilly said, her arm round Sam. 'I'm looking forward to hearing the band again. Haven't heard the lassies since your wedding, George.'

As soon as she'd spoken, she flushed a little, remembering that it was at George's wedding she'd first met Josh, and guessed that Lorna would be remembering it too. But Lorna made no sign and no more was said until the studio was reached and Flo was hovering to greet them.

'Everyone's ready,' she whispered, when she'd exclaimed over Sam and shaken Tilly's hand. 'Some complaining they haven't had enough rest after the tour, of course, but most are raring to go.'

'I'll just say my piece first,' Lorna said, clearing her throat. 'Hope they'll still be able to play when I've finished.'

'They'll be playing better than ever,' George said loyally. 'Mrs Fernie, can I find you a chair?'

Taking a deep breath, Lorna, holding Sam by the hand, moved into the studio.

'Morning everybody! Hope you've all recovered from the tour, which I want to say was one of our best. So, congratulations to everyone. You agree, Flo? George?'

'Certainly do,' they murmured, but the girls in the band weren't saying anything. Their eyes were glued to Sam, and he was staring back, fascinated by them and their strange and wonderful instruments.

'Ma, before you sit down, may I introduce you?' Lorna whispered to Tilly, who obediently remained standing, while Lorna called to her girls.

'Listen, everyone, I'd like you all to meet my mother. Ma, meet the band. Girls, meet my mother. My prop and stay, I can tell you!'

'Oh, go on!' Tilly murmured, smiling at the girls, as they smiled and nodded back. 'But, here, let me take wee Sam, eh? Sam, come over with me and bring your fire engine.'

As all eyes followed the little boy running after his grandmother, Lorna, who had gone rather pale, cleared her throat. 'Just before we begin rehearsing, I'd like to say a few words.'

Eyes swinging back, the girls, fingering their instruments, stared; waited.

'I expect you'll all be wondering about the wee boy I've brought here today,' Lorna began. 'I brought him because I wanted you to meet him. His name is Sam Fernie. And he's my son.'

A buzz of sound ran round the band, then ceased. Silence fell. No girl moved, no girl took her eyes off Lorna, who, now that she'd got out the magic words 'my son' was feeling rather better. Though her cheeks were flushed and her eyes wide and bright, she knew now that she could do this.

'Maybe you'll be thinking I should have told you about my boy before. That's probably true. But you can guess it isn't always easy, managing to do the right thing.'

Looking towards Sam to see if he was listening, Lorna saw that George had gone to him and was playing with the ladders on the fire engine – quite enough to take his full attention, she knew. With a faint smile, she went on.

'Anyway, I've decided that now the time's come for you to meet him and him to meet you. He's no' a baby any more, he's a person in his own right, as well as part of my family. So, it'll be nice, eh? If we all get to know one other?'

Her voice trembling, Lorna picked up her baton. 'Shall we get on with the rehearsal now?'

There was a brief silence before Bridie cried, 'Oh, have a heart, Lorna! We all want to talk to the little guy! Come on, girls!'

'No, wait, how about this?' Trish had picked up her saxophone. 'How about a solo from me specially for Sam?'

'What solo?' voices were asking.

'Listen and you'll find out. Here it comes. If you know it, join in!'

And as George brought Sam over, his eyes large with wonder, the music of 'Teddy Bears' Picnic' rang round the studio, with some of the girls joining Trish with their instruments, while others sang, and Lorna and Tilly, standing arm in arm, were radiantly smiling. And trying not to cry.

After the music, Sam was hugged and fussed over until Tilly said she'd better take him outside to play, the band had to get on with their rehearsal, which of course was true, though no one felt much like it – least of all Lorna. However, they were professionals, they played, they made themselves ready for the evening performance, but when it was over, one by one the girls came up to Lorna and shook her hand.

'We want you to know, we understand what it's been like for you,' Bridie told her earnestly. 'You must have had a hell of a time, eh?'

'Couldn't have managed without Ma,' Lorna answered, dabbing her eyes. 'In fact, we wouldn't be here now, if it hadn't been for her.'

'Between you, you've done a grand job, anyway, bringing up Sam,' Flo told her, to murmurs of agreement from the band. 'And, you see, no one's judging.'

'You bet we're not,' cried Trish. 'It's all a piece of nonsense, anyway, that folk look down on girls who don't happen to be married.'

'Some folks,' Bridie said. 'Not us.'

'I can't tell you how happy you've made me,' Lorna said in a low voice. 'I wish now I'd brought Sam to see you long ago.' She raised her head, put back her shoulders. 'But there's something else I have to tell you girls. Might as well say it now.'

They looked at her with interest. More news? This was proving to be quite a rehearsal day.

'You'll have seen me with Josh Niven?' Lorna asked.

The lovely Josh Niven? Of course they had!

'So, I think I should say that you won't be seeing him any more. In fact, he's left Edinburgh, got a job in London.'

No one knew quite what to say. Was Lorna upset, or not? She was giving no more away, but her girls made sympathetic murmurs anyway. After all, it didn't take higher education to work out that Josh Niven's departure might have had something to do with Sam no longer being a secret. Whatever her feelings on losing Josh, though, anyone could see she was certainly happier, now that the secret was out. It was as though a cloud over her had been lifted, revealing afresh her youth and beauty, and as they left her that morning, all her girls, looking at her, marvelled.

'I've never felt so free,' she said to her mother, Flo and George, as she locked the studio door. 'Somehow, I feel I've been given a new lease of life.'

'You look as though you have,' Flo told her warmly. 'And I think this calls for a celebration.'

'Good idea, I say we should go out for lunch,' George said at once. 'My treat, eh? There's a little cafe round here that might just suit Sam.'

'I don't know.' Tilly was looking dubious. 'He's never been to a cafe before.'

'First time, then! Come on, let's go, I'm starving.'

After the lunch that was a great success, with Sam choosing fish fingers and chips and the grown-ups having something more substantial, George and Flo said they'd be on their way, and Tilly said she wouldn't mind doing a bit of shopping, if Lorna could take Sam home.

'Sure, I can!' Lorna, flushed and happy cried, 'Oh, this has been such a great day, eh? I'm really looking forward to walking out with Sam and no' minding if I meet someone I know.'

Which was why, when she was looking at the window of a stationer's at the end of Princes Street and met the eyes of an assistant, she walked straight into the shop. For the eyes were Claire Maxwell's.

Forty-Nine

As soon as Lorna entered the shop, with Sam in his pushchair holding his fire engine, Claire retreated behind the counter, looking towards an older woman assistant some way off, as though needing protection.

'Hello, Claire,' Lorna said cheerfully. 'Fancy finding you here, then.'

Claire, finally meeting Lorna's gaze, fiddled with some pencils on the counter and said nothing.

'Is this where you used to work?' Lorna pressed.

'That's right.' Claire coughed. 'Got my old job back.'

'Without saying a word to us? Without resigning, or fixing up formalities? What did you think you were playing at?'

'I . . . didn't want to see you.'

'After what you'd done?'

'Everything all right, Miss Maxwell?' the senior assistant called down the shop. 'Need any help?'

'No, thanks, Miss Barbour. I can manage.'

'I'll go for my lunch then, as you've had yours.'

'Yes, Miss Barbour.'

Lorna and Claire remained silent, until the senior assistant, giving Sam a quick smile, let herself out and they were alone.

'Claire, this is ridiculous,' Lorna said softly. 'You working here, giving up your music—'

'I haven't given up my music. I just haven't been able to find a job.' Claire shook her head. 'This is the best I can do.'

'Look, you've no customers at the moment. Why don't you tell me why you did what you did? It wasn't for the money, was it? You just wanted to hurt me.'

Claire, her cheeks dull red, looked down again at her counter. 'That's right,' she said quietly. 'I told you, you seemed to have so much – you were like my sister, and I wanted to get back at you. Afterwards – after I'd spoken to you – I felt bad, though. I . . . hated myself.' She gave a short laugh. 'Mostly, I do, I suppose.'

'Oh, Claire! If only you'd let someone help you!'

'I'm OK now. I've got this job, I can get by.' Finally raising her eyes, Claire swallowed a sob. 'But I'm sorry for what I did, Lorna.

I'm sorry if I made trouble for you with Josh. Don't know if it's any good, saying that.'

'It is good, because I know, in your heart, you didn't really like what you were doing.' Lorna hesitated. 'I did lose Josh, but maybe it was just as well.'

'You told him, then?' For the first time, Claire really looked at Sam, who was crooning to himself over his fire engine, his eyes beginning to glaze. 'And he wouldn't accept your little boy? Oh, I feel bad about that, I really do! When your son's so lovely, too. But you must be so proud of him. I'm so glad I've seen him.'

'Everyone's seen him now. I mean, all the girls in the band. That's where some good's come out of all the trouble. I knew I had to stop keeping Sam a secret, and I told the band this morning. Claire, they were wonderful, so kind, so sweet with him.'

'That's good to know.' Claire took a deep breath. 'Listen, I want to thank you for coming in to speak to me, Lorna. I'm amazed you'd want to do it.'

'Better than that, I want you to come back to the band, Claire. We still haven't got a pianist, so there's another old job vacant for you. What do you say?'

'Back to the band?' Claire's mouth fell a little open. 'Oh, no, Lorna, I couldn't! I couldn't show my face, with everybody knowing . . .'

'No one knows except Flo and George, and they'll be happy to see you back.'

'You know they won't!'

'Once we've explained that you feel differently now, they will. People are allowed a second chance, you know.'

Claire, her face working, put out her hand which Lorna shook.

'If you really mean it, I'd love to come back. I've missed it all so much, can't tell you—'

'Got any A4 envelopes?' a man asked, appearing at the shop door. 'Don't tell me they're in short supply, like everything else!'

'No, I can get you a packet in a minute,' Claire almost sang. 'If you wouldn't mind waiting till I've served this lady?'

'Come in next Monday, and we'll do the formalities,' Lorna whispered. 'Then you can give in your notice.'

'You're sure, Lorna, you're really sure you want me?'

'I'm sure. Don't let me down, Claire.'

'I won't!'

As Claire went off to find the A4 envelopes, the customer opened the door for Lorna, who went through with her pushchair, holding Sam who was now fast asleep.

What a day, she was thinking, her head in a whirl. So much had happened, she could scarcely keep track, except that the thought of Josh was gradually receding. One day, it would perhaps have gone altogether. As she had told Claire, that would probably be just as well.

Fifty

Time went by, pleasantly, serenely, and suddenly it was 1953 and Lorna and Flo woke up to the fact that their band was taking off.

In this new Elizabethan Age, as people were beginning to call the times, after the young Princess Elizabeth had succeeded her father, George the Sixth, the Melody Girls were becoming known and in demand. Not only for the high standard of their playing, but also for their looks and personality, and the new blonde vocalist, Dawn Lamond, they'd managed to find who had been wonderfully admired by all, even Claire. Or perhaps especially by Claire, who had turned over a new leaf, becoming strangely anxious to please, and even a good deal happier.

Everything, it seemed had suddenly come together for the Melody Girls, who found themselves wanted for radio contracts and recording deals, for more tours in Germany, in England, in the far north of Scotland, in Ireland. Even America had been suggested but that had been firmly vetoed by Lorna, even though George had looked glum over it.

'Might be turning down real fame,' he told Lorna. 'America's the hub of everything, our music included.'

'We've got fame here,' Lorna retorted. 'People know who the Melody Girls are now.'

'Not in America, they don't. Just need a bit of extra publicity to push us into the real big time over there.'

'No, Lorna's right, we're OK where we are.' Flo was chipping in quickly on Lorna's side, for she knew well enough why Lorna didn't want to go to America, and George, defeated, said no more.

'Are you still worrying about Rod?' Flo asked Lorna, when they were alone. 'What does it matter if he knows about Sam? Maybe he should.'

'I wouldn't say worrying.' Lorna bit her lip. 'In fact, I did think about telling him one time, but then I thought, no, it's all too late. If I was going to tell him, I should have told him before. Not that I know where precisely he is.'

'There are ways and means of finding out.'

'I know. But I think I'll leave it, Flo, all the same.'

'What you're really wanting is a quiet life, eh? As far as emotion goes?'

'A quiet life, as far as emotion goes, is what I've got, and yes, it's what I want,' Lorna answered quietly. 'Suits me fine.'

But then the piece in the gossip column of an Edinburgh magazine appeared. Full page spreads in other popular magazines featuring the Melody Girls and their 'flame-haired girl conductor' were common enough, but this was different. Very different.

It was Flo who brought it into the studio one morning and laid it on Lorna's little desk. 'Seen this?' she asked huskily.

'What?'

'Somebody's written a piece in *Edinburgh Cross Talk* – you know that magazine, comes out monthly?'

'About the band?' Lorna was leafing through the magazine.

'No. About you.'

'Oh? Where is it, then?'

'I'll find it for you. It's just a few lines.'

Flo found the page and folded it back for Lorna to read. 'I shouldn't worry about it. Probably nobody'll read it, anyway.'

'Now I will worry,' Lorna said with a smile. 'If you tell me not to.'

But then, as her eyes went over the piece, her brow darkened and a deep flush rose to her cheeks. 'Oh, my God, Flo, who's written this about me and Sam?' Her voice shaking, she read the snippet aloud.

'"Rumour has it that Lorna Fernie, lovely conductor of the well known girl band The Melody Girls, has been seen strolling in Princes Street Gardens with a delightful little boy calling her, so accounts have it, 'Mammy'. True, or false? And if true, who would Daddy be? Interesting, anyway."

'Oh, Flo, what a terrible thing!' Lorna had laid down the magazine and was staring at Flo with huge, horrified eyes. 'I mean, it was one thing to tell my friends about Sam, but I never wanted gossip like this to come out about me!'

'Look, that mag's no' read much, and nobody takes any notice of that sort of stuff, anyway—'

'They do, they do, that's why folk write it. It's interesting, like they say. Details of other people's private lives are always interesting, eh?' Lorna was walking round the office, shaking her head. 'But we've just built up a public, Flo, people who really care about us. What are they going to say, when they read that about me?'

'Lorna, you always said you wanted people to know. You said you felt free, that you'd nothing to fear.'

'Like I say, that was only when I was thinking about friends, or colleagues. I remember Ewen saying once, let the whole world know, but I said the whole world had got nothing to do with Sam or me.'

'Maybe it has now. Or, at least not the whole world, but part of it.'

'There'll be letters,' Lorna said drearily. 'Folk will write in, telling me what they think of me. How I've let everybody down, giving the wrong signals to young women, all that sort of thing . . .'

'You're just looking on the black side, Lorna! Wait till the letters do come in and see what they have to say.' Flo put her finger to her lip, suddenly seeming to be lost in thought. 'Lorna, maybe the best thing you could do would be to fight back?' she cried, when she'd come to a decision. 'Give a little interview in another magazine – something more serious, maybe. Give your side of the story, let people see what the struggle's been, but how it's all been worth while and that sort of thing? What do you think?'

Lorna sat down, putting her hand to her brow. 'I don't know, Flo, maybe it might still give the wrong impression?'

'No, I don't agree. I think folk would appreciate what you've done for your boy. I think they'd understand and maybe no' sit in judgement. Worth a try, anyway.'

'Perhaps you're right.'

'At least, you wouldn't be sitting around, nursing more secrets, hoping nobody'd read the gossip!'

'That's true!' Lorna leaped to her feet. 'I'll do it, Flo. Let's choose the right magazine, then, and ask if they'll give me space.'

'I'll get George. He'll know.' Flo was breathing fast, relishing the fight. 'Let's give those folk as good as they get!'

George, of course, knew the very magazine to approach with the offer of an interview with Lorna, which was a rather old fashioned but reputable Scottish journal much read all over the UK. The editor, a friend of his, jumped at the chance to publish something with the lady bandleader who'd recently become so popular, and after a joint collaboration on what should be said, Lorna gave the interview.

It had been George's view that her special problems as a single mother should just be part of a broader picture of her life and that of the girls in the band, without too much emphasis on the down side of bringing up a child without a father.

'But enough to make it clear what's involved,' Lorna had insisted.

'Oh, of course,' George had agreed. 'You'll be able to say how much you've gained from bringing up Sam, and how any woman in your position shouldn't just think of the problems, but take pleasure in having the child, just like any other mother.'

'The truth is, it's all a lot more difficult than that,' Lorna sighed. 'I mean, I couldn't have run the band in the early days without Ma.'

'No need to stress that,' Flo put in. 'All you're wanting to do here is assure your fans that you're an OK person, in spite of what happened.'

'I feel I'll be walking through a minefield, though, and I keep asking, why should that be? Why shouldn't folk accept that these things happen and just be easy about them?' Lorna shivered a little. 'I'm dreading the response, you know. I mean, the letters.'

'As I said before, wait to see what the letters say before getting upset.'

'OK, I'll wait,' Lorna sighed.

As she had foreseen, it was difficult, hitting the right note in the interview, but the woman journalist who asked the questions was not only sympathetic but experienced. She seemed to know just how to get the best from Lorna, allowing her to come over as a sensible and talented young woman, who had faced difficulties with courage and resolution and been rewarded with joy and fulfilment, not only from her music but also in bringing up her boy.

It was agreed that the world was not perfect, things happened that had not been planned, but if the welfare of the child was always considered, all could be well, and Lorna's message to others was to face what came with spirit and hope. And always to remember that even if the world was not perfect, it had its good side. So Lorna herself had found.

Oh, God, is that going to be true? she asked herself, as the questioner thanked her at the end of the interview. What can I hope for out of this?

What she had never hoped for, or expected, was that after the appearance of the interview, there would be sackfuls of letters delivered to her office, almost all of them sympathetic and filled with understanding. Yes, there were some from those who considered her a terrible example to others, but mostly those who'd wanted to write had sent only their best wishes and congratulations on the way she had faced her problems, some even telling of facing similar problems themselves and of how she had inspired them to find the spirit and hope she'd shown herself.

'Keep on playing, Lorna!' one fan had written. 'We love your music and we love you and your Melody Girls.' At which Lorna had burst into tears and had to be soothed by the combined efforts of her mother, Flo and George.

'I never dreamed that people would be so kind,' Lorna sobbed. 'It's just so touched my heart, I don't know what to say.'

'Canna believe everybody's so tolerant,' Tilly commented wonderingly to Cissie, who had been following events with the greatest interest. 'But, there you are, there's hope for us all yet.'

'Might just be that all these folk who've written have been musical, eh?' Cissie asked, but Tilly only pursed her lips.

'Now, when did musical folk appear any nicer than others, Cissie? Look at the way the men won't help the women! Look at Luke Riddell, giving Flo and Lorna the sack!'

Yet Luke had rather surprised everybody by writing Lorna a little note of good wishes. He and Suzie had been so astonished to hear of the wee one, you could have knocked them over with a feather, he said, but, well done, Lorna! To keep on with her band in spite of all, and congratulations to her and Flo and all the lassies, not to mention George, the dog, deserting his old band, but never mind, he'd done well too.

'So, there you are,' Lorna murmured. 'A turn out for the book, as they say, Luke being so generous.'

'Seems too good to be true,' Flo answered. She would have liked to ask if anything had been heard from Josh, but knew Lorna would have told her. As for Rod, Lorna herself had said there'd been no word from him, as she had thought perhaps there might be. But then, they probably didn't take Scottish magazines in America.

'Or, he was too stunned to reply,' Flo suggested.

'If he'd wanted to reply, he would have done,' Lorna said honestly. 'Maybe there wouldn't be much point, anyway, after all this time.'

'Shows the difference between men and women, though, doesn't it?' Flo asked. 'Here we have you who've been looking after Sam all his life, and Rod, who doesn't even know he's a father. Are you listening, George?'

'Hmm?' George answered, looking up from an American music magazine. 'Says here there's a lot more of rockabilly music going around in the States.'

'Rockabilly?'

'Sort of mixture of everything. Country and jazz, plus a bit of boogie woogie and blues. Been around a while, in one form or another.'

'Rockabilly?' Lorna smiled. 'Can't see that being our sort of thing.'

'Should suit the kids, eh?'

'We play for grown-ups,' Flo said. 'But there are always new crazes turning up.'

'And dying down.' George threw his magazine side. 'Listen, have you girls done any cooking? I could eat a horse.'

Fifty-One

Ever since she'd begun to earn what she called 'real' money, Lorna had wanted to move her mother into better accommodation, but Tilly had always said no. She didn't want a better flat, she wanted the flat she had. It was where she'd spent most of her married life; it had its memories of Cam and the two wee boys she'd lost, as well as of Lorna growing up.

'I'm no' moving,' she told Lorna, when they were having a cup of coffee while Sam was out at playgroup. 'And that's that.'

'But the thing is, Ma, Sam's going to need his own room one day, and I want one when I come home, and so do you. We really need three bedrooms now, and I suggest we look for a house. A detached house with a garden.' She gave her mother a persuasive smile. 'You'd like a garden, eh?'

'I'd like a garden,' Tilly agreed, 'but no' enough to move house for one. And there's another thing. I've got my dressmaking customers to think about. They'll no' want to go traipsing miles away to come to me, and they'd have to do that, eh? Seeing as there are no detached houses round here.'

'Maybe you could give up your dressmaking? You've worked hard all your life. Why don't you have a rest?'

'Give up my dressmaking!' Tilly exclaimed. 'What are you talking about? I'm no' old enough to retire!'

'I'm only thinking you might like a break.'

'The secret of keeping well is to work. You like working, eh? Well, so do I. Let's say no more.'

'Well, at least let me look around at properties,' Lorna said, with a sigh. 'And then if I saw something really nice, you could come and see it.'

'I can tell you're dying to look at properties yourself,' Tilly said dryly. 'All right, you do that, but I'm no' promising anything.'

'I know, I know. I'll just get *The Scotsman* and read the property pages. Might ask Ewen to come with me. He'd be interested.'

'Ewen.' Tilly frowned. 'It's time you let that laddie go, Lorna. Time he was married, and no' to you, seeing as you don't want him.'

'He's my friend, Ma. We've always been friends. If he wants to marry, I'm no' stopping him.'

'You are while you keep him hanging on. It's no' fair, Lorna. You've a lot in your life today, you're successful and making money. Just let Ewen go.'

'I can't see why we shouldn't meet as friends, Ma, and if you don't mind, I'll decide when to stop seeing him. Which I've no plans to do.'

'All right, I'll leave it to you.' Tilly bent dark brows on Lorna. 'But you know what I think.'

'Fine.' Lorna rose to go. 'Now, I'll just go and collect Sam, then I'm away.' At the door, she hesitated. 'Do you realize, Ma, Sam'll be starting proper school in September? Can you believe it.'

'Och, no! But he's that bright, he's ready to go now, eh? And wanting to play a saxophone like you.'

'He's a bit young for that,' Lorna laughed. 'But I am thinking of getting him a piano. When we find the new house.'

'Never give up, do you?' Tilly shook her head. 'I tell you, I'm staying here.'

Ewen, of course, said he'd be delighted to help Lorna house hunt, and on his next afternoon off, they began their trawl of possibilities. If she was looking for a detached house with a garden in the Haymarket area, however, Ewen told Lorna she hadn't a hope.

'I know that,' she retorted. 'I know I'm going to have to spread my net. But Ma won't move too far away from where she is now, so there are problems.'

'How about abandoning the detached idea and considering something terraced in the West End?' Ewen studied his copy of the newspaper's property page. 'There's a nice terraced house here in Grosvenor Place – whole house, not yet turned into flats. Pricey, though.'

'Let me see. Why, it's lovely, Ewen! Looks like three floors. And Victorian?'

'Aye, so good-sized rooms. Small sunny garden at rear. Easy distance from where your ma is now.' Ewen grinned. 'Only question, I'd say, is can you afford it?'

'It will go to sealed bids at the lawyer's, I suppose.'

Lorna sat with her finger to her mouth. 'Our Scottish system of offers over a price is OK – until you try to guess how much other people will bid.'

'Haven't even seen it yet, Lorna.'

'No, but I've a feeling it's the one. Let's ring for a viewing.'

As soon as she saw 29 Grosvenor Place, Lorna knew she was right. This was the one, this was the house for her, her mother and Sam. It was on the big side, true, but that meant it had space, they could spread themselves. Each of them could have a bedroom and there were also two spare rooms, plus a tiny room that would be ideal for practising if soundproofed. And then the main rooms were really grand, with fine cornices and plastered ceilings, long windows and original fireplaces. And the secluded little garden at the back was quite a suntrap. Ma could sit there, looking at the flowers she would plant, while Sam could whizz round with his latest cars, and no one could even see.

'I think I could afford to put in a good offer,' Lorna whispered to Ewen, while Mr Rowe, the young man from the lawyer's office, showed them round.

'Is there a closing date for offers?' Ewen asked.

'There is, sir, it's Friday.'

'No' much time, then.'

'Perhaps not, but if you and your wife could reach a decision, you'd still have time to put your offer in.'

'Mr MacKee is just a friend of mine,' Lorna said hastily, as Ewen turned brick red. 'I'm the one interested in the house. I think you have my name there? Miss Fernie?'

'Oh, of course, Miss Fernie,' Mr Rowe agreed, colouring almost as much as Ewen. 'Sorry about that. Now, is there anything else I can show you?'

'No, I'm very happy with what I've seen. Think I'd better get on now with arranging my offer, but thanks for showing us round.'

'My pleasure.' With some relief, Mr Rowe escorted them to the front door. 'We'll look forward to hearing from you, then.'

Outside in the quiet, elegant street, Lorna gave a light laugh. 'Hope that wasn't too embarrassing for you, Ewen?'

'No, no,' he answered quickly, though he had turned away to look back at the house Lorna wanted so much to buy.

So solid, eh? So obviously well cared for, with its fine front door and brass letter box, its wrought iron railings lining the steps, its gleaming windows. How many maids had worked here in the old days, he wondered, cleaning, polishing, scrubbing? No maids now, of course, they'd vanished with the war, never to return, but he supposed Lorna could find a cleaning lady, someone to help, anyway.

It would be a different way of life for her, living in a place like this, but then she already had a different way of life – made by herself.

'What are you thinking?' she asked, touching his arm. 'You've got one of your brooding looks.'

'I was thinking how far you'd come, Lorna.'

'What, from the Haymarket?' she laughed.

'You know what I mean.'

'I've been lucky, that's all. I don't play any better than my dad, but I thought of having my own band and it's worked out for me. So, now I can find a better place for my mother and son to live. That comes with success.'

'You're going to ask your mother to see it, before you go to your lawyer?'

'Of course. I'm going to fetch her now.'

'Lorna, don't be disappointed, will you? If she still doesn't want to move?'

'She told me to look at places, Ewen. I'm sure I can persuade her to change her mind. I mean, wait till she sees the house!'

'It may not be what she wants,' he said gently. 'Why don't you buy it for yourself – if you can – and let Sam join you when he's older? Your ma could come over whenever needed, eh?'

For some time, Lorna stood in thought, before flinging her arms round Ewen and laughing. 'Ewen, you've done it again! Solved the problem. Yes, I think you're right. That's what Ma would like, and I'd like too. Come on, let's tell her what's happening.'

'Hang on.' He took her hand. 'Listen, would you like to come out for a meal with me?'

'To celebrate my house? I haven't got it yet!'

He hesitated. 'I was thinking . . . well, it's my birthday next week, you see . . .'

'Oh, Ewen, of course! Your birthday! I'd love to come for a meal, but I'll have to check my diary. I know there's one night next week we've nothing booked, but it's probably not on your birthday. Would it matter?'

'Course not. It'll just be grand if we can meet. Will you let me know the date? I want to take you somewhere nice.'

'Sure I will.' She put her arm in his. 'Now, let's go and see Ma.'

Fifty-Two

When Lorna met Ewen the following week, she was touched to find that he'd booked dinner at one of her favourite restaurants in George Street. Much too expensive for him, she worried, though he'd had a promotion recently and had now taken over Miss Dickinson's job, she having been transferred to Glasgow.

'I know it's my birthday,' he told her calmly, when she ventured to suggest that she should be paying the bill in celebration, 'but this is my treat, so no arguments.'

'The thing is,' she told him with shining eyes, 'I've got the house! My bid came top at the lawyer's auction. And Ma's thrilled that I'm not going to ask her to move in, but says Sam should definitely come to me when he's older. So, this really must be my treat too.'

'Let's just decide what to eat, Lorna. And drink, eh? I don't know much about wine – maybe you could help me choose?'

'It'll be the blind leading the blind, if I do. I'm no' much of a drinker at all. Let's just have the house red. That'll do me fine.'

The meal at first went well. Ewen had ordered with confidence, the wine, too, and he and Lorna seemed as wonderfully at ease with each other as they always were, until they reached the coffee stage. It was then that a change seemed to come over him. He began to look around the restaurant, at other diners, the waiters – anywhere except Lorna, and to fiddle with his cup, spilling a little coffee over the pristine white cloth and being overcome with confusion.

'Oh, trust me, trust me,' he groaned. 'Can't take me anywhere, can you?'

'Come on, it's nothing to worry about,' Lorna told him, waving away a waiter who was anxious to change their cloth. 'We've almost finished, anyway, and it's been lovely, Ewen, a real treat.'

'Has it?' Finally he brought his anxious gaze to hers, and as he ran his hand over his face, Lorna suddenly realized that more than anxiety over spilt coffee was troubling him.

He had something on his mind, something he wanted to get out. What on earth could it be? Then the idea came to her like a flash of light illuminating everything. Could it be that he was going to propose?

After all these years of being only friends, had he decided, as Tilly had suggested, that it was time for him to marry? And that she, Lorna, should be the obvious one to ask? Even if it was true, as he'd once said to her, that he'd never expected to be the one for her, that he was the boy next door, the one who wasn't special, he might now believe she might consider him. He had, after all, supported her through two unhappy love affairs, been her rock, her trusted friend. Surely, he might think, she was ready to turn to him now.

And perhaps she might be. For the first time, she considered how it would be, to be married to Ewen. Maybe there was a lot to be said for being married to a rock. Someone who'd always be there for you, who'd never let you down.

'Ewen,' she said gently, leaning towards him. 'What's wrong? You're desperate to speak to me, aren't you? Why don't you, then?'

He looked quickly round at the tables nearest to them, saw no one was listening, and gave a long sigh, not of relief, Lorna could tell, but of decision.

'There is something I want to say to you,' he said in a low voice. 'But we've been special friends for so long, it isn't easy.'

'Why, being special friends should make it easier to talk, instead of harder, Ewen. You can say anything you like to me, you know.'

'Can I?' His eyes on her were filled with appeal. 'Well, I should think you're right. I don't suppose what I do will change things for you, eh?'

'Certainly could. But what are you planning to do, then?'

He drank the remains of the wine still in his glass, and set the now empty glass down.

'Lorna, I'm going to be married.'

Married.

She sat back in her chair with a jolt, taking the shock of his words as an extraordinary and totally unexpected blow. Ewen, to be married. And not to her? Not even seeking to be married to her? She felt a strange pain behind her breastbone, which was ridiculous, for if she had actually been considering him as a husband, she still could not think of him as a lover.

So why did she feel as she did? Completely knocked sideways, at the idea of her rock being married to someone else? Because her rock had crumbled? Because she was now clinging on to something that wasn't there?

'Married?' she repeated huskily. 'You're going to be married, Ewen?'

He had been watching her carefully, obvious relief that he'd finally broken his news shining clearly over his dear, honest face.

'Yes,' he said quietly. 'To Pattie.'

'Pattie? Pattie MacDowell?'

Well, of course, he meant Pattie MacDowell. Pattie, who had been Lorna's special friend at the post office, who still worked at the post office and was still Lorna's friend, though they met only rarely. And now she and Ewen were to be married?

Lorna, trying hard to appear happily interested, felt herself failing, felt herself in immediate danger of showing her true consternation, yet couldn't manage to save herself. Ewen to marry Pattie? She simply couldn't believe it. When he had never said a word, never given the slightest hint . . .

'And you never said a word,' she heard herself saying aloud. 'Why, Ewen? Why never speak of Pattie? Why never tell me you were seeing her?'

'I don't know. Suppose I was afraid it might no' work out. It's a pretty recent thing, anyway.'

His look now on Lorna had changed from one of appeal to apology, as though he'd recognized the shock he'd given her and wanted to make amends. Which, of course, was not possible.

'Pattie was telling me one day she was fed up with working at the post office – I'd got the promotion, but she hadn't – and that her job seemed to be going nowhere. And then there was you, you know.'

'Me?'

'Well, you've been doing so well. Making records, being on the wireless, becoming famous, all that sort of thing. Pattie couldn't help comparing herself.'

'Oh, that's a piece of nonsense, Ewen!'

'No,' he said quietly. 'I've felt a bit the same.'

'You haven't! Why, you've done well yourself, Ewen. You've just got promoted!'

'Aye, I feel better now.' He smiled wearily. 'Couldn't call myself a star, though. And people who can, they always think others don't mind, eh?'

'Look, I don't know what to say . . .'

'It's OK, Lorna, I don't want to make you feel bad. Anyway, the upshot of it was, Pattie and me, we went to the pictures and it sort of snowballed from there. She's a lovely girl, you know. Nice to talk to. Very sympathetic.'

Not always thinking of herself, like me, Lorna thought. And as she remembered the way she'd always considered Ewen, more light appeared to be shining down over him and her. How had she seen him? Only as a loyal friend, who'd always be there for her. Who'd never expect anything, but just come up with advice when required. Go for walks, act as a sounding board for ideas and solutions, be prepared to admire and carry a torch without ever expecting anything back.

'I'm the one who's no' special,' he had said of himself, and she had let him think it. No, he'd never been special in the way he meant. Even now, reeling from his news, she couldn't think of him as a lover, but he had been special as a person. Pure gold, you might say, while those he'd seen as special, and so had she, were oh so flawed. The worst of it was, it was too late to make amends. Ewen had found his own salvation, and her name was Pattie MacDowell.

'Ewen, let's go,' Lorna stammered, rising from her seat, tears she couldn't show only waiting to fall. And Ewen, regaining his composure, as hers melted away, called for the bill.

Walking home was an ordeal, for neither could think of what to say. Step by step, they covered the ground to Lorna's flat, where at one time – yesterday, no longer ago than that – she might have invited him in for a goodnight cup of something. Tonight, of course, was different. Tonight, she couldn't invite him in, engaged man that he was, but she did manage to hide her tears and kiss his cheek.

'I'm sorry, Ewen, I never wished you happiness. But I do, of course. And I'll see Pattie and wish her all the best, too.'

'She'd like that.'

'When will the wedding be?'

'No' sure yet, but fairly soon. Pattie says she wants to enjoy being engaged first, but I reckon that'll mean planning the wedding.'

Ewen was hesitating as Lorna stood on her step, swinging her keys.

'This needn't make any difference to us, Lorna, eh? I mean, if you ever want any help – you know, advice and all that – you'll still have me.'

'Oh, yes. I won't forget.'

'I mean it, Lorna. Can't just suddenly change from being as close as we were, can we?'

'No, no, we won't change. Goodnight, Ewen. And thanks for a lovely evening.'

'It was lovely for me too, Lorna. Really was.'

After she'd opened her door and given him a last smile, she saw him walking slowly and steadily out of her life. And then she closed the door and did shed tears, of regret for what she might have done, and the loss of a friend who didn't want to change, but had already changed the minute he put a ring on Pattie MacDowell's finger.

Ah, well Lorna had her own life to live, even if she did feel she was swimming alone in an endless sea where the only rocks there were no longer offered safety. Thank God, she still had what counted. Her family – her mother and Sam – her music and, oh, yes, her new house. Strange how that had for the minute faded from her mind.

Fifty-Three

Tilly, of course, when told of Ewen's engagement, lost no time in declaring that she'd told Lorna so.

'Now, did I no' say, Lorna, that Ewen was ready to be married, but no' to you? And you see, I was right, because he's fixed up with little Pattie MacDowell, and her ma says she's so happy.' Tilly sighed deeply. 'She's got some sense, eh? Good men don't grow on trees, you ken.'

'Ma, Ewen and I could never have been more than friends. We both knew that.'

'You mean, you did. If you ask me, Ewen would have married you any time you said. But he's got sense as well. When he saw he was never going to get anywhere, he found somebody else and good luck to him, eh?'

'Yes, good luck,' Lorna echoed seriously. 'I'll admit, I know I'm going to miss what Ewen and I shared, but he's doing the right thing and I do wish him and Pattie all the luck in the world. OK?'

'Aye, of course.'

Tilly suddenly put aside the blouse she had been stitching and rose to put her arm round Lorna's shoulders.

'I'm sorry, pet, for going on at you. Maybe you're right, it'd never have worked out between you and Ewen. He couldn't have been a part of your world and you've grown away from his. So, maybe he's better off with someone like Pattie.'

'I know he is,' Lorna said softly. Her eyes went to her mother's sideboard clock. 'Ma, you're collecting Sam today from playgroup, eh? Because I said I'd meet Pattie at the West End tea shop.'

'Yes, I'm picking up Sam.' Tilly raised her eyebrows. 'I didn't know you were meeting Pattie, but it's a good move.'

'How d'you mean, a good move?'

'Well, shows you wish her all the best. Just like you said.'

'I meant what I said,' Lorna said coldly. 'She is a friend. I want to give her my congratulations.'

'One of these days, maybe folk will be congratulating you. For more than your band.'

'Hope you aren't going to mention finding Mr Right, Ma?'

'I'm just thinking of you being on your own. It's no picnic. I should know.'

'You had me. I've got Sam.'

Tilly smiled, but made no reply, not liking to say that children grow up, and quickly, too, very soon wanting to lead their own lives. They might come back, might help, give advice, but not stay. And who would think they should? Didn't stop you being lonely, when they'd gone.

Arriving first at the tea shop in Shandwick Place where she'd arranged to meet Pattie on her half day, Lorna was able to watch Ewen's new fiancée approach through the crowded tables. How pretty she looked! Had she lost weight lately? Folk said brides usually lost weight, and if Pattie was not yet a bride, she certainly looked like one. Radiant, was the word.

'Pattie, over here!' she called, from her corner table. 'I've ordered teacake and fancies – that OK? Or are you dieting?'

Pattie, smiling, slid into a seat opposite Lorna, and shook her head. 'You'll never believe it, Lorna, but I've lost a stone, just since I got engaged! And you know I was always worrying about being too plump?'

'You look wonderful, Pattie. Being engaged suits you.'

'Being happy, you mean.' Pattie stretched out her left hand. 'Like to see ma ring?'

'Why, it's beautiful!' Lorna cried, looking at the pretty diamond ring and thinking how well Ewen had done to afford it. Had he been saving for some time? For this particular engagement? Immediately, she brushed that question aside and signalled to the waitress to bring their tea.

'It's really nice to see you, Lorna,' Pattie murmured, as Lorna poured tea and passed buttered teacake. 'Thanks for asking me.'

'Well, I wanted to congratulate you and have a chat, just the two of us. I expect you're soon going to be very busy, eh? With wedding plans?'

'Oh, yes!' Pattie gave a sunny smile. 'Ewen's no' keen to wait, and neither am I. Canna wait to give up ma job at the post office, either. I sometimes wonder just how many stamps I've sold in all these years!'

'You're giving up work? A lot of women are wanting to stay on these days.'

'Aye, that's true.' Pattie was blushing a little. 'But, the thing is, we want to start a family soon as we can. Why hang about? Ewen says. And I feel the same. Seeing your wee Sam always made me feel broody!'

'Never knew that. Must warn you that it's no' always easy, bringing up a bairn. I couldn't have managed without Ma.'

'No, but I've always admired you, Lorna,' Pattie said earnestly. 'The way you've coped, and run your band and been so successful and everything. I'm glad you asked me out today, because I want to tell you that I know you and Ewen have always been special friends, and I understand why. I do, honestly, and I don't want to break that up, so please, if you need any help, or anything, don't think he's no' there for you. He will be.'

For a long moment, Lorna was silent, studying a small untouched cake on her plate. 'I appreciate that, Pattie, more than I can say. It's really lovely of you to think of me like that. But I know things are different when someone marries, and I'd never expect it to be the same for Ewen and me, now that he has you. You come first, you always will, and that's how it should be.' Lorna gave a quick smile. 'But if I ever do need any advice, how would it be if I came to both of you? You're my friend too, remember.'

'As though I could ever give any advice to you,' Pattie said warmly. 'But, come anyway! Don't drift away.'

'And snap for you! First thing you'll have to do, is see my new house, once I've got some furniture!'

Lorna, reminded of Number 29, was thinking of all the pleasant times she should have, going to auctions and sale rooms to find just the right period pieces for her property. Flo and George, who'd expressed themselves thrilled by her acquisition, had promised to come with her whenever possible to advise on the bidding, and when all was complete, there would be, of course, a grand house-warming. That would be some way off, maybe, seeing as at present she had only her own personal possessions to put into her new home, but she had the plans, she had the ideas – she'd get there in the end. Suddenly, life seemed sweet again and she smiled as she called for the bill.

'Yes, you must come round and see the house,' she said again to Pattie. 'Never mind the furniture, come while it's still empty. My blank canvas, I call it, but it looks so nice, I can't wait to settle in.'

'You're going to live in it all by yourself?' Pattie asked, with some concern. 'Won't it be a bit lonely?'

'Sam will be moving in when he's older, and Ma will always be popping round, no' to mention my Auntie Cissie, Flo and George, and you folks.'

Pattie's round blue eyes were soft with sympathy. 'Lorna, do hope you don't mind me saying this, but I'm sure Mr Right'll turn up one of these days. I mean, he's bound to, for someone like you!'

'Ah, the mysterious Mr Right.' Lorna laughed, as she placed a tip for the waitress underneath a saucer. 'Funny thing is, Pattie, strange as it may seem, I'm perfectly happy being Miss Right. I've got everything, you see – my boy, my band, and now my house. What more could I want?'

As they left the tea shop together, they both knew what was missing. Or, might be considered missing, if Lorna wanted to think on those lines. But, then, she didn't. Twice bitten, for ever shy, was her motto, even if no one believed it.

Fifty-Four

Pattie and Ewen were married on a bitterly cold day in January, 1954. The wedding was a quiet one at a Haymarket kirk, with a reception at a West End cafe, and a grand 'going away' for the bride and groom at Waverley Station before they left for honeymoon in London. The only bridesmaid was Pattie's younger sister, which was a relief to Lorna, who had feared she might have been asked, too. Sam, who had been persuaded to act as pageboy, dressed in his first kilt and wee jacket, almost stole the show. Except for Pattie, of course, who had looked her absolute best in white velvet – not to mention, as she said, laughing, her long johns.

'Just glad it's all over,' Ewen whispered to Lorna on the platform at Waverley. 'But don't tell Pattie, eh? Feels like she's been planning this day for ever.'

'She certainly looks wonderful,' Lorna told him. 'I know you're going to be very happy.'

'Aye, if we can find a place to live. Have to find a wee flat soon, or we'll be staying with one of our mothers.'

'You can always stay at my place, Ewen. It isn't properly furnished yet – sometimes wonder if it ever will be – but there's plenty of room and I've got two more tours planned, so I won't be around much.'

'Oh, thanks, Lorna, thanks a lot, but we couldn't do that,' he said hastily. 'When you are home, you'll want to work on your house and we wouldn't want to get in the way.'

'Well, the offer's there, so don't forget.'

'I won't.'

As he was called to hurry to board the train, he gave Lorna a last hug, then ran to embrace Pattie's mother and his own, before joining his bride to wave and blow kisses while the confetti rained.

'There they go, then,' Tilly murmured, as the great London train slowly began to leave the station. 'Make a lovely pair, eh?'

'Lovely,' Lorna agreed and, taking Sam's hand, said they'd better be getting home.

'Which home?' asked Tilly. 'I've asked a whole lot of folk back to mine, so you'd better come as well.'

'Hope I don't have to eat any more of that wedding cake,' Sam exclaimed. 'Currants and icing – ugh! And I hope nobody else kisses me, either.'

His grandmother laughed and said he'd been such a good boy, she'd give him his favourite supper as soon as the guests had gone – beans on toast with a fried egg on top.

'And I'll give you some extra pocket money,' Lorna promised. 'Ma, shall we take a taxi, Pattie's mother's asking? We're all in our glad rags.'

'A taxi? No, what a waste.' Tilly waved to those coming back with her. 'Come on, we'll get the tram. Nae bother, eh?'

But for once Tilly was outvoted and everyone squashed into taxis and drove back to her flat in style, to continue the reception in more relaxed fashion.

'If only I'd got my house ready,' Lorna sighed to Flo and George. 'It would have been perfect for something like this. But I never get any time!'

'Soon as we get back from the next tour, we'll hit those auctions,' Flo promised. 'Then you can get the decorating done and you'll be in business.'

'Aye, because we're all waiting for that house-warming you promised us,' said George. 'And we know you're wanting to invite half Scotland to that!'

'Only the folks who play in swing bands,' Lorna told him. 'No, but seriously, I am inviting all the musicians I know. Even Jackie Craik.'

'Help!' Flo cried. 'You'll be asking Luke Riddell next!'

'Oh, yes, Luke will be coming, and Suzie.' Lorna grinned. 'I've just got to get a few chairs and a table first!'

Fifty-Five

Finding the right furniture for Number 29 proved, however, to be more difficult than Lorna had ever imagined. Buying at auction and sales was not, of course, like buying at a shop. You couldn't just choose what you want, pay for it and have it delivered. No, you had to work through the catalogues, go to the previews, tick off what you liked, work out a bid, then suffer the ordeal of seeing most of your favourite pieces go to other bidders.

'It's all your fault, George,' Lorna told him. 'You won't let me up my bids, so I end up losing out.'

'Fatal to start upping bids, Lorna. Once you've decided what something's worth to you, you stick to that figure. Otherwise, it's all too easy to lose your head and pay out ridiculous money for something that isn't worth it.'

'Shame you can't buy new,' Flo said, 'but I agree, you need to get stuff that matches the house. And what they make today looks so flimsy, it probably won't last five minutes.'

'And priced far too high,' George put in. 'Second hand is best, particularly as I think we should be considering keeping costs down.'

'I'm no' worrying too much about keeping costs down,' Lorna told him.

'Well, maybe you should be. All of us should.'

'What's this, then, George?' Flo asked, widening her eyes. 'An economy campaign? Has something happened?'

'No, no, nothing's happened. It's just that sometimes I can't help wondering if our particular bubble might burst.' He lowered his eyes. 'You know how it is, these fears come, don't they?'

'Do they?' Lorna's brow was furrowed. 'Seems to me we're doing so well, there's no need for you to worry.'

He paused for a moment. 'You remember that time I talked about rockabilly music? Well, it's struck me since that that might turn out to be – like they say – the cloud that's no bigger than a man's hand. If you understand me.'

'No, we don't,' Flo said bluntly. 'Bubbles, clouds – I don't know what's got into you, George.'

'The cloud that's no bigger than a man's hand might come before a thunderstorm,' George said patiently. 'Or, disaster of some sort. One minute, you've a clear horizon, the next, darkness. But . . . hell, I'm not saying we're facing that, of course.'

'What are you saying?' Lorna asked quickly. 'Something's in the wind and you don't like it?'

'Exactly. And the something in the wind seems to be starting up in America. Music that's a mixture of rockabilly and a whole lot of other things. Seems it could really take off, according to the grapevine.'

'Has this music got a name?'

George shrugged. 'Some say rock and roll.'

'But why should we worry about it?'

'Oh, I'm not saying we need. It's not even over here yet. But as we always seem to copy America, it's pretty certain to come. And once it does, who knows how long people will want what we play?'

'George, you're talking nonsense!' Flo cried, in exasperation. 'There've always been different kinds of music going side by side. Jitterbugging music, jive, skiffle, all that sort of thing. This rock and roll stuff, it won't stop people wanting our sort of music for dancing. Nothing will change that!'

George was silent, then smiled and nodded. 'You're right, of course. I suppose I'm only thinking of what might happen, not what will. So, take no notice!'

'We won't,' Flo said, glancing quickly at Lorna's set expression. 'With the sort of money we're making now, I say we have no need to worry. You look for what you want for the house, Lorna, and don't listen to this old doom merchant here. He ought to be going round with a billboard. "The end of the world is nigh", eh?'

As long as it isn't the end of our world, Lorna was thinking, but didn't really believe it could be. George was worrying about nothing, as Flo had told him. Even if this rock and roll stuff did take off, as he'd said it might, that wouldn't mean that she and other band-leaders would be queuing for the dole. There would always be people who wanted what they played, which meant that there would still be money coming in and no need for economizing. 'You buy what you want for the house', Flo had said, and why shouldn't she?

All the same, the more she thought about it, the less Lorna was inclined to spend as though there was no tomorrow, as her mother would have put it. Maybe she had all along been too extravagant? Buying herself a big house she didn't really need? Trying to fill it with furniture that had to be the best? She hadn't been brought up to spend like that, and when she remembered how little some folk had – how little her own parents had had at one time – a great feeling of guilt began to weigh down her heart.

And then, just supposing George turned out to be right, and the attraction for the big bands began to decline, and also their incomes?

Oh, Lord, what could she do? Lorna asked herself, beginning to feel like pressing cold towels to her brow. She could scarcely sell the house in the West End before she'd properly moved in, could she? And if she did plan to live in the house, she'd need furniture. Which brought her back to the auctions and what she would have to pay to get something that suited Number 29. At one time, she would have asked advice from Ewen, of course, but whatever Pattie had suggested, Lorna knew she could no longer do that. Better turn back to Flo and George, then. See what they could suggest.

'Oh, come on, Lorna,' Flo cried at once. 'I tell you, there's no need to take any notice of what George was saying. He even thinks so himself, don't you, George?'

'Suppose I do,' he agreed. 'Which doesn't mean Lorna hasn't got a point. It would be foolish to spend too much, and maybe there's an easier way than auction buying to get what she needs.'

'What easier way?' Lorna asked eagerly.

'Buy from individual sellers. There are no fees, no other bidders to bump up the price, no hassle. And a lot of folk are getting rid of the big old mahogany stuff because it's gone out of fashion. You could get all you wanted, if you didn't mind taking your time.'

'But where do I find these individual sellers, George? I don't know any people with mahogany they just happen to want to get rid of!'

'*The Scotsman*,' he answered simply. 'The evening papers. Comb 'em every day, be first on the phone when you see something you want, and I guarantee, you'll be OK.'

'But you were all for auctions at one time,' Lorna pointed out. 'What's changed?'

'Thought you were rich then, maybe. Thought we were all rich.' George shook his head. 'But now I think we have to be careful.'

'Why, you haven't changed at all, have you!' Flo cried. 'You're still worrying about that wretched rock and roll!'

'Let's say, I just don't think it's likely to go away,' he told her. 'So, best be on the safe side.'

And, staying on the safe side, Lorna took her time about shopping through the For Sale ads. Lived in an almost empty house until she could find what she wanted at reasonable prices, until, by the end of the year, she suddenly realized that Number 29 was ready. Ready for her house-warming, for which she could now send out the invitations. What would she put on those printed cards she'd seen?

Miss Lorna Fernie. At Home?

At home at last, with a house she could be proud of, furniture that looked right and hadn't cost the earth, and enough money to spare to donate to her Christmas charities. At least now she didn't feel so bad about spoiling herself, and if the band's bubble ever did burst, as George feared, she would be prepared. But then it wasn't going to do that, was it?

Fifty-Six

Everyone invited came to the house-warming, and Lorna had invited a crowd: relatives, friends, musicians – pretty well everyone she knew. For once, she decided, she would stop worrying about expense, and booked outside caterers to provide a buffet supper on the first Sunday after Hogmanay, 1955, Sunday being the only day the band people could be sure of coming.

'And has to be after Hogmanay because of Sam's birthday,' she explained to Flo. 'We're going to the pantomime on New Year's Eve, and on New Year's Day I'm having his friends round to Ma's. Thought we'd better no' have a gang of eight-year-olds at the house, seeing as it's all got to look its best for the party.'

'Eight-year-olds?' Flo sighed. 'Is your wee Sam really eight years old? Where have all the years gone? Think I've missed the boat, Lorna?'

'No' if you want to catch it.'

'That's the point.' Flo shrugged. 'George and I aren't sure if we do want a family. So, you know what they say, when in doubt, don't!'

'You're the opposite of Pattie,' Lorna told her. 'She's desperate to start a baby. When she does, I can guarantee that Ewen will be the perfect father.'

Flo's eyes rested on her thoughtfully. 'OK, now?' she asked quietly. 'I mean, with Ewen being a married man?'

'OK,' Lorna agreed. 'We're all three of us very good friends.'

'That's grand. Now, is there anything I can do to help with the house-warming?'

'Not a thing, thanks, it's all in hand.' Lorna suddenly flung her arms round Flo. 'Oh, I do think I've been lucky, don't you, Flo? In spite of everything?'

'If you've been lucky, you deserve to be. All we want now for you is you know who.'

'Ssh, don't even say it!' Lorna cried. 'Mr Right has no' been invited!'

By seven o'clock on the evening of the house-warming, the time when guests were due to arrive, everything was ready. The caterers were in the kitchen, except for one uniformed waitress who was in place to answer the door and another to take guests' coats and show where the ladies could comb hair and powder noses. The excellent buffet was laid out in the dining room, with welcoming punch bowl and glasses in the drawing room, where Lorna, radiant in dark green taffeta, was standing with her family and Flo and George, ready to receive her guests.

'That Josh,' George whispered to Flo. 'He was a nutcase, right? To leave anybody like Lorna?'

'He wasn't the first nutcase she's had to deal with,' Flo answered, at which George grinned and asked her if she hadn't been lucky herself, then? Landing an intelligent fellow like him?

She was knocking his arm and laughing, when the doorbell rang, and Cissie cried, 'Action Stations! The first guests have arrived!'

'I'll go see!' shouted Sam, who was feeling very proud of himself in his kilt, with white shirt and bow tie, and before Tilly could stop him, was away to the hall.

'It's Ma's band!' he cried, dancing back, 'It's the Melody Girls! But they've no' brought their instruments!'

'Hey, we're off duty tonight,' Bridie told him. 'It's your ma's party!'

'Could still have played, eh? I wanted to hear the saxophones.'

'Sam, our rooms here are pretty big, but they're still too small for a band,' Lorna said, smiling. 'The girls would've blown us out into the street!'

'Though I wish they could've played,' she whispered to Flo. 'Our band showing the guys how it should be done!'

With the entrance of the girls, all for once in different dresses, all beautifully made up, their hair elaborately done, Lorna's drawing room sprang immediately to life. There were hugs and little screams of admiration over their leader's house, with even Claire looking relaxed and joining in, and if the band was not quite the same as the original gathering of players, some having married and moved on, it was still, Lorna and Flo felt, their extended family, come to celebrate.

But then the doorbell began to ring non stop, as more and more people came streaming in, bearing flowers and chocolate and bottles of wine, and the hugs and cries continued over the punch and nibbles, to the accompaniment of big band music from the radiogram in the corner.

Whose record was it? The Melody Girls', of course, but then there was one from Luke, and another from Jackie, and even one from Ambrose, the great London bandleader, to which Jackie smartly asked why they were playing the opposition.

'No opposition tonight,' George told him. 'Tonight, we're all just celebrating.'

'Celebrating what, exactly?'

'Hell, do you have to have a reason?'

'Supper is served,' a waiter announced.

And Lorna, flushed and proud, shepherded everyone into the dining room, where there were more cries of admiration, until the room fell silent and the guests began to eat.

'Now, when you've finished that,' Tilly whispered to Sam, who had been happily piling up his plate, 'you'd better be thinking about bed, eh?'

'Ah no, Gramma, I'm no' going to bed yet!'

'Well, you're no' staying up all night, Sam. And you've a lovely wee room upstairs all ready for you.'

'Aye, but I needn't go upstairs yet, Gramma. Ma said!'

'What did your ma say, then?' Ewen asked affectionately, as Lorna, coming up, shook her head, smiling.

'It's all right, Ma, he did twist my arm to let him stay up longer. Just for a while.'

'I wish I could've heard the band,' Sam sighed. 'Specially the saxophones. When I grow up, I'm going to play the sax, like Ma.'

'No' in my band,' Lorna told him. 'Mine's a girl band.'

'I'll have my own band!' Sam cried, and Ewen and Lorna, moving on, said they were sure he would.

'Lorna, you're looking terrific tonight,' Ewen murmured, studying the green taffeta. 'Feeling happy?'

'Happy, and lucky.'

'We think we might be lucky, too.'

Ewen's eyes were searching for Pattie, who waved to him across the room from where she was in conversation with Miss Dickinson. 'Pattie still has to see the doc, but I reckon it's pretty certain we're going to be parents.' He grinned widely. 'What d'you think of me as a dad?'

'Ewen, what wonderful news! Oh, I'm so happy for you!' Lorna couldn't resist giving him a hug, even if her guests were giving interested stares. 'But I must speak to Pattie!'

'Hey, I'm no' sure if it's meant to be a secret—' Ewen was beginning, but Lorna was already on her way, thinking, A secret? Oh, no, there was no need for secrets, surely? There'd been enough secrets over babies, hadn't there? And thank the Lord, Pattie and Ewen had no need of them anyway.

After the congratulations and embraces with lucky Pattie, and a chat with Miss Dickinson, who seemed quite overcome by 'little' Lorna's success, it was Jackie's turn to catch at Lorna's arm.

'Grand party,' he told her, his eyes so bright and his manner so cheerful, she guessed he'd been doing more than justice, not only to the buffet but also the wine. Practised enough to be able to stay in control, however, he was very pleasantly complimentary on all that she'd done with her band, until he came out with a name she would rather have had him forget.

'Sorry about Josh,' he murmured, swaying very slightly. 'I mean, you and Josh. Always thought . . . you'd make a handsome couple, eh?'

'Water under the bridge,' she said swiftly, deciding that was a phrase she'd had to use too often.

'Ever hear from him?'

'No, we've quite lost touch.'

'I did hear he'd moved from Ted Heath to Ambrose, you know.' Jackie gave a grin. 'Never could settle, eh? Fell out with somebody there, too – remember his temper? So, where is he now? Nobody knows.'

Lorna, smiling at Claire, who was passing, said, 'It's of no interest to me, Jackie.'

'No? Well, they do say he's gone abroad. Maybe Italy. Half Italian, wasn't he?'

'Hey, no monopolizing of the hostess,' Luke Riddell called, inserting himself between Jackie and Lorna. He too was looking rather bright in the eye and smiling more than usual, but was as straight backed and elegant as ever, as he drank a little from the glass he was carrying.

'Swell party, Lorna! Must have cost you a fortune, eh? But shows you're doing well, that's the thing. Doesn't it show she's doing well, Jackie?'

'Very well,' Jackie agreed, draining his own glass. 'Long may it continue, I say.'

'As of course we all know it may not,' Luke said softly.

'What do you mean?' Lorna asked quickly.

He fixed her with his dark glittering eyes. 'Been asked lately when folks book you if you're playing the new stuff?'

'No, I haven't. What new stuff?'

'What the kids like,' Jackie explained. 'You know.' He waved his glass. 'Rock and roll.'

Lorna took a step backwards. 'You as well?' she muttered. 'George is full of all that nonsense.'

'Nonsense?' Luke frowned. 'It's not nonsense if it makes money, Lorna. And it's hitting the world big time, believe me.'

'We can make money, too, Luke.'

'Yes, as long as folk still want us. But fashions come and go, you know. Maybe, it's the turn of the big bands to bow out.'

'Bow out?' Lorna shook her head. 'There'll always be people who want dance music.'

'I tell you, the whole scene could shift, dear girl.' Luke glanced at Jackie, who had gone rather quiet. 'You understand that, Jackie?'

'I'm thinking about a young guy in America,' Jackie said slowly. 'Cut a couple of records for his mother's birthday some time last year in Memphis, Tennessee. "My Happiness" one was called, and what was the other one, Luke?'

'What does it matter?' Lorna cried. 'What's all this about?'

'Well, this young guy, everybody's saying, is going to blow the world of popular music apart, because, as they all have it, he's dynamite.' Jackie shook his head. 'So, by next year, we're going to see great changes, over here as well as in the States. And they'll all be led by this fellow, and the young folk, who want something new. Mark my words.'

'So, what's this fellow's name?'

'Elvis Presley.' It was Luke who answered, speaking solemnly. 'Better make a note, Lorna. And keep a look out, eh?'

'Any more of your gloom and you'll be turning my party into a wake,' Lorna remarked, trying to laugh. 'Why don't we all go into the other room for coffee? Or, whatever you prefer.'

Fifty-Seven

Moving around her drawing room, her head held high, her shoulders straight, always her style when facing a challenge, Lorna's mind was still with Luke and Jackie. Talk about looking on the dark side – the gloom they'd cast over her had descended like one great lowering cloud. What had George said about rockabilly's being like a 'cloud no bigger than a man's hand'? A forerunner to a storm, he had suggested. And here were Luke and Jackie talking as though the storm were already upon them.

It wasn't true, though. Try as she would, Lorna couldn't see that her kind of music would be on its way out. Of course, young people might want this new rock and roll, for young people always wanted different things from their elders. But surely that didn't mean that all the folk who came to the dance halls or clubs and hotels now, would want a change too? What, after all, was so special about the new music that was supposed to be sweeping the world? It came to Lorna suddenly that she didn't even know precisely what rock and roll was. So, where was George? He would tell her.

She found him in conversation with Ina and Dickie, both still with Luke's band, both still in love but not yet married, Luke not being keen on employing married couples.

'Of course, it's all right for him to be married to Suzie,' Ina whispered, glancing over at the lovely Suzie herself, who was exchanging experiences as a vocalist with Lorna's vocalist, Dawn. 'But he's just prejudiced against married band players, if you ask me. Says their minds are always on other things, would you credit it?'

'We're seriously thinking of moving on,' Dickie remarked. 'No good looking at you, I suppose, Lorna?'

'Well, not for you,' George laughed.

'And I'm afraid we have a pianist,' Lorna said. 'Otherwise, we'd have loved to have you, Ina. It would have been like old times.'

'Should have come over when you first started up,' Ina sighed. 'And see how well you've done, eh? Luke's green with envy, Suzie's always saying.'

'According to him, we're all due to be bowing out soon,' Lorna said, pretending to laugh. 'Knocked out by rock and roll.'

'Oh, come on!' Dickie cried. 'That's an exaggeration.'

'I still don't even know what rock and roll is,' Ina said. 'Except it looks like jitterbugging to me.'

'Define it, George,' Lorna ordered. 'What are we up against?'

'Well, it's a mixture, really. It's blues, it's boogie woogie, it's big on guitars but has drums and bass, too. And of course a large part of its appeal is the vocals. The singers are tremendously important.'

'Looks like we're up against something,' Dickie muttered. 'At least, bass players seem to be still wanted.'

'But not pianists, I bet.' Ina looked across at Luke who was holding forth across the room to a group that included an admiring Cissie and both Lorna's cousins. 'Maybe I should just stick with Luke as long as he's around.'

Excusing herself, saying she had to mingle, Lorna was surprised to find Claire at her elbow, asking if she could have a word.

'Why, of course!' she told her. 'Like some more coffee first?'

'No, I'm all right, thanks.'

'Well, let's sit in the hall for a minute. You can hardly hear yourself speak in here!'

'Sam gone to bed?' Claire asked, taking a seat on a small bench in the hall and looking, Lorna thought, very pretty that evening. Though a little cagey, perhaps, as if she might have something difficult to say.

'Oh, some time ago,' Lorna answered. 'Ma said he could read if he liked, but he was asleep as soon as his head hit the pillow.'

'An easy conscience, of course.' Claire smiled faintly. 'Listen, Lorna, hope you won't mind but I couldn't help hearing you talking about Josh earlier on.'

'Oh, yes?' Lorna looked away.

'I think Jackie was saying he might have gone to Italy?'

'Are you interested?'

Claire flushed. 'You'll think me very foolish, I expect, but I am. I still am, though I don't have any hope, I know, of seeing him again.'

'Are you telling me you care for him, Claire? I had no idea.'

'No, I never let on. Never told anybody. But I've always felt so bad, Lorna, that I spoiled things for you with him, by what I did. And I suppose I did do that because I was so jealous.'

'Claire, I never knew!' Lorna was staring at her. 'I never knew, never guessed. I always thought there were other reasons.'

'There were, but me loving Josh, that was the main one.' Claire bent her head. 'And then you were so decent, so kind to me, I began to feel terrible. About what I'd done. But I couldn't say anything. I just had to live with it.'

'But you have seemed happier, Claire. Everyone's noticed it.'

'Yes, that's the funny thing. Since you were so nice to me, I tried to be nice, too, and then, I don't know how, I started to feel better. I'm still not over Josh, but I'm definitely better than I was.'

'I'm so glad,' Lorna said warmly. 'And I'm glad you've told me how things have been for you. But now we can put it behind us, can't we? Just keep going, as before?'

'Well, not quite.' Claire was again looking as though she had something hard to say. 'The fact is, I've made my peace with my sister, and she's asked me to go down to London to be with her. Share a flat, find a job, while she gets herself on the concert circuit. At one time, I could never have said yes, but now . . . well, I have.'

'Oh, Claire, that's good! Except, you'll be leaving us?'

'I'm afraid so.' Now that she had given her news, Claire's brow had cleared. 'And I'm really sad. But I do want to be with Hannah, and this is my chance. Who knows, I might get taken on by one of the greats down there! Ambrose, or Ivy Benson, or somebody!'

'You might at that. I'll speak to George – he can put out feelers.' Lorna stood up. 'Claire, I'm so glad things have turned out as they have. Don't worry about Josh. Once you're in London, you'll never give him another thought. Just as I don't now.'

Claire, not looking entirely convinced, smiled. 'Still, I'm sorry to leave you without a pianist, Lorna. Do hope you'll find one soon.'

'I think I might just have someone in mind. Come on, let's go back, and find George.'

Suddenly, everything was quiet. The guests had gone. The caterers had gone. The party was over.

In the drawing room, having tea and cigarettes, only Flo and George were left with Lorna, Tilly having retired to bed and Cissie, with Pippie and Alex, having splashed out on a taxi and returned to Musselburgh. This after everyone else had departed, still calling shouts of thanks at the door, then hurrying out into the frosty night, to drive their cars or catch late trams home.

'Grand party,' George said lazily, blowing smoke. 'You did everybody proud, Lorna.'

'Impressed 'em all,' Flo added. 'Specially Luke and Jackie, and that was worth a lot, eh? I think it's right, what Suzie says, they're envious.'

'I don't know why they should be,' Lorna murmured. 'They're doing well.' She poured the three of them more tea. 'For the moment.'

'Ah, don't say you're still depressing yourself over the future, Lorna!' Flo helped herself to sugar. 'Look, we'll just carry on as usual. Won't even give the new stuff a thought. It could all be a flash in the pan, anyway. We're the tried and tested ones, eh?'

'You're right,' Lorna said, again straightening her shoulders. 'We'll just carry on as usual.'

'Not much choice, have we?' George asked cheerfully, then bit his lip as Flo looked daggers at him, while Lorna drank her tea and said nothing.

'At least, we've got good news about Ina coming back,' Flo said desperately. 'So glad you asked her, Lorna. Claire's improved a lot, but it'll be like old times to have Ina again, eh?'

Wish it could be, Lorna thought. Wish it could be old times again, when there were no clouds in the sky.

Fifty-Eight

But there were clouds, of course. Not great thunder clouds, but those of the 'man's hand' variety; straws that showed the way the wind was blowing. And, oh, that wind was cold.

At first, as Lorna and Flo had promised themselves, they continued as usual, and nothing seemed different. They still got bookings for their favourite venues. They still made records and had a few programmes on the radio.

But when George sought to arrange another London tour, he was asked by a club manager, as Luke too had been asked, if the band was going to include the new style of music in their programme. Something with guitars was suggested, preferably electric guitars, they being so popular. Turned out that one guitar in the rhythm section wasn't quite what the manager had in mind, and though he'd given them a booking, it seemed pretty likely, George thought, that they might not get another.

'Not at that particular club,' he added hastily. 'We'll be all right elsewhere. Just need the older audiences.'

'Older audiences?' Flo cried. 'We've never had to play just to older people!'

'How about the other bands?' Lorna asked. 'They finding this attitude too?'

'Only here and there. But maybe London isn't the place for us at the moment, anyway. The capital always goes for new ideas, eh? I think we should stick with the provinces.'

'And the Scottish capital,' Lorna declared. 'We're still as popular as ever in Edinburgh.'

'Sure, we'll be OK here,' George agreed.

But then the Carillon Ballroom, one of their oldest venues where fans could be the most loyal, asked if they couldn't include a bit of rock and roll now and again. It was this new record, 'Rock Around the Clock', by Bill Haley and his Comets, that had caused all the fuss, eh? Had all the youngsters fizzing and wanting more, and when the film came out next year, the effect would probably be sensational.

'Jump on the band wagon,' the Carillon manager had advised

with a laugh. 'If you'll pardon the pun. Try to replace the saxophones, eh? Buy a few guitars.'

Replace the saxophones?

With those words, it seemed to Lorna, Flo and George, that that was when the small clouds became big ones, and the wind blew coldest of all. For to change the instruments in their sort of band was quite impossible. It would mean changing not only the music they played, but their whole character as a swing band, and they had as much chance of switching to guitars for rock and roll, as of playing minuets with harpsichords.

'Now, we're not to let this sort of thing get us down,' George said firmly. 'As you said, Flo, we'll just keep going.'

'That's rich, coming from you,' she retorted. 'You were the one who first thought we were all going to go under!'

'I never said we were going to go under. There's still a hell of a lot of folk out there who want to listen to us. Maybe not in London, but elsewhere. We'll just have to be careful about venues and see we're getting the right crowd.'

'And the right managers,' Lorna pointed out. 'They're interested in money, remember. We have to make sure we make it for them.'

'We'll make it,' George said with conviction, but Lorna and Flo were exchanging glances. George could put on a very good act when he wanted to, as they both knew.

Meanwhile, whatever the future held, it was lovely to have Ina in the rhythm section again, so thrilled to be in Edinburgh with an all-girl band, while Dickie had been lucky enough to be taken on by Jackie.

'Oh, it's so easy, working for you and Flo,' Ina told Lorna in the office after rehearsal one summer morning. 'I mean, compared with Luke. And don't tell me all these horror stories about swing bands having to go bankrupt, because I know there'll always be audiences for us.'

'Don't worry, we're clinging on to that,' Lorna told her. 'None of the girls is rushing off to learn guitar playing. Dawn isn't singing "We're gonna rock around the clock tonight!" or imitating this Elvis Presley we keep hearing about.'

Lorna began swaying round her office, in the way she imagined rock singers would move, and Ina was clapping and encouraging her, when Trish put her head round the door and called, 'Someone to see you, Lorna!'

'Who?' Lorna asked, coming to a halt.

'Never seen him before. Said his name was Rod something.'

Lorna stood very still, her face turning pale. 'Rod?' she whispered.

'Rod?' echoed Ina.

'Want to see him?' Trish asked cheerfully.

'I'll go, Lorna.' Ina, taking Trish with her, was disappearing through the door.

'Yes, I'll see him,' Lorna answered, her voice sounding a long way off. 'Just for a minute.'

And Rod came in, closing the door after him. 'For more than that, I hope,' he said, quietly. 'How are you, Lorna?'

At first she thought he looked different. But then she realized she was comparing him to the image she'd had in her mind for so many years. Not that she'd called it up so often, but when she did, maybe it had become faded – blurred – so that it was no longer like him. Now that she saw him again and clearly, she knew he hadn't changed.

Put on a little weight, perhaps, but not on the face, which was still as youthful as ever, though Rod must be in his thirties now. And still as kind looking and cheerful as when he'd attracted her on her first day with Luke's band so long ago. Kind? Was he kind? Yes, she believed he was. Just wanted what he wanted, like a lot of people, herself included.

'Rod, why are you here?' she asked, her voice still sounding far away.

'I want to see you.' His previously slight American accent had become more apparent; he seemed much more American now. 'I need to see you.'

'Need? In all these years, you've never needed to see me before.'

'You don't know that. I've been back several times to the UK, usually to see my mother, but I never dared to find you. I knew it would be no good. You wouldn't want to see me.'

'But you've found me now.'

'I called Luke. He gave me the address of this studio.'

Rod's gaze had never strayed from Lorna's face until, suddenly, it moved to the photograph of Sam on her desk.

'Lorna,' he asked hoarsely, coming closer to her desk, 'why did you never tell me about my son?'

Fifty-Nine

The silence was long. Long and painful. Lorna had turned white. Rod was sweating, taking out a handkerchief to wipe his brow.

'Is there anywhere we can go?' he asked. 'To talk? I have a hire car outside.'

'We can talk here,' she said stiffly. 'The girls will all have gone by now. Flo and George didn't come in this morning.'

'May I sit down?'

'Of course.' She watched as he pulled up a chair and sank into it. 'How did you know? Did you read my interview?'

'What interview?'

'In *Edinburgh Cross Talk* – a magazine.'

'I never saw it. Can't have reached America – at least, not Los Angeles. That's where I've been for some time.'

'So, how did you know about . . . Sam?'

'Sam,' Rod repeated softly. 'You called him Sam?'

'Samuel Cameron. Sam because I liked it, Cameron after my dad. But tell me how you knew, Rod. How did you?'

'Josh told me.'

'Josh?' For a moment, Lorna closed her eyes, bowed her head. Josh? She couldn't take it in. Josh, in America, seeking out Rod? It was too much, too much . . .

'Are you all right?' Rod was asking quickly 'You're so pale – can I get you anything?'

'I'm all right, thanks.' She sat up in her chair, straightening her shoulders, putting back her head. 'It was just . . . a bit of a shock, that's all, to hear about Josh. I'd no idea he was in America.'

'He came over from Italy. Been given an offer for a screen test in Hollywood. So he said, but I think he really just wanted to find me.' Rod's mouth twisted. 'When he did, he was in such a rage, I thought he was going to kill me.'

'He attacked you?' Lorna cried, putting her hand to her mouth. 'Oh, Rod!'

'It's all right, he didn't get very far. It was all hot air, as it usually is with Josh.' Rod was silent for a moment. Finally, in a low voice, he went on, 'Lorna, I knew you'd been seeing him. Bob Milnes, a trumpeter in Jackie Craik's band was over in the States for a bit. He told me about you and Josh. That was another reason why I didn't get in touch. Seemed I'd been right – you wouldn't have wanted to see me.'

'Everything between Josh and me was over long ago,' Lorna said coldly. 'I haven't even thought about him for years.'

'He hasn't stopped thinking about you, then. Or, at least, avenging your honour. In the end, he calmed down and told me about our son. Said he was a fine boy and I shouldn't be skulking over in America, I should be in Scotland with him.' Rod leaped to his feet and began pacing the room. 'As though I knew anything about Sam! As though I wouldn't have come over on the next boat if you'd told me about him!'

Turning back to Lorna, he stood over her where she sat, still as a statue at her desk. 'In God's name, why didn't you tell me, Lorna? You know I'd have come straight back from the States. We could have been married—'

'I didn't want us to be married. It would never have worked out.'

'Didn't want us to be married? So you let our son be brought up without a father? How could you do that, Lorna? How could you, when he had me?'

A flush rose to her pale cheeks and she looked away from his accusing gaze. 'I suppose I thought we didn't really love each other.'

'We did! We did love each other!'

'Not enough, though. Neither of us would give in.'

'The truth is, we were too young to see straight. We never gave ourselves a chance.'

Another silence fell, broken again by Rod. 'What did you tell him, then, about me? You have told him, haven't you? He knows I exist?'

Lorna hesitated, thinking back to the time when Sam had started school. Before that, he'd been quite happy to have just her and his 'Gramma', but at school he'd discovered that most other children had dads. It hadn't been long before the question came that she'd been dreading.

'Ma, where's my dad?' Sam had asked one afternoon when she'd collected him at the school gate. 'Have I got one?'

'Oh, yes, Sam, you've got one.' Her voice was wonderfully bright. 'But he's in America.'

'America?' Sam had been thrilled. 'Is he a film star?'

'No, a musician, like me.'

Sam, walking beside her, had looked up at her trustfully. 'So why have I no' got his name, then?'

'There are reasons why I can't go into that now, Sam. One day you'll understand.'

'And one day will my dad come back?'

What to reply to that? Seeing the hope in her son's face, Lorna knew she couldn't crush it.

'He might, Sam, he might. If he can.'

And to her great relief, Sam had said no more.

'Have you told him?' Sam's father was pressing now. 'I need to know.'

Lorna raised her eyes. 'It wasn't easy, Rod.'

'Not when you'd made it so difficult.'

'I did what I thought was best.'

'Never mind, never mind. Just tell me what Sam knows.'

'He does know about you. I told him you were in America.'

'And what did he say?'

'He asked if you'd ever come back. I said you might.'

Rod's eyes lit up. 'Lorna, you told him that? I might come back?'

'I never thought you would, but I couldn't disappoint him.'

'Well, I am back and I want to see him, and he should see me. Where is he, then? With you? How do you take care of him when you're working?'

'He stays with my mother. Without her, I couldn't have managed. She's taken care of him, and I've been with him whenever possible.'

'I see.'

'Don't look so disapproving!' Lorna cried. 'It's worked out well. Everyone says what a fine boy he is and how happy he is, too. And come September, when he moves to a Merchant Company School, he'll be coming to live with me in a house I've bought. Ma will stay over when I'm away.'

'I'm not disapproving,' Rod said heavily. 'I think you've done the best you could, with the help of your mother. You must be very grateful to her.'

'I am.'

'So, when can I see him, then?'

'I don't know. I'll have to prepare him.'

'OK, prepare him. But make it soon. Ever since Josh told me I had a son, all I've wanted is to see him.' Rod suddenly reached across to touch Lorna's hand. 'And you, Lorna. Josh told me you two had parted.'

Lorna, moving her hand from his, stood up. 'Maybe you'd better go now, Rod. I'll talk to Sam and then I'll get in touch. Where are you staying?'

'At the West City Hotel. You want the number?'

'It'll be in the book.'

'You won't leave it too long?'

'No, I want to get this over as much as you.'

He nodded and after an awkward moment, made as though he would offer to shake hands, then thought better of it.

'I'll go, then.'

She went with him to the door, where he stood, looking around at her studio.

'So, the Melody Girls have gone? Got something on tonight, I expect?'

'Yes, at one of the hotel ballrooms.'

'You've done well,' he said softly. 'I congratulate you.'

'Thank you.'

'I can't drop you anywhere?'

'No, I'm all right, thanks all the same.'

'I'll wait for your call, then.'

'Goodbye, Rod.'

'Goodbye, Lorna.'

She watched him open the door of his hire car, glance back at her, smile uncertainly, and drive away. Then she returned to her office and sat at her desk, staring into space, her hands shaking, while her mind remained strangely, completely, blank.

Sixty

Before Sam was due home from school, Lorna went to see her mother. By that time, of course, the numbness that had overtaken her after Rod's visit had vanished, leaving her feeling so dazed, it was as if she were hurtling round – round and round – on some unknown fairground wheel.

Rod back? Rod knowing about Sam? Rod wanting to see Sam? She'd never expected anything like this, yet knew she'd been foolish not to prepare for it. Prepare her defences, make her case for bringing up her child the way she wanted. She had that right, hadn't she? Yet, here Rod was, at the gates of her home, as it were, wanting in, wanting to see Sam, and the truth of the matter was that she had never dreamed that he would care.

'Well!' Tilly cried, after Lorna had burst into the flat with her news. 'Well, so he's back! After all these years, here he is, that fellow who never married you, and wanting to see your son! So you tell him what he can do, Lorna! The very idea, thinking he could just stroll in and tell you what he wants. The cheek of it, eh?'

'Ma, we must be fair. Rod never refused to marry me, I didn't want to marry him. And he never knew about Sam, because I never told him – you know that.'

'Who did tell him, then?'

Lorna sat down and took a deep breath. 'It was Josh.'

'Josh? How did he ever come to see Josh?'

'Josh is in America now. He's hoping to break into films.'

'Oh, my.' Tilly sat back, flicking a handkerchief in front of her face. 'Lorna, this is beyond me. I canna take it in. Josh in America, wanting to be a film star, telling your Rod about our Sam – what next?'

'I felt the same, Ma. I couldn't take it in. But, it happened. Josh went seeking Rod in Los Angeles and as soon as he heard about Sam, Rod came home. Seemingly, he's desperate to see the son he never knew he had.'

'Desperate! I'd give him "desperate"! Should have thought of the consequences before he got you in the family way.' Tilly stood up to do the one thing she could count on in any sudden upheaval, which was to put the kettle on. 'I'm away to make some tea, Lorna. Then you'd better decide what you plan to do.'

'What can I do, Ma? I can't stop Rod seeing Sam. Besides, I know Sam will want to see him.'

'How do you know he wants to see him? Sam's only asked the once about his dad.'

'We don't know how much he's thought about him.'

Tilly, the teapot in her hand, stood in the doorway, her pale blue eyes filling with tears, her lip trembling. 'Aye, laddies do want their dads. Never mind what we do, they still want their dads, eh?'

'Oh, Ma, Sam loves us!' Lorna put her arm round her mother's shoulders. 'Of course, he'll want to see Rod, but we're the ones he knows. We've brought him up.'

'I'll make the tea,' Tilly whispered. 'Be thinking how you'll tell him, then. It'll be a shock, eh, whatever you do?'

Some time later, Sam, now old enough to walk home from school himself, arrived at the flat, calling for something to eat.

'Any wee buns, Gramma?' he cried, when he'd allowed Lorna to kiss him and his grandmother to give him a hug. 'Any flapjack?'

'You and your flapjack,' she said fondly, opening up her cake tins. 'But before you have it, your ma's got something to tell you.'

'What?'

As he busied himself opening his satchel and taking out his homework books, Lorna's heart missed a beat. Another Rod, wasn't he? Now that she'd seen Rod again, the likeness between Sam and his father was even more obvious than she'd thought, their only difference being the colour of their hair, fair for Rod, red for Sam. There were the same blue-grey eyes, though, the same short, straight nose, the same cheerful smile. How strange it would be for Rod to see a miniature version of himself! How comforting, to know for the first time that somewhere in the world there was someone of your own who shared your looks, your family's inheritance, and who would always be special!

'Sam,' she said quietly, 'come here a minute.'

As he came to stand beside her, she held him close, then let him go. 'You know I told you once about your dad?'

His face at once alert, he nodded.

'Well, he's here. He's come back from America on a visit and he'd like to see you.'

'When? When will he see me?' Rod's eyes in Sam's face were alight. 'Is he coming here? Is he coming today?'

'He's no' coming today, we have to arrange a meeting. Maybe at my house, after school tomorrow?'

'Ah, why no' today? I want to see him today!'

'Yes, well, I have to telephone him, you see, and fix it up. It'll be better tomorrow, Sam, when you can be all ready—'

'I can be ready now!'

'Sam, listen to what your ma says,' Tilly put in. 'We'll all go to your ma's house after school and then your dad can meet you there. Now, here's your flapjack. Like some milk?'

'I'd rather have lemonade.' Sam, his brightness fading, sat at the table, working out how long it would be before he could see his father. As Tilly frowned, he added hastily, 'Please.'

'All right, just this once.'

Tilly's eyes met Lorna's. The time had been arranged. Now all they had to do was tell Rod and wait for tomorrow.

What was surprising for Lorna was that she wanted it to come; wanted to see Rod again. After so many years of pushing him to the back of her mind, of thinking she could be happy with someone else, how strange it should be that she should find herself wanting, as desperately as Sam, to see him again. It was only because she'd seen him, she told herself. Once he'd gone back to America, she would be sure to forget him again. Only now she was no longer sure that she had ever, truly, forgotten Rod.

Sixty-One

Standing the following afternoon in the hall of 29, Grosvenor Place, everyone was nervous.

There was Lorna, clasping and unclasping her hands together. There was Sam, straight from school but already hustled into a clean white shirt by Tilly and gazing fixedly at the front door. There was Tilly herself, pretending to be unconcerned, but wearing a touch of lipstick, which she scarcely ever did, and glancing too often at the clock in the corner.

'Four, I asked him to come,' Lorna murmured. 'Five minutes to go.'

'Sure to be on time,' Tilly replied. 'If he's as keen as you say.'

'He's keen, all right.'

Suddenly, piercingly, as the clock struck four, the doorbell rang, making them all jump and look at one another.

'On time,' Tilly said, holding Sam's hand. 'Like I said.'

'I'll go.' Lorna moved slowly forwards, opened the solid, shining front door and took a step or two back. 'Rod, please come in.'

Though he was trying hard to seem at ease as he stepped into the hall carrying a large wrapped box, Lorna could tell he was as nervous as everyone else. His fair hair was well brushed, his light jacket elegant, but his hands on the box were trembling as he looked straight to Sam and for a moment he did not speak.

'Ma, this is Rod,' Lorna said hurriedly, and as Tilly nodded coolly, Sam's eyes on his father were round with wonder. 'Rod, this is my mother.'

'Mrs Fernie, I'm so glad to meet you.'

Setting down his box for a moment, Rod put out a hand, but his eyes had quickly returned to Sam, now standing close to Lorna.

'At last,' said Tilly, shaking the hand.

'And this is Sam.'

Lorna, pushing him forward a little, could think of nothing else to say. 'Sam this is your father' – how could she say that to a schoolboy? How could anyone introduce a son to his father at this late stage? Her cheeks were scarlet, her eyes pricking with tears, she felt the whole scene to be impossible; it couldn't be happening.

But Rod, was already stooping to look into his son's face, his eyes as filled with wonder as Sam's, while Sam himself was venturing a smile.

'Hi, Sam,' Rod was saying softly. 'You don't know how happy I am to meet you.'

'Are you – really – my dad?'

'I am.'

Suddenly, as Sam leaped to take his hands, Rod was laughing, looking up from his son to Lorna and Tilly.

'Has anyone shown this young guy a mirror? He has my face, would you believe? He has my exact face!'

And as he swept Sam into his arms, both Lorna and Tilly burst into tears.

Tea was laid in the kitchen, a large sunny room, painted yellow and white by Lorna, and furnished courtesy of the second-hand shops with a large deal table and some rather suspect chairs. Not that anyone had a thought to spare for a wobbly chair, or even the splendid tea Tilly had put together, though of course they all helped themselves to her scones and fruit cake made with ingredients no longer hard to find, her flapjack specially brought over for Sam. But even Sam's attention was elsewhere, for the exciting box his father had brought had now been opened and found to contain a train set.

A train set! And an American one at that! As his eyes went over the strange looking engine, the carriages and lines, Sam could hardly speak.

'For me?' he asked in a whisper.

'Sure, it's for you,' Rod told him. 'Question is, where are you going to put it?'

'Here,' Lorna said promptly. 'I've got plenty of room.'

'That's a relief,' Tilly murmured. 'I've got none to spare at all.'

'But when will I play with it?' Sam wailed.

'Why, whenever you like,' Lorna said. 'And you'll be living here all the time in September, don't forget.'

'Oh, yes, that's right.' His eyes shining, he turned to look at Rod. 'Thank you,' he said quietly. 'Thank you, Dad.'

It was no wonder then that at the tea table, Sam could only manage to eat while holding at least the engine on his knee, and having the box with the rest of the set close by his feet, while the grown-ups made small talk.

'Such a lovely house, Lorna,' Rod was murmuring, and, 'Wonderful baking, Mrs Fernie. Haven't tasted scones like these since I left Scotland.'

'Aye, well it's nice to be finished with the rationing.'

'Thought it'd go on for ever,' Lorna added.

'Though you wouldn't know about that,' Tilly told Rod. 'Seeing as you've been away so long.'

Time and again her gaze was returning to him, taking in the wide brow, the open, friendly look, the willing smile, and Lorna knew just what was going through her mind. Was this the awful cad who'd caused so much trouble? The absent father, who'd left Lorna in the lurch? This nice, kind fellow, who could scarcely take his eyes off the small boy who was his image? What had gone wrong, then?

Yes, what had gone wrong? Lorna herself was wondering. Why had she let him go? The thought slipped into her mind, as furtively as though it knew it shouldn't be there. Because she knew why she'd let Rod go in spite of her love for him. If she had married him, there would have been no Melody Girls, no career that meant so much, nothing that she'd made her own. And though the old attraction was creeping back – she felt it more and more – she couldn't regret the decision she'd made all those years ago. If only, though, she hadn't had to choose between her love and her music. If only, she could have had both. There was the real regret.

'So, what have you been doing in America?' she asked coolly, as teatime neared its end. 'Playing the trumpet?'

'Yes, but with different bands. Finished up with a cracker – Joe Hunt – terrific chap. Though I've left him now and don't play the trumpet any more.'

'Oh? What, then?'

'The guitar.'

At the look on her face, he shook his head. 'If you can't beat 'em, join 'em, Lorna. I'm with a group, we play rock and roll. But let's leave that for the moment.' Rod glanced at Sam, still fingering his engine. 'I think Sam here would like us to set up the rails, if that's possible? You did say you had the space.'

'Oh, yes, there's an upstairs room I was going to let Sam use anyway, for homework and studying.' Lorna smiled. 'But maybe the train set has priority at the moment. Come on, I'll take you up.'

When she'd left the father and son completely absorbed in the task of setting up the train set rails, Lorna ran swiftly downstairs to sound out her mother's views on Rod.

'Just doing the tea things,' Tilly called from the kitchen. 'You can dry, if you like.'

'OK.' Lorna took up a tea towel. 'So, what do you think?'

'Of Rod Warren?' Tilly pursed her lips. 'Never thought I'd say it, but he seems a nice fellow. No' what I'd imagined at all.'

'What did you imagine, then? Somebody who looked like the villain of the piece?'

'I did think of him like that. Was only natural, eh?'

'So, now you think he's a nice fellow. He is. Just got the wrong ideas, that's all. Which is why we parted.'

'Never thought of meeting halfway?'

'There was no halfway, Ma. He just didn't want me to have my own career.'

'I see your point, Lorna. I always did, because you'd your dad's talent and I knew it shouldn't be wasted.' Tilly sighed and hung up the dish mop. 'All the same, seems a shame you couldn't have come to some agreement.'

'I think I hear the chaps coming down,' Lorna said with relief at ending the conversation. 'It's maybe time for Rod to go. Sam should be thinking about a bit of supper and bed.'

'He'll be far too excited to sleep. And maybe no' the only one, eh?'

Maybe not.

'Think I'd better be on my way,' Rod said, his eyes going to Lorna, who guessed he was hoping she might say he needn't, but she only nodded and put her arm round Sam.

'It's been good to see you, Rod. And for Sam to meet you. Thank you for coming.'

'And thank you for my train set,' Sam cried, and running to Rod, reached up to fling his arms around him. 'Will you come again? Will you?'

'I'd like to.' Rod, releasing him, looked again at Lorna and then Tilly. 'If I may.'

'Come tomorrow!' Sam urged. 'Ma, my dad can come tomorrow, can't he? And I'll come here after school, eh?'

'I suppose that would be all right,' Lorna said slowly. 'If Gramma agrees, Sam.'

'Aye, we'll come here,' Tilly said. 'But you'll still have your home-work to do, Sam. Remember that.'

'Och, it's just a few sums,' he said airily. 'I bet Dad will help me, anyway.'

'Hey, who says I'm good at sums?' Rod asked, laughing. 'But I'll do my best. Goodbye, Mrs Fernie, and thanks again for that delicious tea. Sam, I'll see you tomorrow afternoon, then. Be a good boy for your grandmother now. Lorna, will you see me out?'

At the front door, they stood looking at each other.

'You haven't changed at all,' Rod said softly.

'Neither have you.'

'No, I mean it.'

'Me, too.'

'We're both the same as we were, then, outwardly.' Rod took Lorna's hand. 'Maybe not otherwise. Lorna, can we meet? Have dinner?'

'I'm sorry, I've no evenings free. People are still booking us, thank the Lord.'

'Lunch, then. Can we have lunch tomorrow?'

She let her hand drop from his, but managed a smile. 'I'd like to, Rod. Where shall we meet?'

'I'm out of touch, don't know the restaurants. Can you suggest somewhere?'

'There's a nice little place in Rose Street. Just a cafe, but I think you'd like it.'

'I'll like anywhere,' he said fervently. 'As long as I can persuade you to be there.'

They fixed a time, but when Lorna prepared to close her door, Rod quickly kissed her on the cheek.

'Till tomorrow, Lorna.'

'Till tomorrow.'

Her phone was ringing as she turned away, and Tilly shouted that it was Flo on the line.

'Want to know how things went?' Lorna asked, for she had of course told Flo and George of Rod's return and projected visit to Sam.

'You bet we do!' Flo cried. 'George and I have been wondering how soon we could ring up. Has Rod left yet?'

'Just gone. Everything went well. Sam already adores him, and no' just for the train set he brought, and I think Rod feels the same about him. Could scarcely take his eyes off him, in fact, and he's coming back tomorrow afternoon, to play with the train set. Ma's quite agreeable.'

'Ah, Lorna, that's nice, really nice. To think that Rod and Sam have met at last and it's all gone well. Will you be seeing Rod yourself? I mean, apart from playing with the train set?'

'I've said I'll have lunch with him tomorrow.'

'Aha! Lunch, eh?'

'Don't get too excited. That's all it will be.'

'Can't be sure of that, Lorna.'

Well, that was true enough.

Sixty-Two

'You know what this reminds me of?' Rod asked, when they were sitting the following day in the little cafe Lorna had chosen for them.

Lorna, looking round at the room where the woodwork was white, the tablecloths flowered, and the young waitresses pretty, shook her head. 'Can't say it rings a bell. Better tell me.'

'That little cafe in Sauchiehall Street, where we went on one of our first dates!' Rod's eyes were shining. 'Don't you remember? I told you it was a bit like the Willow Cafe and you said I was clever to know about Charles Rennie Mackintosh. Then, when we came out, it was raining and we ran into a cinema to see *Spellbound*.'

'Good heavens, you've got total recall!' Lorna laughed. 'I never would have remembered all that.'

'Where you're concerned, I remember most things,' Rod said lightly, picking up a menu. 'My word, this looks good.'

'Like to order?' one of the pretty waitresses came up to ask. 'I can recommend the steak and kidney pie. Home-made pastry, you know.'

'Steak and kidney pie? Yes, please!' Rod cried. 'I've been waiting years for this.'

'Tomato flan for me, please.' Lorna smiled up at the waitress. 'With salad.'

'No salad for me,' Rod said firmly. 'The Americans are great on salads, but there are times when a fellow wants mashed potato with butter and a stack of green beans.'

'Yes, sir!' the waitress cried admiringly. 'Coming up.'

After she'd left them, they were for a time silent. It was Rod who spoke first.

'Mind if I ask – I know I've no right – but were you very cut up over Josh Niven?'

'Cut up?' Lorna drank some water. 'Yes, for a time.'

'You really thought he was the one for you?'

'I suppose I did.'

'So handsome, of course.' Rod made a face. 'You know what they say, handsome is as handsome does.'

'I wasn't going just on his looks. We really did seem to get on well. But, thinking about him now, I'm sure we wouldn't have been right for each other.'

'Because?'

'Because he was always so correct, so worried about what folk thought. And then, when I told him about Sam, I know I hurt him, but he never really thought about me, how much I was suffering.' Lorna raised sad blue eyes to Rod. 'Maybe it was just as well I saw another side to him. Just like he saw another side to me.'

'I believe he really cared for you, Lorna.'

'But not enough to accept Sam.'

'He blamed me, rather than you. Quite right, too. I never came out of any of this very well, did I?'

'We both made love,' Lorna said, keeping her voice down. 'I never blamed you for that. Only for having different ideas from mine.'

'Know something?' Rod asked seriously. 'I've changed.'

'Changed?'

'One steak and kidney, one tomato flan,' intoned their waitress, setting down the dishes. 'Hope I haven't kept you waiting too long?'

'Have you kept us waiting?' asked Rod. 'We never noticed.'

'What did you mean, you've changed?' Lorna asked, as they began to eat. 'Changed your views?'

'Yes, don't you think it's possible?'

Thinking of Claire Maxwell, Lorna hesitated. 'Yes, I think it's possible. If the person's got a real will to do it.'

'I'll have to be honest, I didn't set out to change. When I first went to America, I was desolate because of what had happened between us, but I still thought I was in the right. It was only after I'd been around for a while, met the girl bands – and there are plenty over there – that I understood.'

'Understood what?'

'What some girls have to endure, just to be able to play their music.' Rod shook his head, his expression bleak. 'It really brought it home to me, what you and Flo have had to face, after I'd talked to some of the American girls. The prejudice – it was unbelievable.'

'You mean from the men?'

'Well, for some girls there was racial prejudice too, but, yes, I'm talking about men. They weren't just prejudiced, sometimes spiteful, too. Even where their wives were concerned. I tell you, Lorna, I had no idea.'

'As you say, that sort of thing can go on here.'

'I guess men just haven't got used to the idea that women can be as good as they are.' Rod finished his pie and sat back, shrugging. 'I mean, look at me. I didn't want you to run your own band, did I? I didn't want you to carry on with your music, once we were married, which was so completely wrong. It came to me, in America, that I was no better than any of those other guys.'

Lorna, listening closely, was stunned. It was true, she thought, he has changed. This was not the old Rod speaking; these were not the words he'd once have said.

'You believe me?' he asked, watching her face. 'I've suffered a sea change?'

'I think I'll have to.' She gave a cautious smile. 'Just wish I could have met those American girls, though.'

'To hear their stories?'

'To shake their hands. If they brought about this change of heart. The thing is, Rod . . .'

'What?'

'You weren't the only one who made mistakes. I should have told you about Sam, shouldn't I?'

'I guess I wish you had.'

'Water under the bridge,' she sighed, bringing out her famous phrase. 'It's too late to change things now.'

'Why, that's just what it's not!'

Heedless of the stares of the other diners at his raised voice, Rod leaned forward. 'Well, it needn't be! Because I'm not the same as I was. I've changed, so that makes all the difference.'

'What sort of difference?'

'Between saying goodbye and taking up where we left off.'

Lorna carefully laid her knife and fork together. 'I don't know if that's possible, Rod. Too much time has gone by.'

'All right, we start again, then. How about that? We're not too old. We have our lives in front of us. And we have Sam.' Rod's eyes were shining again. 'Come on, Lorna, think about it. In the States, they call it starting over. What do you say?'

'Like to see the sweet menu?' asked the waitress, brightly.

Sixty-Three

They were on Calton Hill, high above Princes Street, looking down at the panorama of the city, favourite view of the tourists, though not of interest just then to Lorna or Rod. Other things were on their minds, rather than picking out the capital's buildings; other things had to be resolved.

Behind them were the sights of Calton Hill itself – the City Observatory, the Nelson Monument, and the copy of the Athens Parthenon, with only twelve columns built, always known as Scotland's Disgrace. 'Would you credit it?' people liked to moan. 'Letting the money run out before it was finished?'

'Shame if they finished it now, eh?' Rod murmured, as he and Lorna wandered by to take a seat on the warm grass. 'Wouldn't be the same, would it?'

'As if they ever would.'

Relieved that Rod was making general comments instead of pressing her to say what he wanted to hear, Lorna relaxed a little, putting her hand to her hair that was so bright in the sunshine, smiling at a little child playing with a ball. But then Rod put his arm around her and turned her towards him.

'When are you going to answer me?' he asked gently. 'We've only made chit chat ever since we left the cafe.'

'Chit chat's easy.'

'Not for me. I've laid out my cards. Now it's your turn to play.'

'I want to, Rod . . .' She stopped, trying to find words.

'You want to, but you're afraid?'

She nodded. 'I suppose that's it.'

'So, what do you have against a new commitment? You know things would be different this time.'

'Yes, I know, but there are so many difficulties, Rod. You're based in America . . .'

'I'm coming back from America. Oh, I'll have to go and sort things out there, say goodbye to my dad, but I'd already decided I should come back here, for my mother's sake. She really needs one of us to be in this country now, and Leland's married and more settled in the States than I am. Dad understands.'

'I see.' Lorna's eyes were searching Rod's face. 'So your brother married an American? Don't think I'm prying, but you were saying you met all those girls. How come you didn't settle too?'

'I had two relationships,' he answered steadily. 'Neither came to anything.'

'Why was that?'

'Because they weren't with you.'

'I can't believe that.'

'Happens to be true. I'll admit, I was looking for a replacement. I never found her.' Rod ran his hand down Lorna's cheek. 'Now I've met the original again, I'm not looking any more.'

She was silent, feeling a stirring of excitement run through her body as his hand continued to caress her face, his eyes intensely holding hers, as the people wandering round the hill faded from her consciousness and it seemed that she and Rod were alone.

'Tell me you want to let me go,' he whispered. 'Tell me you mean that, Lorna.'

'I don't mean it,' she answered quickly. 'I don't want you to go.'

'I knew in your heart you didn't.'

'But, Rod, it's true what I say, there are difficulties. We shouldn't try to rush into anything.'

'Rush?' He shook his head. 'After all the years we've wasted, I think the time has come to rush. We made mistakes, OK, we did. But everybody deserves a second chance. And this is ours.'

They were very still, lost in each other, until Lorna suddenly leaped to her feet. 'We mustn't forget Sam, Rod. He'll be home from school soon.'

'I haven't forgotten him.' Rod, breathing fast, took her hand. 'Come on, let's go get the car.'

But in the car, parked at the foot of Arthur's Seat, he did not at first start the engine.

'We've a few minutes yet, Lorna.'

To be together, to be alone. To let their mouths meet in a long, long kiss, that was the sweeter because it brought back memories of other kisses long ago, and a love that had meant so much. And when it was over and they'd drawn apart, they knew they need say no more. The love was theirs again; the commitment was made.

They were silent as they drove back through the West End to Number 29, each on such an emotional high, words seemed impossible to find. Yet, of course, they had to descend from the heights, they had to think of practical things.

'What do you think he'll say?' Rod asked at last. 'I mean, Sam.'

'Rod, he'll be over the moon. It will be exactly what he wants. For you to stay with him and me.'

'Think everyone will be pleased? Your mother, for instance?'

'As a matter of fact, she likes you. She was surprised, when she met you.'

'Oh, Lord, she thought I was the villain of the piece, did she? How do I convince her I'm the hero?'

'You won't need to. I think she's going to welcome you.'

'As my mother will welcome you.'

'Rod, I'm looking forward to meeting her.'

'We'll fix it up.'

They had stopped outside Number 29, but were making no move to leave the car, savouring the last moments of this special time together.

'I'll have to tell my girls,' Lorna said thoughtfully. 'They'll be thrilled. So will Flo and George. Might think it's all happened so quickly.'

'Not at all. It began long ago.'

'I mean, our starting over.'

They both laughed and Rod pressed Lorna's hand. 'Tell you what I meant to ask – what happened to that other fellow you used to know, the one who was just a friend. He still around?'

'You mean Ewen? He's still around, but he's married and about to be a father.'

'Still your friend, I bet.'

'Yes, he always will be, his wife too. They'll be happy for us, I know. Pattie was always telling me to find Mr Right.'

'Hope she thinks that's me.' Rod sighed and looked at his watch. 'Shall we go in, Lorna?'

'Yes, let's go in.'

Sixty-Four

As Lorna had forecast, Sam was ecstatic when told his dad would be staying on in Scotland, coming to live with him and his mother at Number 29, playing with the train set every day! And if he was put right on that by his grandmother, who told him his dad would have other things to do, it didn't matter. He was just thrilled to have a dad of his own, and to see his ma so happy, for he always knew when she was happy and she was happy now.

So were other people pleased for her.

Tilly herself, who said as soon as she'd laid eyes on Rod, she'd seen it coming – he and Lorna were going to be lucky, second time around. Which didn't stop her from buttonholing Rod and warning him to make her daughter happy this time, or else!

'Mrs Fernie, it's all I want to do,' he assured her, and Tilly smiled and said when he and Lorna were married, he could call her Ma.

As for Flo and George, they said they felt like the Cheshire cat in *Alice in Wonderland*. 'Just one big grin,' George said.

Flo, hugging Lorna, whispered that they'd always known things would work out, once Rod had come back. 'And we always liked Rod,' she added.

'So did I,' Lorna answered. 'Liked as well as loved – is that the secret of getting things right? Wish they hadn't gone wrong before.'

'Got there in the end,' said Flo.

And Ewen? When he came round to Number 29, he had news of his own. Pattie had had her baby early – a lovely little girl they were going to call Jennifer after Pattie's mother, but her second name was to be Lorna, and would Lorna herself please be godmother? So dazed was he at his sudden fatherhood, Ewen could scarcely take in meeting Rod or Lorna's news, but when he did, his smile was wide and genuine and after he'd shaken their hands he declared he'd never been more pleased – except of course over the birth of his wee lassie.

'I'm very glad to have met you,' Rod told him. 'I know you were always a good friend to Lorna, and I'm grateful.'

'Always tried to put me on the right track,' Lorna murmured. 'Didn't always succeed, but that was my fault.'

'On the right track now,' Ewen told her, blushing a little. 'And now there are four of us to be friends, no' two. Let's all meet when Pattie's up and about again, eh?'

'What a grand chap,' Rod commented, after Ewen had departed. 'You've some pretty good friends here, Lorna.'

'Don't forget the girls in my band. Oh, they're so thrilled, Rod. No' to say surprised!'

Weighed down as they were with worries about the future, it had indeed been an amazing surprise for the Melody Girls to have their leader suddenly so radiant, so happy, now that Sam's dad had reappeared in her life. And what a nice guy he was, then! They couldn't imagine him ever letting a girl down, but perhaps he hadn't. Seemed it was true, he and Lorna had just had different ideas and now they'd agreed to agree, with Lorna keeping her band and Rod finding what work he could.

Of course, he was a guitar player, he had a chance to be a part of this rock and roll revolution. Had even seen the great Elvis perform in Memphis and boy, was he something else. The embodiment of the future, said Rod. But what about the band? What about us? Lorna and the Melody Girls were still wondering.

Keep going was Rod's advice and George's, and if bookings dried up, as they might, look elsewhere. To the provinces, or the seaside, for holiday shows. Anywhere, where there were more traditional audiences. Just take it as it came, that was the best thing to do, and was after all what others in the same boat were doing, so the grapevine reported.

There would always be a place for the big bands. Always those who'd want to listen to their music, instead of to Elvis. Or, maybe as well! Keep heads up, shoulders back, just as Lorna had always done, and let the music go around and around. As Rod said, sometimes it was best to let the future take care of itself.

'Ours, too?' Lorna asked teasingly.

'That's already taken care of.'

'Seeing as I'm writing wedding invitations, I thought it might be.'

'I suppose you're asking the whole world and his wife?'

'Well, your father and mother, your brother and his family, my mother, my Auntie Cissie, my cousins, Flo, George, Ewen, Pattie, and the baby, and everybody in Scotland who's ever played in a swing band. It's going to be a thoroughly musical wedding, and if it's in the papers, folk will see what we can do.'

'Not some sort of musical farewell, is it?'

'No! It's more a hello. A hello to our new life, whatever it might bring. To us, and Sam, and Ma, and my Melody Girls.'

'Feel we should be drinking a toast. Got any champagne?' Rod held out his arms. 'Only joking.'

'As though we need champagne!' she murmured, going to him. As though they needed anything, was the thought in both their minds, except what they already had. Their music, their families, Sam, and each other.

No wonder the future could take care of itself.